THE DEADLY VEIL

THE DEADLY VEIL

NELSON MCKEEBY

Published By: 4 Horsemen Publications, Inc.

4 Horsemen Publications, Inc.
PO Box 417
Sylva, NC 28779
4horsemenpublications.com
info@4horsemenpublications.com

Cover & Illustration by CD Corrigan
Typesetting by Autumn Skye
Edited by Charles Miano

Library of Congress Control Number: 2024950648

Paperback ISBN-13: 979-8-8232-0745-4
Hardcover ISBN-13: 979-8-8232-0746-1
Audiobook ISBN-13: 979-8-8232-0748-5
Ebook ISBN-13: 979-8-8232-0747-8

Contents

FOREWARD

Sunstar and Darkfather

Sunstar Nine sat the device she had fashioned on the chart table of the cockpit top where the command crew normally clipped down maps when underway. It was a simple object, but for Sunstar, it allowed her to look at the face of God without damage. It consisted of six wooden sides, lap-straked like a fine boat, enameled black, one side having a small hole drilled into it and another having the eyepiece to a broken rangefinder set into the edge. The box was magical because properly positioned, you could look into the eyepiece and see the sun in all of its glory.

When you are named for the center of your people's religious belief as Sunstar was, your travels through the ecumenical wasteland of human society afloat on the *Oceans-of-the-Lord* were ones of constant introspection and discovery. It required moments of calm reminding one that the truths existed no matter what port your ship was docked in. The port did not matter, as there always burned above the head the answer to existence, the ever-guiding star that the gods and the God declared was the center of the proximate universe and from which all life sprang.

Sunstar looked to the docks, recently bloody with her comrade's life essence, the very edge of a revolution in a land that she had never visited before. She was from the far west, a land she was likely fated never to visit again, and had left her last lash on *Voyage Respite* when she had seen a prism of light touching the captain of this ship, Javier al-Rasheed, as he stood on deck debating with himself the nature of his crew's comfort. *Remarker's* Captain, in her mind, was the very definition of a proper leader. Firm one minute, bemused the second, with an inner glow and the approval of the gods, he was like Jack Nimble in the stories, two thoughts ever in one mind, clawing for victory but finding compromise with each waking minute.

And despite the challenges of the world's ocean, and the violence of naked aggression put forward by mankind, she had found a home.

"Is that your Sun-Box?" came the deep voice of one of the *Remarker's* newest crew.

Sunstar Nine turned and looked into the dark man, the new Quartermaine who had been called on by Captain al-Rasheed's wife. "Quatermaine Darkfather. It is my sun-box, if that is what you ask, though courtesy allows all to look upon god inside."

"May I?" he asked gently, but there was something wrong in Sunstar's mind with the man. Her sense of humanity screamed a little when she watched him loading supplies and dunnage for the *Remarker's* second trading voyage. He had a deep beard whose color could be deep gray or a darker black. A scar from a saber sketched his face, and his eyes were a brilliant, impossible blue such as you only found in the deepest jungles of the Halo's Core, adorning unrecon-structed tribals who traded rare wood with the great king-doms but otherwise peered from behind huge-palmated leaves, hiding from the sun in the canopied darkness of their homes. Men and women who did not mind a taste of flesh, if you were crazy enough to venture into the twisting paths of their jungled homes without the protection of the bright sun overhead.

It was a whole minute before Sunstar said, "You may."

The Darkfather bent to the viewer on the sun-box, peered in, then carefully manipulated it to catch the true form of the greatest star. He held its gaze for a long handful of min-utes, before standing up and nodding. "It is a fine device you have fashioned."

Sunstar nodded. There was no need to refute or agree. The sun-box was the best her art allowed, so fine that it could catch moons and other satellites that swung about Ocean in their lazy, endless path, drawing circles in the sky. Instead of remarking on the compliment made by the Darkfather, she addressed the skeleton that danced above the grave. "You served the princess?"

The Darkfather laughed. "So many questions not asked, for the one that finally spills from your lips."

"I ask for the safety of the ship," she replied. "I ask all crew where they were before, and how they arrived here. Why should you be loyal to *Remarker*?"

"Does the Princess's word not suffice to see me to this appointment? Does she not own this ship?" The Darkfather parried, turning to stand at the cockpit top's railing and watch the activity of the crew preparing to leave on the morrow.

"Until the past month, I did not know the princess either, only the captain and this ship," she said.

"You are not Cycus-born," the Darkfather said.

Sunstar laughed. "Neither are you."

The Darkfather nodded. "You are correct, but I have lived in this land for many years, longer than you can imagine. The people of Cycus are normal to me. I admire them."

"Normality," Sunstar said, "is a condition of recognizing that the banality of now is a preferable contrasting condition to the horror of yesterday or the promise of sameness for tomorrow. Our dimensions for that normality revolve around the stories we are told that create the borders that define our lives. What is your normal, Darkfather? You see, the stories that define *Remarker* are the stories of her crew. As an officer, I listen to those stories. What is your normal that we should trust you?"

The Darkfather shrugged, "To some, steel beasts belching fire may be normal, but those stories you spoke of were told while this ship faced volcanoes, great storms, and the vagaries of human conflict. Many years ago, I had a daughter who brought me a book from her school. It told a story of great beasts that walked the land, and she asked me if this could really be. I told her if you lift away the veil of history, many things are possible and have happened. You have to keep your wits about you and look at the cursive the book is written in to see if the story makes sense. For her, great beasts are the story that she told herself in the darkness of night to entertain her mind."

"Do you think your daughter's beasts are real?" Sunstar asked, sensing an ennui from the new Quartermaine.

"I do not know. My daughter and they are gone, as are my wife, the land I was born in, and everything else. All of those stories are part of a deadly veil of the past I no longer care to lift." The Darkfather waved at the docks and said, "It is the now I live for. You seek stories of the past. I work to make this story continue forward, if only for one more voyage."

He stopped, looked down at his hands, and then said, "What is pomp, rule, reign, but earth and dust? There were stories told while *Remarker* challenged the seas. Stories that predated your birth and whose missive flow into the minds of every person in this land. If you want to know my story, then perhaps you should contemplate all the stories hidden by the veil of time. How a land was invaded and overtaken, but whose rule was subverted by those banalities that now you discuss. How a wood-fisted ruler had a son brought low. How that son married in ill-favor and had a daughter who was fated to be a playing piece on a fatal game board, but who arrogated herself the role of player instead of piece."

"And thus, we fought on the docks for our ship, and, in turn, for that daughter. Yet none of that explains your role, which seems to be hidden by that deadly veil you mention," Sunstar said, probing.

The Darkfather turned to consider Sunstar. "My spirituality is an ebbing tide that flows out from my soul in the form of boring lessons taught to children whose polite disdain is a sign of exasperated boredom. It forms a straitjacket around me that entombs my heart and robs me of the right to contemplate the meaning of my past. Yet there are stories to tell, if you wish to hear them, the story of a land that hatched this improbable ship and its valiant crew. My past is an overflowing cardboard box of experiences that takes the form of old pictures, letters from friends, military awards, and snippets of half-remembered poetry quotations jotted on the back of restaurant napkins. A velvet box contains a star made of bronze. An empty scrapbook ready to devour my history yet never filled. I will tell you these stories as we prepare this ship for its journey, but you must question if the stories are accurate, at least to me. They are all great land beasts that entertain a long-passed daughter. I offer them to you, Sunstar, to consider and accept or reject as you are wont. If the last voyage you took was the story of Javier, this then is the story of Nazira, the princess who became Dominar."

Sunstar nodded, looking back at her sun-box. "So you say, but also the story of Darkfather, no matter how you claw at the veil that these stories part.

"As you say," Darkfather replied.

Chapter I

Nawaz the Conqueror

"As if I need this now!" Nawaz screamed and shoved the simpering servant to the floor.

Admiral Jazira stepped up to him and whispered in his ear. "Calm, Dominar," he said. And Nawaz became calm because that was Jazira's job. To remind him, ten-thousand cannot rule millions unless the millions will it.

The servant cowered on the ground but was able to pass a few words. "My Dominar, the young master is down hard, sir." Cycuns spoke common like they were trying to gargle walnuts, and it was just one of the things that annoyed Nawaz.

"What does this mean?" He asked the Admiral. "I cannot deal with my idiot son's constant injuries on the playground. My cousin is demanding to have my seat in the Kemeyan council, the great bank is playing games with the treasury, the Camellia fleet is restless, and the regiments are spooked over the damned Guisarmes and their private bodyguards!

My son must deal with his witless incompetence on his own!" He stopped and looked at the sunset and the coming storm that the weather watchers said would flail against the coast and likely cause damage to the fishing fleet. Too many problems to solve, and only one body and mind to solve them. He kicked the servant as hard as he could, then yelled, "What is different from this pratfall than all the others?"

"Dominar, he had a fit, but he did so as he was climbing in the courtyard. He fell quite far and was seriously injured." The servant climbed to his knees, his face bruised and his face bloody, the effects of the kicking causing him to breathe in short, fitful breaths. The admiral grabbed the servant by his cassock and lifted him. "Speak sense. Is the boy awake, or dreaming? Does he breathe?"

The servant cried out in pain at being manhandled, then said, "The museif despairs and says the boy is in alhayaat alnihayiya. I do not know what this means, but it is with a serious face he says those words."

The admiral turned to Dominar Nawaz and said, "I advise you to look into this now. The boy may be feeble-minded, but he is the heir the Guisarmes agreed to, and they may demand concessions to agree to another."

Nawaz considered. "My son is not just bruised and crying for my attention?" He asked the servant, who was still being held up by the Admiral.

"No, I have seen. The wound is horrific," the servant replied.

"Lead me to him," Nawaz demanded.

The servant regained his own feet from the Admiral's grasp and hurried into the hall where he was blocked by Benson al-Youseffi and the museif, Drakma Bey. They were Cycuns, and his constant shadows ensured the dustari was kept. "We have heard of an accident. Drakma Bey has been at the boy's side, and it is serious." Benson al-Youseffi was huge, dark-haired, and dressed in the finest.

Nawaz owed a bow to al-Youseffi, as he would soon marry his daughter and seal the contract between the two people. "Alnaasih Benson, we are going to the side of the boy. Will you come with us?"

Drakma was like a pine to the al-Youseffi oak, thin and towering. He was not even Cycun and spoke common with the lilt of a dancing master. He said, "I have the boy in his chambers ... being watched by competent hands."

"Then let us go," Nawaz growled.

The so-called "palace" was anything but one. There was a castle, poorly built, and a series of low wood and masonry buildings connected by covered walkways. Nawaz had been to the Core and seen a real palace in his youth and intended to have one himself. He banged out of the residence and into the open Bailey and became enraged again at the lands he had taken. "Suffering simps and graylings!" he yelled.

Solders from a guard post ran to them. The leader was one of his most doughty fighters. He was dressed in fighting leathers and had a talwar at his side. "Master, we saw the accident."

Nawaz stopped the procession and embraced the ranker. "Good, follow me, and stay ready."

"My men and women are always ready to defend you, Dominar," he replied.

The swelling entourage entered the outer Bailey and barged forward, led by Nawaz. A boy was standing under the covers of one of the open hallways. "My Dominar, your son is this way."

"Lead me, servant," Nawaz said.

"Petrov, sir," the boy said.

"Do not care," Nawaz said, grabbing the boy's collar and spinning him around. "Where do I find my son?"

The boy squirmed a little and started stuttering. "Second wooden hall, my Dominar."

"Child, go empty the butts in the dungeon and get out of the Bailey," Nawaz said. The servants in the castle were dumb keena farmers for the most part, useful only for being bent boys in a blue circus. At least this Petrov item had found the information Nawaz wanted somewhere in his mind. And as things stood, the child would find the dungeons safer for the next several hours.

The Dominar turned and stormed out of the Bailey to the flats where the halls were lined up, turned, and walked to the second wooden hall in the first column. He burst into the doorway and saw his child in swaddling, his head wrapped and bloody. The minders were around him, keening and crying like washer women around a drowned fisher. Nawaz walked up and kicked the first one of his son's attendants as hard as he could. "Tell me what happened before I invert the lot of you."

The eldest of the minders turned and said, "Dominar, the young prince was climbing the trellis above the outer hall when he took an episode and fell. We feared he was dead, but he is instead senseless."

He turned to Drakma Bey. "Now, you worthless boot licker, tell me the truth. Will he ever be better?" Nawaz asked.

"There may be ... problems. His skull was crushed. The brain was exposed. It may be, though, it would be better to, well, let him go and seek an alternative to the heir." Drakma looked nervously at Nawaz, who was staring at his son.

"Damn that boy," Nawaz said. "He looks like his mother swaddled as such."

The admiral stepped in and said, "Do not think of your former wife. She is safe from harm."

"The god's strike me down with fire," he yelled and turned out into the vestibule, then onto the colonnaded boardwalk. The admiral, Benson al-Youseffi, and Drakma Bey followed him out.

Benson came close and said, "This could be a sign. Abelard could pass, leaving room for a child by your new wife, Griselda."

The admiral laid a hand on Benson. "Damn you man, he has a child laying in the bed, not an heir."

Benson pushed the Admiral's hand away. "You do not touch Jazira. You do not have that power."

"You simp, Benson, because your battalions surrendered without a fight and were not shown the qabr with you thrown in ass-to-face!" the Admiral yelled. "My sailors can still take Tariq Castle from you any second I give the order."

"Then come do it, kadah. You have not yet measured your sword against mine, and I hear your sword is blunt!" Benson yelled at the top of his lungs.

Quietly, Nawaz said, "Stop."

There was silence except for the wind of the upcoming storm.

"Drakma Bey, will my son live?" Nawaz asked.

Drakma Bey looked troubled and did not immediately answer.

"Silent are you, Drakma? Does your cheater's heart say that this is a good thing for us? Will my son live? But if he does not, is that good? Should I do the mother's duty to him now?" Nawaz said.

Drakma looked confused. The admiral, who was Kemeyan, said, "he does not understand the term." He turned to Drakma and said with a stern tone as if the man was a schoolchild, "He is saying should he kill his own son."

Drakma closed his eyes. "Do you ask me as the priest … or the practitioner of the healing arts?"

Nawaz looked at the priest. "You know where you go if you lie to me, Drakma. You answer as the one you wish, and I will do what I wish," he replied.

Drakma always looked like he would bend in the wind, straight as a reed of wisp and almost skeletal. His bones had the appearance that they would pop out of his face if he grimaced, while his eyes were bugged and protruding like a puffer fish.

"While I appreciate the position of strength of the al-Youseffi, one house is not twenty-three, and many of the houses agreed to your current son taking the crown of the Dominion, and his sire being next, as a way to assure stability without war. If your son dies … there may be chaos. He must live, somehow," Drakma said.

Nawaz said, "And will he?"

"Will God's fire strike?" Drakma asked in return.

Nawaz yelled, "Do not play word games! Not now, not if you want to stay away from the Island. I will have you screaming for years at the hands of the Mistress. Walk a careful line."

Nawaz stood straighter and sucked in a lung of air. "My Dominar, you have broken many things. The island is a threat, and I know this threat myself, but it must be balanced. The walls that held the island of Cycus in check are destroyed. The scholars are gone. The leaders of the family battalions have died or been driven into hiding. The order of our land hangs on a knife suspended over our heads by a string. Much more chaos and the knife will break." Drakma looked to al-Youseffi, who laughed.

"You have vapors, Drakma, the al-Youseffi have the al-Dinni and the al-Cinci in our camp. No other family comes close to the power of the three, and they support our Dominar, Nawaz. If any of the other families make even a mouse's squeak, they will die and see their lines extinguished," Benson al-Youseffi said.

The storm was starting to rake the coast, and Benson had to pull in his immense way-cloak to avoid the slow spatter of water wandering in from the open portico. Drakma seemed like he wanted to speak, but kept looking at Nawaz for permission.

"Admiral?" He turned to al-Jazira and asked.

The admiral looked at the Dominar and replied, "What has changed? The only thing that cut off a civil war was making sure the smaller houses felt safe. You cannot take sides with three of the twenty-three and think the lesser houses will not pull out of the Cycus 'dustari. Many of the agreements in the dustari are meaningless, designed to provide a defeated kith a cloak of victory snatched from defeat. Knowing who will be the ruler for generations to come is more than this to them. If your son dies, then the dustari will have to be negotiated fresh." He then reached out to his Dominar. "The life of your son, though, is in other hands than ours."

Nawaz looked at the Admiral, then at al-Youseffi and Drakma Bey. "Admiral, take al-Youseffi and Drakma to the meeting room and wait for me."

The admiral saluted and gathered up the two other courtiers with his eyes. Al-Youseffi seemed like he was going to protest, but the Admiral put his hand on his talwar and shook his head, and the grizzled warriors behind him came up on their heels.

Benson al-Youseffi bowed, "My Dominar." He then turned and left with Admiral Jazira and Drakma Bey.

Nawaz turned to the soldiers. "Warspike, you have seen many wounds. This scholar offers me only doldrums, not open seas and a good wind. Tell me the truth, will my boy live?"

The warrior stared ahead and tried not to look at his lord, but Nawaz could see he had pity in his eyes. "So, my boy will die?"

Warspike nodded.

He turned and entered the room where the minders were working at busy work, the child having no need of healing, and looked at his child, heir to the Camellia throne. Something caused him to tear up and start to cry.

Warspike came close to him, comprehension on his face. Nawaz looked at his loyal comrade from endless fights, who had spilled blood with him and followed him into the horrors of war for years. "Warspike," he said, "I love my son, but he is part of a plan I have had since we first stormed ashore on Lesser Cidalies. Abelard was to follow me and be the ruler of this land. He was to marry a great woman from one of the core ward islands and have children who would be, in every sense, the continuation of the Camellia throne. His mother died knowing his future. I broke this land intending that he take the throne when I was done. I killed and burned for him to be my successor. Yet he was never worthy, was he?"

Warspike let his hands fall to his sides. "Dominar, there is no answer to the will of the gods."

"Then why do they not show me the God's fire? Why not punish me? Why do they target my son? Abelard may not have been who I wished, but he was my son. Damn the Gods. Damn them all." Nawaz said.

"Dominar, do not say that. If the gods cursed you and they could be got, I would get them. Yet they cannot be got. They serve their own masters, and we are but ants to them," Warspike said in his graveled voice.

"Loyal, Warspike. Do you have children?" Nawaz asked.

"Seven, my lord, I have moved them all to this new land. The oldest is now in the Life Guards," he said.

"Have I treated him well?" Nawaz asked.

Warspike nodded. "You have made him an ensign and I will be saluting him before my days are done."

Nawaz nodded. "I will have to see my son to the next world and take the consequences. You and I may see the end of our days fighting these people, bringing fire and the sword to them. I am sorry I led you to this."

"Dominar," came a soft voice from the corner. He turned and was surprised to see a tiny wisp of a woman standing in the corner of his son's chambers. She was dressed as a herby from Kemeya, wearing the white dress of the order and the gauzy veil, but she was anything but. She was a demen.

Nawaz gritted his teeth and bowed to her. "I did not know you had left the island."

"The deadly veil is the shadow of your line, Nawaz al-Nabeel, now styled Dominar of the Camellia throne. You have contracted with us, and we have contracted with you. This is a danger to our contract, so I am here," she said.

"So quickly?" Warspike asked, but Nawaz shook his head and the warrior backed off.

"You do not question me or my sisters, Nawaz," she said.

"I was not. Your ways are yours," Nawaz said. "I made the compact. I am supporting it." He turned to the warrior and said, "Warspike, take your men and women, and the minders, and leave us to speak."

Warspike nodded and collected the group. They left by the main doors. Nawaz turned to the woman in the white dress and said, "Speak freely, mistress."

"This is not the time to burn Delphi and keen the shanty of the lost for the boy. There are healers concealed in the people of this land who peer into the darkness, just as my kind does. Sayid, if you wish, I can bring one, but you must forget him when he leaves. It is the way of the gods of Kemeya." Her tone was dulcet but dripping with acid that no son of the lesser Cyclonidaes could ignore.

"Do not conflate yourself with the gods of Kemeya, please. I do not mind your god-like powers or your derision of me and mine, but your pretending to be our gods would make it hard for me to protect you if the more religious of my warriors discovered your calumny," Nawaz said.

The woman shrugged. "I will comply, but do not for a second believe you are the dealer of this hand or in control of the fall of the cards. You accepted my offer when your conquest started, and I aided you. The price is the Island of Silence and the captives passed to me."

"I am already being blamed for what happens to the captives," he said.

The woman in white scoffed. "They are being tortured and broken. That is fear. As long as you hand us enough captives, their use is effective in keeping the people of this land in terror. It is not the worst thing that has been done."

Nawaz looked at his son. "God's fire."

"Precisely," the woman said. "If you doubt that was us, give me reason to test that doubt."

"I do not. Yet my son," he said.

The woman walked up to the boy wrapped in swaddling. "To you people, this is death. To us, it can be cured. A tabib of select powers could do it. One who waits outside will be our tool."

"Who is this healer?" Nawaz asked.

"A criminal whose safety depends on me. He will make no error, for it would be his undoing. We call his sort forlorn, soulless ones, in your old tongue manfi or allaena'. So consider him a tool, nothing more," she said in dark tones.

Nawaz touched his talwar. More than once, he considered striking down the woman, this 'wahash shaytaniun qadhir' as the stories said, to slay her and bury her body under the cloudy sky so she would remain hidden from the gods, if indeed she was of their lands. Making up his mind, he stepped to the door and yelled out, "Warspike!"

Warspike approached, "My Dominar."

"Call out the guard utisa. Lock down the castle, no one into the Baileys. Check the gates for a visitor seeking to heal my son. If there is one, bring him or her here." Nawaz said.

"I will do this," Warspike replied and turned, yelling to his men.

Nawaz returned and took up his child's hand for a few seconds. "My son, I give you to the future, but I wish it was not so." He stood crying softly as he waited, ignoring the veiled woman in white.

After ten minutes, Warspike arrived with a dark-skinned man in tow. He had a deep scar on his face, a heavy beard, and was short but with wide shoulders and heavy-set features. He had a dark cloak and a rusty, old yataghan on his waist. The woman in white said, "You may call this man Darkfather. He will cure your son. I have business to handle for an hour, but I will return." She turned to the man called Darkfather. "You will do this or suffer. Do you understand?"

The man nodded. The white woman stared at him for a long minute, then turned and left past Warspike. Nawaz turned to the man called Darkfather.

"Do you know who I am?" Nawaz asked.

The man nodded. "You are the Dominar of Cycus."

"Can you save my son?" Nawaz asked.

The man called Darkfather turned and looked at the child. He approached, placed his hands on the child's head, and closed his eyes. After a few minutes, he opened his eyes again and said, "Dominar, while Hesperia is not present, you and I must talk."

"Who is Hesperia?" Nawaz asked.

"The woman who left. I lured her away." The Darkfather replied.

"How did you do that?" Nawaz asked.

The Darkfather shrugged, "That is not important. Instead, we have a short time to talk about your son. He is dying."

"I know that. Tell me how to save my son. This Hesperia women will kill you if you do not make this happen." Nawaz said, his hand menacingly on his own talwar.

"She thinks she can kill me. However, you must have knowledge and agreement for me to try to save your boy," the Darkfather replied.

"Enlighten me, shaytan, and do so quickly," Nawaz ordered.

The Darkfather looked at the boy. "Your son has a severe traumatic brain injury. I can save him, but I am not a healer, merely someone who can heal. In my land, it would take months or years of subtle treatment to repair what has been damaged. Specialists would work on him, and he would require arcane medicines and complicated machines. I have none of these tools, skills, or knowledge. My skill would be in the saving of his life and returning him to the normal functioning of the average human being," the Darkfather said.

"Then do so," Nawaz demanded.

The Darkfather hesitated, then lifted his hand from the boy. "The brain is a complicated instrument. I have looked into your son's mind and seen he already suffers from what your people call d'alsare. If I repair the wound, he will suffer worse tortures. He will be unable to control his emotions. Fits of anger will rule him. He will have trouble speaking and will, at times, speak in gibberish. Demons of the mind will torture him. Sometimes he will suffer fugue, and other times mania. His life will not be a pleasure, and nothing in all the Halo will cure him."

"Then you feel it is better my son died?" Nawaz asked.

The Darkfather stood up from the child. Warspike, listening in to the discussion, also stepped forward, but Nawaz motioned him back. The dark man noticed the interchange but seemed to ignore its meaning. "No. If it were my son, I would want him healed, and then I would spend my life making sure he could be what he would be. However, being the leader of a great land ... that is too much to ask. It would be like exposing a person with a burn to the heat of the sun."

Nawaz shook his head. "It cannot be. He must take the throne and have an heir. I can do much to transfer power and wealth to a child of his and even his grandchild, stripping my son of many of the tools of power, but I am old enough I will soon lose my grip and not be able to steer these things."

The Darkfather nodded. He turned to the child and placed his hands on the young man's broken head and again closed his eyes. Nawaz grew concerned and lurched forward, but Warspike grabbed him. "My lord, it is dwimmer. To not interfere. He is a practitioner of the arts."

Nawaz turned and tried to shake himself free from his soldier's grasp. "What is this? Dwimmer? Child's nonsense!"

"Not nonsense lord, look!" Warspike said, and indeed it was true. Abelard's skull had been noticeably deformed, broken like an egg. A soldier learns to see wounds like that on the battlefield. He or she learns what they look like from seeing them visited on friends and enemies alike. Yet here, he watched as the crushed skull was mended. Soon it looked whole and strong.

The Darkfather looked up and said, "He will not wake for a few days, but mind my warning. He is healed but not cured."

"You will have whatever reward you want, warlock. I would have you in my court." Nawaz said with tears of joy.

"No, you will not. You must forget me and you will. But take my truth on this. Hesperia is a criminal and what she does on her island is evil and will result in no good for your new nation. Even her own people would condemn the acts she takes." The Darkfather stepped away from the boy, who was stirring in pain and muttering. He went for the door and was stopped by Warspike.

"The Dominar says for you to stay, warlock," Warspike said menacingly.

The Darkfather turned to the Dominar and looked at him. Nawaz approached him at the door. "Is your name really Darkfather?" he asked.

"You will not remember my name even if I tell you," the Darkfather replied.

"Then why not tell me?" Nawaz asked. "You saved my child."

"That may not be a kindness. It certainly was not for the best except for your heart," the Darkfather said.

Nawaz did not respond, only looked at the man with a deep frown. Warspike said, "Warlock, answer the Dominar."

The Darkfather looked at him and said, "I was the baron of Darkfather mountain, but you may call me simply Darkfather."

Warspike looked at the Darkfather and asked, "Who are you and what are you doing here?"

The Darkfather shook himself from the man's grasp. "I am a messenger to say your son has been healed."

Warspike and Nawaz turned to see Abelard sitting up. They both knew this was not all for the good, but they could never explain how it happened. Despite this, both agreed to never trust the white lady again, and they never did.

Chapter II

The Loss of the Longshore Explorer

She was known as "Greylord Almuzlim Jabal al'ab" in this far land. In her youth, she had simply been known as Finn. Greylord was a war name that gave her cache. It was meaningless, a bit of salesmanship that had gotten her hired to guard the woman who had left her homeland and married the heir to a warlord. She was kith now to lady Irula. It was a fair and honorable task.

"Ka pupuhi nga hau o te ao i tenei kaipuke iti ki te rangi," she said to herself in the language of her homeland. It was a little poem. No one else could possibly understand it. It was her private language now that she had been away from home for so many years, and speaking it all was just a private kernel of pride.

Irula, Queen Dominar of the land of Cycus, looked over from her bed where she had retreated when the storm had grown difficult. "What is that Greylord?"

Greylord replied, "Something from the language of my youth."

The Queen nodded. "Yes, my mother told me to not inquire into your past, a curious thing for the High Moderator of Canus Cragia?" She looked to the rocking floor, and asked, "Can you tell me what it means, it is beautiful."

"It is hard to translate into this tongue. I do not speak that well. Say it means 'the winds of the world blow this little ship into the sky.' 'Rangi', though, means more than sky. Heaven? I say not well," Greylord said.

The Queen nodded, then threw up into a bucket. When she had wiped her face clean, she said, "Heaven perhaps. The people of Cycus say heaven is in the sky."

"Kuare," Greylord replied. "It means lack of ... the word is no good." She said,

The Queen nodded. "Yet I understand. No, these people are admirable, just poorly led."

Greylord looked at the queen. "You have another child?"

The queen did not reply.

Greylord carefully stood and walked across the constantly tilting deck to a place where she could "lock in" next to the queen. "Your mother sent me to protect, and I serve for silver, yet you can rely." She hesitated then said, "Tell me your truths my liege, or else I cannot plan to protect."

Irula reached over for a boxwood tea bottle and tried to take a sip. Some spilled on her dress, but most went into her mouth. She gagged and looked green for a second, then swallowed. "I have not spoken of truth since I arrived on this island. So much is different. I long for conversation that is complicated and has any truth about it."

"'Korero honore' we say, 'speak with good talk,'" Greylord said. "He tamariki taku korero i tenei reo. Kua mamae toku mana."

"I do not understand what you say Greylord, but I understand that you find the language hard to follow. I do as well, and it was a tongue I studied early. The reason we struggle, though, is our languages are simple. They actually speak a combination of three tongues. The old tongue, the modern tongue, and the tongue of business, or trade talk. And the people of Cycus will speak the three at once sometimes," the Queen said. "When you learn Eurabanni you must follow all three versions, or you are not truly literate."

"Kaore au e marama ki o korero," Greylord replied, then said in the tongue of Cycus, "This is right. Queen Dominar, worry no. Tane-Abelard will not harm you now that Hungawai-Nawaz has died. Abelard needs you. He needs your daughter. And you are liked." Greylord reached out and put her hand on the Queen-Dominar's shoulder.

Irula shook her head and said, "I am not liked, you are wrong. Do you think Nawaz's wife will be so inclined to protect me? You know what she has said about me and my daughter, and now that Nawaz lies dead..." The queen let her voice trail off.

The ship heeled in the storm and sent Greylord crashing into the bed frame where Irula had taken cover. She righted herself and locked in again, cursing under her breath about the weather gods and their ill humor. When she was composed, she said, "Griselda was not able to make Nawaz cast you off and seek new marriage for son. She could not make it happen. Power exists only when it can make something happen."

"Perhaps the storm is affecting my mood. Nazira seems to not mind." She pointed to the smaller bed where her daughter slept, and Greylord had to laugh. The girl was five and had climbed all about the cabin as it bounced and rolled in the waves.

"The child has fire in her. Horses, climbing, exploring," Greylord said, but then added, "But she is not without a mind. She will read soon."

"Her father cannot read. Did you know that?" Irula retorted.

"It is rumored," Greylord said. It was not safe, even for her, to criticize the mercurial Abelard, and it would be worse, Greylord felt, with his father dead and the crown of the Dominion firmly on his head. She glanced at the young princess, sleeping in her bedstead. Greylord looked at the child, who for once was not exploring every nook of the ship, considering how knots were tied, how doors were hinged, or listening and understanding the words of her elders. She was an unusual child, like a brilliant adult who had returned to life with all the previous knowledge retained, and was remembering instead of learning. A brilliant, scary child. Her gaze fell back to the child's mother with a raised eye. Protecting the child meant somehow getting Abelard to accept her, even love her. The mother had to see that. "Speak not of your husband so forcefully."

"You are my protector, Greylord, and the only being who could repeat what we saw is four years old and asleep. Can you pour me some more tea?" Irula held her protected cup up and pulled its top open.

Greylord poured tea from the wooden tea canteen; they had and decided against a service for herself because of how little was left. The heaving boat could not support a fire safely, so hot tea would have to wait until the end of the storm. She returned the tea canteen to its safe carrier and instead took water from her belt canteen to sate her thirst. "The captain guiding the ship on the longshore," Greylord said, motioning at the door. "He could hear us talking of your husband."

Irula laughed, but then grew stern. "If Captain al-Rasheed violates our privacy, I will order you to behead him and throw him to the sea."

"His son and wife?" Greylord replied.

"Them also," Irula stated without mirth.

Greylord frowned at her. "You do not mean that Queen-Dominar."

She drank but a sip of tea. "No, I do not mean that. I am tired and sick, and this procession has drawn my spirit wan. All of those people looking at me, hoping I was the answer to some question they could not put voice to. Then the power-hungry asking me what I would support and who I would fancy at court, like what I support or who I give favor to matters. And then the darkness that is wrapping its arms around us."

The ship swelled again, harder than the last time, and they crashed back down after a second of feeling their stomachs fly. "What darkness Queen?"

Queen Irula considered her answer. "History has been erased here, but not entirely. There were always truths that were not being uttered. Even if you light a torch, there exist shadows if you cannot deploy it well, and I feel those shadows as I speak to the people."

Greylord again placed her hand on the Queen-Dominar's knee. "You see, you are the daughter of the Moderator. You were trained to look into shadows and wonder what was in them. Do all the people of the lands of Codis Aletia practice what the moderators of the Canus Cragia teach? Is not your own queen mired in madness?"

Irula drank more tea. "Perhaps that is it. I should have been moderator of my own small mountain fastness rather than thrust into the greater world to be a princess of this great land."

Greylord laughed. "I have been to the core, seen the great cities and their trembling towers. Cycus is not so great as that."

"I do not see them that way, nor does my mother. The core is powerful, but they are in decline. In a few generations, the nations in the outer Halo will be their equal in trade, and if they can be united by a strong leader, then Greenlandia and Emporia may find that they can no longer dominate the sea lanes in the north." Irula paused and seemed to be searching the wood of the ship. "It could mean a new order, or it could mean war."

"Not in our lifetime, Queen-Dominar. What do you call in your tongue the future-telling that has no way to change the present?" Greylord asked.

"Prognostication," Irula answered.

"Then perhaps you would feel more at ease to leave that horrible word to those who deal with fancy," Greylord said.

A shuddering crash, louder than the constant pounding of the storm, shook through the boat. Irula and Greylord looked at the groaning timbers, then shared a look with each other. For any of this to matter, the ship they were on had to survive the unseasonable storm.

Greylord shook herself. "Ignore the issues you cannot change my Queen-Dominar. Abelard was not married on his own desire. Feel it I do in my heart. This means, not that you lack power in your place. Nawaz was boorish, terrorizing of his son—a thing I shuddered to see, yet he was looking for a person that was worthy of the crown and not finding. Perhaps he did not see who he should have? You!"

Irula made a groan and said, "Yes, I am the brood mare assigned to produce the heir, and said heir is four years old and is sleeping in a jumper at my feet, such power I wield. Old ground. Why send me to visit all the towns of this strange land? Why the procession?"

Greylord shrugged. "I cannot say, my queen. Perhaps the darkness obscures. Nazira is future, though, that much I know. You could be present. And they seemed to treat procession as important." Greylord said.

The door burst open in a spray of water and the captain, Reza al-Rasheed, stumbled in with two sailors, all clutching baggy clothing. Al-Rasheed slammed the door closed, then yelled, "You will get into these now. We have lost our driver, and the steering sheets are torn."

Irula sat up. "What does that mean, Captain?"

"There is an uncharted island. We will not be able to keep ourselves from catching up on the rocks. And we cannot launch a boat. Our only chance is to take to the waves," he said in obvious terror.

"An uncharted island?" Greylord said with incredulity.

Al-Rasheed replied, "Uncharted but not unknown." He threw a bulky canvas rig at her. "It helps you float and keeps your head above water. Get into this now." He then turned to Irula. "Hand me your Child!"

She did. He took the small girl and put her into one of the canvas rigs, tying straps and fitting a collar device around her neck. Then he said, "Get up, Queen."

She did. Greylord watched as the captain manhandled Irula quite roughly into the same canvas rig that her daughter was wrapped in. Her daughter ended up face to face with the queen, carried on her chest. "As long as your head is above water, her head is above water, understand?! Do not fight the vest when you go into the sea. The long-shore currents carry south to a beach at the headlands of the island. If we abandon now, you will be swept to shore and not to sea. Do you understand?"

Irula yelled, "I understand!"

As soon Greylord and Irula were wrapped, the sailors, fear in their faces, started sticking things into the pockets of the rigs. Bottles, bags, little boxes. It was all tucked into the outfits until they could barely move. "What is this?" Greylord asked.

"When you reach shore, you will need water, food, shelter, or you will die on the beach. No one dies on the beach, you understand?" The captain yelled. "We go inland and hopefully find a dwelling. If not, we start a fire and shelter from the weather.

"Are you wearing one of these?" Irula asked.

"No," Reza al-Rasheed said. "There are not enough, and someone needs to have their arms and legs free to swim and tow the rest of you. Now shut up."

The sailors dragged Greylord, Irula, and Nazira snuggled to Irula's chest onto the storm-threatened deck and jammed them into the bars of a capstan. The captain's wife and child, dressed in the same rig as Irula, were also brought out, and the sailors started to put on rigs themselves. All but the captain, the first officer, and one of the crew, who wore only kapok floats. They ran lines through the rigs of the crew and passengers, then yelled, "Stand up!" Despite the screaming volume of the captain, it was hard to hear him over the maelstrom.

They all stood up. The ship was now going almost vertical as the wave caught it, but on the down pitch, Greylord could see that the island they were headed for was quite close and seemed to be rushing forward at them like a horse loose from its reins. Even in the sheeting rain, it was easy to see that the ship was lost. It would not hit the beach; it would crash into the great cliff and rocks.

There were no more verbal commands. The three unencumbered crew tied off the people in the canvas rigs. They shoved, pulled, and manhandled them as a group to the edge of the ship. When the inclination of the vessel was almost vertical, they pitched with main force all the passengers and crew into the water, then followed themselves.

Greylord found herself bobbing in the great storm, yet her face was clear of the water. She was only a meter from the queen, but she was absolutely unable to reach her with her hands. She noted the sailors who had canvas rigs crossed their arms around their chests, so she did as well.

As a wave rose up, she could see that the passengers were being dragged by three swimmers: the captain, and the two officers. Each of them was pulling their own bundle of humanity, the weak strength of a human against the massive strength of the storm. Yet, as unequal as the struggle seemed, it was apparent the tactic was working. The ship could be seen crashing into the cliffs, but the small cluster of humanity was caught in the longshore and swept into a beach rather than off to sea.

Then the surf caught them. Ropes parted. They tumbled end over end. Greylord reached out and enclosed the queen in her arms and then they were broken from the rest, small lines parted by the great force of the waves. Holding onto Irula, she tried to surf the swell to shore and finally ended up tumbling end over end in the waves. She lost her senses in blackness.

The Queen was slapping her awake perhaps a minute later. "We must get ashore," she yelled. Greylord nodded and helped the queen and the child into a dense forest. She heard, even over the storm, yelling. It took a minute before she had the queen safe. She then looked at Nazira and asked the child, "Is the princess safe?"

Nazira looked at her and said, "I do not want to do that again."

The Queen yelled into the wind, "A miracle, but we must find the rest!"

"Stay here. I will be back," Greylord said.

Greylord had her yataghan, so she drew it from its sheaf and went to the edge of the forest where the screams were coming from. The rest of the crew had landed further north on the island, just past the cliffs on the black sand beaches. Despite the terrible storm, there were people there, uniformed men and women with swords of their own, a few with black firelocks. They were wearing regimental colors, brown and black, but Greylord did not recognize their crest. And they had the crew lined up on their knees. Two had been beheaded by the soldiers, their bodies leaking blood into the surf.

Greylord looked into the eyes of the captain, Reza al-Rasheed, on his knees next to his wife, who was still wearing the rig with their child, a black-haired boy, attached to her chest. He saw Greylord and mouthed something to her, then burst forth, head butting the soldier in front of him.

There was a minute of bloody struggle and two of the soldiers themselves fell into the surf, mortally wounded, but the ship's captain was restrained again. Over the sound of the storm, Greylord could hear a bashi scream, "How did you get here? Who do you work for?"

Al-Rasheed replied, "We are in service of the queen, you bastard."

There was a scream, and one of the sailors on the end was beheaded by a soldier. The soldiers then wrestled the child of al-Rasheed from the captain's wife and held him into the air. Greylord felt anger fill her soul, but there was nothing to do. She had to protect the queen. Dying here on this beach as a gesture to the crew of a coaster was not an option. She kneeled and began to pray, but no more of the sailors were killed. Instead, they were dragged into the forest off the beach. When the beach was clear of soldiers, she crept out into the maelstrom and approached the bodies of the sailors. If left for the waves, their bodies would be dragged to sea, so she threw their heads up into the forest, and dragged each one above the surf line, lining them up.

She had no way to perform the rights of the dead, but instead, she could safely keen a dirge to the dead, the storm being so loud that the normally piercing ululation of pain would not be heard. Into the storm she yelled, "te kaituhi o to tatou ao, me pehea koe ki te tango i enei taitamariki me nga wahine. Ko te Kapene tana wahine me tana tamaiti! Karangatia koe mo to pene toto! Engari whakaorangia ratou ki roto i to pukapuka o te ora ka kite i a ratou ka kitea te matekore ki te tangohia e koe!"

She then searched the bodies of the dead, finding what she could and making it into a bundle. She would witness them and speak for the dead to their families. She would lie to them and say they had died in gentle bliss, the lips of praise for kith and kin on their lips. Then, someday, she would avenge them. "Ae ka ngaki ratou," she said in the language that only she could know on this land far from the harbor and beaches that bore her. The land she may never find again but embraced in her heart as if each time she woke it was before her. Grasping up the bundle of personal items, she turned back to where she had hidden the queen.

Irula was covered under the canvas rigs, protecting young Nazira from the storm. She gathered them up wordlessly and packed the supplies from three rigs into a bundle that could be easily carried. Irula noticed her stern face and said, "Greylord, you are crying?"

"The water from the storm is on my face." She replied.

"What happened?" Irula pressed.

Greylord leaned close to the queen's ear. "We are in danger, lady of Canus Cragia. I vow to save you, but remember this for me, my place is the beach of Whenua Koura in the south Escalades. There is a mountain by the harbor, and at its peak is a bench of lava stone. It is there I want my final rest. Do you understand, Lady Queen?"

Irula nodded. "And I want only my daughter to be safe. She cannot leave this land, it would be death, but if I fall, see that she is protected. These people brew a poison that cannot last, but when it strikes, she must be protected."

"I swear, my queen. We must leave here now. There is more poison than you can believe. I have just seen some with my own eyes." Greylord rigged a carrier for the child, then tucked the possessions of the fallen sailors into the carrier to form a counterweight so that Irula could carry it easily. "The possessions of the sailors," she whispered to Irula. "I will return them to the village of the Rasheeds, but if I cannot, please take them for me and tell them their kith-fellows fell peacefully."

Irula nodded, but said, "That is not my way. They will know the truth, but otherwise, they will have the knowledge of how their relatives fell. Did they all perish?"

"I fear, my queen, they did, or all will soon meet death at the hands of the residents of this island. They were soldiers," Greylord replied.

"Soldiers? Then they should follow orders. I am the queen now! Nawaz is dead," Irula said, abandoning the whispered conversation to fight the storm with her words.

"Queen," Greylord said. "They cannot know, and they killed the sailors when they heard the plea of the captain that he was your partisan. We must go and assume those who would normally be our succor have their hands turned against us."

The forest was heavy, as if no humans' back had bent to clear it for wood or built pathways for walking. The storm was abated by the trees, but not completely. Greylord cut a path when needed with her sword and helped Irula over the stygian chaos of life that stood in their way. The island grew out of the sea, like many islands, and they climbed for a while until they reached a wide forested plateau. There were viewpoints, but nothing to be gained by looking out, as the wind and the clouds obscured any intelligence to be had.

Greylord decided then to follow a small crest line in hopes that she was not merely going in a circle, lost in the wild forest. The crest line ran for a kilometer or so, then ended in another flat, and an open clearing. She started to skirt the open space when she heard a voice in her head and saw a small girl in white standing in the storm, reflecting the cracks of lightning. "Do not run, aunt," the voice said.

Greylord shook her head and stopped. Irula said, "What is it?" She pointed into the clearing at the girl and the queen gasped.

Despite the tearing wind and sheeting rain, the girl walked forward with calm assurance and stopped within a few meters of them. She said soft words that rang in their minds as if spoken in a drawing room. "You should not be here." Though she was tiny, perhaps 150 centimeters and perhaps 45 kilos, her eyes showed she was no child at all.

Irula stepped out into the clearing, clutching her daughter. "Yet we are."

Another young man, pale and ghostly, heavyset, and with jowls despite his youth, stepped from the forest close by the ghostly woman and said, "Mistress, do not start. It is for your good we say you are in danger and should not be here." Then his face softened and said, "You carry a girl!"

Greylord stepped forward when the man pointed out the child in her care, her yataghan flashing in the storm, and yelled, "Ka whakarerea tatou e nga wairua!"

The girl said, "We are not ghosts."

Irula put her hand on Greylord's shoulder and said, "Then who are you?"

"We are the damned of the island of silence," the man said.

The girl replied, "I am mistress, and this is Oban, my brother."

Greylord stood still. "E mohio ana koe ki taku korero."

"No, I am not privileged to know your noble tongue, aunt. I am the Mistress Silence. My lover watches from the hedge and is gainsaying me his own talent with tongues." The girl looked up and said, "Hesperia is coming with soldiers. We must flee and hide you, or else you will become one of us, and that is a terrible thing."

The man named Oban said, "Let me take the child." His eyes were warm, and his voice was trust itself, so Irula did what she never thought she would do. She released the child to the man, who took her in his arms in a protective hug. "I vow no harm will ever come to her."

Silence scolded him. "Do not vow brother."

"I do," he replied.

"Then so be it. But we must flee." And indeed, she reached out and grabbed Greylord, and she felt the urge to flee.

She turned to Irula and grasped her hand, leading her through the clearing and back into the forest.

The flight took on a preternatural flavor. The storm was a chiaroscuro of shades, while the water falling from the sky was now a pastel of soft patters that the canopy of trees created from the great downpour which showered the upper leaves. They followed a path that seemed trackless, yet the man, Oban, and the woman calling herself Silence were able to figure the constant changes. At one point, they stopped, and the ghostly woman said, "My lover says we have, for now, passed out of the immediate danger that Hesperia represents."

Greylord asked, "Is your lover real or spirit-kind?"

"How can spirit-kind love?" She laughed. "He has hands and lips and a brain that can be touched. He is no imaginary lover. Now follow my brother and I."

They followed a climbing path that led to a cave. The woman ushered them into it.

"What is this place?" Greylord said.

"It is a cave," Silence said.

"No, this island," Greylord replied.

"Your queen should know, it is a place her husband's father let to a great evil. Wahash shaytaniun qadhir walks the woods. Here they make alamiwat alahya' with fiendish delight and horrible schemes."

Greylord said, "Wahash shaytaniun qadhir? Alamiwat alahya'? What does that mean?"

Irula reached out suddenly and hugged Greylord, a move that confused the warrior. "I do not know the meaning of the words. I, like you, were not born to the Cyclonics or educated in their ways, but the words hold a terrible meaning." She looked at the girl and said, "I may be queen, but I do not know what these words mean or what this place is."

Oban walked deeper into the cave and put the girl down. "Let us build a fire. When we are warm, we will follow this cave and take a boat to the mainland, where you can return home. Do you want that?"

Nazira nodded seriously, and said in her young voice, "I have had enough of storms and odd doings. Home would be nice."

They all watched as Oban, ignoring the import of their discussion, pulled tinder, great wood, and a fire starter from a corner of the cave entrance and started a small blaze. When it was burning the queen turned to the woman who called herself Silence, and said, "What is this place, no riddles or ancient sayings that you Cycuns cleave to? Tell me the truth, for if you are Mistress Silence, I am a daughter of the land of Canus Cragia, and truth is the only currency I trade in."

Oban said, "The cave is the home of my sister's lover. She has not introduced me, but I see his reflection often."

Irula stated, "Again, not the cave, this island."

The woman nodded and bowed a dancer's bow. "The true mistress of this island is Hesperia. She is a visitor also, not of these lands. My people use the old tongue, as does your warrior-protector, to express meaning that cannot be found in the common. 'Mutarsid' is she. That means fanatic, a hunter who will do anything to catch their prey. And her prey is horror. She seeks to make humans more." She stopped, then said, "My lover is her slave as well, though I do not know why. His powers hide the evil, but he cannot be free."

"More than what does Hesperia intend you to be?" Irula asked.

"Just more." Then in Irula's head, a voice rang out, "More than we should be."

Irula turned to Greylord and said, "Did you hear that?"

"I did not, Queen, but she spoke in my head as well. I know what she did, not how she did it." Greylord walked to the cave entrance and peered into the storm. "How is this possible?"

"Tools of dwimmer?" The girl replied. "Why she is not visited with God's Fire I do not understand, but she flaunts the rules of the gods with impunity and rules this island with horror. I do not know how she does this. My lover says it must end."

"How?" Irula asked.

Greylord said, "My liege, she must be destroyed." She turned to the Mistress Silence. "That is why you cannot escape, why your lover who cannot be seen is bound. She prevents your leaving and hides you from the gods."

"In essense," Mistress Silence said.

Oban had the fire going and said, "Draw close to the fire. The storm is hours from ending, and the temperature is falling."

They all gathered and were surprised with bowls of stewed beans and rice from the fastidious Oban. That was followed by a tisane of mint in mugs of laminated boo-wood. Greylord warmed better than she had been warmed since she left her homeland years ago. The storm could not enter the cave, and the fire drove away the cold.

A scream came from outside, and some sort of horn blast sounded into the sky. The Mistress Silence lost her detached visage and grew fearful. "They have found us."

Greylord yelled, "Then this Hesperia will meet the agent of the Great Author, the daughter of Whenua Koura. And she will despair."

Mistress Silence placed her hand on the warrior's arms. "She may indeed do this." She turned to Oban. "Take the queen from here with her daughter. Get her back to her kith."

"Sister, I do not wish to leave you. Come with me," Oban said.

"You made a vow, but so did I. You protect the child. I protect this island. I cannot leave with you, not when the people of this place suffer," she said.

He nodded and put out the fire, then rushed to his sister. He was a huge man, and she was a slight woman, but the resemblance between them was obvious as they embraced. He then turned wordlessly, crying, and grabbed the girl, Nazira. "Follow me, Queen," he said.

"Not without Greylord," she said.

Greylord looked at the woman she had been hired with coin to protect, and pulled from deep in her pockets a coin. Five grams of silver; such a small thing. Meaningless really, unless given meaning. "Here is my life," she said.

"What do you mean?" Irula asked.

"You paid me silver to protect you, now I return the silver and say flee. It is the way of Whenua Koura. It is my life. I buy my life back from you, and I spend it as I wish. 'Kia maumahara ahau ki te kaituhi nui e tuhi ana i tenei korero ki runga i tana pepa i te rangi.' That means you must tell the Great Author, the God of Whenua Koura, to remember me, but to do that you must live. Goodbye, remember the memorial to the Rasheeds. I will make my own memorial to them now." Greylord kissed her sword and started to turn, but Irula stopped her.

"And here is my memorial. I will quit this land, for truth is where I belong, but before that, I will see that the evil of this island is expunged, though I do not understand it. Whatever deal my husband made, or his father before him, will not stand. I promise this." She reached out to Mistress Silence and grasped her hands. "I promise this, Mistress."

"Then I will owe you as well. We make this debt. Now go, Queen, take my brother and my child and live." She, too, was crying as she watched her brother and the queen disappear into the cave.

The horn screeched again. "This cave must remain hidden." The Mistress kicked sand on the fire and walked to the entrance.

"Then we will meet this Hesperia in the storm. I have only my sword, but you can have it." Greylord said.

"My silence is my weapon. I am the Mistress Silence. Hear my voice and fear." The girl said.

The two women, child and adult, strode into the storm and thence into the forest. Silence and Greylord advanced to the horns. They walked a hundred meters, then were met by a dozen soldiers and the ruler of the Island of Silence, Hesperia, dressed in a white set of leathers and wearing a veil that hid her face. She stepped forward and yelled into the wind, "The sailors tell of a queen and her child! A true catch. Where are they?"

Greylord stepped forward as well. "Where are the sailors of the boat who tell you this tale? What has happened to the Rasheeds?"

"Met the Qabr, bitch," came a yell from one of the soldiers.

Greylord stared at the soldier, then turned back to Hesperia. "What does that mean?"

Hesperia laughed. "Who knows? What do any one of you in the Halo mean when you speak? There is no one on Ocean who can put five words together with any meaning. Bog, kako sovražim ta svet." She then looked at the girl Silence. "What did you tell these people, child?"

Silence remained mute. Then one of the soldiers yelled, "You terrible child!"

Hesperia turned and yelled, "Keep your men and women in control Bashi!" Yet she grew confused for a second. "What did you say, child?"

"She said nothing. Speak to me. The Rasheeds are dead?" Greylord asked.

"Oh, the man-child is already being put through the change. Children make the best subjects. The Rasheeds, as you name the sailors, were too old and violent for the work to be effective, but the child was perfect for it." Hesperia then shook her head again. "Bashi, quiet that child."

The Bashi stepped forward. "The child said nothing. I will deal with her though." Then he stopped and turned. "What is this?"

"I am no child," Mistress Silence said.

All the soldiers seemed distracted, turning and looking around as if their inner selves were being bothered by some form of persistent gnat. Greylord saw her chance and launched herself forward with a yell, "Mo-te Rasheeds!" She felt the inner peace that is a promise of right action and collided with the bashi, who was looking around for a voice he could not find. A slash with her yataghan and the bashi spun with her neck cut. Another soldier tried to clear his mind but ran into her blade. He was dying but would not realize this for a few seconds, so she spun and caught another distracted soldier flat-footed, cutting her deep at the leg and again at the wrist.

A loud blast came, and Greylord felt a punch to her stomach. She was not stoppable though, not for a punch, and she turned and took another soldier. They were parade ground quality, not warriors, and had no idea that murder stalked them in the cavalcade of rain. Another fell, then two more as she danced with death, letting the author write her story the way it should be written. As she spun, she yelled, "Kaituhi rangimarie, murua ahau i enei oranga e mau nei ahau, engari awhinatia ahau kia nui ake!" Then screamed as another fell to her.

The soldiers were all dead or dying when she turned to Hesperia, but saw that she held some sort of twelve-sided solid in her hand. With a sweep, the woman took Greylord off her feet and began to crush her with an unseen force.

She walked up to Greylord as she gasped in pain and let the force lift for a second. "None of them mattered, girl. Twelve dead soldiers are like twelve lost fruit. Your valor was misplaced. You should have taken me when I was distracted. Now I will take an hour crushing you. See this? Its dwimmer you cannot understand. Such a terrible name for a thing with so much power. I can take the air from your lungs, crush your organs, rip your skin."

"Dwimmer," Greylord said.

"Primitive girl, tehnologija actually, but dwimmer is acceptable," she replied. Then the pressure returned. Greylord could not breathe and knew this was the end.

Something, though, distracted Hesperia for a second. She turned and yelled, "Shut up, girl," and the pressure let up. Greylord kipped up and swung her sword, taking the woman's head, then fell to her knees.

Mistress Silence was at her side. "Help me up, child, my legs are hurt," Greylord said.

Silence was crying with hiccups and stutters. "Oh, warrior, I cannot help you up. Your wounds are mortal."

Confused, Greylord touched her chest and leg. Gaping holes were coursing blood. The girl was right, there was no use. She was gone. Silence grabbed her, the blood spilling on her white dress. "What is your name? I never caught it."

"Greylord jabal al'ab almuzlim," Greylord replied.

"No, sister, your real name. I see the beach, the mountain, though I am not a practitioner of readings. Tell me your name and your God."

Greylord coughed. "My mother named me Tangata Toa."

"Tangata Toa, your mother shines on you and would be proud of how you acquitted yourself. If the Queen Dominar does not carry your silver to Whenua Koura, then someday, someone will. I promise." The girl leaned close and kissed Greylord on the cheek.

A dark shadow appeared next to the Mistress Silence. "I will take the silver to your final resting place."

Darkness fell on Greylord, born Tangata Toa, but in the black, she heard a voice. "Sister, stand free."

"Are you the Author?" She asked.

The voice replied, "You can call me that. It is all the same. The Mistress Silence and the Darkness can hear you still though, and that must not be. Step up and seek my hand. There is an island waiting for you beyond."

And she did.

Chapter III

Ghalibia

The people of Cycus did not celebrate birthdays like some foreigners did, but the 15th year of a person in the court of the Dominar had meaning. It was the year you were recognized, and the extent of your world defined as you were presented to court. Her father had little patience for court ceremony and allowed various relatives and courtiers to handle all the pageantry and process that came with ruling a great realm. Nazira, chafing under her father's dictatorial edicts and disinterested malevolent rules that controlled her waking hours, had looked forward to the court ceremony where she would be assigned title, rank, and know where her place would be in the world.

The day of the ceremony, she had Oban dress her in the highest of court fashion in a gown borrowed from the dresser and worked on by her friends in secret. She had no jewels, did not possess a wooden torque of family like her half-sister and brothers, nor was she given a talwar with a sateen frog as a young knight of the realm. She was a princess, whatever that meant, but had none of the material proof of station that her half-sisters and cousins did.

A traditional dress would make a statement she felt. It was useless, clunky, flowing, hard to walk in, and hot in the summer heat, but she loved the thing for what it represented. It was her announcement of freedom and her taking a place in the world where she had even the smallest control of her destiny.

When the court ceremony came, she had made sure each fold of the gown was precisely creased, that each wrinkle was steamed from the fabric, and that the seams had been stitched and waxed carefully. The dress was deep royal black with a green shawl rather than the court parti-color. She had to get creative with the signet, with no warrant to have one made by the office of rank. Instead, she had found one on the backing of a chair, which she had stolen in the deep of the night. She had smashed the chair, then carved out the wooden Camellia orb, which she fixed to the canvas backing. The orb was given white, red, and green enamel to match the ruling house's colors, and she had then placed it on her neck. Lacking a sword, she had modified a metal-tipped, wooden fire poker into a walking stick, common among knights that did not gainsay a martial air.

She looked into the mirror and was terrifying. Proudly, she went to the door and was stopped by her grandmother.

"Out of my way, Griselda!" she yelled, hoping that traditional court petulance would carry the day. It did not.

"I am Dame Griselda al-Youseffi dd' Tariq and am not your grandmother, child, nor will you be going to the ceremony." Behind her were two of her house guards, armed and armored, as if they were going to war.

Nazira looked the soldiers up and down with a sneer. "You needed two Guisarme trash to handle little princess Nazira?"

"I am Guisarme trash, girl, and I bought them to show your face to. Tamale, Crete, your heads if she enters the presence chamber during the ceremony. Guard the doors. Understand?" she said.

The two guards held their left fists up in the archaic manner of the old families and then returned them to their sides. Receiving no answering salute from the old woman, they turned and left down the main passage.

Dame Griselda turned back to Nazira. She was dressed in parti-color, the mix of red and blue from the traditional flag of Cycus, and green from the Dominar's crest. From her blouse she pulled a small, curved dagger and, fast as an adder, grabbed Nazira by her dress-front, dragging her to her side. Looking her in the eyes with her terrible clove-scented breath, she said, "The dress is nonsense, and you will never wear it again." Despite her age, the old woman was strong and used to physically abusing people of lower station. Nazira had seen it herself, though never been the subject of her wrath. She could lash her throat with that blade and Nazira would die, choked out on her own blood.

Slowly, deliberately, Griselda brought the dagger to Nazira's throat, but instead of cutting flesh, she separated the fabric that held her torque in place. It clattered to the ground, and she kicked it away. Several functionaries were in the hall by now watching the tableaux, and Oban appeared in the door to her rooms and squeaked, "Dame, do not do this!"

Griselda ignored them all and slipped the dagger between the dress and her cotton camisole and cut away the shoulder seem until it was loose enough to fall away.

While she worked the dress, the old woman did not release Nazira, instead holding her close to her face. She did not even look at the damage the knife was doing to the fabric. She held Nazira transfixed with her eyes, adjusting her grip on her as the dress fell away, her left hand cutting the fabric without visual direction.

When the top of the dress was cut away, she lifted Nazira's camisole with the blade. The crowd was growing in the hallway, and Oban was now on his knees crying and begging the old woman to stop, but no one stepped forward to save Nazira. Instead, Griselda traced the blade down the skin of Nazira's stomach to her fancy, voluminous, black dress bottoms. "Do you know what would happen if I cut your fundaments from your body?" she asked.

Nazira looked at the woman with all the hate she could throw at her. She refused to cry or react, but she was completely in the woman's control. "You would be tortured by the Dominar."

Griselda laughed. "I would be executed certainly, but not by the Dominar. You see, the only thing that matters about you is your ability to have a child of the lineage of the Dominar. I could cut your nose off, remove your ears, chop your fingers from your body, but if I did not harm your ability to have a child, perhaps I would pay a fine, and nothing more. But I am the wife of the old Dominar, Nawaz, and that means I have power you will never have." She pushed the blade into the fabric of the dress bottoms and cut it free, using her right foot to tear it away from Nazira. Her beautiful dress was gone, along with the torque she had worked so hard on. It was gone with whatever childhood she had clung to. She stood exposed in her camisole and sirwal and nothing else.

"Run and hide, girl," Griselda said, and Nazira ran, but not to hide. She ran to think.

There was no one to console her. All of her friends were either involved in the ceremonies as guests or servants. Standish was getting her sword and being given the rank of ensign in the Marine Guard, being three years older than Nazira. Being a ward of the Dominar, she would be a major in ten years and a colonel in fifteen. Gullen was being inducted into a dancing academy where she would be able to rise in ranks as a scholar, while the rest of her friends were in the pantries working for the feast that supported the ceremonies or accompanying their families to be in the crowds of attendants and middle ranked people who would watch the events from the outer Bailey.

A favorite place for Nazira was the Hall of Statues. Her father and most of the court avoided the place as most of the statues were damaged or defaced, old Guisarme heroes overthrown by the new order before her birth. Sometimes, very old courtiers would sit in the sunshine of the portico and look over the city, but that was more a memory of her early childhood. Now it was likely to be empty, and a perfect place for a person to sit and think.

She ran down the rear stairwell to the first level of the kitchen to avoid the public halls. No one would care if she was naked, many courtiers preferred in the heat of summer to walk the halls without clothing, and it was common for younger courtiers to exercise and show off their athleticism in the large Bailey, but there was a special shame in being deprived of all but her camisole and pants on a day when everyone else was dressed in their finery. She could feel the shame in her soul and did not want to let others into that feeling of helplessness. By taking the servant's portico, she was able to avoid the most busily trafficked parts of the old palace and avoid the presence of chamber hallways where important families carried out "corridor politics."

The Hall of Statues was the last portal off the promenade, across from the back service hall, and required only a quick dash to reach. Nazira made the move without being noticed but found the hall occupied by a brooding, dark man with a black tunic and pantalones, a scholar's hat, and heavy boots, wearing a disreputable yataghan. He had no house signet and was woefully underdressed for the naming day.

"Who are you?!" she demanded.

The man stood, bowed, and then returned to his seat. "You do not know me."

"You obviously do not know me," Nazira replied with anger.

He looked at her, then back at the statue he was considering. "On the contrary, you are Princess Nazira d' Camellia. And dressed below your station. I knew your mother and met you when you were a small child."

Nazira thought for a flash second that the man was a Dartian noble used to being rude as part of the tenor of the court. Yet he was so unremarkable and utterly unmemorable that it came to her she had met him before and simply formed no memories of him.

Then it came to her. He was not some exotic Dartian noble, just a sad dancing master who educated a few of the lower-ranked families in the palace. "You are Master Darkfather," she proclaimed.

"Clever girl, I estimate that your father will fear for his throne before you are finished," he said. Then he stood, took the robe that was on his lap, and wrapped it around Nazira. The move was so gentle and avuncular that she could not protest it. "It is a hot day, but the robe will do for your modesty."

"The people of Cycus are not concerned about modesty," she said, gripping the light cotton cloak about her. The Dancing Master nodded and returned to his seat. "You are more than a girl of Cycus."

Nazira looked at the statue the Dancing Master was gazing at. "What are you doing here anyway?" she asked again.

"Learning Princess," he replied. "Your father is not in favor of learning, but I would commend it to you."

"What do you mean?" She asked.

"Nothing, my Princess." The man bowed his head and went back to studying the statue. "Just the wandering mind of an old man who knows too many people and remembers their follies before they came to power."

The carving was one of the larger figures and obviously a man or woman, rather than something more fantastical. Like many of the older figures, its face and head were vandalized, and it was now more of an abstract than a true representation of a human. "Why this one?" she asked.

The man looked at her and said in a distracted tone, "I am sorry, Princess. You mean this question for me?"

Nazira motioned around the room as if to say, "Who else?"

"I think it is Gulzar al-Omid d' Guisarme," he said.

Nazira rolled her hands. It was sign in the palace for "more than that." He seemed to understand the gesture and said, "Do you read my princess?"

"Everyone reads," she replied.

He laughed. "You father cannot, nor could many of your grandfather's partisans. Reading is a thing for priests and servants. I am not surprised you can read though."

"Why is that, Dancing Master?" she asked. The man was making her cross.

The teacher waved at someone behind her. She turned and saw that it was one of the Life Guards, an ensign, likely sent to spy on her. The woman hesitated, then came to them. The Master said, "Tea for both of us, bring a big pot, a cushion for the princess, and look into what the kitchen has for noble fair and bring us two plates."

The woman looked at the dark figure sternly and replied, "I am an officer of the Life Guards!"

Darkfather bowed his head. "I am sorry, ahh, Ensign? Would five silver cover your services?"

"I am an officer!" she replied in chagrin.

Darkfather made the sign for an apology and said, "I am so sorry." He pulled two five-silver coins from his pocket and held them out. "Ten then, and five more for whoever actually brings the tray."

The officer hesitated, then took the coins and left. Nazira watched and then scolded the Master. "You should not have done that. Roshana has her stripe new and tends toward anger at being made to look silly."

"I hardly call fifteen silver for one meal and tea silly. Many of the commons in Cycus Port do not see fifteen silver in a month and consider themselves well off." The Dancing Master seemed calm about the guard, calmer than Nazira would be. "It is a lesson well learned by the Ensign if she wants to make rank in a palace regiment. Do not assume a person with a sword is one thing when they could be another."

"And you could get the Ensign in trouble?" Nazira asked.

The Dancing Master considered like he wanted to know how much to say. He finally shook his head. "No, I have no power here I care to use. If she gutted me like a fish, likely she would make a few minor families mad whose children I tutor, but considering my situation, not very mad. So even I must be aware of this lesson. Do not make unneeded enemies, make friends." He then waved at the statue. "Though that is not a guarantee, as this person found out."

A pair of servants from the lower halls, Misti al-Ziba and Karzen Kall arrived pushing a trolley with the Ensign and two troopers from the Life Guard ranks. The Ensign said to the Dancing Master, "My Captain says the Princess is to remain in this room. Her servant Oban is sending new clothing up."

"That is good thinking, Ensign." He removed from his tunic a card. "My Carte d' Visit. Please call on me if I can assist you in the future. What is on the bill-of-fare?"

The Ensign looked at the senior servant Misti, who answered, "Steamed saffron rice tahdig, kuku sabzi, and yogurt cucumber pudding. The tea is Allo Cella. Shall I make you a plate, Lord Darkfather?"

"Only tea, and if you leave the servlets, I will prepare our plates, as it seems we will be here for a while," he said, looking at the ensign.

The ensign nodded. "I have guards out at the entrance. You may use the water room next door as you see fit." The group then withdrew, leaving the room empty again except for Nazira and the Dancing Master.

Darkfather stood and looked at the two carts. "There is a cushion here for you, and one for me as well. Shall we have tea in front of this poor statue?"

Nazira took a cushion and settled it down, then received tea from the odd man. He looked more like a rogue than a teacher. He had dark hair, dark skin, a thick beard, and a deep scar across his face. He was unarmed but wore a frog and scabbard.

He took tea in a clumsy manner. Taking two stoneware cups into one hand like a pair of eggs, he grabbed the lacquered service and poured tea into both cups as if the steaming liquid could not harm his hands. Putting the service down, he ignored the second cushion, instead setting the cup on the stone bench and resuming his pensive position. "I am curious," she said. "Your accent is not Dartian. Where are you from Dancing Master?"

"Please call me Darkfather, Princess. There is no need for one of your rank to maintain formality with one of my rank in private, or such privacy as we have," he said.

She sipped her tea. Allo Cella had a smokey, nutty flavor and was said to be "bracing" because of the way it could keep a person awake for a day if you drank several cups. The dark man had a scar on his face, a battle wound of some sort, and shaved his head bald, but kept a long, black beard. His clothing was not descriptive of any affiliation. There was no pin or medallion, no patches, and no rank she could find.

"So educate me, Dancing Master. How is a man with no sigils of family, no national attachments, who avoids even telling a student where they are from, allowed to wander freely in the palace?" Nazira asked.

The Dancing Master laughed and sipped his tea. "The best way to teach is to force the student to ask the right questions and to seek information to inform their own answer. Let us instead turn to your story."

"I have no story," she replied.

Darkfather leaned into her and waved his cup at the statue. "You have a story. You just do not know you have one. Before you were born, your story starts in the dim recesses of time. And when you die, your story continues on in the children you have, the people who you change for better or worse, and the imprint you leave on the world. You cannot see what will happen, but you can look into your past and connect to the present."

"Ok, why break an old statue?" she asked.

Your Grandfather was Emir Nawaz d' Kemeya. He did not become the first Dominar of Cycus because everyone agreed he was a good master. He took the lands with a small force of soldiers when this man died of God's Fire. Yet this man died. His memory was powerful, so Nawaz had him and his line erased."

"I have never heard of him," Nazira said.

"Showing Nawaz was successful. Would you like a meal?" he asked.

She looked at the food. "Never have I been served a special meal. I had feared my coming of age would be ignored after, well, my grandmother reacted badly to it."

She stood, walked over to the food on the servlet carts, and ladled out two plates, handing one to the Dancing Master. He took the plate and looked a little sad. "They did not give you a meal. They gave me a meal."

"How do you know?" she asked.

"Let us get back to you. How many people do you think live on Cycus?" he asked.

She took her plate and sat down. "A million?" she said.

"A million is good. Probably low, but it does not matter. A million people on 25,000 kilometers of land. 4,000 soldiers from a land with a population of 125,000 living on 9,000 kilometers invade a land of a million people and Nawaz wins. Now he has a million people he has to dominate. But the million people had just lost the heads of their 23 families, the Guisarmes. And that, if you only knew, is what rules your life. Nawaz erased the dead leaders with a chisel and hammer but could not erase 23 families ready to resist his usurping of the prerogatives of the Guisarmes. And that is where the illiterate invader made a deal with the highly literate Guisarmes to avoid a terrible war. He did it ironically on paper, and then he worked to add teeth to his side. The rules, though, he had to follow were simple. None of his relatives from Kemeya would be imported to hold power in Cycus, only his firstborn child, your father. And your father would marry who he was told, and he was told to marry a woman from another land in hopes of civilizing him, and as his father married into the Guisarmes. I do not blame you for not knowing all this, but you must figure it out because these laws, these marriages, these tricks and compromises, are the logs and plaster that form the walls of your world," he said.

"I do not like your lecture or your tone," she said.

He smiled. "Do you remember an accident on a ship as a child?"

He looked intensely at her, putting his plate aside. "No, I have never been on a ship," she said.

Darkfather said, "Terrible things happened there, but you were shielded from them. I knew your mother ... served her, in fact. You could remember her if you find your situation dire. She was able to bend the rules of the Dominion and escape with her life, though she could not take you with her."

"Tell me about my mother, Dancing Master," she asked, suddenly seeing the man as more than just a prissy, dark-souled teacher, but someone who might have knowledge she could use.

"Your grandfather married a Guisarme, but the Guisarmes were jealous, petty, and they could not decide who Nawaz's son should marry. So it was decided to marry her into a line of religious scholars from a foreign land. The thought was she could tame the illiterate and venal aspects of Nawaz and his children without leading to civil war among the Guisarmes," Darkfather said, sampling some food from the trays. "Abelard was married to your mother in the same way that a tomato is subjected to cross-breeding to make its orange color stand out more. The hope was you would retain the decisive leadership of your father, and then gain the intellect and sanctimony of your mother."

Nazira looked to the statues in the room, many defaced, but some still beautifully captured works of art. So many lies, so many people telling her self-serving stories of her mother and why she was exiled. Was this man telling the truth? She closed her eyes and tried to commit his features to memory, and found it was impossible. A scar on his face and a dark, shadowy countenance was all that she could conjure, though she only had to open her eyes and stare into his to be connected again to his features. What an odd man, that could be so lacking in character as to be forgettable in seconds, but had so much to say.

She opened her eyes and looked at the Dancing Master. "I do not think you are lying to me."

He laughed. "You should assume I am lying to you, then go find the truth."

"Are you lying to me?" she asked.

There was a pressure on her consciousness that eased, and she seemed to focus in better on the dancing master as his face grew troubled. "I am not lying to you, but believe me when I say you must find a teacher to survive the coming years. I still owe your mother much from the years I served her. I owe your mother's mother much as well, though she has passed to the beyond. I could not come near you. The guards around you are too strong, or else I would have applied to be in your service." He paused for a second, then stood and approached her, placing his hand on her cheek. "Your mother is a great woman, a woman who seeks truth and knowledge and lives in peace on an island of scholars. Send a message to her when your need is dire."

Three soldiers and the ensign came into the room, the ensign holding a set of manacles in her hands. "Time for you to go," she said.

Nazira stood, threw her plate to the ground, and yelled, "I will not be taken in manacles!"

The ensign stopped short. "Princess Nazira, the manacles are for this man, Master Darkfather."

There was silence as one soldier took the manacles from the officer and the Darkfather stood to allow himself to be fitted for the mental retainers. As the soldiers worked the wooden and hemp devices to the dark man, he looked at Nazira and said, "You are fifteen. You have very little time to learn much that is kept from you. You asked why a man without sigil could be free to roam the palace, but I am not free, I was allowed to eat my final meal here in this room of statues, many of who I knew in life before their stone likeness was defaced. My final meal. Now you know a fact that did not make sense to you from context."

Nazira turned to the Ensign. "Release this man and have him brought to the chambers of my tutor."

The ensign stopped assisting with the manacles. "Princess, he has an order to be strangled that has been signed by your father. Only your father may set that aside."

"Then bring me to my father!" she yelled.

The ensign shook her head. "I have orders to restrict your movements from the Presence chamber."

"From Griselda!" she screamed, falling into tears. She hated crying, but this was infuriating that the first man willing to actually teach her would be dead and out of her reach.

The rest of the people in the palace would be attending the ceremonies or working to make them a pageant, but you could see the executions from the portico railing. They would fire a serpent the minute before they would occur, and another serpent when the last of the doomed were dispatched. She stood tensely looking at the ensign and her retinue, measuring the minutes that the dark man would be walking through the back hall, down the servant's steps to the gardens, out and around to the first tower, and then through the tower to the torture chambers. She had watched the executions before from the hall of pollards and knew the doomed were gathered into a room where they have their wood and hemp shackles checked, where each was given a teacup, shaped with a long wooden stem to allow a person with their hands bound to drink it. The tea was Junebug boiled black, and the hated dungeon master Petrov would adulterate it to make it biting and vile. It was a running joke, and you could see the effects of the drink on the faces of the doomed.

The first shot rang out, and she ran as fast as she could, clutching the dark man's coat about her. The guards were surprised and yelled at her to stop, but she ran down the hallway, turning left instead of charging to the Presence Chamber. The grand portico had a view of the Bailey of the Doomed.

The guards were on her heels, so she spun and threw the coat from the dark man at them and resumed her run in her cottons. She doubled her speed, if that was possible, and passed startled servants and soldiers who looked at her dumbfounded. At the end of the hall, she turned into the grand portico and reached the point where you could clearly see the execution space, although not up close like most nobles viewed it. She looked out and saw men and women, their faces shrouded, being poked and heckled by the Life Guards, with the sinister presence of Petrov and his son. They had lost their last apprentice and were looking for a new one, but had also gotten a new and sinister little sot who used to belong to the west wing of the palace, a little disgusting snot from the al-Cinci clan.

Then the guards were on her. She felt one slap the back of her head, and the other grab her by her waist, so she turned to grieve them as she was being grieved. They were armored in leathers and household half-mail, and they were larger than her by a head and a half, but she had learned a lot from Standish these past two years, who was a master of the deadly arts in all manners.

She reached out and scratched the face of the first guardsman and screamed, "Poison!" Many of the palace nobles loved to test horrible mixtures on the servants of opponents, and it was not uncommon to have the medico summoned to try and save a writhing cupbearer and partisan of one of the many factions who had gotten too fresh with a pretentious noble. The soldier backed away and screamed herself, while the other soldier drew his sword.

The ensign arrived and pushed Nazira down and kicked her in the stomach, screaming, "She is a little girl! Grab her!"

"Stop!" yelled a new man, Regnal Bish. Bish was a minor courtier who darkened the hallways providing inexplicable services to the Camellia throne. He was the source of much humor because he had crazy eyes. He bent down to the mewling guardsman and said, "You are not poisoned." Then he looked at the ensign, "If you kick that girl one more time I will break your ankle."

The ensign stopped kicking Nazira. "Someone needs to teach this snot a lesson like they are teaching that dancing master."

Regnal Bish picked up Nazira and said, "Go to the railing if you wish to watch the ceremony."

Nazira cursed him under her breath and went to see the men and women, the doomed, being poked and shoved around into a rough line. Behind her, Regnal Bish said, "Ensign, they are killing Master Darkfather, but there is no reason for you to chortle. You could be one of the doomed someday yourself."

"Maybe you also," the Ensign growled. She sounded angry enough to fight Regnal Bish.

"Possibly I will be next to you. Now shut up, Guardsman," he replied with a purr, his eyes wandering in the air, but you never really knew what he was looking at.

Nazira looked down at the doomed. Some could not stand, had broken limbs, crooked backs, and horribly mangled fingers. They had come from the dungeons and been subjected to the question. But some were straight and healthy, standing tall. There were rules supposedly, who could be tortured, and those rules were violated often, but some people could be executed but not put to the question. There were rumors of more vile places where worse was done, but they were whispered rather than spoken to outwardly.

Once the doomed had been poked and prodded into a rough line, Petrov turned to an empty galley and yelled, "Will any of the doomed be redeemed?"

There was no one to answer, so it was just another cruelty visited on the doomed. Her father never visited the executions, and never pardoned or exiled anyone. If the doomed arrived to the Bailey, they were going to die.

Usually, there would be a pause while fruit drinks and pickles were sold to the crowd, but with no crowd, no one to sell them anything, and thus no profit for Petrov, the usual wait for people to get their snacks was limited.

Each of the doomed had their shackles locked into a rack and then had the strangulation garrote placed around their neck. The garrote was then fed into the master wheel that allowed twenty doomed to be strangled at one time. The process horrified Nazira, and she never understood how people thought it was fun to watch, but among the families, betting on how fast the garrotes would cause the doomed to collapse in the final throws of death, or which doomed would be the last to stop twitching was popular, and Petrov had started in recent years adding numbers to the racks since the doomed could not really be told one from another in their shrouds.

With all the doomed lined up and in their garrotes, the youngest executioner al-Cinci was handed a drum by Petrov's petulant son, and then Petrov nodded and began turning the master wheel to the cadence of the drummer. Each time a drumstick hit the tympani of the drum, Petrov spun the wheel once, which pulled slack from all twenty of the doomed a millimeter at a time. One turn per second, one millimeter per drum beat, meant that the first signs that the garrote was choking off air from the doomed happened quickly. There were screams for the next minute, but then the air was cut off and the sounds stopped, with struggles seen in the doomed as each tried to figure out how to get one more breath.

In the third minute, half would be silent, and the crowd would be yelling encouragement by the number of the victim. Now, with no one present, there were no cheers. The fourth minute would pass and only a few of the doomed would still be offering resistance.

That was when it grew ugly. Nazira looked at the doomed, hating her father and everything about her life, as the dark man was dying in one of the shrouds. This was where the strongest were spending the very last seconds of life, but where some would be reaching the point where the garrote was ready to decapitate them in a gruesome fountain of blood.

This was when the virtuosos would lean over to Nazira and her friends, forced to watch from time to time by the matrons, and give them a colorful discussion of what was about to happen. Sometimes, they explained, a person with the right sort of neck would remain alive, but at some point, the garrote would bite in, and they would be beheaded. When the head just rolled off, there was no excitement. But sometimes the head would explode from the body under a fountain of blood. That would result in a series of cheers because it implied the person had been alive until the garrote cut their head from their body.

Nazira was prepared for this, but the last body slumped without drama. For ten more minutes the bodies were left, and then each was detached and thrown on a cart. She turned and saw that Oban was now present. "Damn you all," she said to Regnal Bish and the ensign. Then to Oban, "Take me to my rooms."

Oban clucked, "Princess, let us dress you for the halls."

"No, Oban. As I am dressed," She said to the ensign, "You may follow me if you wish."

Nazira knew this lesson would sink in. She would no longer allow others to teach her, she would seek the truth herself. Her life was not a game, and she was not a piece on a game board.

CHAPTER IV

The Acts of Dame Griselda

Griselda sat in the presence chamber. She had a busy night, and it would be busier still before dawn crept its hoary hands across the city. A messenger had just come and handed her a note. It was in old speech, but that was not a useful way to conceal its meaning. Many people spoke and read old speech. No, the messenger had tried to use context to produce a message that the disloyal coven of idiots who inhabited the broken court of Abelard 'Arba'a 'Aashar' would have difficulty understanding.

She scoffed. 'Arba'a 'Aashar,' as if thirteen idiots pre-dated him.

But the paper she had been handed said it all:

Taeud aldajajat 'iilaa altufaah, wayughadir aldiyk bialsafina.

Only, her agent outsmarted herself as well. The words meant that the hen returns to an apple... She meant to write, taeud aldajajat 'iilaa alshaati, or "the hen returns to shore." Still an effective communication, and maybe the error would provide more security to the message, though Griselda never assumed a message handed to her had not been read by half the palace before being placed in her hands.

She looked at Phelm. He was two-twenty kilo mass, two hundred centimeters tall, and dressed in the al-Youseffi livery of green and gold, looked a bit like a guardsman of the Life Guards whose official colors were yellow and green. "Are our people ready in case this is not as we planned?"

Phelm nodded. "It will be as planned though. We will take the princess from the dock as she returns from *Remarker*. We can take *Remarker* as al-Rasheed does not sail on this tide in a few hours. If not, he will be forced to turn back because of a storm that is lashing down on Cycus. And if he sails that ship into a storm..."

"He dies by the sea and is not our problem anymore," Griselda said.

Which left her mercurial and mentally stunted stepson to deal with. Someone had completed a puzzle box and then not left it for others to admire but had instead scattered the pieces about the floor, and some were still missing. Well, her stepson was not the mental giant who needed to know that what they had was a box missing its pieces and that they all must be found. She could guide him through this. It was her life's work, keeping her husband's idiot progeny from destroying the nation in a venal fit of temper.

Abelard styled 'Arba'a 'Aashar' entered the presence chamber and stopped short, nearly causing the Life Guards in their green and yellow finery to crash into each other. She could see that he expected a midnight levee, which was more about self-congratulations than actual work, and which she knew from long observation Abelard preferred. Normally the room would be filled with petitioners, courtiers, lawyers, priests, nobles of the great families, regimental officers, and commoners. There would be tea and gara, maybe some wine or beer to drink with distasteful comments of the religious impropriety. Cigars from the core may be broken out when he entered, leaving the great room with a hazy atmosphere, and perhaps, in the corners, the more apostical would be sipping palm rum mixed with juice as a tonic.

Instead of the crowds of the levee, though, there was just Griselda, her guards, and three other notables surrounded by their personal staff. The three notables included Priest Domingus bar Calad, who stood in front with eight men and women of the piety, taking center stage as it were. Then Chief Justicar Colonel Abrams Taffez and a group of lawyers had clustered to the right, trying to both be present and absent—making Griselda smile at their idiocy. Finally, Bank Master Youti al-Presence was to the left with four bank clerks. They all held great stacks of banking books in their wrinkled hands and affected banking caps to protect their rheumy eyes from the glare of the gaslights flickering in the chandeliers.

Griselda sat on the throne mount with Phelm, her guards of the al-Youseffi, and a woman wearing a red, flowing dress and a headset of the great bank

"What, I mean, what you say?" he yelled. It was his speech problem. No one "noticed it," but all noted it. He calmed himself though and took control of his anger. "What is this?"

"My Dominar, there has been a problem," Domingus said, bowing with a crazy flourish. He was dressed as all the simps did, a bright white bleached linen thawb, parti-color swallow-tailed coat in blue and orange, with a turban of some sort of worsted incrusted with shells and jewels. His torque of office was valuable shells and cerulean. At his side was a talwar that Griselda doubted the man could draw without emasculating himself.

Griselda noted that Abelard's soldiers soldiered their positions through the hallway. Gone were the warriors of Kemeya. Now all the Life Guard were born on Cycus, but despite the lost anger they had gained professionalism. Abelard had not ordered them to move into their positions opposite the al-Youseffi, but instead, his Bashi had made a slight wave with his right hand, and the Life Guard had taken their positions. Another wave and the guards would open fire with their firelocks and then wade into the three small masses of humanity arrayed around the throne mount, slaughtering everyone in the room. Everyone but Griselda, herself, and her partisans. If they tried that, then the island would rock with revolution like they were Denuvani simps.

"Make this quick. If there is no levee today, I have a man in the dungeons who needs to meet a fire-heated poker!" Abelard yelled.

"I am sorry, Dominar. The man Javier al-Rasheed is gone. Your daughter has rescued him, and he has attacked and stolen a pirate ship. The *Remarker,* I am to understand," Domingus said.

Abelard walked up and struck the priest in the face with a closed fist. The man fell back into the arms of his acolytes, nose streaming blood. "You told me not to kill him, priest. You said wait! What reply do you make that keeps your head on your worthless shoulders?"

Domingus rolled onto his belly and sat on his knees. He wore gows which protected his bony knees but could not both hold his nose and remain stable. The blood gushed out onto his thawb and stained the floor. "My Lord!" he screamed.

Griselda calmly stood up and walked to Abelard, placing her hand on his shoulder to calm his rage. "As your idiot counselors have left the tea to rot on the docks, I have been finding out what happened."

"Griselda, do not interfere," Abelard said. She knew he could not punch her, but she also knew it was possible, nonetheless. Let him hit her and she would own the Dominion in a week.

"No, Abelard my child. I will soon have your daughter held, and the final pieces of what she has done are coming into my possession." Griselda set a purring tone with her stepson.

Abelard puffed up and yelled at her, "Then tell me, what has she done?"

Griselda nodded. Keep the shark circling, looking for answers, and you can take the tuna from its very mouth. "Under the nose of your councilors, she took a loan on the fiscal estate she holds." Griselda said in an even tone, delivering a kick to the fallen priest while Phlem, taking his cue, picked him up from the floor. "Your damn father and his distrust of you. Look around, the season is past when you can let that little cretin-girl run circles around you. She has played her game. Her stone is resting on the board, but know, we use it to our advantage. We knock her stone off the clay and replace it with our own."

Abelard was not ready to listen. He stormed over to Youti al-Presence. The simpering man was the son of a Guisarme who Nawaz had executed on the battlefield. His eldest brother and sister had been dragged to the imagined horrors of the island of silence. Yet the simp was loyal, or too scared to act.

"What is this about a loan?" Abelard asked.

"It was not from the banks of the Camellia. It was from the Great Bank!" Abelard put his hands around the banker's neck, causing him to cry out in pain.

Griselda advanced again to his side. "Let Youti down, Son. He does not have all the answers, I do.

Abelard swung around and seemed to notice the woman in red for the first time. Her dress was long and sumptuous, and she was covered by ostentatious jewelry. Indeed, she was only a meter from being outright apostolical, given the extravagance of metal on her body. "Then it was you!" He yelled. "Step forward and explain."

The woman flowed forward like she was a great king rather than a coin counter. "It was us, and it was good business."

"Tell me!" Abelard yelled.

"Abelard, dear. Calm yourself. This is the Great Bank. They are not our enemy." She turned to the woman and said with a sly tone, "Not yet, at least."

The woman genuflected; a barely adequate motion of her chin and not the practice that was accepted in Cycus. "The wealth of Nazira was laid to her by Nawaz and recognized by the bank. It can be used as collateral, for nothing more, until she or her heir takes the throne. You have used that collateral as her guardian, but she called back your control, paid off your debts, and borrowed a large sum on her dower rights," the banker said in purring tones.

Youti al-Presence approached cautiously. "She paid the Dominion's debts. We are not immediately in trouble," he said. "She could have burned the entire land to the ground simply by withholding the principal and keeping us from servicing."

The banker smiled. "Indeed, it was the one thing she could do with the principal. Use it to pay the debts accrued under your administration, my dear Dominar. Of course, there is another issue that your banker is not saying…"

"What are you not saying, Youti! Tell me what you are not saying!" Abelard screamed, slurring his words and rubbing his forehead with his left hand.

"Dominar, the balance. She now holds the balance. She cannot know about the payments in sinister, the deal you made with the al-Youseffi and the al-Cinci. That money-sinister came from the interchange of funds on the principal of Nawaz's fortune that Nazira now holds in chief, and since she is married, the child will hold distaff. In twelve months, unless Nazira confirms the debt and returns to paying the Guisarme's geld, there will be no payments." Youti explained.

"What have you done, banker?" Abelard asked the representative of the great bank.

"I did nothing, Dominar. Your money was not entrusted to you. It says so right in the papers your father signed. It was able to be used by you as long as your daughter was in your partisans and not in her majority. When your daughter passed her ghalibia, she entered into control of the money, pending the entail, even if she did not exercise the rights until today. And from where the bank sits, she did you no harm. She paid off a vast debt and, in turn, created issues of liquidity of her own that she could have used to destroy the dominion and your banks. Priljubljena Banka does not play games with contracts, it honors them," she said with finality.

"Then you will see her change her mind after I strip the skin from her back," Abelard said calmly.

"My sorrow, Dominar, but you will not." The banker's tone, Griselda thought, was like a teacher scolding a student. "The bank has hired a protector for her. Until her child is born and her situation is settled, we will protect her. If she violates her contract with the bank, then it will not be you who takes vengeance on the girl," the banker said.

Abelard laughed. "That is still easy. This protector gets the same as your daughter. Stuffed in a dry well, up country."

The great banker said, "Priljubljena Banka will not permit this."

"Then you go in the well with them," Abelard said.

Then Chief Justicar interjected, "My Dominar, the bank would destroy us if we killed one of their kith. And the protector is not just a mercenary. It is one whose kith cannot be named."

"What cannot be named?" Abelard asked, confused.

"My son," Griselda said, turning him physically and putting her hands on his head to ensure he was looking her in the eyes. "Assassins. The bank has hired an assassin. If we move against this 'protector' before his or her contract is up, they will murder every one of us. How many of them are on Cycus? I can assure you if we kill even one of them, then the next ten ships that dock at the port will have a hundred more, all disguised as commoners."

The banker stepped to Abelard's side. "We of Priljubljena Banka are not kith, but you should treat us as if we were. No banker is harmed. Ever," the woman said in low tones.

Justicar Taffez helped first Youti al-Presence to his feet, then the priest Domingus. As he did so, he said, "There is the procession."

"What?" Abelard asked.

"My Dominar," Taffez said calmly as he worked to stanch the bleeding of the priest's nose. "The heir must be shown, and now that Nazira claims pregnancy and marriage, it is the best time that can be imagined. Put her in the veil, then put her on the road, away from whoever helped her plan this.

Let her try to line up her partisans and guards in the public glare of procession. When the heir is born, then we can fix the bank with a new minority heir," he said.

Griselda laughed. "Taffez, you idiot, I have to say you are thinking. The child cannot control the money until he or she reaches ghalibia. And Nazira need not raise the child, only birth it."

The banker in the red dress shook her head. "The child would be a minority under her mother and father, which is, as I understand, Nazira al-Youseffi and Javier al-Rasheed."

"She is NOT an al-Youseffi. She is not a Nabeel either," Griselda yelled at the banker. Then she calmed. "Neither of her parents will be alive, my dear banker. Not once your own protections drop and Nazira falls either to the blade of the assassin or to my own blade if that does not happen," Griselda said. "Or if she dies in childbirth or before giving birth at the hands of someone outside of the family, the same issue. No minority, just passage of the line to my daughter. The money as well."

Domingus looked worried. "The families will not accept the murder of the heir. It would break the Cycus 'dustari. And I doubt that they would see your daughter as the heir of Abelard."

"Who said murder? God's fire," Griselda said. "Knives slip. Bad food. So many ways to die and not be murdered." Griselda then turned and noticed her son-in-law was standing, now ignored in the room he had controlled just a minute before. "Let the families vote for the heir if needed. They won't vote for al-Cinci."

Abelard said in a soft voice, "I did not order anything yet. My head hurts and the voices are screaming in there again. I remember my father holding my hand when I was young. So sad is what a father must do to their child. So sad."

Griselda looked at the bashi leading the Life Guards. The Bashi looked at the Dominar and nodded. He walked up in martial order and asked, "Would the Dominar like to retire to quarters?"

"It is said, Bashi al-Kansi. Do you have a child?" he asked.

"Three Dominar," the Bashi responded.

"If you have to kill them, do it quickly," the Dominar replied in a low voice.

Griselda touched her stepson again. She felt nothing but contempt for the lump of a man who raved in the hallways and slurred his words constantly. She nodded at the Bashi again and he helped the Dominar return to chambers.

Griselda turned to the others in the room standing in disarray. "Back to your duties. Or do nothing. That is what you lot are good for."

They left, and Griselda looked to the banker. The woman was so sure of herself, tall and loverly in tens of thousands of silver coins worth of dress and jewelry. Green zumarud and blue jawharat zarqa' cut to precise angles to catch the light and flash as she turned. An eahira who was paid by the day for her services. No kith but at the counting house, so sure her power was limitless. "I took your positions. You take mine," she said.

The banker bowed. "The bank takes its own position."

Griselda nodded. She turned for her next duty but stopped. Over her shoulder, she said, "Do not assume that if this goes wrong, I won't have you horribly murdered, abused for days by my partisans. I may be willing to fight the Priljubljena Banka just to have a shot at making you beg for Phelm here to cut your throat." She looked to the side, caught the banker's face, and saw fear in her eyes.

Her soldiers dispersed and Phelm turned to follow her down the grand stairs and out into the Bailey. Her people had someone held for her. She walked down the cardinal path and turned off onto the distaff that led to a doorway in the side of the wall. She was tired, but this had to be done. She let Phelm open the doorway, which led to a well opening and a space where a man was tied to a chair with two of her partisans behind him. "Who is this?" she asked.

Phelm cleared his throat. "The minder of the princess."

"Your name?" Griselda asked.

"Parm al-Zudio. I am on the staff of the butler," he said.

"Listen to me. You were the minder for the princess, yes?" Griselda asked.

"Yes," the man calmly said.

Griselda nodded, and her partisans produced a chair. "Why are you not scared?" she asked.

"I did nothing wrong, Dame Griselda. The butler knew of my work and knew I did it well," he said.

Griselda nodded. "I need to hear from you the truth. Lie, and you will be punished. Tell the truth, and you will be rewarded. Simple as that."

The man nodded. "I have been the only minder for the princess, and I have done my duty well, Dame Griselda. I have no reason to lie."

"Good, then tell me what you know of the princess, be detailed," Griselda said calmly. It was a false calm.

"I was tasked by the butler after the princess passed ghalibia to ensure the princess did not become pregnant with, as he said, anyone who was a philanderer or of low birth. So I assayed to follow her on her reveries and assure that none of her contacts could see her with child," the man said.

"What reveries?" Griselda asked.

"Well, the princess often took to the less used spaces of the castle and palace with her friends. But I had intelligence that most were women and that she had relations with one woman in particular, which were quite innocent," the man said.

"In that it was not, how do you say, consummated?" Griselda asked.

"Oh, no Dame Griselda, they consummated many times! However, Major Standish—that is her rank now, at least— she was not a major when she was doing all the consummations, could not leave her with child. I know the rumors are that she is, well, special in that way, but the physician assured me that she was not so … well … equipped is a word I might use. Their consumptions could not result in children," the man said.

Griselda frowned. Exactly how Nazira was able to marry al-Rasheed was an important blind spot in her chaperonage. But the man was not wrong that a princess who owed dower respect to the crown was almost never prohibited from relations inside of her gender. Griselda was married young, so the issue never presented itself, but many in the palace followed the practice. "So this was the extent of her reveries. She had a lover among her coterie?"

"Well, to start," he said.

Griselda put her head in her hands and felt a pain starting behind her eyes. "Did her reveries extend past the hidden corners of the palace and castle?"

The man nodded. "Oh yes!" he exclaimed. "She was older, of course, when that started. She still consummated with the major a lot, but she started leaving the castle in disguise. She is quite clever. She started consummating a few guards and some kitchen staff."

"Women?" Griselda asked, head in her hands.

"Oh no, but she was quite responsible," he said.

"How was she responsible?" Griselda groaned as she asked.

Parm al-Zudio said, "Oh, she used two hands, one she put on the man's..."

"No!" Griselda said. "She had dalliances with lots of men as well as women?"

Parm shook his head, "No, she consummated with me and women in a way that would not leave her with child. They then turned a blind eye to her leaving the castle. I mean she was very safe and very clever, and I warned all the staff that she was, how do you say, in contact with that they would be burned in a fire if they asked for it or went further. They all understood. The rule was only when she offered, and nothing to make the princess, well, gravid is a word?"

Griselda groaned again. "Gravid is a word, Parm al-Zudio. So that was the extent of the, how are you calling it, consummations?"

"Oh no, Dame Griselda," he replied.

She looked up into his eyes. The fool really did not know what he had done. "Tell me."

"Well, she would go into the taverns on the docks. She did not consume unfit beverages, but she cavorted with those that did. And she consummated in a safe way with several. Interesting people, a pirate, a knight from the regiments, a scholar who was writing a book. Always women, or men who she consummated in a safe way." He actually looked proud.

"And you allowed it?" Griselda asked.

"I intervened when needed. Naseer al-Dinni was hot after her and wanted more than just the normal consummation. So I doctored his rum and beer drinks," Parm al-Zudio said. "Well, you know how people who chew qat cannot ... well, if they are men, they cannot... I am not sure how to say this, Dame Griselda," the man explained.

"You do not have to," Griselda said. "So you doctored the drinks of 'Jinn of the High Seas?'"

"Well," Parm replied, "him and others, but to tell the truth, I need not have done that. She was strict on how they acted. And she was always protected by all her friends. Now some of them would take on the more lustful of her companions, and they did some things... let me tell you, if I wrote a book, it would sell! But the princess... she never had the chance or seemed to care to have one. I am sorry if she felt bad though, considering how many of her friends she met in the taverns were not able to, well, be consummated because of issues..."

"Let us press on. If you were so careful, how does she get, well, you call it gravid, but I say pregnant?" Griselda asked. She looked at Phelm standing next to her and saw that he was looking straight ahead as if he was ignoring all of this. But that muscle in his face that twitched when he was angry was twitching. *Good*, she thought. *Be angry, Phelm.*

Parm al-Zudio said cheerfully, "One of her special friends, it turns out, was not interested in her the way the others were. At least he was not always pestering her for consummation. He was Javier al-Rasheed. She met him when Captain Naseer al-Dinni had fallen out from the rum. His crew dragged him away, and his second officer introduced Nazira to al-Rasheed. Now, he is technically a knight, whereas Naseer is from the right kith, but is a pirate."

"What do you mean, al-Rasheed is a knight?" Griselda growled.

"The rule the butler gave me was no children from dissolute sorts without rank. And no children outside of marriage. And no marriage but to one of rank." Parm al-Zudio stated with idiotic tenacity.

"Let me understand," Griselda said. "Al-Rasheed gambles."

"All the time. Loses a lot of money," Parm said earnestly.

"He is said to be insane," she stated.

Parm shook his head. "Not insane. He has an imaginary friend. It is quite humorous, everyone plays along."

"He is a whoremonger," Griselda said, disbelieving what she was hearing.

Parm shook his head, "Oh no, they never charge him. Strangest thing I have ever seen. He does not, to my knowledge, run with the men in the capital who charge for that sort of thing, but more than one of the women who console lonely men and women have consoled him to my knowledge, but never for money. Never saw anything like that. If that sort of traffic would not charge me a handful of silver, I would be on the docks every night. If you ask me, that is the crazy part. He did not use any of that, well, let us call it lucky wealth, when he started seeing the princess."

Griselda shook her head. "Seeing? How could he be seeing her, what does that mean?"

"Well, they started talking in the tavern, and Nazira and her lot were pretending to be chars. Far as I know, he did not know better than she was a char. Anyway, they started reading together. Going to the games and playing shuffle. Dancing at the Covenry. Walking and talking. There were no rules, you understand, stopping that. Woman can pay court, and he is a knight," Parm al-Zudio said.

Griselda shook her head at the dullard and his inability to read the room. "So how did she get pregnant?"

"Well, like she should, she married him," Parm al-Zudio replied. "Could have been the first night, but they consummated so much it was only a matter of time." He paused, then said, "I felt sorry for Standish. She did not take it well. Nothing to be done though."

Griselda stood up without a word and left the well room. Phelm followed her. She looked at the warrior and said, "Take care of them."

"Them?" he asked.

"The guards as well." She turned her back and walked to the palace with a bad taste in her mouth.

CHAPTER V

The Remarker Plot

Angela was imposing in her leather armor and chain coifs. She dropped a scrap of paper from her clenched fist and walked into the stairwell up to the main porticos. Gullen looked at the retreating warrior but was distracted by Petrovson giving a nasty sneer.

"Like to get a hold of her in the dungeon alone," he said. He was a difficult sort whose father had struck fear in the palace. Petrov Petrovson was every bit his father and liked to wear his bloody leathers through the honored halls of the palace. When Gullen was appointed his apprentice, it was a horrible day followed by many things that could not be unseen.

"Major Standish would see to your yatadalas if you accosted her without a battalion at her back, and most of the guard would do the same," Gullen replied. She bent and picked up the paper.

"What did she drop?" Petrovson asked.

Gullen showed him the paper, which was five by eight centimeters and made from low-quality scap. It had a bunch of letters and numbers scrawled around it in ink. "She draws on paper all the time, nonsense."

Petrovson peered at the paper. "You grew up with her, I remember that. Oban-Bey was your tutor. I used to watch your lot play in the courtyard from the Firthing Tower."

"What of it?" Gullen asked.

The crude man laughed. "I bet you were shocked to be handed over to a man like me for your job in the palace."

Gullen sniffed in disdain. "Every child in the creche gets a preferred job in the palace. Why not me?"

Petrovson laughed. "No, I mean you probably thought with your neat writing and airs you would get better than a dungeon master. I mean, my father was THE dungeon master, so I apprenticed under him. You, though, ran with the quality ... the princess no less. And then they stuck you with me."

"Lister al-Cinci is from a great family," she said. "He is your apprentice!"

Petrovson guffawed so loudly that people in the lower hall turned from their work and stared. "Lister is an al-Cinci, but he is the idiot son of an idiot flower monger Abd. Not a real al-Cinci, or else he would be an officer or a clerk."

Gullen shrugged. It was true that her position in the dungeons had been an insult. It was because she had beaten the simpering al-Youseffi whelp to teach her some manners. She was not going to confirm that to the so-called master of the torture rack. She withdrew the scrap of paper. What Petrovson did not know was that their little group had their own childish secret code, a code that allowed them to pass messages without Dame Griselda or her nasty lot finding out. The flattened paper said, "meet in the hall of statues."

You just had to know how to read it. She crumpled it up and put it in her working coat pocket.

"If you knew the game of the dungeons, you could make money, be important like my father," Petrovson said.

"How could I make money cutting the yatadalas off of some idiot who ran afoul of Abelard? It is vile work," Gullen said.

"You and I, we do not have a kith name. You were an orphan, and my father was not the man people invited into their family homes or sponsored marriages with. If you were nice to me, I would cut you in for the silver," Petrovson said. "The guard caught Javier al-Rasheed last an hour ago."

Gullen's knees almost buckled. Nazira, her patron and friend, had secretly married Javier and was pregnant with a child between them. He was a dashing navy officer and a scoundrel who was famous for helping command the frigate *Constellar* through its tour of the Halo. "It is interesting that al-Rasheed needed to be caught. I saw him on the docks yesterday."

Petrovson smirked. "Oh, his past is catching up to him, and before they slice the last piece off of him, there will be a sack of silver on my belt. We could share."

Gullen knew exactly what Petrovson meant by share. "You must excuse me, Master."

"Why?" he asked.

Gullen said grimly, "Because I want to spend the rest of the day relaxing, given that you called Lister and me in late."

"Not myself, but the Dominar's secretary. Dominar Abelard returns on the late tide from his sport and will see to al-Rasheed with us. You be there no later than twenty-four," he said.

"Of course," she said, then turned to the stairs up to the portico.

Everyone met to talk in the Hall of Statues. It had benches, was fifty meters long, collected a nice breeze from the sea in summer, and was heated by braziers in winter. The statues and tapestries soaked up sound like a wild sponge soaked up salt water, so you could be ten meters from another person and not hear what they were saying.

Standish was standing by a brazier alcove, warming her hands and looking out at the thick clouds above the port city. She nodded to Gullen and said, "They say a big storm is coming, a few days away. I have news from Nazira."

Gullen took out the scrap of paper with the coded note and threw it into the fire. "They captured Javier."

Standish laughed with a dark chuckle. "I captured Javier. He was not hard to find."

"You cannot take your pain out on Nazira's husband," Gullen scolded.

Standish's face grew angry in the firelight. "I did no such thing. Nazira commanded it."

Gullen chuckled, herself. "Then our beloved Nazira has a plan?"

"Not one that I approve, but one that I fear must be. You have heard Griselda and the al-Youseffi talk. She is dead when she has an heir. And taking flight with Naseer al-Dinni, that was good for no one to be a pirate's flame." Standish handed Gullen a leather envelope.

"What is this?" Gullen asked.

"Instructions and money drafts, all you need. Nazira and Oban-Bey have been busy when we both took the yoke of adulthood around our necks. Only, now only her best friends, you and I, are free to pull the trigger on her damn complicated firelock," Standish said. "I have been summoned to meet with the Dominar when he returns with his retinue over what to do with al-Rasheed."

Gullen slipped the documents into her coat pocket. "I have been summoned as well, for my first torture and dismemberment. Petrovson is so pleased over that. With the Dominar in the chamber, I will not be able to ignore his orders or walk away. It will be my knife that flays Nazira's love's skin from his body." She saw that despite her veneer, Standish was sad. "I am sorry, Angela. I know you and she were ... special."

"More than special," Standish replied.

"You know it was never to be. Nazira belongs to the Dominion as the heir, at least until they steal it from her. And then if they do, she will be dead. At least with Javier, her duty to have an heir can be achieved," Gullen explained, placing her hand on Standish's knee.

"Anyone else can marry who they want, why not Nazira? She cannot possibly love Javier. He is an end to a means," Standish said.

Gullen looked at her childhood friend. Growing up in creche under the same dancing master was a close bond. There were two score-odd children of destiny in the palace creche, all carrying important kith names that indicated to the world no matter what skills and knowledge they would attain, no matter how hard they worked or what they achieved, they would be important people in the Dominion. These children with names like al-Cinci, al-Jouseffi, and al-Nabeer, form a traveling circus of pomp, living part of each year in their countryside landed-estates, and part of each year in the Cycus Palace, the great folly of Nawaz I, First Dominar and warlord conquerer of Cycus.

But there was one child who did not travel to estates because his home, first and last, was the palace. Kemeyan practice was to surround a child-of-destiny with other children to form a coterie, which would teach the child to rule.

It was supposed to be unrelated children who worked for the palace, but none of the other kiths, being Guisarmes, followed the practice. Nazira, granddaughter of Nawaz, though, had her coterie selected exactly because they were not attached to an island clan.

There was Angela, orphan of a Denuvani jute merchant who had died over a business deal with the al-Dinni; Clathy, whose father had brought her from the trailing island of Semini to do the books for the Dominar; Saad, whose father was an officer with the Life Guards; and Abadi, the child of an officer from the Docks Regiment. And, of course, Gullen was a founding adopted by the palace to fill out the entourage of the princess.

Like all important children, Nazira had a dancing master to teach grammar, rhetoric, astronomy, and logic. He was supposed to teach athletics, acrobatics, and music, but had no skill in these three. His name was Oban-Bey, and he was either incredibly strict or absolutely lax in turns that changed with the wind. All of Nazira's group would be taught and shepherded by Oban.

And although they were sisters in the creche, Standish and Nazira had gone past that. Though Nazira, Gullen believed, never took the relationship as a romance. Standish, though, did, and dreamed of a life that could never happen.

"I think she loves Javier," Gullen said gently.

Standish clenched her fists and said, "Be off. If this works, I will be at sea and we will not meet again, at least for a year. Protect her."

Gullen touched her hands and left.

She knew the face dancer, which is why she was needed for this one task. All of her other labors were to hand signed documents to bankers or pass currency to the people who paid for sinister hands to work in dangerous matters, but the face dancer was different. She knew him because of a favor she had done for him, a favor that saved a child he said he did not care for from a horrible end at the hands of an al-Youseffi. As they all had learned from the creche, favors were a currency in the streets of the port of Cycus, and the best way to get favors was to first do them in turn.

"You travel a strange path, artfal alqadar." The face dancer said.

'Atfal alqadar' was what they called them, the children of the creche who were from the great kiths. Children of destiny. They were the children who were 'arba'a aashar' or 'first born,' meaning not that they were the oldest but, instead, were saddled with being the children who would inherit titles, lands, and wealth, children who were now coming of age and taking their place in the ruling families of the land of Cycus.

The face dancer and Gullen sat in the lowest of dives, a tea shop that served more date gin and palm rum than tea. A place where the idle smoked hooka stuffed with tanbul nuts and the cigars were cut with imported qat leaf. Or sometimes the patrons bought tea, but the qat was infused in the glass of what should be a wholesome drink. You could tell the tanbul smokers and the qat chewers in that they would sit looking at the rickety wooden tables in the dive twitching, unable to collect their minds, thin from the ravages the stimulants took on their systems, occasionally getting into paranoid screaming fights with each other as they crossed some threshold between stupor and paranoia.

"I am hardly atfal alqadar," Gullen said.

"Al-Cinci, Al-Youseffi, you run in rare circles," the face dancer said.

Gullen laughed. "I work with an al-Cinci who is anything but rare."

"Poor Lister. He has sold out to Daniella the Red Hand. And one of her lot sold out to Naseer the Pirate. Or maybe I have it backward. It is no matter. Tonight, they kill Javier al-Rasheed on the rocky beaches of the port, unless they kill each other first," the face dancer said. "So many betrayals all looking to gut one rather dashing playboy and naval officer."

Gullen pushed a folder to the face dancer. "One more betrayal than your spies have told you about."

The face dancer pulled the envelope forward and opened it. "Ah, I have a part in this play! I will be playing the role of the renowned Devious. I think I will wear false teeth."

"Do you understand it? Do you know what is to be done?" Gullen asked.

"I seem to be taking the name of another man and then waiting for you to distract your fellow dungeon masters and take Captain al-Rasheed to this pirate ship *Remarker*. But I must remind you, *Remarker* is owned by a man who will not hesitate to kill al-Rasheed," the face dancer said with a chuckle.

"Naseer no longer owns the ship. My master Nazira does," Gullen said.

"Does Naseer know this?" the face dancer asked.

"No, but he took the boat without paying. I merely paid for what he took and transferred the ship to my mistress. The *Remarker* is now a tea trader."

"So Javier al-Rasheed is now a married tea merchant captain. An error ends in laughter, I am afraid. I do have one concern. I owe you this boon, and your proposal for payment is acceptable, but the role you cast me in is one of taking the name of a very dangerous man, Devious. Will he not be angered by my deception? Even a face dancer must be concerned with repercussions." The man waved his hands expansively as if the reprobates in the tea tavern would represent a danger if they discovered he was taking the name of another.

Gullen put her head in her hands, then looked back up and said, "On my honor, I guarantee that Devious will not object to your impersonation. In fact, as far as I know, he is leaving Cycus and will not return for a long time."

Chapter VI

The Taximan Sings

As the cutter carried Nazira to the docks, leaving her husband and her best friend to fling themselves into the seas of eternity carrying a great burden, she started to get lulled into a false sense of daydreaming calm by the boatswain calling the sculls. Surprisingly, the cockswain sang the cadence in the old tongue, which dragged her mind further into a stupor.

"Ta'arjah almijdhaf wahafr altifl," the lead sailor sang in vibrant deep tones, looking for other boats or even ships that could hull the cock boat and send it down. Fatalistically, the oarsman replied, "natajidif ealaa shati akhar!" They had an odd tonal way of carrying each phrase that made the words alien in their rising and falling cadence, as if they had learned the archaic form of trade in some mystical shore on the far edges of Ocean. As an inmate of the palace, Nazira's experience with the varied patterns of speech that the Halo offered was comprehensive. Visitors to court spoke the trade tongue in a hundred ways, some almost impossible to understand. And running the docks she has further heard the trade speech twisted by drunkenness, dolor, and imbecility, yet never had she heard the ancient trade language spoken in such a saccharine manner. It was like their tongues were spinning toffee candy in the form of sounds and sending it out into the universe.

"Have you ever heard such singing?" She looked at her body servant Oban, who sat in an upset and turgid mood. She knew that only Oban's loyalty held his tongue over her moves that sent the father of her child into the great seas of the Halo risking death and financial ruin. Rolling half the dice and expecting victory was what he called it.

"Adfae sighar alma', hafiz ealaa tadafuq majadifik lil'amami!" came a bark from the cockswain, and the oarsman replied, "fam almawt hu almakan aladhi nadhhab 'iilayh jmyean ealaa 'ayi hal."

Oban finally snapped out of his funk, or at least pretended to be content. "They sing a song from Kemeya. It is a pirate's drive chanty, a violent song for violent men."

"Then these men are pirates?" Nazira asked.

Oban shook his head. "No, they are just taximans, but they have learned the song from someone who speaks the old tongue as the pirates do. Or so I assume."

Nazira nodded, letting herself relax as the boat sculled through the water. "I cast all of our dice on this, my dear Oban. Many innocents may die before this is over."

Oban set his hand on her shoulder. "My young princess is tired. Shall I massage your hands?" Her caretaker was moon-faced, heavyset, balding, and dressed in the loose robes of a servant, with the white and green parti-color pattern that announced him as a servant of the Camellia Throne. While he was maddening in many ways, Oban had been with Nazira since she could remember. Her mother had left when she was tiny, a distant thought dragged into her reality by current events, but her servant Oban had stepped into the job of raising her, asking nothing. He fidgeted, warned, harped, predicted, and fussed, but more than once he had taken savage beatings from court masters, until they realized that disliked by her father or not, she was still the princess of Cycus and heir to the Dominar's titles and wealth. Oban was her shield and conscious that had allowed her to survive until she could take matters into her own hands, but in doing so, she may have killed them all.

She smiled at her caretaker and offered her hands, then closed her eyes and found she was triggered to revery. The past swam into view as the taximen sang, and the present left her as she daydreamed in a cloudy reverie.

The cutter she rode sliced through the waves of the harbor like a wren flew through the summer air, slowing and almost falling out of the air until a new powerful pull of the wings lifted it back into the stream and propelled it forward. Each oar moved into and out of the water with precision to the cadence of the soulful song. They cut the water with a powerful push, and, like the wren, seem to stop and start with the effort of the skulls.

The oars crashed into the water and heaved the cutter forward with each downbeat in the song's stanzas. Nazira felt her thoughts and knew that she was dedicated to a terrible purpose. She had indeed cast her dice into a viper's pit with no guarantee that any would read twelve and carry the day. Yet she knew it was the only way she would see the next year out. If there had been a better solution, some more elegant way forward, she would have taken it.

She considered Oban, who sat next to her and worried with her hair. He was the caretaker who had raised her through her lonely and hard youth. His presence was, as much as anything else, a sign to Nazira that time marches on. Oban was a sad man, dedicated and fussy, with great strength, but he worried all the time at things no one else could see. Where he had come from and what he was, Nazira did not know. Standish had speculated on his back-story throughout their childhood. They had noted how the man made her father nervous, but why he should disturb the great Dominar was never apparent. He was a burly man, and immensely fat. But he moved with a dancer's grace and was immensely strong. He complained often, but his complaints were never for himself, only for Nazira.

He interrupted her reverie. "There are people on the dock."

Nazira looked out into the darkness. There should be people waiting for her on the dock; the comment made little sense in and of itself. Then Nazira saw that the people on the dock were the wrong people, and the right people were hanging from the cargo cranes, stretched out and lifeless like limp, dried fish. Corvids and sea vans were already gathering for their feast of human flesh, only waiting for the light of the torches to leave them to their super.

The dead were pirates, hired by the former crew of the *Remarker*, and were not a serious matter to Nazira in the basic thread of events, any more than the grass that was trampled by her sedan was an issue of worry. Yet this was the first event that had not gone to plan in the past month, since she had realized she was pregnant and launched her great game. The oarsmen had their backs to the spectacle, but the cockswain could clearly see the harvest of death blowing gently in the harbor breeze. The next song verse stuck in his throat, and he looked at Nazira with fright.

"One-two-three," she said, "keep rowing!"

A second passed and then Nazira's cross face overcame the cockswain's fear for his life, and he began calling the rowing cadence. She turned back to the dock and looked carefully. It was Melinda standing with a gaggle of soldiers, her husband Bostwick, and a few serious-looking courtiers. A welcoming party, as it were. She was not scared of them. She could only die once, and that was her fate at the hands of her father, but she hated losing. It made her angry in the depth of her being. Somehow, she had to see this play and meet it in kind.

The cutter turned into the dock and slid roughly into place; the oarsman listing their sculls at the last second, lacking orders from the shaken cockswain.

Melinda flashed her eyes at Nazira and said, "I could have you killed right here. I could have these soldiers tie you to an anchor stone and toss you in the harbor. I could have them flay your skin and feed it to you!"

From behind her came a calm voice, "No, you cannot." It was the courtier Regnal Bish al-Beijus, a colorless and minor functionary in court, usually assigned to carry messages by her father to other courtiers. Someone who did not matter any more than the dead pirates hanging like a horrible harvest of brown peaches from the gantry crane on the docks. Colorless was the best description Nazira could come up with for him, although he was not invisible, merely drab. He wore particolor as was expected in court, but the colors he always chose were grey, black, and brown. He was such a non-entity that he could be standing in a room an hour and you would suddenly realize he was present when his gaze fell on you. Although he was technically a knight and entitled to stand armed in the presence chamber, he did not select a talwar or yataghan such as was preferred by true fighters, but instead, had a drab, blue-black kirpan suspended from a doughty and unbecoming frog attached to a leather cast-er-belt. Yet here he commanded the Dominar's favorite bas-tard, Melinda al-Cinci d' Courtage, like she was an errant service maid.

Nazira waited for the explosion from her half-sister, her well-known temper tantrums being the single defining characteristic of her personality, but there were none. Instead, there was a slow-boiling steam, as if a limestone heating rock had been thrown in a hulling pot when it was cherry red and all out molten. It made itself evident through the tensing of Melinda's wrists and the flexing of her neck muscles. Nazira could hear her perfect teeth grind into each other like masa stones kneading dried slake corn.

Regnal Bish continued, "My apology at this correction, but your sister…"

"Half-sister," Melinda snapped. That was an angry point. Melinda's kith was al-Cinci. She was not in the line, instead being a second viola to Dame Griselda al-Youseffi and her daughter and granddaughter. If not for Nazira, the direction of precedence fell on the al-Youseffi and not the al-Cinci bas-tards. Melinda might be beloved of Abelard, but she was not important. Not really.

Bish bowed his head at the correction offered by Nazira's half-sister. "Thank you, high born. Your half-sister is now mother to the heir apparent and protected by laws that not even the Dominar can break. She is the recognized line, you are not. You may not touch her."

And that, Nazira thought, was a dressing down that would make Melinda furious. The Dominar, Melinda and Nazira's father, had four children, but the only one through a line recognized by the Clanute Superior, the Priesthood, or the old guard that held onto power since the days of the Dominar's father, was Nazira. Melinda could essay angry expositions about the fact she was the eldest child, she could scream and beat servants, lose her cool in the presence chamber, and tip over tables at state dinners, but none of this made the laws defended by the conservatives any more liberal to her desires. She looked at the calm, dignified courtier Regnal Bish, and then to her hyperventilating sister having a meltdown under the torches that lit the dock, and knew she was far from understanding all the issues she faced, but this one she did understand.

Melinda had power amongst the radicals, but no power where it counted, at the center of the Dominion. It was possible she could be named King of some portion of the Dominion where the al-Cinci name mattered, but she would always have to rule under the watchful gaze of the Dominar. And the next Dominar was Nazira's son or daughter.

Bostwick looked at his wife's anger and seemed like he wanted to protect himself from it. He shook his fist at Bish. "Regnal, you had best be careful of my wife and I. We are bad business."

Bish nodded. "As you say, Lord Bostwick." Then he turned to the commander of the Life Guards. "Let us take the Princess to her accommodations." The commander was a Bashi in green and yellow, with an orange stripe on his jacket. He had a dozen medals but otherwise was a non-entity. He took Regnal Bish's orders without complaint.

There were two sedans. One was Melinda's own, but the other was less luxurious, and its drive team was not as well coifed. She considered the vicuna and realized that while Melinda's wore bangles in a striking manner, they were bandy-legged and not physically in their prime. They were prancers from the Dominar's stables that were kept for their wool and were used only in court functions. The nondescript sedan had vicuna of a completely different caliber.

They were broad-shouldered yamalids, strong, jug-headed creatures with poor wool used by farmers for cartage and plowing. Regnal Bish extended his hand to the nondescript sedan, and even aided Oban into the cart with her. "Dame Melinda, you may follow us if you want."

"As if," she yelled, then stalked to her own sedan. Half of the company of Life Guards formed around her cart and escorted her up the draw away from the docks. Nazira watched as they left until Regnal Bish pulled up the window screens and blocked her view.

He got into the sedan and closed the door. "We will let your half-sister withdraw far enough that she does not come up with any form of mayhem."

Nazira looked at the crazy-eyed man and said, "So my father has sent a functionary to collect me?"

Bish turned and seemed to look at her. You could never tell. "I assigned myself this duty knowing that your half-sister intended to execute you on the docks."

Nazira nodded. "How nice of you. You should go into business rescuing damsels."

Regnal Bish shook his head. "The issue you face is not if you will be executed, but when, at least at this second, as I understand it. As long as you carry the heir legal though, you must be protected and indeed shown off to the Dominion."

"Shown off?" Nazira yelled.

Bish hit the front of the sedan, and it began to move. "You will find out soon. I dare say your games with finances have caused more than a few headaches. You managed to save your lover's life, but at what cost?"

"Husband, I married him," she said.

"And the priest who married you is hanging in the yards of the castle." Regnal Bish replied.

"Damn my father!" Nazira yelled in anger. "Damn my father to hell and back."

"The Princess should remember past events that, though she is invulnerable, for now, others are not. Others can be quite vulnerable. You have played an impressive game, but people who underestimated you are no longer quite so gulled by your act. In fact, I will be your companion until at least your child is born, and I no longer see you as a child," he said as they bumped across the cobbled road.

The next morning a deputation arrived.

Chief Justicar Colonel Abrams Taffez, the Priest Domingus bar Calad, and the Bank Master Youti al-Presence looked like three singers from a funeral dirge, each with long beards, craggy faces, sunburned noses, and graying hair caught in crazy wraps held in place by fish bone belners. Each wore a chest of silver's worth of sumptuous linen shirts, particolor swallow-tailed coats, and had their heads wrapped in jewel-studded turbans. They had great delicate chains of scrim-shell and cerulean weighing their necks, formal knee gows for genuflecting before the Dominar, and indicated their knightly status with long, curved talwars, carried in jewel-encrusted lambskin scabbards hanging on chintz froggings clutched onto brightly dyed sisal belts. The court dress always minded Nazira of the display of peacocks, especially since the women at court fashioned themselves in more simple clothing that reflected some aspect of their chosen cultural background. Nazira herself saw inner court dress as nonsense. She had always dressed in the ways of the outer court as a timesaver. She usually wore a pegged linen dresser with a kilt and tunic over top, wool in winter and linen in summer. If she was in chambers, she preferred a simple blouson and favored a half jacket for warmth in the halls of the great castle she had grown up in.

She could have dressed in the finest kid and showered herself in shellback and roseru, carting twenty kilos of the finest on her small frame, but the waste of money in court was enough, and Nazira did not want to participate in the farce that far, even if her dancing master said it was the language of the court. What language? A tongue where silk or satin were consonants and scrimshaw, shellback, alluyria, or roseru were vowels? A language that had courtiers standing across from each other considering the meaning of a topaz stick pin while the business of court flowed around them ignored? Regnal Bish, who stood beside her, was a non-entity in court wearing dark particolor and a swallowtail of gray, and no one admonished him for being tone deaf. They chittered behind his back, over his eyes and his stooped posture, but otherwise ignored him.

The tableaux was set in the farthest hall in the rear portico of the palace. It was a place where vendors drank tea with the buyers to supply the palace with taffeta, glass and wood cups, cotton sheets and coverlets, baskets of keena and split pea, plus a thousand other things that allowed the dominion to house its ruling class in comfort. The room had a cockpit of sitting cushions underneath a large parasol, softly steaming censors giving off the scents of commiphora mixed with serrata. Nazira would have preferred this to happen in the lesser presence chamber of her quarters but had not come unarmed. She had Oban prepare a service cart as a tea service made from clear blown glass, a traditional stone kettle on an alcohol paraffinated-gel fire, and cups of pure silver. The cups in particular discomforted priest Domingus, who was notably el-dari.

The three great men stood in a cluster near the verges of the room and had brought six Life Guards, two each, who wore the torques of personal protectors. They nodded at

Regnal Bish, who sat on a wool tuffet near the chamber's fireplace but ignored Oban. Bish seemed to be occupied and merely looked into the fireplace while he fiddled with manicuring his fingers.

"Tea for five, Oban. Please be seated, my father's knights, we have just enough cushions, though I am happy you did not bring Dame Hailee and Mortisa al-Cinci with you, as I would have had no place for you all to be at ease." Nazira smirked. By treating the portico room as hers and them as her guests, she took on the duty of service and the custom of 'alturuq alqadima,' which meant roughly the "way we used to act." Instead of hearing the three sanctimonious harpers play their weary tune, it would force them either into formal politeness or dishonor by breaking the traditions of court behavior in a very key way.

And she had done it in a way that would hopefully put them on their back feet. In naming the missing members of the council, she was taunting them in a way that they could not politely respond. In the old manner of discussion, passed down from the days before the Dominars or even the Guisarmes, one came to a negotiation either as oneself or as a group with no one missing. Nazira had called out that the missing members of the council, Dame Hailee who was Seigner for Interior, the Dominion's high constable, and Mortisa al-Cinci as the Warden, had created a social situation where the three members of the council who had appeared could not really claim the authority of the Dominar's Council. They would each speak as one of the five, but not as the whole five, at least in the manners of court.

The absence of the Warden and the Constable meant nothing in reality, but it was a way Nazira could throw some small roadblocks into the pretensions of these great men, and inform them that she had grown to adulthood watching the games of state. Her father ruled with a closed fist, ignorant of any subtlety of court communication, breaking glasses like some great scaled monitor let go in the glass cupboard. She was reminding them that she knew the ways of court, and saying quite plainly, "Why are you three here, and not all five?"

Taffez and Domingus took the astirkha cushions while Youti was, for some reason, taking a servant's stool. No one elected to cozy up on the divan pillows with Nazira. An uncomfortable silence settled over them as they all directed their attention to Oban and his preparation of the tea. It was the power of the ancient ceremony, the human desire for warm stimulants, and perhaps an element of the olfactory in the process of "waiting for tea." It left words unsaid, waiting for the process of bringing the water to boil and steeping the leaf, then pouring five portions.

The nature of the service was part of the ceremony. In her chambers, Nazira had her prized personal service. It was made from cheap copper and was a gift from her husband. The copper was ancient and would have looked appropriate in a peasant's cottage or fisher folks' den anywhere in the land, or for that matter, on almost any island of the Halo.

This service, though, was sumptuous. Oban had borrowed it from the kitchens, where it was used for tea service of the highest political importance. It was not part of the regular trade. A commoner could not order one in a dry goods store.

Oban was always fascinating to watch as he made tea. First, he cut blocks of paraffinated alcohol taken from the metal fireproof into useful sizes and placed them in the fire pan on the cart. Next, he measured out a liter of water from a decanter into a glass retort. This was a "cheaters portion"—meaning that the servant expected to drink the tea as well and thus five cups were actually six. It was not a compliment in the inner court that the servants drank tea, but a sign of caution. A servant was a taster whose sudden discomfort from drinking tea could signal an attempt at poison. This was never a concern in the outer court and in peasants' households, as no greater sin existed than the adulteration of tea. It was an essential element of tea service to the powerful.

Oban arranged the blocks and then lit them afire with a sparker. The flame rose up, and a look of surprise sketched the faces of the three men. Oban had likely spiked the fuel somehow to make the flame burst out like that; a bit of theatrics. The hot fire though, burning blue in the copper cooker, melted and lit the paraffin quickly and then settled down into a more reasonable flame.

Oban took out from the pantry box of the serviette a sealed jar marked "Dukhan," which was a north shore tea that Nazira always kept because her childhood friend Standish preferred it. If Nazira was attempting to show pride in her tea selection, she would have sent out for Mlik or Rwyal tea, both approved by the Dominar's kitchen for service to the elite, but the smokey Dukhan tea was excellent, and anyone who did not approve of it, did so out of personal pique rather than sensible taste preference. From the tea can, Oban measured 12 grams onto a scale, then placed the dried and crushed leaves into an infuser and lowered it carefully into the heating water. Unlike Mlik or Rwyal, Dukhan seeped at a little less than 90 degrees, requiring care by Oban to see that the water did not boil. He achieved this with a temperature ball and a small water service, allowing him to introduce a small amount of water to the copper teapot.

Once finished, Oban measured out six cups of tea and delivered five to Nazira, Bish, and her guests. Oban placed the glasses on a japanned tray and then took them to the guests. Regnal Bish took one at random and sat it down on the ground. Justicar Taffez took the furthest cup and almost spilled the tray. Master Youti dithered over the cups and finally selected the first one he had favored. Dominos genuflected in prayer for a second, then took a random cup.

Ordinarily, in the inner court, it would be up to Oban to take the last and drink before the watching guests, but, instead, Nazira took a cup and immediately sipped the hot liquid and waved Oban back to his corner. The tea ceremony of the inner court was not ridiculous. Poisoning was common, but Nazira did not fear Oban, and the tea service had been selected at random from a dozen like it stored in the sanctum of the Cycus palace. Taking her sip allowed each of the paranoid prelates the opportunity to drink the tea, and perhaps, find a better mood.

"Hospitality is served. Now, explain your reasons for demanding this meeting," Nazira said.

The three prelates looked nervously at each other, but it was Domingus bar Calad who spoke after a short silence. "There are rumors of your actions and rumors of those rumors. We have amassed much information, but it is time to hear from your own mouth about the truth behind the extraordinary events. For example, a prisoner of the dungeons seems to have escaped, two of the dungeon masters were injured in an explosion, and another is outright missing."

"Oh, is that all you want to know?" Nazira asked.

There was another uncomfortable pause. "No, the money. We want to know about the loan," Domingus replied, looking like he had eaten a bad oyster. He looked down at his silver teacup and put it down like it was poison.

"I took out a loan with the bank syndicate on the money that is part of my inheritance, which I receive when I am confirmed to be pregnant with the heir to the Dominion," she said.

Youti al-Presence leaped up and spilled his tea. "How dare you, that money keeps the Dominion fiscally sound!"

Nazira laughed. "Then you are not doing your job, are you Youti!" She looked at Domingus and drank deeply from her tea. "I happen to know my bequest is a tithe of the fiscal accounts. Where is the rest? How can one coin in ten bankrupt the Dominion?"

"And what did you do with the money?" Domingus bar Calad said.

"I used it to steal a pirate ship and outfit it as a tea trader, then I buried the rest of it in the mountains," Nazira replied.

Youti al-Presence yelled, "To the deep you say, damn your eyes!"

Domingus Bar Salad slapped the ground with his foot and rose from his seat as well. "Youti, regain your composure." He then turned to Nazira. "Dame Nazira, unlike the honorable Youti al-Presence, I do not care what you have done. The law says your child is heir to the crown. The money in the Barrister's account is preserved for your use, to raise your child until the age of their majority. Its wastage is unethical and a shame considering the limits of the Dominion's resources. However, it is not actionable nor an issue that I care about. Instead, I am here to give you the Dominar's orders to prepare for procession and, otherwise, I do not care to talk to you.

"What is this procession nonsense?" Nazira asked. "Have I broken the law, Domingus?" Nazira asked. "Have I done anything that is against the Great Statutes?" Nazira knew that each man had his weakness, and Domingus had a weakness for the letter of the law. Her comment made the man's jowly, pug-like face close in like he was trying to swallow his own chin.

"Dame princess. Your mother was in a similar position, and she was able to negotiate a way out of what she perceived was her own jeopardy. She even was able to push some of her agenda on the Dominar. Yet she survived. You have risked your life to protect an insane courtier like this al-Rasheed item. And then put your life in more jeopardy with what I hope is the truth about your pregnancy." Domingus said, leaning forward and using his teacup to emphasize his words.

"Are you saying, on your oath, that Melinda is wrong? That I am safe? That when my child is born, I will not be murdered?" Nazira said, drinking her smokey tea deeply after she spoke.

"You could have married who you were told to marry, then as long as you had children, you would be safe. Do your duty!" Taffez yelled. "Damn you, woman. Now you will do what you are told until the child is born. And what you are told is procession, and you will take a damn veil, that is certain. You will smile under that veil. You will show off yourself as a mother to the heir, and you will think about all of your sins and how you can make each one right."

"I am a broodmare?" Nazira asked. "And as for the veil, I will not take it. You cannot force one on me."

Taffez seethed. "Dame Melinda has no power to bedevil you, but we have your number. You think crazy eyes there is going to protect you? You asked if you were a broodmare, and the answer is yes, and as soon as the pup is squeezed out of your awful thighs, crazy eyes there will be seeing you off to the nether world and the heir will be with a brood nurse never to hear your name again. We won't be making a mistake like was made with your mother."

Nazira looked at Regnal Bish and considered him, seemingly ignoring the discussion and sipping his tea. Was he not just a guardian, but her killer? It seemed unlikely. He was a functionary, but not one who collected heads.

Domingus yelled at Taffez, "Will you be silent or so help me I will have your torque!" He spun around and pointed at Youti al-Presence and said, "Be seated al-Presence, unless you want me to call anathema on you. Your closets are dark, but the gods shine lights where they will."

Youti al-Presence stamped his feet in anger. "Ohhh, Domingus, you step too far. There are ways you can suffer as well."

Bish said quietly, "Enough confusion." He then stood from his chair and advanced between the three prelates. Gesturing to Nazira, he said, "She is your broodmare. Her husband cannot protect her. She has no power and no partisans. And you have already given her no choice on taking a veil. Your conduct is unseemly." He then turned to Nazira and said, "Procession is a tradition for the people. Your mother held you in procession and was feted for it. The people, they demand it, and it will allow us to get you away from court and on the road where we can protect you. Everything else is a song for another day. These men forget that there is time for all to settle, and a deed done now cannot be undone later. Not if it is a terminal deed."

Domingus bar Calad swallowed deeply, looked down for a second, then waved his fellows to their seats. He stared at the silver cup on the floor like it was a venomous snake. "The law says that you must go on a tour to show the people of Cycus that you are the mother of the heir. And while your loan is technically legal, it places you in jeopardy outside the law, unless you are pregnant with the heir and under the bans of the veil." He bent over, picked up the cup, and returned it to Oban, who accepted it with a bow. He then turned to Bish, the last person standing, and said, "My dear Regnal, you must yourself take your seat. You have one role here, a role none of us would have assigned you to, but your role has nothing to do with loans or procession. Only the assembly of the Princess's personal guard and the logistics around moving her from one place to another. That is your role. That and protecting one under veil."

Bish stood his ground. "Just so you know, my masters are not you and your coterie here."

Domingus waved his hand. "And just so you know, your limitations are known to me. Do not expand yourself in a way that violates those limitations."

"My dear Domingus, you say you know where my limitations are, but if you wake up late one night and hear a noise on your terrace balcony, please consider the dangers that exist in a misestimation of my, well, let us use your term, limitations." Bish then bowed his head and returned to his seat.

Domingus settled into his seat and said, "Princess, your cooperation is needed for this, not that ways could be found to do without it. The veil protects you. No one can move against a man or woman decreed to the veil, just as you will not be allowed to move while you wear one. Greater minds than yours have considered these issues."

"Then tell me of this procession," she asked of the prelate.

Youti al-Presence waved at Oban and shook his cup at the servant. Oban took the cup, filled it with tea, and returned it to the bank master, who took it down in one scalding drink. His mouth obviously burning, he flung it at Oban, who caught the hot cup gracefully and returned it to the service. The habit of drinking hot tea to show physical mastery was not one of court, but of the docks, and Youti did not have the skill or perseverance to do it. He tried to speak several times, nursing the burns in his mouth, then finally was able to start. "It is an ancient right. When the new heir is decided by the ancient laws, or in our case by the Cycus 'dustari, that heir is taken from town to town to be seen by the people, and to allow all the families and groups of the land to understand that this is the next leader of the realm."

"And my mother did this?" Nazira finished her tea and nodded to Oban, who collected her cup.

Domingus bar Calad interrupted Youti, who was still having problems speaking, "Your mother took you on procession. The details are not important. What is important is that you are commanded by both the Dominar, your father, and by the prelates and committee of five, to take the veil and undergo procession. There is money for this, it can be had through Regnal Bish, and you may spend the money you have taken as well. You should quit your scheming and plan for a loyal showing of fealty to the Dominar while on procession. If you think that your life is in danger, try making the men and women who can save your life happy."

"Such as you, Prelate?" Nazira asked.

Domingus nodded. "I represent the priests in this realm. That is not a force to cast aside."

"No, it is not, Prelate. I will do as I am told," Nazira said.

"That would be best," Domingus said, standing. He motioned with his head to the other prelates, then turned to the silent rank of guards and said, "I believe we will be leaving." There were no rankers in the soldiers, who all wore the green leather breastplates of Life Guards with the crests of the Interior Battalion. They were fusiliers, with firelocks on their backs, but also guardsmen with septum and falchion.

Domingus walked to the door and motioned, followed by the others. Bank Master Youti al-Presence followed him immediately, but Colonel Taffez hesitated. "My people have taken into custody Gullen, the former apprentice Dungeon Master, who I believe aided Javier al-Rasheed in his escape. I could have her thrown from the top towers onto the rocks. I could have her abused in any number of ways that our lord the Dominar would enjoy. However, I instead will have her sent to you unharmed. Do not let the Dungeon Masters Petrovson or al-Cinci have a chance at her if you want her to remain jointed and with her teeth still in her head."

"Petrovson is a thug, and the Dungeon Master al-Cinci is an imbecile," Nazira retorted.

As he left the room, Taffez said, "Exactly, just remember that."

Oban, fussy as ever, wiped his bald head clean of perspiration, and went first to clean up the broken glass, then return the survivors of the service to their cupboard. Nazira watched Oban work methodically on the cleaning, then said to Regnal Bish. "You will shepherd this procession?"

"I will," he replied.

Oban turned and started to clean the remains of the high tea. Nazira watched him work and then stood and joined him in clearing dishes.

"I want my own retinue, not yours," Nazira stated flatly as she collected cups. She turned and looked at the courtier, who seemed to be looking into the fire.

"That would make sense," he said.

"Bring me Gullen as my first servant," Nazira said sternly.

Bish stood up and bowed. "I will get on that immediately. Be careful in the halls, Princess. The scores are unsettled, and someone may wish to remove some dice from the table before the next hand is rolled."

"As you say, however, it appears you are my protector, so you will have to protect." Nazira dismissed Bish with her hand. He looked into the sky, nodded, and left the protocol room as well.

Oban finished packing the serviette and then braced the princess. "Is my princess happy?" he said as if he had heard not a word of the previous conversation with the prelates.

Nazira considered that. What was happiness? Could she even understand the meaning of the word? "Who was the man that rescued Javier? You have never told me how he was procured and set to task."

"My little princess." He stepped back and folded his hands in front of him. "My loyalty to you is deep as time and strong as iron, but there are things that you must not worry on. They must not trouble you. Who cares how the vegetable hash is made, as long as it is savory and healthful?"

"I do not like having dice hidden from me, my dear Oban." He remained standing silently in front of her as a soldier waiting for an officer's command. Sometimes Nazira would look on Oban and become sad. He was so loyal, so loving, he never asked things for himself, but instead dedicated himself to raising Nazira, the child of a Dominar who only existed to birth an heir. Who was otherwise a useless shoot off the Dominar's family tree, the motherless sop to the iron-willed demands of a now-dead grandfather and a document the average subject of the domain did not know existed. Her position was not to rule herself, but to provide the heir and continue a line into the future unbroken.

Oban sighed. "He is called Raqisat Alwajh, and he is one of the few of my land who can travel without censure or struggle. I ask only that his secrets remain his."

Nazira looks up at Oban. Now this is interesting, she thought. This shows dice that have long been hidden by the cup. "The old tongue, it means 'face mover,' does it not?"

"Face dancer, a person who changes his face and voice to meet the needs of the moment. A type of actor, but instead of placing one of the six masks of drama on their face in the form of porcelain, he wears a face that is convincing because he becomes the person, or creates the person from whole cloth," Oban said.

"And like you, he comes from the island?" Nazira asked.

Oban's bald face turned red. "The island should not be on your lips, lady. That is a veil that should not be lifted by you, I beg. Such a deadly veil, not something that should be lifted"

"My mother, you, this face dancer, all of this connects to me, but you say it is a veil that protects me, that my ignorance of this place is safety. Yet others know of it. They speak of it in hushed terms." Nazira motioned to the sea beyond the room's colonnaded facing. "Fifty kilometers by boat, I could charter one and make landing in a few days. So what is the mystery? What does it need a veil for?"

Oban looked down at the floor. "The veil protects it, and you. For me, do not delve into this place anymore." He stopped.

"I sent word to my mother. Do you know this? Javier has written instructions on how to locate her," Nazira said. "And you once said she has everything to do with the island."

"She does. Your grandfather and she made a deal. The deal shamed your father. She is the hand of mercy to Nawaz's hand of pain," Oban said. He dropped his hands, turned, and carefully closed up the serviette and unlocked its spoke wheels. "I must return this to the kitchens."

"Will she lift the silence?" Nazira asked, putting her hand gently on his shoulder. He was tense, shivering almost as if in fear of his life, but Nazira knew he had no fear for himself, only her, and whatever in his past produced him. It hurt him to have her tear at the wound he had, long since its cutting, sealed with stitches and honey. Yet beneath the swaddling of bandages, the cuts were deep, angry, and filled with pus. "My dear, you have cared for me my entire life. I must learn of the silence laid on you, but I will not task you with it. The one you call Raqisat Alwajh, he will be rewarded if he ever asks. Can you communicate this to him?"

Oban could only shrug his shoulders and shudder silently. Nazira put the palm of her hand on his cheek and kissed him gently.

A clatter from an attention stick indicated that a person wanted to enter the room. Nazira said to Oban, "Be off." He nodded and pushed the cart to the entrance of the chamber. A guard stepped in his way, so Nazira said, "He is taking the serviette to the kitchens. You may usher in whoever commanded you to break the silence of this room.

Oban left, and the guard nodded, then ushered a woman in a black cassock of a scholar, wearing a green shell necklace-of-the-court. She was not a knight despite the necklace as she did not wear the rampant lion of one of the orders on her breast, nor was she armed, but she did carry the wristbands of one of the council, a sub-prelate or omarisa. She also held in her hand a newly made lacquer-painted torque and a fine leather book. Like many, she was probably metal-shy, her rings were made of fine wood set with stone, and her tiara was twisted vine, all signs that she was pious and avoided showing metal except when it was demanded by work or rank.

Despite this piety, she did not look like one of the dowdy functionaries that worked for Domingus bar Calad. She was young, only eight or ten years older than Nazira, but she was poised and had an open expression on her olive-toned face of someone innocent of the world, yet her composure showed Nazira that she was past the throws and passions of youth.

She entered the room and genuflected. Despite her trappings of rank and signets of being a member of the court, Nazira did not know the woman. That itself was an oddity because Nazira had grown up playing in the presence chamber, eating in the great hall, and pursuing the activities of kids in the gardens. She may not know a person of court by cordial contact, in that she held friendly conversations and could place them into a kith and clan with precision, but she could recognize the rank and face of everyone who waited on the mercy and bounty of her father, the Dominar.

When the woman rose from genuflecting, she said, "My princess, I am Ribea al' Jin, the new scholar of the Great Tower."

"What happened to my old tutor Dastgir? Is he retired for incompetence?" Nazira asked.

Ribea looked nonplussed. Nazira knew she was young-looking, and that her voice did not carry an automatic weight like her father's did, but she could surprise and put off balance many people by the sharp cadence of her tone. The comment made her sound petty, but also like someone who could lash out randomly if made angry, which was a minor application of power Nazira had learned in her most powerless times. Many powerful adults would stop in their tracks in hearing displeasure in her voice. People did not really know or understand how little she meant to her father. The Dominar did not care if she was happy or mad, and certainly would never have acted against anyone who made her cross, he only cared that she was physically able to have a child. However, most of the court did not really understand this. They imagined, or so Nazira thought, that she could whisper in her father's ear and send people to the boneyards of Chakroun-Denal.

"My princess. I am not aware of Scholar Dastgir's current tenure, only that I have been asked to come from the school at Musca Sharjari and act as your master of Procession, a great honor bestowed on me by your father," Dubai said.

"And you will be my guide?" Nazira asked.

Scholar Ribea looked like she was about to do a dance. "It will be fascinating. Your first chance to be seen by the people of Cycus. Twelve stops in the procession, six months, then returning to Cycus City for your shutting-in and the birth of your child."

Death in childbirth, Nazira thought, was the result of her shutting-in. Sadness through the Dominion but fealty to the new heir. This was the work of more than her father. "Who set this schedule?"

"I am to understand Dame Griselda al-Youseffi d' Tariq has arranged the procession. She interviewed me for this just three days ago, so I rushed to the capital as I understand we leave in under a fortnight." The Scholar did not realize that her free way revealed much.

She was a spy at best. Dame Griselda was the wife of the first Dominar, the stepmother of the second, and her own grandmother in fact, if not in birth. Unlike her father, she was intensely clever, but like him, she was not burdened in any way by empathy. Griselda was rumored to be many things and to have many powers, but the font of her power seemed, to Nazira, to spring from the simple fact she was the daughter of the greatest of the twenty-three families of

Guisarmes. So few lived through the invasion, and almost none of that era still lived to this day.

Nazira had heard all about that compromise since she was a child. It was the defining element of her life. Yet despite that naked power of the Dominars', father and son, Dame Griselda had fought for the power of the al-Youseffi. Nazira was technically named Nazira al-Youseffi on the roles of state, though she was actually without house, sept, kith, or clan as the future heir-mother. Her son or daughter would likely also be considered an al-Youseffi as well. That was power in the palace, and power the translated into strength in the hinterlands.

Nazira said, "What is this book you have?"

"This book... it is amazing." She handed it to Nazira. "From the old library..."

Nazira cut her off. "The library my grandfather burned to the ground with the librarians in it?"

"My princess, so dramatic, there is no record of that happening," she said.

Nazira laughed again, feeling the cool texture of the leather covering on the book. "Because my father burned the storybooks and the people who wrote them also!"

Scholar Ribea blinked at Nazira, then said, "You must see this as the exciting thing it is. Only one other procession has ever been tried since the Dominion was formed. You have much to do yourself to prepare for this." She handed the torque over to Nazira as well. "That is your torque of office. It was your mother's."

Nazira stopped. She was growing cross, but the torque was something that she could feel a connection to. Somehow, she remembered the beautiful piece of jewelry. It was made from seeds gathered on an exotic island by the hands of her mother, lacquered in shellac collected from the same trees on which the beads grow, and then tumbled in sand, before being woven into a matrix of fine jessap twine. She did not know how she knew this, but she was sure it was true. She could almost see her mother wearing the beautiful piece while holding her in her arms.

Nazira softened her tone. "What should I prepare for, Scholar?"

"Your retinue. You will need an entire staff. Has no one told you this?" Ribea asked.

Nazira retrieved the chamber's attention stick and banged it against a small wooden gong by the fireplace. A guard ducked his head into the room. "Tea for two, please." The guard ducked away, then returned with three cups of tea on a tray. He set the cups, these made from common fired clay, and let them each take one, then retrieved the third, drank from it, bowed, and withdrew.

"Please have a seat. One of the cushions if you like, please." Nazira got up and took the second chair. "I have to say Scholar, I do not hear the Cycus Cryer from my window, so perhaps you will tell me what I should know that has not been told me."

Scholar Ribea sat on a large cushion. "You will need a dresser, bodyguards, a banneret, a knight of the chamber, and a recordist. You may want an almoner and a prayer mistress. Drovers certainly; you will be expected to have a retinue." The scholar handed Nazira the book. "This book was in the library of Musca Sharjari. It contains a mention of the old forms and how the people before the Dominars celebrated the coming of a new generation and the selection of the next King. Scholar Bayal al-Hindi wrote it with some definite cunning. It is an enjoyable read."

Nazira opened the book. "Thank you, Scholar. I seem to have many duties to attend to. Can you excuse me?"

"I am happy to help you. Please simply send word to my office." Ribea turned to leave. "Thank you for the tea."

Nazira followed her to the entrance, then told the guards in the hall, "I will return to my quarters."

She stopped short as a dour woman in gray staff cloth of the lower halls appeared, holding in her hand a veil of green silk. "I have been asked to veil you for your trip to the to your apartments."

Nazira looked at the slip of shiny cloth. Such a little thing, and so much portent in its meaning. She looked at the servant who held it forth. It would be so easy to yell at the woman who held it, kick her in the shins, force her to humiliation, but something inside of Nazira pushed the desire down. "Can you aid me in putting the veil on?" she asked. The servant bowed and passed around her. The veil went on her easily in the physical but was a terrible weight on her soul. In the court, a veil was a symbol of submission, a way of saying that you accepted the orders of the Dominar and were not to be harmed, as your task was not political. A child was veiled. An old scholar or artist may be veiled. It was a special type of humiliation. One was commanded into a veil, and that did not sit well with Nazira.

When the piece of cloth was hanging from her face, Nazira thanked the servant and returned under guard to her apartments.

Chapter VII

Aleab Almahkama

Melinda's idiot husband was blocking the hallway. Oban chuffed as the man stretched his right hand to impede her progress, but Nazira waved him down with a flick of her wrist. "What do you want Bostick?"

"My name is Bostwick," he purred with a self-satisfied hum. "The veil is an improvement, my lady."

Nazira looked him in the face. There was a long silence as she held his gaze, a silence she could tell was eating at the courage of Melinda's idiot husband. Emasculating a weakling was so easy it should be illegal. She could tell her defiance was torturing the man inside, but it was almost like he had been born to be tortured in this manner. Melinda had married the man because of his money and his name. The al-Cinci were not a top-tier family, but they were large, and many of them worked in the capital in various sinecures as minor functionaries of the Dominion. If a mercenary wanted a sword license, they had to get it from Devon al-Cinci and his Fighter's Bureau. If you wanted approval for a new Macadam turnpike to the highlands, Beatris Remanda al-Cinci was the head of roads and highways. The second dungeon master was an al-Cinci as was the First Serpent and the Master of the Mews. Looks and family were what Bostwick had, but nothing underneath. No spark ignited him, and iron barrel howd strengthened his soul. He was a flesh puppet who never asked who was dancing his strings or why he danced at all.

His gaze caused him to start sweating and turn his head away.

"I repeat Bost-swill, what do you want?" Nazira said.

"Bostwick," he corrected.

Nazira sneered. "That is what I said. Get on with it, or do you think I won't cut your yatadalaa away from your little rsujiq?"

He continued to look away from her but started sweating. "I have a message for you."

"If my half-sister wants to tell me something, she can do it herself," Nazira replied.

"Naseer al-Dinni demands to see you." Bostwick lowered his sharp chin and looked about where her stomach was under her dress.

Nazira thought that this was unexpected. Idiot Bostwick carrying water for the so-called "Jinn of the Seas?" "What does the former captain of the *Remarker* want?"

Bostwick stepped up from the wall and took on a half-hearted sneer. "You stole his ship, and he feels you stole your own hand." He lifted his right hand and waved it in front of her. "That is a great debt you owe him."

"A debt I owe him?" Nazira asked.

"He told me if you place the dower of your child onto him, he may be able to save you from the blade of your father." Bostwick seemed to think this was clever as a small smile gleamed out of his pugnacious face.

"Let me get this proposal settled in my mind. I took his ship. I took most of his crew. I almost got him with an explosive trap, and he feels that he has something to offer me in exchange for my dower rights? And that this would extend to my father, who has never held back from killing a man who challenged him before?" Nazira threw all the acid she could into her voice, but Bostwick seemed unable to decode the meaning of her tone, only the meaning of the words she said, and maybe not even that.

"I am the messenger, but I will not be the last, just the most cordial," Bostwick replied.

Nazira pushed him aside and continued down the hall. Over her shoulder, she said, "Bamwell, you are about as cordial as a verruca but twice as smart."

He yelled at her, retreating back, "I am twice as smart as a verruca, you will see!"

The palace was a cluster of towers standing over a series of Bailies and low-hung galleries. No one really knew when Cycus castle was first laid down, but the deepest levels were claustrophobic, dark, and sometimes dripping with water. Tunnels, ramps, and rooms long abandoned and dark, not even being piped for gas or having sconces, crisscrossed and ran in odd directions, like the builders were unable to decide what they wanted to make and had been trying to create a corn maze rather than a place where people lived. Newcomers to the castle and palace had to be warned that downward sloped corridors would lead into the lower maze where they might become lost and never come out.

For Nazira, though, nighttime allowed access to the world of the lower mazes, and she knew their turns like she knew her own hands. She and Standish would spend hours exploring, returning to their beds only at dawn, gaining a reputation for laziness among her father's servants. Once she and Standish had found the moldering remains of a courtier, a knight who had foolishly left the main corridors of the great castle to plumb the depths in search of whatever people looked for when they found death. The man had been stripped of flesh by the rats, but otherwise, his bones were articulated and his clothing, armor, and even his sword had survived the days of entropic disintegration.

The dead man was, in fact, a common meeting point for the children of the castle, those who were never allowed to roam the streets of the city, though Nazira had in her teen years learned to leave and enter the castle at will. And it was here that she found herself, the smell of Bostwick's cologne still in her mount. The tunnel had a breeze, communicated somehow from the outside into the upper tunnels into the dark depths, and several people had already arrived with tinder and match wood to start a small fire for tea.

It was Gullen and Clathy who had arrived before her. Nazira removed her veil, throwing it to the ground, and then rushed to Gullen, who was her age and one of the castle children, hugging her.

"Regnal Bish said you were to be saved." Nazira looked her friend in the eyes and smiled.

Gullen, whose father had been a wright, said, "The guards caught me when I returned to my rooms." Motioning to Clathy, she said, "We have Goat Isle tea, smokey as a barn fire and strong enough to make even our old playground seem happy. I hesitate to ask, but what of al-Rasheed?"

"Javier got away." Nazira replied.

"I saw. Lister al-Cinci and Petrov Petrovson were not close enough to the fire for my bomb to take them out," she said, taking a cup of tea from Clathy d' Semini, the daughter of an accountant in the actuarial office. "I got one of Naseer al-Dinni's people, but no one else."

"Do not fear Gullen. One adversary at a time. Naseer has no more crew and no more ship, so he can be ignored," Nazira said, sipping her tea.

Clathy d' Semini looked into the dark tunnel, then said in a hushed voice, "Daniella de Tomei al-Fortuna and the last of the al-Dinni seem to be at each other's throats and ignoring you. They are both done with Naseer. Blood is flowing in the city, but no one is sure to what end. Hammond got away as well, but he is not of the same stuff as the others." Clathy was obviously nervous in the deep tunnel, not being a child of the castle.

"What of Oban's agent?" Nazira asked. "The one who helped you."

"The one who pretended to be Devious? Who is Devious, his name is often said, but I have never met the genuine article?" Gullen asked.

"Never you mind who Devious is," Nazira said. Devious was known in the castle and the city, but Nazira was one of the few who knew all about the man and his stealthy antecedents. "Consider Devious a mystery. In fact, the man who played Devious is just as much a mystery. I could not get anything from Oban on him, but I am happy he got away from the beach."

Clathy shuddered. "Nazira, this is not the game it once was. There are things here I do not feel safe doing." Gullen looked disgusted at her fellow cabal member, but Nazira put her hand on Clathy's shoulder.

"Clathy, you are not from the castle, but you have to know that things are deadly serious now. We are not children anymore. I am pregnant and my father will kill me if I cannot find a way out. Gullen was not just a Doorkeep.

You know where she was sent when she came of age, what they do there? People are fighting and dying in the streets because of things I planned and made happen."

Clathy tugged at her black hair and reached for her tea. She drank a bit, trying to brace herself, but could not get herself under control. Nazira grabbed her face and looked at her eyes, trying to will courage into her soul, then dropped her head. She turned to Gullen who was furious at their friend. "Should have sent her with the Tea Merchants and kept Standish."

Nazira fixed Gullen with a disapproving look and then turned to Clathy again. "Nothing will happen to you; this is not your thing, and I should not have included you. You cannot stay in the castle though; you might give us away."

"Where will I go?" she asked. "They told me I was to be your body servant on progress."

"Does your father have a farm in Semini?" Nazira asked.

"My uncle does, winter kale, short corn, and walnuts." She looked at Nazira with a hopeful look.

Nazira pulled Gullen close. "I need you to help me figure out who is on my procession that I cannot trust, but first I need to get a message to Clathy's father Yesha. He is to call his daughter to his farm to help with the harvest. Make sure that Yesha knows this comes from me as the princess, and I expect him to act as if I am his liege, not a little girl playing in the corner of the presence chamber.

"That may be difficult," Gullen said. "I have found that the adults do not see us as fully birthed."

"That is because we call them adults and assume we are children. You tell him I am trying to save his daughter's life, tell him to smell the wind and if he thinks I am wrong, ignore me. Hell, promise him patronage, I could care less. I cannot risk Clathy breaking on us."

"I am sorry, Nazira," Clathy said, crying.

"Do not be. You knew me when princess meant nothing to any of us. We just had to grow up quicker than you. Your father is not in the castle, he does books, and your family is farm stock, not gentry." She lit a taper and stuck it to the wall for light, then extinguished the fire and hid the old tea set they used behind the knight's skeleton. She then hugged Clathy and watched as she disappeared into the darkness.

Gullen and Nazira stood in the flickering light of the taper for a few minutes, then Gullen said, "Should I kill her?"

Nazira thought for a second. Clathy was an old friend, and usually loyal, but definitely had reached the end of her bravery and usefulness. She was like a sputtering breach charge, something to be kicked over the side of a ship rather than allowed to roll around until it detonated.

"Leave her be, for now, Gullen. Her whole life has revolved around finding some minor position in the castle, finding a knight to marry, and getting a plenary title. I think about how shy Standish was when we were young, like an ungainly giraffe, all power and grace that she could not see in herself, but stately innocence. I remember you, quiet, serious, the one in our group who knew things, could find out secrets. I remember Saad and Abadi, shy boys and children of the barracks, and how Saad had such a crush on you he brought you flowers picked from the gardens until the garden master had him whipped, but he took the whipping and never said your name. And how smart Abadi was, how he knew more than the teachers sometimes." Nazira felt the steel running through her heart, the cold grip of icy winter then gripped her brain in its clawed fist. This was no game of stones, yelling to the sky on the rock pile, daring the God of Fire to strike the sinners as they walked below them on the merchant's path.

Gullen's facial expression did not change, it never did. "I remember the beating Saad took, all of them, by the counselors for your father who could see no humor in kid's games. And I remember Abadi and his mother being dragged away, and we never saw them again. Do even you know, my princess, what became of our eternal friend? Did Abadi deserve punishment for the crime of his mother? Is his skull even now stacked with the bones of the traitors at Chakroun-Denal? You wish for a childhood we never had, one in books read to us by Oban as we all gathered for our sleeping parties in the low firth. But there never was a child's life to be had for us, not like one we deserved. And I say to you, you do not know what I saw when my father died and left me to be apprenticed to old Petrov."

Nazira reached out in the darkness to comfort her friend. Petrov died eating a meat pie, and no one dared move his body for eleven days. That was how feared and hated he was. Yet that was poor punishment for what the man had done to her friend. Nazira knew the reason she could not kill Clathy, even though Clathy could bring her downfall. Because Saad had been beaten for stealing flowers. Because Abadi was dragged away with his mother for some crime she still did not understand. Because of all the friends of her youth, only Clathy had been given a real childhood, and her childhood had come because she had not lived in the castle, and her father had been a colorless accountant, while her mother worked as a computer at the docks, and no one considered them worth being cruel to. Clathy had never seen the horrors, and that was not something to be vengeful over, but to value.

"Clathy will not be harmed," Nazira said, spending all of her force of will to overcome the sadness in her heart that she actually had to say that to herself more than Gullen. She reached for the taper and put it into the hand carrier to light their way out. In reality, they did not need the light. They knew exactly where they were going.

Gullen and Nazira slipped out of the castle by the Circum Valus doorway in the North Keep which, due to inept design, locked out but not in. Every child in the Keep knew that it was the key to freedom, but somehow generations of adults never figured that out, the information magically failing to jump the age gap between junior and senior status.

They wore the clothing of docks, dark, drab, loose fitting. Most dockers wore coveralls that they covered with short jackets when they left work. Heavy hobnailed boots were the constant complaint of the shopkeepers, but the salons and inns simply put up with the scratches in the wood veneer of the floors or replaced wood with ballast stones taken from ballast piles of heavy coasters that transported grain.

Workers wore knit beanies when they shifted cargo, or else straw-brimmed hats in the heat of summer, but at night the beanies went into their pockets and the brimmed hats were left in lockers, to be replaced with cockades. While they preferred bright tweed jackets, the gray-colored ones Nazira and Gulen affected were not too unusual. Dressed in such they looked like the smaller dockers called "shifters" that moved cargo in small holds.

The street near the castle was dark. The walls attracted strange folk, and there was an impermanent nature to the structures that huddled near the palace and its castles. The Life Guards would every year or two tear up the hovels but they would return. Nazira went to one of the squatters who sat around a small fire cooking dock rat and gave her a few boos of copper. Ironically, the woman called herself Junkfire.

"You have grown," she said. "Rat?" she offered. Nazira and Gullen took a piece and pulled some bread from their shirts for the woman.

"How does it look?" Nazira asked.

Junkfire shivered. "Strange sorts around. Very strange." She then said, "Things ain't settled since the gang mistress got blowed up. No mistress, no. Yet you should know one of them has dwimmer and has been on about you."

"Dwimmer?" Gullen asked, looking at Nazira, who shrugged.

"What is dwimmer, madame Junkfire?" Nazira asked.

Junkfire was a face from Nazira's childhood, a person who lived on the edge of society, that would protect her on her early explorations into the world's underworld, but as kind as she was, there was never a clear attachment to objective reality. She was an inlander who had great mats of hair on her head and wore every piece of clothing she owned. Despite this, she was actually employed like most of the people in the margins of the town. She collected, sorted, sold, and burned trash. She made her small house out of trash, had a cart made of broken wood, and crushed shells for the gardens of inns.

While petty crime was common, the people of the verges also were concerned with each other, and a number had appeared from their corners and shadows and begun to listen to what Junkfire was saying. They were all known to Nazira who had hidden here when she was smaller, playing with the children of the ramshackle community, but they had their own worries and own lives and could not be considered friends.

Bitter, who hunted for niter in the honey piles, was wet from a pail bath. He had constant jitters and sallow skin but cared for the children of the ramshackle verge. "The man who you seek is there."

Nazira turned. The dark man was right in front of her, causing her to start, then pulled her hidden karambit and charged the man. He turned and did not so much run and stride away. Gullen yelped and also drew a small blade. "Step back Naz," she yelled, not daring to call her princess on the dark streets.

The dark man turned a corner, which Nazira was forced to take wide to avoid ambush and skidded into a drover carrying boxes for the night trade. Impossibly, her quarry was still walking briskly and gaining distance on her. Perhaps it was the early pregnancy that was slowing her up, or the lack of exercise she had suffered, but as the street grew more crowded with night trade, he seemed to magically be able to pull ahead.

He adroitly dodged some drunks from a bar which Nazira had to literally bull through, which her petite form was not perfectly able to do. How Gullen avoided them she could not guess.

Nazira had grown up on the streets of Cycus port, playing in the mass of humanity pretending to be a waif of the under docks. She even cut purses and essayed hot foots of the merchants to pack the battery, a dangerous game for a bored child of nobility. Yet this dark man behaved like the city was air, and the people of the night no more difficult to navigate than a light misty breeze.

Again, he cut a corner tight, and she was forced to take it wide and came face to face with the man. He held an old, black yataghan and yelled a strange tongue, "Zdaj ni čas." His face was impossible to view in the darkness of his cowl. She felt Gullen collide with her, and they both fell to the ground. The man made a light appear, some form of a clever hooded candle, although she could not see how it was designed. "Do not be scared," he said, and she was not.

And that scared her more than the sword. Before she could get up, he said, "Someone follows you. He always follows you. Yet his effect is mixed. You are the center of a storm."

And he was gone into the darkness.

Nazira recovered and helped Gullen up. "Who in the hidden world was that?" she asked.

Nazira looked into the darkness. "I saw him at the levee. I thought he might be a watcher from Dame Griselda or one of Daniella's people stalking me. Now I am not sure what he is after. His face, though, is familiar."

Gullen leaned down and breathed deeply. "I followed one of Griselda's, she works in the kitchen and is stalking you. Though I doubt she is all that effective."

"Why?" Nazira asked.

Gullen stood up and laughed. "I dropped a teddy into her tea." Gullen added, "She threw up into the porridge."

"Gods," Nazira laughed as well. "Dark strangers, sneaks in the kitchen, and I hope they did not serve the porridge! We have to get on with things before Regnal Bish shows up as well."

"I am afraid it is too late," a man said. It was Regnal Bish, nearly invisible in his dark parti-color against the patterns of the brick walls. "I am, indeed, now here."

"You cannot stop me." Nazira said, startled. Gullen drew her knife again but put it away when Nazira shook her head.

Bish said, "I do not intend to stop you."

There was silence, an extended tableaux of indecision that made Nazira uncomfortable. She felt the warm bone handle of her bodkin in her hand and wondered if this was the time to drop the annoying courtier in the alley where his death would look like a random mug. Cycus City was dangerous. People died in the alleys, their bodies uncovered by the lamplighters as they came through to extinguish the gaslights.

Just as she was clearing her mind to kill the unfortunate man, he burst into movement and the bodkin was lost in the darkness. Nazira felt her hands tingle, and while not shocked, she never was shocked, she felt surprised. How had the man taken her knife from her with such ease? Then it came to her.

"You are an assassin," she said, rubbing her wrist. "I have been blind to you until now. Is the man we chased also an assassin?"

Bish said nothing and his face remained blank.

Nazira pointed at the knife sitting on the ground. "No one moves that fast. No one. You are an assassin—I mean a member of the guild of course, and the man we were chasing is one also, don't deny it."

Bish picked up the bodkin knife and offered it to Nazira. "Have you ever met an assassin?" he asked.

"Of course, I have," she replied.

"Where?" His face exposed no emotion. "What is his or her name? Is this other man one, and if so, how do you know?"

"Gannet Vries, he holds court at the Fairhaven," she replied and took the bodkin.

"And let me guess. When you are supposed to be tucked into the deepest room in the dungeons of the castle, instead you are listening to this twaddle marker steam on about being a certified killer?" A bit of humor leaked into Bish's voice. "Princess of the entire realm, dressed like a common docker in your canvas and hobnails, skulking around the dark corners of the great city; it is almost unbearably droll, do you not think highness?"

"I used to have Standish and Gullen at my side," she said. Standish, her loyal lover who could never be her wife. How she missed the huge warrior and her ferric protectiveness.

"Yes, show me this Fairhaven so I also can meet a real assassin," Bish said with a wry tone.

"I have things to do," Nazira replied.

Regnal Bish said earnestly, "If you indulge this for me, I will help you do these things in a safe manner. What are you on the docks for anyway?"

"Looking for hirelings, you suggested this after all," Nazira replied.

"Then we will find them for you. I have no reason to interfere, I have two tasks," he said. "Protecting you is the one that is most important, and one way to protect you is to teach you about the world."

"What about killing me?" she asked.

He looked at her, then at Gullen. "Put away your knives and show me to this Fairhaven."

Fairhaven tavern was misnamed. It was not fair, it was not a haven, and it was not even truly a tavern. Instead, it was a place where a poorly coordinated four-piece band played distended and laborious sea chanties that sounded like three ship crews singing three different songs had crashed head-long into each other during a roaring storm. Where a tavern had sturdy wooden tables and inviting chairs, Fairhaven has planks of rough, splintery wood laid across jittery trestles of softwood birch, always threatening to collapse under the elbows and drink glasses of the drunk clientele. And where a real tavern would serve tea, fruit drinks, tonics, and elixirs, Fairhaven had fortified beer or fortified wine with no other service. Not even tea.

Its charm was that a silver went a long way when the menu was priced in tithes and dozens. In fact, a silver would be quite lonely in the mass of copper and brass that was evident on the tables.

Nazira took the lead and entered the tavern from its back-alley entrance. The establishment was one large room, probably converted ages ago from a cargo storage or some sort of warehouse. Despite the volume of the room, it was packed with the common workers, hobnail dockers, quarter-bodies, heavers, cottagers, and all the rest of the common people who lived and struggled on the streets of the Dominion.

In one of the best-lit corners, there was a large man decked in mail with leather pauldrons. He was surrounded not by the working crowd that filled most of the tavern, but by a less "employed" and more unruly group of streeties, vagabonds, gill-steals, and quarters boys, none of which were even close to savory. Yet something made the group exciting to look at. They did odd jobs in the shadows, work that might be thuggish but which made the streets work. Gannet Vries, with his armor and his falchion resting against the table, was a master of the street enforcers, someone who intimidated people who intimidated people for a living. Oddly, people felt safe in his sinister presence.

Bish stopped Nazira from sitting down at a central table and instead walked to the place where Vries held court. For Vries, it was unprecedented. People were invited to his table, they were allowed to enter his circle. They did not simply walk up and stand in his orbit without leave. It was an affront to the easily offended man.

As Bish stepped to the table, the congregation silenced, and Vries said, "What do you want short-pants."

"Sorry, I could dance all night, but I wanted to see if you were the cream in the tea," Bish said softly.

"What did you say, sirrah?" Vries stood up and threw his arms out in a threat display.

"You are an assassin yeah? Kill people for money?" Bish laconically said.

"You think that is funny?" The big man came around the table pushing people away from him. "Do you want to see what a master of the guild of assassins can do?"

Bish looked down at his brass chain which said he was a courtier of the Dominar and slowly removed it. He handed the chain to Nazira and simply replied, "Yes."

There was a sudden burst of movement, blindingly fast, and Vries ended up on the floor of the tavern while Bish was standing, seemingly untouched. Vries clawed his way to his feet and yelled, "How dare you."

"Son," Bish said laconically, "that was all I needed to see. If you want to end it here, I am happy to leave you with the field."

The big man again tried to rush Bish, but Bish simply stepped to the side and seemed to catch Vries by his clothes and help him pass by, crashing him into cheap furniture. By now, the entire tavern was gathering around. Fights were common at Fairhaven. Nazira has seen dozens in her day, but most were slug tests where one or both patrons battered each other into a bloody mess. This was like going to an arena fight and finding out the bill-of-fair was a dance troupe. None cheered, instead there was a murmuring silence as the most feared man in the bar was handed his ass by a slight, gray-haired, bookish elder. Three more times Vries jumped up and charged, and three more times he was deftly thrown to the ground by Bish. Finally, he charged so hard that he fell into the hardwood of the serving bar and knocked himself out.

Bish turned to the tavern and said, "Even an assassin can meet his or her match. However, do not elevate yourselves above this man, and awaken him with gentle friendship. With honor to you and my own soft sayings, there goes he, and there could always go me or you."

He then looked at Nazira and said, "Shall we retire?"

Sandbagged, Nazira nodded. They both turned and left the tavern by the rear exit, passing by the odiferous jakes and the people huddled under the eaves passing haze sticks between each other with gravid desperation. When they reached the alley, Nazira turned Regnal Bish around and said, "So is he not an assassin?"

"I did not say that my princess. I merely made a lesson to a young woman on the difference between claim and reality. You carry yourself with dignity and courage, but your learning of the streets, great though it is, is incomplete. No one has taught you about the people of this land and the difference between boast and reality, not in a systematic way," Bish said.

"So I should take lessons from you before you kill me?" she said.

Bish laughed. "If my duty is to kill you, and I agree your half-sister believes this, then the issue would be time and place. And until that time and place is reached, and I assure you the Dominar's orders to have you shown off in a procession are ones that I and others will follow to the letter, perhaps it is best to assume I would not only protect you as I claim is my duty, but treat you like any other person of rank and do my best to advise and educate you. I am, after all, no matter what you think, a knight of the realm."

"A hitman," Nazira said, sullen but considering.

Bish laughed again and let his crazy eyes wander the alley. "All knights are hitmen. Our blades go where the

Dominar would have them go." Then he raised his voice. "And Vries, do not attempt stealth to sneak up on me, I might find reason to deal harshly with you."

Gannet Vries was emerging from the Fairhaven tavern with a handful of his followers, but to Nazira, they did not seem sinister. "Mistress Nazira, I have been informed you were more than just a butterfly in the net of Fairhaven. I did not know this man was your creature."

Nazira said, "Assassin Vries, do not concern yourself. This man is no more my creature than you are."

"Please, Princess, I am no assassin. Not one of the order, at least. I am not one of them." Vries looked scared like he was in mortal danger.

"You do not need to be sorry or tell me that," Nazira said. She turned to Bish. "Vries, I have seen you for years here and known the work you do. Can I suggest you take my trade and give up the streets for a more honest profession?"

"I will my Princess. My group has been fighting for the street gangs after your husband saw off Daniella, but the candle in that is falling to a nib as the war winds down with no winner, just street squabbles and nameless dead. I would take your coin and be loyal." Vries said.

"Will you take the orders of my associate Gullen, though she is young?" Nazira asked.

Vries nodded. "I swear Princess."

Nazira turned to Regnal Bish. His eyes were less disturbing now that she knew him, and if you looked carefully, it was actually easy to tell where his attention was drawn. Familiarity leads to favor and reconsideration, Nazira thought. "Will you see to the details of bringing Vries and his associates into my little cabal? I can assure you I feel his character is worthy of the position."

Bish looked like he was considering it, they said, "I will do so my Princess."

"And the dark stalker. If you see him, please arrange a meeting with me." Nazira asked.

Bish bowed his head. "I will do this as well Princess."

Chapter VIII

On the Camellia Throne

The next morning Oban woke Nazira early, before dawn when only the castle and palace staff were stirring. "Lord Regnal Bish is waiting to take you to the marshaling yards."

Nazira sat up. In the table game of her life, this was one of the moves that could see her advance her position, or lose ground that would never be made back. It had been a late night for her in the catacombs of the palace, but she had taken time to lay out a precise outfit, gathered in secret, for just this day.

It started with a fresh shift, but unlike her linen, this one was unbleached cotton with the three lines signet of the land of Cycus. Not the Dominion, but the ancient kingdom. No one would see her shift, but Nazira had chosen to do as she and Standish had done as children, create and wear outfits that made them grownups, put together with as much precision as they could, but legitimate from the first layer of their skins outward.

Over the shift went tough west soft cotton pantalets secured by a worsted belt in sable, tucked into brown rugged regimental boots.

Over her shoulders, she pulled a jacket that soldiers called a "Five and Seven" for reasons that were beyond Nazira. And on the top of the jacket went the green and yellow swallowtail coat of the Last Guards, upon which she fixed a sigil for a Captain of the Cycus Brigade. And as a final touch, to fill the last requirement of a knight of the realm who was adopting the role of an officer of the army, she placed a small bone-handled blade into a cross sheaf that was firmly attached to her shoulder belt.

Then she let Oban hang a veil of worsted on her face. An absurd touch, but it made her look sinister instead of demure when combined with the uniform.

Dressed, she motioned for Oban to open the door for Regnal Bish and was shocked at what she saw. Bish also had worn regimentals.

"You have anticipated me, Lord Bish," Nazira said.

Bish bowed. "You give me too much credit. The idea that I can follow the machinations of your mind well enough to predict your dress on a given day is proffering me credit far past my intellectual capacity. I elected to wear this uniform, as is my right, just as you elected to wear yours, as is your right."

"You are a knight. Should you not dress as one?" Nazira asked, retrieving her gloves from the bedstead.

"Despite being a knight sworn to Dominion, and despite the rank in the family of the Beijus, the first title I ever held was Ensign of Utisa 4, North Shore Battalion. I still am carried on the rolls of the battalion, even though here my knight rank, humble as it is, outranks my military accomplishments. What about you, though, how can you justify a captain's serge and a position in the Cycus battalion? I do accept that you are also a knight. That would be something that any Justicar would assign you without question. But a Captain of Infantry? My princess, that rank might cause consternation." Bish crossed his arms and looked out the window like a male teacher might when faced with a daughter student.

Nazira pulled the leather waterproof orders case that officers wore tucked into their coats and presented it out. Bish walked up and took the case and opened it, pulling a creme piece of scap with red and black letters on it. He whipped the document out and used both hands to carry out the roll, flattening it into a flat plane, brought it to his nose and smelled it, then held it ridiculously close to his eyes, moving it right to left. After a few minutes of examination, he returned the document to its case. "A very clever piece of legerdemain, my dear princess. Legal also, though perhaps the letter of the law is not exactly maintained. Your friend Standish is not noble, is she?"

Nazira smirked. "An orphan of a Navy officer, but a bastard as well. She was raised with me as a companion."

Bish nodded. "Then she was matriculated into the military?"

"As an ensign, when we were sixteen. She happened to drill with the Last Guards, and by chance, the Cycus battalion." Nazira replied, putting the orders cylinder back into her jacket.

"Shopkeepers and old men who play soldiers on the battery each weekend," Bish commented.

Nazira held up her finger. "Now Lord Bish, a long-standing battalion of long and honorable service."

Bish smirked, "Elevated to colonel by your father using some form of, well, sleight of hand?"

"My dear lord, no sleight of hand needed. She was rewarded for the capture of my husband and the delivery of him to the dungeons, and she was already a captain, so my father made her a major in gratitude. Is that not common enough? My father made an ensign a lieutenant one time when the man directed his urine stream with great precision onto the back of my lord al-Suleaomon, who had himself collapsed during a drunken revelry. Is it not the right of the Dominar to promote? He may not, by the bans, appoint an officer to rank. That is why the knights are outside of the rank system. He may promote, though, an officer one rank in special need." Nazira smiled with her clever recitation. "Besides, she would be an honorary major anyway as master of marines on a tea trader."

"And then Major Standish of the old men and women's battalion, who is also Major Standish of Marines of the newly minted ex-pirate tea trader *Remarker,* appoints you a captain in return," Bish countered.

"She is the head of a detached marine company of the rank of major, which indeed gives her the right to appoint officers ad hoc while away from port. She wrote this letter, post-dated it, and made me a captain. Sadly, I must be confirmed by the commander of the Dominion Guard and likely I will be dead before they meet, but it is such a small present for the doomed pregnant girl, do you not think?" Nazira said with wry humor.

"Pedantic nonsense," Bish replied.

"Legal fiction, my dear Lord Bish. Very legal," Nazira shot back.

"Then let us test your legal fiction, my dear princess. We must see the companies and select two for your procession. I was going to use my rank to say the right things before the soldiers. They can become grognards when the letter of the rules of parade is not maintained. However, far be it for me to stage-direct your drama. Lead the way," he said with a flourish.

Nazira knew the way to the marshaling yards. They were the largest space inside of the walls and were a constant center of her childhood play, the one protected place where she could run in good weather and play ball with her friends. Standish especially loved watching the fusiliers practice drills, as the Life Guards had a completely mounted company armed with firelocks. The screams of the sergeants repeating team and platoon orders, the flash and smoke of firelocks as they fired on the age-old target bunkers, the screams as the soldiers engaged in tussling melee with wood-sheathed weapons, and the occasional rush of medics to remove soldiers who were injured in the scrums. They would take water to the exhausted soldiers, and when the food trucks came out with the large vats of stew, Standish, Nazira, and her coterie would run bowls of food to the soldiers along with the big hunks of black bread that the capital commissary fed them.

So when she stepped out onto the training field, it was not as a newcomer entering a strange arena, but as an adult returning to the playground of her youth. Only this adult faced fourteen companies of Dominion soldiers in their parade uniforms, some of whom could remember her as a child, running them water as they trained under the hot summer sun.

As soon as she entered the parade ground, Nazira stepped out, walking fast enough that Lord Bish was forced behind her by a step. She could hear him trying to keep up for a short time, then accepting that he would have to fall in at her back like an adjutant.

She marched across the field, removing a set of papers and a small banner from her inner jacket pocket, and made a straight line for General al-Dinni, who was standing at the head of the various battalion officers and their adjutants. When she reached the general, she could sense the old woman's confusion, she had been the barracks commanding officer for years and was mostly a functionary—so she came to attention and said, "General al-Dinni, please accept my orders to form a new service battalion designated the 1st Fusiliers Battalion, Last Guards Utisa, Cycus Brigade, through draft ordinary of Capital assigned companies of the Dominion Brigade."

General al-Dinni blinked at the princess. She was somewhat sandbagged and looked in shock at Bish and his uniform from a backwater unit, and back to Nazira dressed as a company grade ranker from what amounted to the city volunteers. "You, well, you have a veil?"

Nazira said, "Yes, my general, I have been ordered into the veil. My procession, you understand."

The General looked at the orders, then at Nazira, and Bish again, trying to do the math in her head. Finally, she fell back on formality. "Captain, err, what is your honorific?"

"Saeid d' Cycus my General," Nazira said in a loud ringing tone as if she was an ensign. There was a muttering in the ranks. No one had ever bothered to give Nazira a title or a post that she might use as an honorific, so she had done what countless young women drafted into service each year did. She had affixed what amounted to a nickname to herself as an honorific, which presented a commoner of military rank problems that were not easy to work out. She could have claimed al-Youseffi or even the Kemeyan family name al-Nabeel, but neither felt right. They never had.

"Princess," General al-Dinni said. Then she caught ahold of herself and took the papers. "Very good Captain, it says you may draft a company of sixty fellows from the Life Guards and Dominion Brigades. And here I see you have the master of horse and foot signed off on the formation of the new battalion under the Cycus constabulary brigade. And I also take note of this final document, a draft by name. Very good Captain."

Nazira came to parade attention and saluted, "Thank you, my general." She knew the expectation that she would simply choose a single company from the two brigades in barracks, but she had read the orders for the procession simply called for a draft of men and women, not for a unit. There was a significant advantage to be had in gaming orders others thought of as routine. Sixty hand-picked soldiers were better than a unit whose quality varied across a spectrum of personalities. In this business, at least, she needed to break a unit in fast.

The unit commanders began barking names, and fusiliers started leaving their old units and forming up into a company square. Her funding was for a composite unit of all ranks, so she could not simply choose all long service rankers. She did not want that, anyway. Instead, she had chosen a half squadron from each of the battalions, led by men and women she remembered from the parade ground. Soldiers who seemed to her had tried just a little harder and had risen in the ranks as she had watched them. The commander of the newly formed battalion marched up to Nazira and said, "Your orders?"

"Train and prepare for procession. I will inspect your unit in ten days. And I am not your commander. You outrank me, Major. Not when I am in uniform. When I am in my role as princess, I am, of course, the commanding general," she said.

"Very well, Captain. We will do our best," he said, turning and yelling for his sergeants.

Nazira turned to the general and saluted again. "My general, permission to retreat."

Looking even more sandbagged, she replied, "We have assigned the 2nd Battalion of the Life Guards to your procession as well with the compliments of the Dominar. Does this meet your desires?"

Nazira stood, holding her salute. That was a trap, she thought. Her guards were her guards, but the battalion assigned to the procession was entirely the prerogative of the Dominar. To say otherwise would prove she was nothing more than a noble playing soldier. Her veil, ignored by Regnal Bish in the polite fashion of court, was being eyed by the General and her officers. The military is not commanded to wear a veil; it was unheard of. A veil was a type of political ownership, a sign of one who is commanded to obedience by the Dominar, a symbol of a Knight who gained their position through politics. Veils were either dismissal or deadly serious. And hers was the most deadly veil one could wear.

Nazira did not take the bait. Let the General order her to answer, or let her order that she remove the damnable veil to see her eyes and face, see how serious she was. Everyone would note if the General tried to lift the veil or ordered Nazira, technically here Captain d' Cycus, to answer the question whose answer was such a political grenade. Finally, she broke.

"Of course, Captain, that battalion will be the one assigned. Good day." The General saluted in return.

Nazira lowered her salute and then turned, nodding to Regnal Bish with an exaggerated dip of the head to defeat the loss of facial communication that came with the veil and started to withdraw. Lord Bish came up to her side and said, "Very clever, Princess. You made a custom unit of soldiers who seem interested in your safety, and you obviously think this is a victory."

"I did. The game can be won by points after all," Nazira proudly said.

Regnal Bish stopped Nazira at the door to the lower tower. "Are you willing to take counsel from me?"

Nazira laughed. "Are you not my murderer? Is a murderer who a princess normally takes counsel?"

Bish looked into the sky. "You act as if an event that may happen in the future is vouchsafed as certain prediction. You play your schemes, yet you are consumed by this thought you are already lost. I give you creed for your bravery, but not the sense of your own preservation by using every tool at your hand to seek victory."

"Then say what you are to say, crazy-eyes, and let me be on with my day!" Nazira replied.

Lord Bish laughed out loud. "I am the butt of humor because my eyes do not track. Crazy-eyes they call me. It is not unlike wearing a veil, is it? But people see my eyes and do not see me, do they not? And they follow my eyes for hints of my mind, but the hints lie without the tongue lying, does it?" He smiled, and said, "Very well. You assure yourself of the quality of the follower, but fail to assure yourself of the quality of the tea you will serve your followers when they march at your side."

"Details," Nazira said without conviction.

Bish scoffed. "Wise princess, become wiser. Life hangs on the details. A kilo, sometimes two of provender each day for each soldier. A liter, perhaps as much as eight, of water. A draughter to calculate the supplies, and a drover to care for animals that carry the provisions, tents, and gear for camp, medicine, and even luxury items that maintain morale; so many details that must be collected. If you leave this all to faceless men and women whose track record and providence you do not understand, or if you let these people act without understanding their quality then your hand-picked soldiers will lose their pay, their health, and possibly their life." He paused for a second. "They won't ever be loyal if your table is crooked."

Nazira simmered for a minute, then looked closely at Lord Bish. "If this concerns you, teach me how to make this right. What should I do, and why would you wish me well?"

Bish smiled. "Perhaps I am as crazy as my eyes. Or perhaps I am concerned for the good soldiers who you may harm. Or perhaps I secretly admire you and hope you learn where the snake pits are in time to save yourself."

Nazira then stuck her finger in his chest. "Then teach me, Lord Bish."

He nodded at her and said, "Follow me."

She turned and followed him. Instead of entering the lower tower, Bish took her down the east wall and into an arched door well. The well led to a series of galleries in which people were at work stacking boxes, cooking food, sewing cloth and leather, and in one darkened corner, furtively forging metal, a priest in prayer to placate the gods. In one space, clerks were busy writing, filing, and retrieving papers. It was this open room that Bish turned into, and then walked down the line of workers with the stacks of paper, stopping at a woman's desk that seemed to have not just sheets of scap spread across her desk, but wooden boxes marked with carefully stenciled numbers.

"Wakira, my love, how is your place in the sun?" Bish asked.

The woman was older, maybe fifty, with beautiful, long, black and gray hair and a thin, hawk-like face. She wore a magnifier on her head like a hat band which was swung up above her hand and a shoulder. "Regnal Bish with your killer smile. Is this your daughter?" she replied.

Bish shook his head. "No, I am sorry. It is Princess Nazira."

Wakira looked her up and down, then rose and tilted her head. "My princess," she said.

Nazira nodded, and replied, "Please call me Captain Saeid d' Cycus and treat me as if I were a junior officer."

Wakira looked at Regnal Bish, who waved his hands in acknowledgment. She then shrugged and said, "Ok Captain, what do you want that cannot be handled by indent or order? We are busy here."

"I have just stood up the 1st Fusiliers, Last Guard," Nazira said.

"Never heard of it," Wakira replied.

Bish leaned over and whispered into her ear. She looked daggers back at him and said, "Ohh, the procession. And you are a captain in a uniform that has never learned logistics."

Nazira nodded. "That is right, I do not have a clue, and you can teach me. Is that a problem?"

Wakira stood up from her desk. "No, Captain." Her emphasis on captain was almost angry. "Idiot nobles with no experience and officers appointed for their ability to drink are not uncommon. If the regiments were really tasked by them, they would be in trouble. Yet we do what we can and if you want to learn, then power to you and honor." She stood and walked into a small alcove that contained boxes filled with small books. Reaching into one box, she pulled out an old book bound in green leather. "Written 43 years ago, by the great scholars of the Republic, the Logistics, Weights, and Measures book. The forms in the back, if copied and returned to us, would assure your needs would be met without one silver penny in five being taken. The tables in the book will say how much food, what type of shelter, and how to keep a safe camp."

"And I should learn this is ten days?" Nazira asked.

"Obviously impossible," Wakira said. She stepped out into the main gallery and said to a worker in the nearest desk, "Have Brandon come here."

Brandon turned out to be a young, short-haired clerk in a kaftan of muslin and gaberdine, a soft keffiyeh holding a business-like shemagh of patterned cloth in place, and a much over his side filled with pens, pencils, protractors, and sticks of conte. He also had a silver notes case tucked into his upper pocket, the cases bursting from the sheer quantity of office scap that it had been forced closed over. In fact, every pocket he had showed folded, rolled, or loose papers poking up. The only oddity of his precise dress was his sleeves, which had tea stains on them despite his otherwise precise grooming. He stopped before the trio, bowed his head, and said, "Captains, Chief Administrator." His voice was soft and shy, though he filled his use of the term Chief Administrator with great reverence.

Wakira said, "Junior Administrator Brandon. I am assigning you to the upcoming procession. This captain, the one with the long hair, is to be your line command. Address her as she is dressed because she is also, by my knowledge, a princess and an owner of a tea merchant. Please walk her through step-by-step at the end of the workday of your progress and keep a support diary for her perusal."

"Of course, Chief Administrator," the young clerk said. He nodded, turned, and left for the main hangar.

"Does this aid you sufficiently Regnal?" Wakira asked.

"You have, as always, Wakira, exceeded my expectations in your skilled handling of the world of scap," Bish replied.

Chief Administrator said, "Yeah, sure." She turned and walked into the main hangar.

Bish bowed slightly before Nazira. "I understand you attend levee?"

Nazira nodded.

"Then that is where I will escort you," Lord Bish said, turning to leave the hangar.

The presence chamber was said to be the center of the Dominion, but it was not the formal place for consideration of law, charges, defense, and precedent that existed in the era of the Republic. Nazira knew no other life than the regular meeting of the Levee of the Dominion, her father sitting on his wooden throne, banks of placer mirrors bathing the room in a sparkly, almost sensual light, the hand bars divided the room into standing and walking channels, bars that were removed in the evening to allow the powers of the land to meet for drinks and discussion.

Her father ruled the levee with benign neglect for formality or process. The ruling body was himself, Chief Justicar Colonel Abrams Taffez, Priest Domingus bar Calad, Bank Master Youti al-Presence, Dame Hailee who was Seigner for Interior, and the Dominion's high constable, and Warden Mortisa al-Cinci. Leading to the dais upon which the ruling body stood was a broad carpeted walkway with three broad genuflection points marked by lines on the floor, and a bar stand where the petitioner could address the luminaries. To the right was the gallery of the knights, where the nobility of the land that held military and civil dynastic assignments stood, and where at any time a quarter of the land's leadership could be present. By practice that predated the Dominion, the leaders, now known as knights, stood for the duration of a levee, but could leave to the outer gallery and return as they wanted

On the left of the walking channel were three sets of chairs. One was reserved for the members of the Dominar's family. The second was provided for people who may be asked to answer questions on subjects, and the third was for commoners who were given five minutes, then ushered out if there was a pleading of interest. Otherwise, the final cluster of seats tended to gather the same crowd of older Cycus townies who were at odds during the day.

Nazira walked in and went for her seat in the family gallery when she was stopped by Seignior Hailee. "A damn wrench you threw in the Dominion, did you not?" She then stopped short. "A soldier are we now?"

Seignior Hailee was older, with short-cropped steel grey hair and a deeply cleft chin at the bottom of a long, hanging face. Nazira ignored her dig about her livery and replied to the first accusation. "You mean that I took a loan out on my own money?"

"Damn you, child. You did nothing to earn that money!" Hailee replied.

"Nothing?" Nazira scoffed. "What did my mother do? That money was passed to me from her. She brought that money to the Dominion!"

"And lost it when she fled," Hailee said angrily.

"And it rested on me, allowing you to take the proceeds and pay off every sloth that comes to the levee. I merely used the proceeds for what I wanted, nothing stolen. The money was mine, and you were stealing its working power!" Nazira did not want to fight this woman here, in the minutes before levee, but she would not back down to her, not if it cost her everything.

Oddly enough, it was Taffez who came to her rescue. With Mortisa al-Cinci in tow, he approached and said, "Seignior Hailee, shall we delay the Dominar any longer? Perhaps this is better to discuss in chambers?"

Hailee looked at the empty throne, then back at Taffez, before stalking away. Taffez tilted his head to Nazira, while al-Cinci ignored her, and they both went to the dais.

Bengan al-Youseffi was the only resident of the family section today. Bengan was her grandmother's grandson, a cousin by court standards. Griselda al-Youseffi rarely, if ever, came to levee, but no levee was held without her. Instead, there was always some member of the al-Youseffi around to monitor proceedings.

Bengan was perhaps the best of the al-Youseffi kith in Nazira's mind. He had rare sandy blond hair and piercing green eyes and had been educated better than most of his peers, having grown up in Cycus instead of Castile Tariq. In fact, Nazira remembered Standish beating up Bengan al-Youseffi, his sister Teagan, and Process al-Dinni when the gang made fun of her for her great height, but that both Bengan and Teagan reacted with good humor to their beating, humor that most of her al-Youseffi relatives would never have been able to muster. This did not make her trust Bengan, but did make her feel less like hiring a thug to slaughter him in the street.

She approached her chair and looked him over. He was always well dressed in court finery, including a yellow linen thawb, a particolor swallow-tailed coat of serge and wool, and knee gows of plush. Around his neck, he had a delicate chain of scrim-shell and cerulean with the Sea Lion Rampant of the al-Youseffi. On his head was a fez of brown satin set at a rakish angle.

"My cousin," he said, "are you not newly married?"

"Does this matter?" Nazira quipped, sitting down next to Bengan.

"I was going to say," Bengan pulled his face closer to her, "that you got a healthy boy for your bed. I have had many a sporting contest with Javier al-Rasheed, and I can say he has an eye for ball games. Bit weird in the head though."

"Thank you for your assessment, Bengan, and thank you for your approval," Nazira replied.

"Oh, you seem to have gone all forward on him though. How much was the ship you bought him?" Bengan asked.

"I did not really buy it for him. I more like stole it for him, but outfitting a pirate for trade is quite expensive. It takes about S4,200 silver a year, almost 20 chests," she said, pulling a notebook from her swallowtail military coat.

"Yet you have S20,000, do you not?" He leaned over again and whispered.

Nazira looked over at him. "The escrow pays S20,000 a year, but who says I borrowed on it all or that I did not spend it on the dogs?"

"My Grandmother says," he retorted.

"Our Grandmother, Dame Griselda. How does she have this intelligence?" Nazira asked.

"I wonder," Bengan said, then turned as the Dominar came in.

"Dominar Abelard XIV, King of the Cyclonidees, Lord Cycus, Admiral of the Camellia Fleet, does deign to hear petitions, draw forth all." The barker yelled from the corner, and Nazira's father trundled in. He was a large, loud man, with a red face that always seemed on the edge of exploring, and tiny piggy eyes, who never could quite get clothing that fit his girth.

Nazira listened with interest as various people pre-sented problems that had obvious solutions but which were gummed up in tradition and anger, or whose problems were simply the result of miscommunication. The advisors to the court tried to guide Abelard, but he was like a bull in a dressing room, knocking into things and constantly cross. Bengan said under his breath, "Your father hates these levies. Why does he not let my grandmother take them on?"

Nazira looked at Dame Griselda, her daughter, and granddaughter, Bengan's sister, all sitting in the noble seats. *No*, Nazira thought, *her father might hate the idea of the levies, but he would never hand them over to the woman who was technically his stepmother.* "Your Grandmother is Cycus-born you know, Bengan."

Bengan replied, "So what?"

"Melinda's mother was an al-Cinci," Nazira replied.

Bengan screwed up his face in a point, something that he was far too old to do, in Nazira's opinion. "You talk in riddles, cousin."

"Had no one told you anything?" Nazira asked.

Bengan laughed. "Oh cousin, they predicted today you would be in veil and that crazy-eyed Bish would be following you."

"Why though?" she asked quietly. There was supposed to be a low murmur among the viewers of the levees. It kept some awake, and it hid the boredom some felt.

"Look at this next lot, Cousin," Bengan changed the subject.

Indeed, they were diplomats of the Corveen, the Halo's most powerful nation-state. They were dressed in blue overcoats, shirts and slacks of gaberdine, hip boots, and had the splashy sun symbol of their people. Their skin was pale white, and their hair was long and black. "This matter's Bengan, if our traders are to gain access to the core islands and the

Sea of Calms. My father's counselors have been working for months to get these people into this room."

Bengan said, "He should have done it with less silly people."

The three diplomats bowed. "Dominar Abelard, I am happy to meet you at last. I am Statesman Ranjit. To my left is Doctor Sergious, and to my right is Commodore Buell. We are happy that our agreement has reached your eyes."

Abelard was in a petulant mood, no doubt in some ways because of herself, Nazira thought. It made her sad sometimes when her father was angry. She wanted to be his daughter and be loved, but that had been a ship that had sailed long ago, never to return.

Nazira shook it off as her father spoke. "You state we will be immune to marque, and subject only to the flag reference. What do you mean by that?" She wished she could explain that the marque issue was if Corveen warships would respect the right of the ships of Cycus to travel. It was in their favor. She could see her father was cross over the issue.

A hand sat on her shoulder. She looked over, and it was the Butler. "You must come with me."

"Why?" she asked.

"You are disturbing the Dominar and he must get this negotiation right," the old butler said. Nazira was about to make the poor man's life miserable, but then she realized he was right. Her father was cross because she was here, and it could hurt the nation. She hurried out of the presence chamber, made a wrong turn, and walked right past the guard station into a room full of waiting petitioners.

They all stood as one. One, a farmer by his looks, said, "My lady, why are you crying?"

Crying, she thought, how absurd. She reached up to her face and realized her veil had shifted absurdly and revealed her eyes, which were indeed tear-filled. "The dry air," someone said, and it was her voice.

An older woman stepped up and adjusted her veil. "You are pretty, Princess. Why are you veiled?"

Because, she thought, *it is a way to break me. Only I won't break.* "Gentle-woman," she replied, "it is tradition for a princess who is on procession to be veiled."

"No, it is not." An even older woman said. "I remember the time before, the fall of the old order. They died in a fire, and then there was the upstart, who now is our Dominar, the gods save him." She stopped and spat a brown liquid on the floor. She was one of the older generation that actually chewed some varieties of tea. "Gods save him, Princess."

Two guards rushed to her side. "My princess, this is the common waiting room. You should be in the noble cloak-room." The Life Guard looked very anxious.

Nazira waved him off. "Back to your post," she said, then thought better of it. "No wait, send a runner to the Draughtsman's office, have the Draughtsman Yesha d' Semini report here with his table, a blank book, receipts, and ink pens. The guards looked nervous, but Nazira had been ordering around soldiers since she was nine. "If you do not believe I have the right to have the Draughtsman of my choice here, say now, and we will discuss it with your colonel.

Without another word, he saluted and ordered a junior to carry out the task. A functionary had entered the room and asked, "Princess, what are you doing here?"

"Starting my procession early," she replied.

"This is not acceptable. If you do this, I will have the guards remove you, forcibly if needed. You are not only under veil, but you are not authorized to hold a levee," he replied. The man was dressed in court finery, sateen robes, a pental-wood torque of office, pockets with notebooks and pencils, and padded pants for genuflecting. Yet as official and stern as he seemed, his eyes widened with fear and he seemed caught in a conniption.

From behind Nazira came the voice of Regnal Bish. "You will not touch the Princess."

"Not your play, Regnal," the man replied.

"Look around, Brishal. How many of these commoners will be called for the levee by the butler? And what possible harm can come of the princess holding a levee of her own here? And then consider what type of winter you will see from my and mine should you confront us!" Just as he had come from nowhere, unseen, his voice was forgettable, almost soft, yet she could feel the weight of sinister threat from the colorless, wild-eyed courtier with his absurd dagger around his neck.

"You push, Regnal." The functionary stamped his foot and turned and left in high dudgeon, passing Yesha d' Semini the draughtsman and Nazira's childhood friend. He was holding one of the large scap books that served as court records and a scribe's case filled with the tools of the writers' trade.

"Princess Nazira," Bish said, "conduct your affairs."

Nazira nodded. "Yesha, please open the book and enter the note that I am enrolling this levee." She looked up at the crowd and said, "Friends, I have time to proceed with your issues, but we must be quick about it. In order of your ticket, step forward. If you are here adversarially, please know I will not allow catfights in the gallery." She reached over for the docket box, pulled the first wooden chit, and said, "Seven-four."

An old couple stepped forward, one a grizzled man and the other a bent-backed woman. They both genuflected deeply, then the woman said, "Princess. We hold the curry on a dom in the fourth carry. The sewag on it is passed by a bit, but we cannot work. It is just not in us anymore. We do not want out in the street."

She looked over at Yesha d' Semini, who shrugged in confusion, but Bish said in a clear voice, "Curry is street tongue for ownership. A dom is a place, probably a small house, usually with farmland that must be worked. Sewag or sometimes sesag is the tax debt on the farm. So the couple is too old to farm and is running into tax debt and may lose their farm."

Nazira nodded. "Good sires, is this accurate?"

"Long and short, my princess," the woman said.

"How much is the debt?" Nazira asked.

The woman pulled her hood from her head and looked at Nazira with gray eyes. Her skin was dark, craggy, and filled with honor lines. She held her husband's hand tightly and looked like she was about to be swallowed whole by a drag-onfish. "Fifty-something. It has backed up three years now since my beloved was spiked in the field. We have no one left. They are all gone. It is just us, Mistress."

"So no one stands to have the land?" Nazira asked.

"No one, my princess," the woman said.

"Yesha," she turned to the draughtsman. He nodded at her, pen ready to write. "The man and woman in posses-sion of this land are to meet with my regimental logi. The Regiment will purchase their land and give them lifetime tenure. Soldiers, too, may apply for the right to claim the land on end of service if they or their family works that land during the lifetime of these two. Designate this couple stew-ards." She turned to the man and woman. "I have little I can legally do about this, but this may work. You retain the house until you both pass. My regiment will take charge of farming and paying taxes, and you will get a stipend. If this does not work out as I intend, return to my regimental commander. Take this letter and ask at the barracks for my people. Do you understand?"

They both bowed, then turned and left. Bish stepped to her side and whispered, "You cannot buy everyone in the room. And they have nothing to sell."

Nazira shrugged. "No matter. A soldier's family will work the heck out of the farm, and when the old couple pass, it will go to the soldier as steward after them. I just hope it is enough to save the farm."

Bish nodded and stepped back behind Nazira.

Nazira looked out across the room and saw a man who seemed to rowel her mind, a hidden, deep memory of her youth hidden by the darkness of time. He was dark-faced, cowled, had a deep scar on his face, and had piercing eyes. Unusual of the people, he was likely a knight. He was armed with a ratty yataghan frogged to a belt of canvas. Nazira stared at him for a second, then lost interest and called, "Next."

The cases were simple in basis, but difficult because often there were two or more people arguing for access to the same property, angry over some trespass, or simply befuddled over a life issue that had no clear solution. In five, she could solve one without the laying down of finances. Some she could solve with money in a way that maintained equity and did not drain her accounts, but for most, there was no easy way to decide who was right.

As she handled cases, there was a growing number of courtiers—knights, lawyers, accountants, jongleurs, advocates, logisticians, vendors, boleros, bonivides, chambermaines, dancing masters, and soldiers, watching the process that normally they would not be able to see, an actual hearing of commoners. Nazira, herself being a courtier, felt she knew exactly what they were thinking. Here are the issues of the small people, the people who never get heard. Justice, if it exists for them, comes from street gangs and guilds and happens deep at night when the city guard withdraws from the city streets. The law that was practiced was one of financial transactions and sometimes, if the people were lucky, the concepts of Cycus equity. Equity did flow through many of the petitioners' requests, but that was like two ships trying to share the same channel. Ships, unlike the lives of men and women in the realm of the Cycus Dominion, had a book of rules that each captain followed to ensure they did not collide in harbors or even the whole of the sea. It was like that for many things. Tea masters followed a widely agreed set of rules on how to grade and sell their tea. She could walk into the library of the tea master of Cycus Port and read not only those rules but also a range of agreements made between tea masters and a listing of all people who could claim to be masters.

There simply was no such thing that existed for the lives of men and women. The Camellia throne was, in theory, a court of equity. It balanced the needs of the people who came before it. But it was, she realized, hardly effective. Her father was vainglorious but had no idea of consistency. Even handling a few hours of claims and requests among the people taxed Nazira intellectually. Most of these people would never be able to be presented in court or have their questions heard.

A man stood in front of her. Soldiers were throwing trash in his well. Were they? Nazira had no idea, but she had a note written to the palace Master Armsman to report to her what was happening. If he refused, there was nothing she could do. A pair of egg vendors discussed the difficulty of getting their eggs through the gates to the shops they served.

The traffic in the morning was intense, and the soldiers were too slow. Could that be happenstance? Would there be a solution that really should be the egg vendors starting earlier for their appointments? Was there a way to make the processing of people from the countryside entering the city easier? Was this even an issue for court? Could it be handled in some other manner?

Then the piercing idea that she was being watched again settled on her mind. She looked up and the same man was staring at her. She had completely forgotten he was in the crowd of commoners, sitting amongst the masses as if his rank did not matter. The courtiers were careful to avoid close contact with the petitioners, hugging the walls like they might catch the plague, but he sat in their midst, staring. She thought for a second, a flash of time, that she knew the man, then it left her and she forgot about him again.

After six straight hours and fifty petitioners, she was done. "If I can hold another levee good folk, before my procession, I will," she announced. Then she stood, bowed to the people, and left the waiting chamber. As she left, she stopped by Draughtsman Yesha d' Semini's table and said, "Yesha, you are now my scribe-in-chief. Write orders to have you promoted to writing master and attached to me. Then dispatch the current orders I have issued to the appropriate people." She paused, then said, "You will need a staff?"

"My princess, what do you intend I do? To be honest, you need not employ me. I am on the rolls of the palace," he replied.

"Finish your work here and then meet me in my sitting rooms on the eve. I intend you to be attached to the retinue of procession, and you will have to do a great deal of work for me," she said. Then she nodded to Regnal Bish and left the chambers.

Bish, a bemused look on his face, looked at Nazira as she walked. She noted the attention, causing her to say, "Do you think I am stepping outside of my power?"

Bish laughed. "My princess, no one, and I mean no one in the court, cares about anyone who was in that room awaiting petition. That is why they are in the room. They are led to believe the Dominar will intervene for them. If they had coins in their purses, they would have been assigned to the main levee and the nobles' chambers. Nothing you did in there will even be noticed."

"Except by the commons," she said.

He ducked his head. "Except by the commons, my princess."

"Yesha will be my scribe-in-chief," she said in a tone she hoped displayed a resolution of spirit.

Bish turned the corner into the portico hall with her and said, "That can happen, and will. I will arrange for it."

"His staff?" she asked.

"Princess. You have no experience of these things, but let me tell you that you have spent only a tithe of what you could spend. You could encrust your pantalettes with jewels and order up a pack of ringleted vicuna, and no one would notice nor care. I admit that if anyone was looking at your expenses, they would be shocked at what you were spending money on, but no one with any perspicuity of vision will note the direction your silver is flowing." Bish arrived at the doorway to her chambers and nodded at the two guards standing there. "The princess will have visitors through the day and eve. She may not leave these chambers, but she may have any visitors she wishes. Tell your ensign when she carries out the inspection."

Nazira noticed that the guards were goggling at Bish and her as if they were aliens, then realized they were both in ranking military uniforms. They had not changed since she had visited the parade grounds that morning. "Guardsman, attention to orders."

They snapped to with her order, their armor and weapons ringing with the sudden change of position. Bish laughed again, then said, "I had forgotten my uniform. Good day, Princess."

Nazira entered her chambers and found Vries and three of his men, former thugs from the docks, now in the finery of the palace. Three soldiers of the Life Guards stood with them, eyeing the newly minted bodyguard with contempt. What the soldiers did not know was that Nazira had known Vries for a decade. He may not be the assassin he claimed to be, but she had seen him hold court in the dockside bars and offer up a rude, rough form of justice that may have lacked grace and considerations of decorum, but which kept warring gangs and visiting scalawags from tearing each other to bits.

Gannet Vries was a huge man, a meter or more tall and 125 kg in mass, but he did not have the cut muscles of a showquin from a jongleur's show. Instead, he had an oddly square jaw and looked almost portly. Yet Nazira had only seen only one man best him in hand fighting, and that was Regnal Bish.

The guards might not trust Vries, but Nazira had seen him control the violent docks without mass murder, and that said a lot for him. She looked at the sergeant and his soldiers until they grew uncomfortable. "You can withdraw to your station outside of my rooms, sergeant."

"Princess, this man is not vetted," he said.

"He is vetted by me. Now, you are not instructed to remain in my quarters past when you are dismissed. I cannot ask you to leave your external posts, and I appreciate and value your presence there. But unless you want to watch me undress, and then explain said viewing of the princess in her camisole to your captain, you will kindly withdraw." She put her hands to the buttons on her uniform blouse as if she were going to strip in her presence chamber. The Sergeant nodded and withdrew with an unhappy look on his face.

Nazira looked at Oban and said, "Tea for our guests." Vries looked uncomfortable, but watched Oban as he made tea, then took the copper insulated cup from the beat-up service into his hand and said, "Thank you, Master Oban."

Oban bowed. "Just Oban, Assassin Vries. Please have a seat with the princess."

Vries sat and said, "I am not an assassin, my princess." He motioned for his two silent companions to also sat as Oban equipped them with tea.

"I know this now. I suspect that assassins are fictional and you were using the fiction for your own purpose, Mister Vries." Nazira accepted the tea from Oban and drank from it immediately. Unlike a formal tea, where Oban might be expected to make and consume a cup first, the informality of the setting made the tea service closer to the warm, simple ceremony of the outer court.

"Begging your leave, Princess. The Assassins are not a fakery. They exist, just not how I claimed to be one. Claiming the mantle, so to speak, got be off with less throat slitting ... if you understand how that goes. You should look to Regnal Bish for an assassin and ask him the long and the short of it, my princess." He drank his hot tea down in one tilt, and Nazira could feel the burn in her own mouth, but it did not seem to bother him.

"Your bodyguard is four teams of three. We have three teams of three covering your apartments at night. And my followers are four and fifty-four. Your fine Master Bish has arranged for training with the regiments for our people, but I can say that they are not happy." Oban was hovering around, so Vries handed him the empty copper cup. "My princess, there are some who have left my service when I chose to follow you, and they will be paying the cost soon."

Nazira shook her head. "Are they taking up with our enemies?"

"They are, Princess." Vries looked at the other two enforcers and they nodded.

"Mister Vries. Inform them that you will not target their families, but that their betrayal of you is a betrayal of me. I want you to understand that I order outrages if outrages are to be ordered. You are welcome to ask for mercy, but not for destruction." Nazira stared at Vries and hoped he got the point.

It seemed he did. He dipped his head, then said, "My princess, if this is what you say, it is how it will be done."

"My friend, Vries. I knew you before you knew me as a princess, and I note and appreciate your honor and that your honor has been violated. When the time comes, I will let you decide who pays and what the bill handed out is. And there will be a time. Your honor matters. There is just a time for it to be paid off," she said.

He nodded. "Princess, your guards will be in the uniform of your regiment, but in an emergency, they will provide a hand sign to you with the left hand, long finger up on right breast. May I be excused to see to our guards?"

"You may. I will be retiring early. This uniform is tiring to wear, and I am almost asleep."

Nazira woke with a hammering on her door. Oban lit a taper and dragged a fire poker from the fireplace as the portal burst open, revealing Regnal Bish, Vries, and three soldiers.

Bish said to Vries, "Guard the room. Princess, did you have anything to eat from the kitchen?"

"I did not," Nazira said, climbing from her bed and putting a cloak on. "I retired without eating. Oban made me tea from my service."

Bish looked at the disreputable tea service the Princess favored. It was bashed copper with a wire basket pot for steeping. The cups were likewise of copper and not kept well-shined. "Then you are lucky." He stepped to the windows and looked out across the courtyards. "This evening a tea cart was prepared for you along with a curry of duck."

Nazira stepped to the window herself. "I would never eat duck, and I do not have tea trays in the evening. My own service and Oban make a better setting."

"Which tells me the principals in this matter did not know your habits. The trays, uncalled for, were eaten by staff of the lower halls. Three are dead, seven are fighting for their lives, and three more are seriously ill," he said. "There may be others coming from the lower hallways, it is not known who all ate from the trays with your meals and tea."

"I will go to them," Nazira announced.

Bish closed the curtains and said, "You will not, my Princess."

"Vries, prepare to escort me to the medicals. Oban, dress me and prepare my guards for the visits," she commanded, ignoring Bish, who shrugged and stepped aside.

When Nazira was dressed, she arranged her guards and some servants into a formation. She was in such haste she almost forgot her veil, but Oban supplied it before she ventured forth. Dressed, surrounded by her followers, and in high dudgeon, she entered the hall like she was a Dominar herself. Courtiers pressed to the walls or fled the main corridor altogether as Vries, eight personal guards, nine soldiers led by an ensign, Oban, and five servants plus Bish glumly taking up the rear charged down the transactional hall to the portico, then took the service stairs down to the Medicals. Two young men in nursing surplices were standing in the portal to the healer's room but were gently displaced by Vries and his guards.

Nazira strode through the opening and to the lead medical, an old woman named Juene al-Numbra, and said, "Scholar Juene, how are the poisoned?"

The woman bowed. "Princess, none of your people were affected."

"I do not care, Scholar. I understand they were poisoned drinking and eating provender intended for me." She waved into the room and said, "That makes them my people. If a shot aimed at me from a firelock hits another, it is myself who is indirectly to blame."

"I understand, my princess," Scholar Juene said. "This is not something you want to see though. Even those we hope to save are affected. The poison affects the nerves. It is brutal. It would have been easier for the poisoner to outright kill."

"Show me them, Scholar," Nazira said.

Scholar Juene bowed. She turned and walked deeper into the medical, followed by Nazira, Oban, Vries, and Bish. There was a growing sound of yells as they walked down the corridor. A portal with a heavy wooden door marked with the word "Ward" stood at the end of the hallway. In the heavy double door was set a smaller door, as if giants used the main set and regular humans used the smaller. She pushed the small doorway open—it was hinged to swing both directions—and stepped in, holding it for Nazira and her followers.

The room was a scene of horrors. More than a dozen people lay in beds screaming, hands and arms twisted, fouled sheets and stench assaulting the eyes and ears. Dead were lined at the end of the room, one of which was cut open revealing the internal form of the stomach. A score of healers of various grades and specialties, possibly the entire staff of the medical, was performing tasks, obvious and obscure. One of the screaming women in the bed nearest them sat up with great difficulty and yelled, "Damn you, Princess! Damn you and your line."

A healer, befouled like Scholar Juene, rushed to the Princess and said, "Do not take note of such speech, it is not them, but the poison."

Bish stepped forward and said, "It is likely prentice weed."

"How would you know, sir?" Juene asked. "Are courtiers now chemists?"

Nazira lifted her hand and gained the attention of the group. "I believe Regnal Bish has this knowledge. It would be best to use it." She turned to the museifi who had approached when her patient yelled at her. "Museifi, return to your patient. No utterance of theirs will cause me worry, just their safety and return to health."

The man bowed. "Thank you, Princess." He returned to the patient.

Nazira braced Juene. "What can be done?" The screams were starting to tear at everyone's composure.

"Prentice weed, my princess. It is hopeless unless the dose was very slight. It may take weeks, but all in this room will die." She looked at one patient as she spoke.

Nazira followed her vision and saw that the writhing form as a girl, not more than fifteen. Her skin, like toffee, and her hair, black and glistening, would have been appropriate on the finest of dolls. Yet here she was, screaming and twisting in the bed. Nazira clenched her fists and said, "The horror." She grabbed Vries by the arm and said, "The

Butler is to come here. If she will not come, drag her here. The Usher as well. This room, now. I do not care if they are in bed clothing. Here, now."

Vries nodded, turned, and left. Nazira pointed at Bish and said, "Where is my father?"

Bish shook his head. "Princess, this is horrible to see, but the Dominar does not look into the doings of the lower halls. Unless soldiers or nobles are killed, then this is no more than the cost of doing business."

"Horrors!" Nazira said. "Horrors!" She grabbed Bish by the arm and forced the man to follow her into a corner, away from the rest. "Is this the work of your people?" she asked him pointedly.

Bish looked back at the room filled with writhing people. "Princess, I do not know what you mean."

"Assassins use poison, do they not?" No one could overhear her in the din.

Bish considered, his eyes pointed crazily into the corner where two shelves holding healing supplies stood attached. "If there were assassins, they would not use this poison. They would, in fact, take the use of this poison as a crime beyond almost any other. A patron would not need to offer much bounty for them to seek out the culprit and wreck them in a fury of vengeance."

There was a silence in the middle of the screams, a silence of thought as Bish and Nazira considered each other. The usher then ducked into the room through the small door and announced, "How dare you summon me, Princess! You are veiled and a child, not one who ranks here!"

Nazira turned from Bish and noted Vries and three of his heavies were entering the room after the man, who was indeed dressed in a gown for sleeping. She had known the usher only a short time, as he had purchased his position only recently, but disliked him almost immediately. She strode forward and with the palm of her hand slapped the usher in his bearded face.

The usher looked shocked for a second, then cocked his fist to hit Nazira back, only to be stopped by six blades wielded by Oban, Bish, Vries, and the three enforcers who Vries had recruited to her side. "Let him land the punch if he wishes," Nazira said, and the blades all withdrew.

"She is veiled, Usher!" Bish growled through his teeth

"Not in a sick house!" Scholar Juene yelled, "Not as these people lay dying."

Nazira turned to the patients in their beds writhing, then at the ruddy-faced, hirsute usher, and finally to Scholar Juene. She bowed deeply to the healer, and said, "Outside all."

Oban spoke up. "My princess, I can aid the healers."

Nazira nodded. "Do what you can." Then she motioned to Vries, who took the usher by hand and pushed him from the medical. Once in the hallway, she said to the usher, "Do you control the lower hall servants?"

"I let the butler handle that," he said.

"Fool!" Bish interrupted. "Do not lie."

The usher looked at Bish. "Crazy eyes, you are not above my rank. I will break you if you are not careful."

Bish reached for his kirpan. "Be careful Odger al-Lucci. This is not the time to test me."

"Enough," Nazira said, fatigue in her voice. "Usher al-Lucci. I want you to investigate this poisoning and report to me what you find."

"You cannot command me, Princess," he replied.

Nazira nodded. "I cannot? Then you are dismissed. Leave my presence now. And in the future, if you see me, bow and stay bowed until I leave a room you are in."

Anger crossed the usher's face, but he seemed to have no answer, so he turned and stalked down the hall of the Medico to its entrance and stormed out. In doing so, he passed the butler, who was walking alone to Nazira.

The butler was older, bent from labor, and her face was filled with worry. She walked slowly, but when she reached the princess, she sketched an appropriate bow. When she rose, she said, "My princess."

"Butler Caelia. I have just had a dissatisfying conference with the usher. Will you give me the same?" Nazira said.

"Likely, my princess," the butler replied. "It is a long night and many of my people lie dying. There is no time, and no will to deal with your temper tantrum as well."

"Would you speak to my father like this, Butler Caelia?" Nazira asked.

"No," she replied but said no more.

Nazira looked down at the floor. The night was wearing on her, and she could still hear the screams of the stricken loudly in her head. "Perhaps I have approached you wrong. I want to help, and I want answers. How do I achieve these goals?"

"Answers," Caelia said. "Two members of the kitchen staff are missing and being sought by the Life Guards. It appears they are the ones who introduced a poison to the tray of food and tea intended for your chambers. It was consumed by the servants, as is the custom when you did not call for it."

"The families that cannot enter the palace?" Nazira asked.

Caelia replied, "They cannot listen to this. There is nothing to be done."

"Warn them, give them the option, then open a room off the portico for the rest to remain," Nazira said.

"Is that an order?" the butler asked.

"Yes," Nazira replied.

The butler nodded. She bowed, entered the small door to the medical, then shortly exited. "I will do as you say here. Will you accept the expense?"

"Of course I will," Nazira said. "Regnal Bish holds my purse strings. Look to him for the costs."

The butler turned to Bish, and he nodded. "Is there anything else the princess demands?"

The wails of the dying still echoed in her mind. "If any member of the family wants a boon, expresses a loss that can be made good. I ask you speak with Regnal Bish and between the two, see it done if you feel it is asked for in good faith. If they wish to accuse me to my face and yell their hatred, then arrange for this in private audience. Their relatives died because someone wanted me to suffer. They have that right."

Butler Caelia bowed. The woman was inscrutable to Nazira, but she felt that it was understood by her that the dead were to be avenged, and their families succored. She turned and left without giving away her feelings over the attack.

Regnal Bish put his hand on her shoulder. "Princess Nazira, you should go to bed."

"There must be more I can do," she said.

"My princess, no more travels through the palace at night. No more visits to the docks. Whoever essayed this travesty did so with the intent you die screaming in agony. That is more than simply a move to the throne. It is hate," Regnal Bish said.

"Have you ever wanted to return to Beijus, leave this life behind you, stalwart Regnal?" Nazira asked.

Bish considered this. "We all wish to set aside our deadly veils and return to the time when we were free and happy."

Nazira reached up and felt her veil, forgotten so often now, the sign of her captivity. "Vries, leave a guard for Oban when he decides to return. Let us see me back to my sleep. Dreamless, I hope."

Chapter IX

Kurdial Qatil

R egnal Bish woke in his simple chambers in bayt kaz-bara. The structure was an old counting house that his order had taken due to its sturdy construction and proximity to the palace in Cycus Port. The rooms were formerly for storage of spices, with thin slip windows desired to air the rooms without allowing thieves to enter. They had the original clinker doors, heavy and brooding, with the doorstop and cross beams moved from the external to the internal door sets.

Handasuh had entered his room, likely through the air vents, and was sitting on the foot of his bed rack. She regarded him with stern purple eyes, then proceeded to lick her fur impudently at her shoulder. Bish clicked his tongue at her and went to a small hamper he kept for the purpose of measuring out some kibble into a finely carved oaken bowl. He placed the bowl on the ground and clicked his tongue again, causing his visitor to unwind herself and step down to inspect the offering. She circled the bowl three times, sniffed it, then looked at him with accusing eyes. "E-yawel," she said in a tone that stated Bish had failed in his duties.

"I have no fish, Handasuh. I am sorry," he said. His clothing was hung on a dowel rod of pine, either on wooden rackpinnes or in a canvas travel-all. His needs were simple, and he did not keep much or a wardrobe. The bed clothing he wore went into a basket by the hanger, and he took the water he prepared the night before and took a bath with a fresh washing cloth. Handasuh decided that the kibble in the bowl was the best she would get and tucked it with a loud crunching down that belied her dissatisfaction with the morning repast. Bish smiled as he washed himself. She would never turn down food.

He took from his rack a silk top and pants. He did not wear them for luxury, but because they turned aside knives well, and were light and cool. He then put on his black cotton thawb and sirwal, and then followed it with his par-ticolor swallowtail jacket.

Around his waist, he wrapped a woven belt and attached a frog for his kirpan. He then used a looking glass to appraise his appearance. Once satisfied, he left his chambers and went down to the common room.

Instead of seeing every member of his coven in place, there was only Trace, their mistress of the house.

"Where are Wevern and Luthers?" Bish asked.

Trace took a wooden bowl and scooped into it a serving of potage. "Eat and have tea, Regnal." He nodded, took the bowl, and sat at the table. As soon as he sat, Trace delivered him a great mug of tea.

The potage was keena grain and barley with half milk and lath. Whatever it was, the meal was hot and well prepared. The tea was fresh brew common tea, something from the market for those on a budget. It was not bad, and Trace had added a touch of hickory branch to balance the bitter tones.

Trace came over with her own meal and tea, then sat down and said, "Your coven-mates tell me that last night was a long one for you."

Regnal nodded. "Someone tried to kill the princess with poison." He took another spoon of potage and more tea from his giant mug.

"Occupational hazard?" Trace asked.

Bish shook his head. "Not this way. No one can expect to get to a veiled princess with something as simple as poison. This was a message."

"That was what Wevern and Luthers said. They said that a message should be met by a message." Trace replied.

Bish looked up at the house mistress. The guild was based on the pillars of secrecy and the connection of the brethren into covens of three, with three covens forming a conspiracy led by a master. The word assassin was never spoken aloud, however, each member of the guild knew and accepted that was what they were. "Is this their task on this morrow?" he asked.

"You have been distracted," Trace said. "You may not be able to complete your task. The Master of our Conspiracy feels that there are perhaps issues you are wrestling with."

"And she communicated this to you?" he asked.

She nodded, drinking her tea. "Is that not my role?"

"Your role is to make tea and breakfast," Bish replied.

Trace laughed and took his plate. "As if. Wevern says the day will be long for you. The procession leaves tomorrow, and you have much to complete today."

"I do," Bish said, standing. "I will eat in the market for the mid, and likely have dinner with the princess."

Trace nodded and handed Bish a piece of scap. He opened it and said, "That is a surprise, and is indeed my first stop. Thank you for this."

"Widdinger sent it over. They have one of theirs on the man," Trace said.

"Indeed," Bish replied.

The marketplace was the normal bustle of mongers and buyers. "Business," the master of Cycus port said, "shall be carried out on the tables of the marketplace each day between the first and last rays of the sun." No money was to change hands at any other time.

Almost no one followed the rule, but that did not make business in the light of day unpopular. It just did not stop business in the darkness of night. Bish entered the great forum and looked around the edges for Catheir, one of his order, who was in his conspiracy but not his coven. She was a young woman who styled herself in practice a courtesan, but she did not do actual business. Instead, she took the arm of nobles when they plied the forum during the days. The nobles, male and female, relied on her to give them a sense of class, and she dressed herself accordingly, like an untouchable dame of the great families.

That Catheir was from a family of drays people, and not being noble at all did not matter to the merchants who hired her. It was like hiring a big warrior with an axe, or a little accountant with a book of figures. They were all cosmetic statements on how they saw business being conducted in the open spaces of the forum. And if the same man or woman who was on a merchant's arm one day showed up on the arm of another a day later, it was all part of the fiction. Like wearing a green cravat or a red and blue beret.

Bish moved through the market forum to where Catheir stood. He nodded at her, and said, "I have a note you have received intelligence of Naseer al-Dinni. I know he has sought money from his kin and was in touch with his cousin, the General."

She smiled at Bish. "Brother-of-the-Knife, it appears he wants to form a new crew and seek revenge for the loss of the *Remarker* and the embarrassment he was shown by your charge, the Princess Nazira."

Reverting to formal speech, he said, "Sister-of-Blade, his old crew is scattered. Absorbed to the gangs, fled the lands of Cycus, or dead. He has, I know, tried to contact the princess through Bostwick, her half-sister's husband, which hardly speaks to the former pirate's intelligence."

"The master of our conspiracy wants you to warn the man off. It is said the princess does not like her veil, but it is useful, if you see my meaning." Catheir nodded to a passing merchant.

"Why does our master allow this game piece to roam the streets if she is worried by its actions?" Bish asked.

Catheir drew forth a fan from her sleeves. It was cool, so the fan was a mere prop to cover her lips as she spoke. "The Master of our conspiracy feels that we are coming into a time of strife. Naseer al-Dinni is an embarrassment to his entire kith as a pirate, but dead in the depth of night, he could rally them to the cause of someone more decisive and dangerous."

Bish smirked. "The most dangerous and decisive person in the mix now is Griselda, and the Dinni are not likely to match with the Youseffi."

"Your blindness is because you are too close, which is expected by your brothers and sisters. Could not Nazira take the throne if the Dinni were to suddenly rally to her side?" Catheir said. "It is noted you admire the young princess. Is she not having her birthright stolen by those who misread the Cycus 'dustari?"

Bish looked out across the traders at their tables, exchanging wooden chits representing all the products of the dominion. "Since when has the order lowered itself to politics?" he asked.

"Since when has it not? If you kill the princess when her child is born, it will be because our order interfered in politics," Catheir said. "It will be on the orders of others and not our personal choice, but the guild is not just the silent regulator that its founders chose, but a hand that reaches out to keep balance and prevent wars."

Bish nodded. No one could reasonably follow the cant, but he still felt vulnerable speaking it in public. "I believe in our consensus. What do my coven friends say?"

"They believe that Nazira should be queen, just as you seem to have fallen into," Catheir said. "We act by consensus, as you say, and your coven is exerting a power influence on the Conspiracy, which is noted by the whole guild. My warning, though, is that we may not arrive at any consensus before the acts of others define the reality." She pulled a leather sheaf with a set of papers in it from her dress. "Naseer al-Dinni cannot be removed from the board. There is no consensus. But he can be sent away, where his fate can be his own. Is that not a good solution for you and for the rest of the Guild?"

"Killing someone is always the last choice," Bish quoted the guild mantra. He accepted the paper sheaf and leafed through the contents. "Passage on a frigate as a guest of the rulers of Dartia."

"The best that can be done, Regnal. He is in the forum now, and you are a known partisan of the Princess. He has demanded through many channels to meet her, and meeting with you will suffice we think. Save his life, get him on this ship." Catheir turned to leave, but Bish stopped her.

"What of the poisoning?" Bish asked.

Catheir turned back to him and touched his cheek. "Brother Regnal, tell Wevern and Luthers that they should not break too many dishes chasing the rats, but that the consensus is firm despite the short time between the crime and now. Your coven can prosecute this crime with forceful vigor. Any hand, to the third hand, may feel the wrath of the Guild and you will be supported."

Bish grasped Catheir's hand and lowered it from his cheek. "Tell our master I am not lost in this. I will do my duty, but I believe we have found a gem in the rocks of the creek."

Catheir nodded. "I will tell her this. Now go save that man's life."

Bish walked slowly through the market forum until he saw Naseer al-Dinni sitting at tea, alone at one of the lesser tables. He changed his direction and walked directly to the pirate, placed a penny on the table, and then sat across from him.

"Regnal Bish al-Beijus," The pirate greeted him. "You have come up in the world."

Bish smiled. "Not so much Naseer al-Dinni."

"Captain al-Dinni," the pirate said.

"You have a new ship?" Bish asked.

Al-Dinni grabbed his goblet of tea and drained it. They held it in the air. "I am the Captain of the *Remarker*."

A tea monger came by and asked, "What can I serve you?"

"My dear tea monger," the pirate asked, "there are so many of you, yet you never fight over tables. Why is that?"

The man said, "Who wants to know?"

Naseer al-Dinni pushed a five-gram silver cartwheel onto the table. "Indulge me."

The tea monger swept the silver cartwheel from the table. "We stand in rank, and the next table to signal for tea is assigned to the next one of us. Then we serve our customer from one of the brew steads of the forum. Anyone who breaks this is in trouble."

"Anyone who breaks this is in trouble! How wonderful! Here is another coin-of-silver, bring us a pot of Mlick tea. And a cup for my crazy-eyed friend." The pirate turned to Bish and said, "They take their turn or there is trouble. Is this not a fine system?"

"For sheep and mongers," Bish said.

Naseer al-Dinni slapped his mug on the table. "Not just for sheep and mongers. Nazira was mine."

"Who says this?" Bish asked.

"I do. I was the one who won her," Naseer said.

Bish nodded. "I do not understand, but nonetheless, she is married and with a child. By the way, she has taken the veil as well. If you had claim, which I doubt, the claim is gone. I am here to stop you from your path of self-destruction and offer you a way out."

"She has taken the veil? What does that mean for me?" the pirate said.

Bish smoothed a wrinkle from his particolor swallowtail jacket. "If you do not believe that the veil matters, then by all means, try something. You will find the veil deadly if you try."

Naseer sneered at Bish. "Then give me my due if you do not want me to exact terrible revenge. You will return my ship to me! You will allow me to torture Javier al-Rasheed to death and burn his body for my amusement! You will give me back the hand of the woman I love! What other way out do you have if I decide to wreck this house of paper you have made? I want what is owed to me!"

Bish looked at the pirate for a long while, while he held his tense pose. When Naseer did not back down, Bish put his hands on the table. "I thought pirates elected their crews?"

Naseer replied, "They do." The pot of tea came, and the monger poured out two cups. Naseer grabbed one, swallowed it down in one draught, and motioned for another.

Bish ignored the challenge and also ignored the tea. Voices of the dead yelled in his head, so he could not, in fairness, quench himself with the tea until they quieted down. He pushed the cup away and said, "Captain, let me explain to you something. I know you spoke with General al-Dinni, your kith-mate. I do not care. I know you have had at Bostwick with coins. I do not care. Last night, though, more than a dozen souls died screaming, poisoned by someone, perhaps you."

"I did not poison anyone," he said. "How could I poison anyone?"

Bish looked over the crowd. "It could be said you have made many such arrangements, could it not? Do you believe when facing the stake that Bostwick will keep your confidence? Perhaps I will interview him and see what he has to say about poison and secret instruction for you."

"What have I done to warrant the stake, damn you," Naseer said, pounding the table.

"Be calm," Bish said. "The forum may have ears, even here at these tables."

"Then what do you offer? Tell me now so I can counter," he asked, quieter.

"This is not a negotiation, Captain al-Dinni." Bish took the leather document folder out and said, "Passage to Dartia and a sack of silver if you take any ship from there with the intention to warp to the Core."

Naseer sneered. "I really do love her, you know. Damn al-Rasheed and Devious to the fires."

"There are no guarantees, but al-Rasheed, Devious, and the *Remarker* were last seen entering a great storm, and they did not find port where expected. They are likely dead, at least that is what I am assuming," Bish said. "Your new ship awaits a passenger though, and you are alive, as long as I see your back right now."

Naseer got up and started to leave, but turned and said, "Do not count al-Rasheed out, nor count him trustworthy. My warning for you, Regnal Bish al-Beijus."

Bish nodded and watched Naseer al-Dinni get up and leave the forum. A small waif-child came to his table and asked, "Follow him?"

Bish looked at her. "Report to the mistress when the Dartian Frigate and that man both depart the port." He then hesitated and asked, "It is getting colder. Do you have a situation?"

She nodded. "The mistress found some of us places in a chantry." Then she looked to the sky. "Some will fall back to the docks."

Bish touched her hair. "Off," he said to her, and she left into the crowd, an invisible person. *Poor thing*, he thought, then stood from his table.

There was added tension in the forum, tension Bish normally would have delved into, but with Wevern and Luthers on a terrible task, he was forced to leave it to Catheir and her coven. He did put in a few appearances where he was expected to be seen, a party to celebrate the end of a loan, two coming-of-age gatherings, and torch passage, but he was not expected to linger at any event. Merely note who was there and the mood of the attendants. It gave him an hour to consider his troubled mind and the terrors of the night before, cleaning his senses for logical thought, as he had been taught.

The order he belonged to funded itself by loans. In the guild history, there was some point when ascetic monks in a secret society lent the first silvers to a small shopkeeper and, in turn, took some of their profits. Now, the little loans were part of who they were, long past when the deity they used to worship had been subsumed and lost in time.

Yet, unlike the corruption of the gangs and their usurious form of lending, the guild celebrated a farmer or shopkeeper whose loan was ended. We never forgot a loan, but once paid, there were no surprises.

Chapter X

Procession

The day the procession was set to leave was blusterous, with great sheets of rain coming down. The column was forming up in the parade grounds: 60 mounted fusiliers, 20 close bodyguards, cooks, camp assistants, drovers, musicians, her scribes and runners, bannerets, dressers, and for all Nazira knew, jugglers and jade smiths. She looked over at Gullen, who nodded and came close to talk under the cover of the downpour.

"We could ride to the first town with ten of us faster than this menagerie will move in the rain," Gullen said.

Nazira laughed. "It is a procession. That means the Dominar shows off his continuity with the future, pregnant old me. And he has to pretend that I am a big deal."

Gullen looked at Ribea, who was soaked to the bone and running from person to person with a large book. "I looked into the mistress of ceremony."

Nazira looked straight ahead. "Did you listen to the water pipe symphony?"

"I listened under doors and into the mouse-holes of the castle," she replied.

"And?" Nazira asked.

"She is under a lot of pressure. Melinda has her reporting on you, as does Taffez and Domingus. So the question is not if she is spying on you, but who is she not spying on you for." Gullen leaned close to Nazira. "She can drown in all this mud."

Nazira looked at Gullen closely. "She won't though, at least until I have considered the matter."

"Of course not, Princess," Gullen replied.

"What about the retinue?" Nazira asked.

Gullen closed her eyes like she was reading a book from the back of her eyelids. "The bodyguards are loyal to you. There is no chance they are feeding information to anyone or are a danger to you. The soldiers are not exactly loyal, but they were picked randomly. I doubt anyone's hand has been in and about them. Everyone else?" She opened her eyes.

Nazira finished her sentence. "They are all likely bent in some way."

Gullen nodded. Then she looked purposely at Regnal Bish.

The knight was dressed in an oil cloth but still had not affected one of the preferred weapons of the knighthood. He had a walking stick, but no firelock or any other warlike material on his body. Nazira said, "He is his own problem. I cannot figure out if he works for my father or for the bank."

"I do not see why you would stay your hand. He has admitted he is against you," Gullen replied.

"Not really. He has hinted at what he is, and if his hints are true, eliminating him could bring down disaster." She paused. "I am not my father. I cannot kill my way out of my problems, nor enlist a foreign power to prop my regime, such as my grandfather. I need allies, not enemies."

Gullen nodded and went to prepare the wagon for the princess.

The procession was like a slow-moving inchworm stretching out two kilometers. At first, it stopped and started a dozen times before even getting out of Cycus City and the port complex, but by the first day, it had, like some sort of semi-intelligent sea creature washed up on land, figured out how to flop and gyrate in a matter that generated a forward motion back to the sea. It was not pretty, but the column seemed to gain some form of intelligence as it sorted itself out, and the rear elements stopped falling back into the distance, while the forward portion of the worm became mindful of how far it led the main body of the procession.

Gullen walked next to Vries as the procession moved slowly down the road. Nazira looked at the two, so different, yet each very loyal in their own way. Bish did not seem to like either of Nazira's chosen guards but did not try to send them away.

Vries was towering, nearly two meters, and, since Nazira had brought him on, had affected a khanda of immense proportions. He wore banded armor of metal plates and leather bracings with mail coifing, while his cover was a conical war helm sat on the white linen wrappings of a tuft. Every eye was always on Vries, his mass and arms creating a preternatural dread, even in the hearts and eyes of warriors and knights.

Gullen was, by comparison, almost invisible. She was dressed in handmade shift of black sisal, a wool coverlet, and a satin veil through which only her dark eyes peered. Of the two though, she was by far the most dangerous.

The master of the procession was Ribea al' Jin, scholar of the Great Tower. She was in her forties, dressed in the black gowns of a scholar before the coming of Dominion, dowdy, covered in chalk dust, and topped with a great five-sided hat. Her knowledge of subjects was endless, and all that knowledge had no lock on the gate that ran to her mouth. She seemed born to lecture. And this was her first chance to show her talent to someone who seemed to care.

In fact, Nazira found the history of the lands fascinating. While others in her entourage would drift away from the "royal carriage" when Ribea al' Jin became engrossed in a story of the past, Bish notably saying, "Why should I listen to what I lived through?" Nazira had a sense as she listened that the young scholar was painting a picture that might not look nice when hung on the wall—the memory of the Dominion. Oban himself seemed to confirm this when he said, "The Violence of History." As far as Nazira knew, Oban was insular and completely unread on any subject except tea and how to get bedbugs out of mattresses. Yet that one statement made her wonder what went on underneath her caretaker's aggressively bald head.

"The procession is one of the few old government practices that remain intact after the fall of the Republic to the Dominion under your grandfather. The Republic had a practice known as 'noble procession,' where a newly elected 'First Citizen' would hold 40 grand meetings, introducing the people to their newly formed cabinet, and being hosted by a representative from the region. The first Dominar dropped this process, but instead replaced it with a tour of the heir. Your mother was the first to make the new procession, when she was gravid with you. And now you are to make the tour in your own stead." Ribea pointed to a nestled community on the coast they were riding to. "That is Reskin-Gild, the port where our fishing fleets hail from and your first stop."

"Why maintain the tradition?" Nazira asked.

"Now that is a question that can be answered, but which no one would answer. No one sane," Ribea said.

"Gullen!" Nazira yelled.

Gullen turned and walked back to where the cart and team were resting in preparation for entering the city. She bowed her head silently to the pair.

Nazira looked at Ribea, locking her gaze into a vise. "Ribea, I respect you and want to hear great things and wondrous doings from you. In fact, I need you to do more than be a simple-molly taking me on a walk through the butter house. I need you to guide me to truth."

Oban looked worried at his mistress, and then saw that Gullen had removed a small blade from her shift. He suddenly stood up in the cart and left in scared haste. Nazira smiled and said, "Forgive Oban. He is less knowledgeable of the nature of negotiations in the world that is life and death. I forgive him though. I am giving you a chance, a choice. In ten months, my father will take my child and kill me. See that man over there, Regnal Bish? An hour past when my child is taken, I will be dead at his hands, by the order of the Dominor, our lord."

"My lady princess..." Ribea said.

"Be quiet, my dear, this will happen quickly. If I believe you will be a loyal servant who tells me the absolute truth about what you claim to know, the history of the lands of Cycus and the Cyclonidees, then you will be a member of my retinue and will never have to fear what you say or write. If I do not believe you, in fact if it seems to me like there is a motive other than truth behind what you counsel me on, then I will have no reason not to have Gullen make a tiny cut on your neck, ever so small, and then I will watch you bleed out here on this hill."

"My princess. The lords of the Cycus, the Dominar…" she said, starting to cry.

Nazira stepped out of the cart. "I know. This is not fair. I know you have a child and a husband in Cycus city. I know you have been told what to say and what to do on this procession. In fact, I know that Petrovson and al-Cinci, the dungeon masters, dragged you down into the dungeons and told you that a horrible, long death awaited you if you did not do as you were told. You were to fill my head with nonsense and watch me the way only another woman could, to assure I did not get ideas or wander away. Does this make sense?"

Ribea fell to her knees. "Please, Princess, you are said to be kind. Please do not do this."

Nazira dragged the sobbing woman from the cart. Guards, drovers, cooks, householders, all the people in the column of the procession did not seem to notice, all looked out at the town and the ocean as if the tableaux was not happening. She grabbed the woman's head and turned it to look at the ocean. "I am kind. They would kill you in a cave after great and painful torture. I will kill you with a single prick of the skin, letting you gaze off on the beauty of the sun. They would take your kids and slaughter your husband as they watched. I will report to your husband and children that you died bravely serving the crown."

Gullen moved closer, the knife held loosely in her hand. A few of the retinue started to turn and look with worried expressions. Nazira felt this was power, the understanding that here she terrorized one person to make the others both fear and accept her. She was not the kith of the Dominar who married a playboy and bred without permission. She was, in fact, a wild card whose behavior was iron underneath a lace of silk. As the knife moved closer, she whispered into the terrified woman's ear. "If you follow me, it is for life, and that means my life stands before you, just as your life stands before me. If you refuse and I do not kill you, you will die in that dungeon because they won't trust you. But if you join me publicly, then I will give you what you want, your heart's desire."

The knife pressed against the woman's neck and she said, "Save my husband and children. Please save them."

Nazira nodded and Gullen removed the knife, hiding it and in the same motion removing a bag filled with the clink of silver coins. With a furtive move of her hand, the coins were tucked into Ribia's bodice. "Four-hundred tolars of silver. Not for you, but to see your husband and children from the capital and into hiding. Vries will take the money from you, and he will ride back to the capital and arrange for their safe hiding among the street gangs. Do you believe me?"

She nodded.

Vries turned from his looking at the ocean and caught Nazira's eye. Nazira nodded, and Vries looked at the sobbing woman and nodded to her. She smiled wanly and felt the coins concealed in her bodice. "Now for an assignment. I need a scholar to do something for me, as it happens. I want you to have Vries return with books from the library on my mother and her marriage. Who did she know, who were her servants and partisans, and I want you to write me a story of the time before I was born. Does this make sense, scholar Ribea?"

The scared woman nodded. "As you, my princess, commands."

Nazira stood her up and said, "Come to my table tonight, Ribea, when we sup with the mayor of Reskin-Gild." She turned and called out, "Oban, I will walk for a while. Can you sit with scholar Ribea and keep her company as we enter the city?"

Oban nodded. He walked over with his funny waddle like gait and helped the sobbing scholar into the wagon. Nazira took a walking staff and set out ahead, telling the trailblazer, "Let us leave this place behind. Dinner in the city will be welcome after the day's travel."

The trailblazer nodded and blew his sounding horn, allowing Nazira to take the lead before calling the rest of the retinue into order. Bish fell in beside Nazira. They walked in silence for a while, then Bish said, "Very pretty theater, but what do you expect a scholar to do?"

"My dear Regnal Bish, what could you mean?" Nazira replied.

"Even I can say there are more spies in this retinue, and more dangerous ones, than the poor Ribea. Even if you make her your creature, what then?" he said.

"Do you really want to know Bish?" Nazira asked.

Bish laughed, his crazy eyes looking at everything and nothing. "Is there harm in me knowing?"

Nazira smiled. "Of course not. How did I know Ribea had visited the dungeons and was made a creature to watch me?"

Bish shrugged, "My Princess, I confess to not have access to your intelligence network. My job, though, is to keep you alive."

"Until it is not, I understand, my murderer. The honest answer is I did not know she was a spy. I grabbed her at random as someone who would fold under threat no matter who she was. I was just lucky she turned out to be a spy. Now Vries will save her family, and those who see her will see either a saved spy who owes me everything and how well I treat her, or they will see me slaughter her with no mercy if she betrays me." She looked down to navigate a difficult part of the road. Looking up, she used her walking stick to motion back at the retinue. "They will make more mistakes now, be more likely to come to me for protection, and they will think I have them under observation. I will play each of the spies and offer them their dignity, or death."

"You cannot play me, Princess," Bish advised.

"You are not a spy, my dear Regnal. I intend to capture your heart and make you my loyal servant before the procession is done. Or else," Nazira said.

"Or else what?" Bish asked.

"You will kill me. Is that not your job?" Nazira replied.

Bish turned and kept walking, apparently considering the issue deeply. "What brought you out into the open?"

Nazira replied, "I saw a dead man."

Bish was looking at the sky, or so it seemed. You never knew with him. "Tell me of this dead man."

"The other night when we recruited Vries and his gang, there was a man in a cowl watching us," Nazira said.

"I had not noticed," Bish replied. "You have seen this man before?" he asked.

"You have as well," Nazira started. "On the name day they executed the criminals, the execution I watched from the back portico. The dancing master named Darkfather. I saw him in a crowd. He was staring at me."

Bish put his right hand to his chin. "There was a dancing master some years back. An old one. I do not recall his fate."

Nazira laughed. "Ten years has dulled your memory, my dear Bish. I cannot say I was much aware of you back in my childhood, but I remember you knowing the man, and knowing he was killed by the dungeon master Petrov. He told me he served my mother and that she was in a shipwreck."

Bish halted, but did not look at her. Behind them, they could hear the drovers and soldiers calling a halt to the entire procession. "What did he tell you of this shipwreck?"

Oban hurried forward from the sedan carts. "My princess, why do you halt?"

Regnal Bish turned to her servant and said, "Oban, have you told our princess stories of your homeland? Is this entire mess caused by your loose lips?"

"Master Bish, no, I swear. There is little for me to say, none of my own secrets, certainly," he said.

"What is this?" Nazira asked, but Bish waved his hands in her face.

"Are you not loyal to your princess?" Bish asked Oban, looking in the direction of the town below.

"I am loyal," Oban said. "The answers to those questions are not mine though. When my princess asked what island concealed her mother, then the answer was hers and I spoke it. She has never asked about the island or the shipwreck."

"Tell me what is hidden from me, Bish," Nazira demanded.

"My dear princess. There are things at play that must be explored, but I promise you that when the exploration is ended and the secrets revealed, I will make sure you get told all there is to know. As a favor to me, do not torture poor Oban. He is a locked door that may hold information for you, but which you may have to break down to get what you want to know. Let me look into this Darkfather character you claim to have seen, and leave Oban his secrets," Bish said. Then he hesitated and said, "And do not remove the veil. You may not think so, but it has protection for you."

Nazira nodded, but talked around that comment. "Can you find him, meaning the Darkfather?"

Bish replied, "No one hides from me for long. Not if they are stalking you. And keep the veil, consider it armor."

She stared at him angrily, then turned and ended the conversation.

The procession wound down onto the verge of Marsh, and across the Faithful Causeway to the Isthmus Mordigen, where the city of Stanis Review stood. The gates of the city were thrown open, and in front, lining the path forward, where a few commoners and a small retinue of mounted knights and nobles. At their head was a man Nazira recognized from court, Major Tedjen al-Myrra d' Stanis, the current eminence gris of the third most powerful family on Cycus. His colors were drab and gold, so all of his retinue looked to Nazira like caramels. A second was an old woman, Dame Griselda al-Youseffi d' Tariq, looking like she had a lemon under her saddle.

Nazira, still on foot, held up her hand in a fist to designate "stop," and picked up Vries, Gullen, Bish, and the Scholar Ribea to follow along. They walked the last hundred meters, and when they were close, a horn sang out and the crowd took a knee, all but Tedjen and Griselda.

"Princess," Tedjen said with an effusive wave.

"You once told me that Stanis Review was a great city, and I see now you were right. Will you tour the city with me?" Nazira asked.

Tedjen bowed and pointed to a set of white-washed carts drawn by large, strong looking dromeds. "Your battalion has taken up positions along the route. I may say we will be safe."

Nazira laughed. "Is there any reason to be concerned?"

"The citizens are like citizens anywhere, not aware of their luck in regard to their masters. Tedjen was a popinjay. I have a cart for your plebes," he said.

"Tedjen, child, enough flirting with this child. We have duties to the procession. They must see this girl, your people.

They need not hear her speak. She is a doll being placed on display," Griselda said.

"Oh, Griselda, you are too serious here. Nazira and I will get along famously," Tedjen said with an effusive chuckle. "Besides, she is in the veil. Woe to the man or woman who breaks the boundary of the veil of a princess. Is that not what it says?"

"Take heed, Tedjen," Griselda growled.

Nazira interrupted her grandmother, "So long as the cart has room for my advisors, I am fine with your arrangements, Major Tedjen."

Tedjen looked cross for a second, staring at Griselda, then cleared his face like a char wiping scum from a wall. "Oh my, the cart I had planned for us was two and two footmen. So much better than the bigger carts. Of course, your dear forbear, the incomparable Griselda, will have a cart all her own for her contemplation. But you and I can get to know each other alone while the crowds goggle."

Nazira laughed again, though this time it was fake, and she felt obviously so. "Now Tedjen, you know I am married!" The veil she left unsaid.

The noble-major shrugged. "To a man who never returns again, you are married, but leave it to me to chaperone you from the slick characters in this city who might see a slight bit of sheer cloth no hindrance to ill machinations. However, there is a cart for six we can use. It is in the van, though."

Nazira stepped off and headed for that cart. "I am sure the drovers can arrange our little convoy in an appropriate manner." She turned and saw that Griselda was burning like a torch. "Perhaps my jidat-bialtabaniy would like the two-seater. It does seem a nice cart for my beloved 'grand-mere.'"

Griselda pointed her walking stock at Tedjen. "Major Tedjen, my trusty Phelm, pike sergeant, and Mister Bish in the main cart with you and the princess." She turned and pointed the stick at Nazira. "Do not presume, Princess, you have any say in this procession or that your veil protects you from me if it comes down to that. I will have Major Tedjen strangled half out of his life, then violated in ways you can only imagine in your worst dreams if you do not behave yourself. So your behavior keeps people from hell, that and my good humor." She turned and walked to the cart.

Vries said, "Princess..." He was clearly ready to fight. He had squared up with the partisan of Griselda named by her, Phelm, a huge man with a falchion made of steel and no fear to affect a metal breastplate. Major Tedjen's own partisan named to ride in the cart was standing next to the mountainous warrior looking to their liege and then to the Princess.

Major Tedjen shrugged, smiled, then turned and followed Dame Griselda, motioning to his pike sergeant to follow. Bish stepped to Vries and said, "Perhaps you can organize the rest of the carts to make sure the Princess has protectors?"

Vries looked at the big man a second more, then turned when another hand, Gullen's, touched his shoulder. He retreated away and began to shove and push people into carts with obvious ill favor. Gullen looked at the warrior, shook her head, then turned to follow Vries, but stopped when the warrior said, "Time comes when you are mine, girl."

Bish calmly stepped up to the big warrior and slapped him. The courtier was a head shorter than the warrior and older, though in a vigorous and sun-touched way. Yet the slap was hard enough to resonate across the field by the city gates and cause silence in its wake. "Ask your patron what it means to square up with me, Mister Phelm." He looked down at the warrior moving his hand to his huge sword, then back to his eyes. "One more centimeter and I take your hand."

For a second, Nazira saw calculation in the mute guard's mind. With a hand she gave the 'chop' signal to Gullen, telling her to turn away, but did not herself give ground. Regnal Bish was not her friend. He worked for powers that she did not understand, but several times now he had taken action that a partisan would. For a courtier who worked in the shadows and did not expose themselves to others, his actions were a show that his allegiance could not yet be noted for any party, and may be subject to recalculation.

The tableaux was broken by Griselda, being helped into a cart by Major Tedjen, yelling, "Get on with this!" Phelm blinked, removed his hand from its position near his falchion, and said, "Saved by my patron, little man. Know, though, that you earned a special place when the walls break on this."

Regnal Bish bowed. "Off to your master, little man."

Phelm turned and went to the cart, followed by the pike sergeant who looked like he wanted to run away and hide under a bridge. Nazira walked to Bish. "Be careful, my killer. You seemed to be calling out the al-Youseffi."

He shook his head. "Dame Griselda al-Youseffi would have that man tortured if he threatened me or knew he was making an ass of himself. My young princess, I have said you must learn the world, and so you must. That man is a tool in a box of tools. The tool does not decide when to hammer the peg. It waits for others to wield it."

He gently took her arm and escorted her to the wagon. "What you saw was a power play," Bish said as they walked. "Major Tedjen wanted to be seen with you because he is weak and there is unrest here in Stanis Review. Griselda reminded him that the power of the crown is held by the al-Youseffi and that she will let him have some, but if he grasps, he will suffer. That was a conversation between the al-Myrra and the al-Youseffi for future relations, and you were just a puppet."

Nazira did not respond but wondered again at Regnal Bish's motives.

They approached the white-washed cart and Nazira saw that it had three passenger benches. One bench faced backward, and one faced forward. Between them was a forward-facing bench that was higher than the others and intended to allow people to see its rider. Griselda and Tedjen were facing backward, while the rear bench, facing forward, had been chosen by the pike sergeant and Griselda's partisan Phelm. Bish helped her onto the highest bench, then took a seat to the right of Tedjen, who turned and touched the shoulder of the drover.

The caravan had three small, three-person carts, one of which held Gullen, Vries, and a drover, and the other held Scholar Ribea, Oban, and another drover. Then there were four six-passenger wagons that carried three soldiers and three courtiers each. Three companies of soldiers, one from the Last Guards, one from the Life Guards, and one from the local regiment Tedjen nominally led, spread out on the sides. A soft drumbeat commenced, and the official presentation convoy siphoned through the gates of the city and into the crowded city.

"Tradition says we make small talk when in presentation to the people," Tedjen said, making himself heard over the rising din of the crowds.

Nazira nodded, looking at the people who were straining a line of uniformed men and women, trying to see the cart and its people. "Then you may select a topic, Major."

"Your former husband then," Major Tedjen said. Griselda laughed at the proposed topic.

Bish replied, "Major Tedjen, no one knows the fate of the stalwart Captain al-Rasheed."

Tedjen said, "My intelligence said he rushed off with no crew in a captured pirate and blundered into the mouth of a storm which sank three other ships. I was to understand he was more courtier than sailor."

Nazira looked at the Major and scion of the al-Myrra with acid in her eye, but she answered in a vigorous tone. "He was a veteran sailor when I met him, from the last great expedition. He held a cadet and then an ensign position under Admiral Ramon d' Galli, was a sailing master, and was awarded the *Orbit of the Moon*."

Tedjen said, "I wonder if the *Orbit of the Moon* allows one to float when the currents of Ocean drag them to the far side of the world?"

Nazira frowned and looked out at the crowd. They were pointing at her and yelling something she could not hear. A sea of faces. Indeed, she had thrown her lover and the father of her child into the winds of the Halo to seek wealth and fame enough to save them both, knowing what Tedjen perhaps did not, that there was a piece of her love that was broken. Did he break in that great storm and die yelling incoherent orders at the winds? Was the great pirate ship *Remarker* smashed to float-wood by the great waves and winds of the storm that killed so many others that it was called the century storm? She was about to cry when she realized that was the goal of Tedjen. The venal man was performing for Dame Griselda. Nazira looked at the acidic old woman and saw her crooked smile and piercing eyes. Something in her burst, and she stood up and leaped from the wagon, Tedjen's and Bish's hands grasping for her but failing to hold her in place. She turned for a second as the cart moved on, unaware of her abandonment, and yelled, "Let us test this veil for its durability in a sea of hands!"

Turning back, she stormed to the line of guards and the people who reached their hands out. She had seen parades and knew that the Dominars and the earlier Guisarmes ruled from afar. The people followed the theater of the ruling families like a stage show that had to be watched from sea glasses, reading lips because the actors were too far away to hear. It was how things were done.

When the pirate captain Naseer al-Dinni was courting her, he would call her his "zakhrafa." It was a term for a magical or powerful ornament. Treasure to be hunted and hoarded. The common people would use the term for a foolish thing to seek, but pirates took it to mean a literal object of magical power. If her veil could protect her from death, and if she was indeed a magical ornament of power, then she could walk into the crowd safely. Or it would all be proven wrong in a second and all these guards and the use of her as a shuttle stone in a game of makuk maknasa was simply a way to hide how deadly this veil was, and how she had sent her lovers, former and new, to their deaths in her own vanity.

Nazira walked to the crowd and imagined it was a typhoon, and each hand was a tendril of wind ready to smash her dead upon the rocks of a distant land. Let them grasp her deadly veil and destroy her now if that was what they intended.

The hands, though, were not, it turned out, grasping claws, but were reaching to her in greeting. She recoiled for a second, then chose to stay away from the crowd by a meter, but let them touch her hand and she walked down the road. She had touched only a few hands when she felt a powerful body behind her, quietly looking at each person she contacted. She did not have to look to see it was Vries, and he had some of his bullyrocks by him but was not interfering with her contacts with the crowd.

Then Regnal Bish joined her side with Gullen and Oban. She caught their faces from the corner of her eye and saw they were neither fearful nor angry, just concentrating on the people in the crowd. And she noticed Ribea, who had been fearfully staring at her after Nazira threatened her life, was now in some sort of transposed awe, adding her own person to the retinue that protected her but did not stop her.

The guards on the way kept the crowd back, but could not stop the hands from reaching, nor could they stop Nazira from meeting that reach. Nazira saw two Dartian women screaming as if translated to hysteria by some mental disease, and one held forth a small child with a huge spray of black hair. Nazira stared for a second, then grabbed the child, who was himself smiling and having fun with the noise. She leaned to the two women and said in question, "Your child's name?"

"Malthus," they both yelled.

Nazira kissed the child and held him up to the crowd as a talisman. She looked at Ribea and said, "Take these women's names. Malthus gets gifted an apprenticeship, if he wants one, when he is ten and six." Ribea nodded, then stepped to the women and pulled a book of blank scap from her tunic. Nazira hugged the child again and returned him to the screaming parents.

She moved down the row of people and took a second to look at the cart where Tedjen and Griselda sat. Tedjen looked struck with real fear. Fear for himself or for her, she could not tell, but the fear was real, like a spear to the stomach. Griselda was different. There was no fear, only anger, a simmering rage that was greater than the normal disgust she held on her face when she looked at Nazira.

Nazira turned back to the crowd. One of the men in the press yelled, "Where is your husband? Who is the father of the child?"

She was about to answer when Vries did it for her with a blasting voice. "She is married to the great tea trader Javier al-Rasheed. Your neighbors down the coast, the Rasheedi, are the kith of the Princess Consort!"

The screams redoubled. Nazira shook more hands but was shocked at Vries and herself. She had never really considered Javier's family. He was an orphan, raised in an orphanage. That his name meant a family, and that this family could be someplace and acknowledge Javier as their own had never entered her mind. More so, that boastful and vain Vries, a man who lorded over the docks as a muscle for hire, pretending to be an assassin, could know that the Rasheedi lived near Stanis Review. There were new things to learn even about the people around her, and she knew underestimating them was an error she would not repeat.

After a few hundred meters, she grew tired. Grabbing her belly, she waved and let Regnal Bish escort her back to the carriages that had been slowly keeping pace with her. She climbed back into the carriage with Bish's help, then returned to her seat.

Major Tedjen said, "That was extremely dangerous, my princess."

"And will not be repeated," Griselda added, but her comment was muffled by Regnal Bish taking his seat.

"It will be repeated each time we take parade in this procession," Nazira said.

Griselda was about to protest when Regnal Bish interceded. "Dame Griselda, there is no way to prevent the princess from greeting the crowds."

Griselda snapped back, "Her mother did not."

"You will notice that your grand-mere is not Irula d' Canus Cragia, and that Irula did not last long as Dominar Consort," Bish replied.

Griselda seemed like she wanted to respond but choked it back and looked at the crowd. "I knew a hunter who liked to play with his game before he slaughtered it. What do you suppose causes this tendency?"

Bish ignored her, but Tedjen said, "I am happy I shall not be responsible for your safety when the procession moves on to Tariq. I am intrigued, though, that I will be present to see you perform during the rest of the procession."

Griselda looked at her seat companion with shock. Bish though cut her off and said, "I did not know you were going to follow the procession past your own environs."

Tedjen shrugged. "I was mistaken in my choice, and I now amend it. I have relatives in Tariq, which I understand is the next stop." He paused a second, then asked, "Where do you go after that?"

Regnal Bish rolled his eyes. His mis-aimed vision always left Nazira uneasy, because it was impossible to see where he was looking. However, sometimes, such as now, he could tell he was using this fact to look at one person while answering another. It was Griselda who drew his attention, but Tedjen answered. "We are not stopping in Tariq but in the adjacent town of Crosswell. Tariq, though, will probably outnumber the al-Setti. Then to Yavne, across to West Harbor, down to Litcheon, and finally to Remida. There are some other stops, but they are transitional."

Tedjen smiled. "This will be exciting then. I hope to see what other events you plan, Master Bish."

Chapter XI

In Your Head

There was a minute in her life when the direction changed and it all fell apart. Ribea al' Jin had left the keena farm for school. The expenses for her education had been paid for by her uncle and brother and had settled down with the intention of paying them back, knowing the cost had sent them back into debt. Knowing what she owed, Ribea had studied hard, collated and presented papers, gave lectures, and soon was teaching. She had chosen to have a daughter with a man who worked in engineering in Cycus Port. She was now of age and studying at Musca Sharjari, bills which Ribea and the engineer were sharing, though they were cross kith and neither had the stomach to join with the other's family.

It seemed like the world had handed her everything when she was sent to the Tower of Scholars in the capital and handed the role of Master of Procession. It was the chance to break out of the pack—do something memorable that would set her reputation for life. She had prayed for such an assignment, and here it was, the project of a lifetime.

But that turned out to be a hubris that tore at her soul. No one cared about history, no one cared about the beautiful extent of knowledge which one could discover and detail. They cared about intelligence designed to pull down another person, and Ribea was nothing but another cog in a broken machine, grinding keena to flour noisily as it self-destructed around her. She was to write reports on a pregnant girl, no older than her daughter, and betray her smallest secrets to a handler who wished her harm.

They had not asked. A woman with a torque that announced herself as a partisan of the al-Youseffi had her grabbed from the hallway of the tower, dragged into a side room, and set upon Ribea three vile creatures with stinking breaths and apostolical suits of chained mail, armed with sharp, curved daggers. She was not to be a scholar, but a spy. The princess Nazira was her subject. Report in writing or die slaughtered like a sheep taken for meat.

She had done as ordered, her pen held in a shivering hand, knowing that this betrayal was to save her life, but not seeing it as anything honorable or scholarly. She was a cheap betrayer, and not really the mistress of a great procession.

Then Princess Nazira had discovered her betrayal, and again a large man with a knife had held her while she was threatened with terrible death. Death if she betrayed the princess, and death if she did not.

Who should she follow? What should she do?

The procession had stopped in Crosswell because the great Hôtel d' Tariq was here rather than in the home city of the Youseffi, Tariq-Makajudran. Ribea knew this was some subtle play of local politics being carried out by

Dame Griselda and noted that in her diary. The city of Tariq-Makajudran was the second city of Cycus.

She sat down with her book, the one she was writing for Nazira and her unborn child that would tell her of the people who she would soon rule. Each town they passed through was more than yelling crowds and simpering officials. It had a past, people who achieved amazing things. Rumors and stories of the amazing and miraculous. Unique details of how they prepared food, the gatherings and the remembrances they participated in, the unique arts they produced, and the special little ways they talked when they stood together on the street. Ribea was simply not very creative, but when she wrote the truth, it was like the gods we pushing the words out of her stylus. Piles of scap notes led to twenty pages of neat print, and each page seemed like it belonged where it was, a story of humanity. Her lack of creativity left her only bothered by the titles. *Processions* was the name that immediately came to mind, but it lacked flavor. She would come up with another. It compared and contrasted the nine towns visited by Irula d' Canus Cragia with the child Nazira during her procession with those same towns more than a decade later when Nazira herself was taking her unborn child to be seen by the people of this complex and wonderful land. A decade or more had seen changes, many not pleasing to the eye, but the book would be the truth. It was her life's work, after all. The capstone of her studies. One part written when she was fresh from her studies, before her daughter was born, written at arm's length as a minor functionary in the court of Nawaz. The second part, when she was inside the inner circle and could see and hear who said what, and how it was said. No one may read it and care, but it would be published for the benefit of later people who wanted to know how the people of Cycus were ruled.

Ribea held up the book to the light. She was preparing the perfect copy for reproduction and by perfect, it had to be exactly how it would look as copyists would forever reproduce even obvious mistakes. She knew scholars who were not so precise because, obviously, redactions and commentaries could be added, and if your book was popular and there were hundreds of copies made, they would likely all reside in libraries whose book lists were known. A scribe could show up, redact the imperfect book, note the redaction on a cover page, and no one would care.

Ribea cared. 541 pages. 122,379 words. 91 drawings. 206 figures. 16 maps. It was her dissertation, and she had produced it in less than ninety days. In a thousand years, no one would remember Ribea. Her bones would be dust, and that dust would have long been blown by the winds of time into disassociated nothingness. But this book could, if she was lucky, still be read long after she was gone.

The room that she let was not that comfortable. A stone pottle gave off heat in the corner. Most large buildings in Cycus used radiant air to heat themselves from a central heating room, but this town used saltwater run through concrete and stonework piping. The pottles had fascinating stopworks to hold hot water as it radiated out its heat, then released it and let more water flow through it. The room, though, could become humid, and Ribea had hung blankets around to protect her books. She had written about the difference between towns that used hearths, air columns, pottles, or other more arcane ways to heat or cool themselves, and she had almost used her research into this to form a new chapter of *Processions.* In the end, though, she had chosen against this. It was itself a book, and one she loved, but not one that should be hidden amongst the larger subject of the procession of Nazira, daughter of Abelard.

She looked at the glass and realized it was nearly eleven and well past darkness. It was close enough that she could turn the gage, which she did, putting the tag in to show when she had done it. The clock was manual and very old-fashioned. Her own home office in the Tower had a newer clock wheel, but she had used worse in school.

Now was the time when she had to face the demons and address the shadows in her mind. Only, these shadows manifested themselves as horrors in human form. She took her book, placed it in the cork carrier she had made for it, then wrapped the cork in canvas, and inserted it into a wooden book carrier. Then she took from hiding the scandalous tin and percha box she had found, waterproof and even fireproof, and slipped the wrapped tome into that container. The book would survive, even if she did not.

She next gathered the folders of her notes. There were twenty books in those, and someday she would revisit them. But now, she prepared them to be sent tomorrow to her daughter. For the rest of the procession, she would be working from more limited notes, filling in extant details from contemporary notes. She had purchased a dozen scap notebooks, and they would do. The goal would be to take the procession book, which did not include current events, only the details of the towns and the people they would meet, and add a book where the occurrences and speeches of the people could be memorialized.

Ribea shook her head. Not the time to let her headspace wander to thoughts of future work. Now was the time when the nettles were plucked, and they could burn her. Perhaps fatally.

From her clothes trunk, she laid out her scholar's robes and the finery of procession, and took out simple sackcloth and trousers that would make her look like nothing more than a char. Ribea had used the trick in school as no one notices chars, for the most part. They come and go, cleaning and sweeping. They run the walls with caustics, scrub the floors with Primitive Stone, and wash the linens, but rarely are seen are commented on. She had obtained a bucket, put some boxes of Primitive Stone into it, and left her room.

She walked down the hallway, and as if to prove her point passed right by Vries, his immense sword rested on his shoulder, without comment. She was just a char. No one cared. The hôtel in Crosswell was an immense structure of masonry. Only the Dominar's castle in Cycus port was larger. Ribea had thus had to explore earlier to find the exit the chars took, but it proved similar to what existed elsewhere. The chars would pass through the kitchens to a tradesmen's gate, only having to undergo a short inspection by the butler's staff, and no inspection as they left unless there were concerns of pilferage.

And indeed, it was easy to get out. The kitchens had their own stairs down from the residential spaces and were alive all day and night, but the bustle was not one that was targeted at guarding the house. Each person in the kitchens was concerned with chopping onions, cleaning grill stones and cookers, bringing in wood to feed the cookfires, stoking the water heaters, preparing trays of food, brewing tea, or moving supplies about the pantries. This was made worse by the hundreds of guests, both in the main house and camped in the stables and rushes, that were the result of procession.

The guard at the door looked at her with a dull eye. His glaive leaned on the wall, and he was drinking an immense mug of tea. Ribea nodded to the man, and he just turned his latchkey and let her out.

The kitchen led to a back alley jammed with wagons, but even in the darkness of night, there were dozens of people to conceal herself. In the day it was bright with sunlight and crossed by boxes and crates of food and other supplies. At night it was just where the staff had their tea and entered the hôtel for work. Ribea wove her way out into the main street through the relaxing workers and joined the crowds of people still awake.

The note she had been delivered by a Life Guard was to meet in a tavern, but when she saw the one chosen, she took a pause. It was not a clean place for taking tea and meeting with the public, but one of the few places where one could get spirits. Most towns had these houses. They usually served beer and wine and served food as well. This tavern was not that sort. Above the door was the word SHARACK. It meant a place to drink distilled spirits. Ribea hugged herself and entered.

Indeed, the tavern was seedy in the extreme. There was a fighting pit where humans and animals could bloody each over for sport, a long bar with stools, and a pile of people passed out in the back of the establishment, their pockets turned out, sleeping off the effects of drink. Crosswell was that sort of town despite hosting the hôtel of the al-Youseffi. Or perhaps it was a reflection of the great family. Stanis Review, their last stop.

At the doorway, a bullyrock said, "Half penny." Ribea dug into the pocket of her char costume and took out a penny. She handed it over, and the man shrugged and gave her two wooden coins. They were marked "sharak wahid," meaning one drink. She smiled at the small bit of pride that made a grog tavern print tokens for palm wine using the old tongue rather than using more modern usage.

As she entered, she stopped short. In the back of the room was a man in dark clothes. He had the look of a Dartian, swarthy, bearded, with a scar on his face. Of all the people in the room, her attention was drawn magnetically to him. He was staring right at her, his eyes blazing like lit coals.

A hand touched her side. "Scholar," she said. It was the woman who handled her, though lacking the silver torque or fine clothes she has been wearing as she had her knifeman slide his blade on her throat. She squeezed Ribea's arm hard and guided her to the table where her huge thuggish assistant sat amongst six other angry-looking men and women in the clothing of miners. Unlike the other miners in the room, they stood out because they were unwashed. Ribea knew this was an amateur mistake. Miners always washed before they ate, it was just what they did.

The woman jammed her into a seat next to the biggest thug, who put his arms around her with cloying familiarity. She struggled, but he put his tongue in her ear, then whispered, "Scholar, do not be uppity. We are friends, no?"

The handler smiled and said, "Oh, the scholar is our friend. Now tell us what you have."

Ribea screwed up her courage. "They discovered I was your creature. I will be killed if I help you more."

"Who told you this?" the woman asked.

"Princess Nazira herself," she said.

One of the women, dressed as a mine seeker fresh from work, smelling of tailings and mine damp, said, "That Gullen item who tried to blow up Petrovson is likely the cause of this."

The handler shrugged. "It does not matter. Tell us what you have, Scholar."

Ribea shook her head. "Killed by you, killed by her. It does not matter."

"Good enough," the Handler said. "You will tell us, but you won't like it. I think Ruggers here gets his wish. You like Ruggers?"

Ruggers began to run his hands over her, and Ribea felt revulsion. At least her book was almost finished. If she had to die, dying with her work done was all she could hope. The idea of death rang around in the darkness of her mind, but she could not quite admit it was the end.

The group stood up and pulled her out of her chair, then guided her to the door in a closed pack. "The alley off the causeway, best place," the beast called Ruggers said. Her Handler nodded.

As they passed the bullyrick, Ribea said, "Help me." The man stared at her and shrugged. No help would come for her.

Once on the street, they started to sing an evil drive-shanty, pretending to be sharak-soaked and jolly, but Ribea was held hard in the grasp of the one called Ruggers. They laughed and yelled witticisms into the air. Just a group of rum-soaked men and women seeking to shake off the dangers of the mines and celebrate one more day of living. She saw their game and knew they felt themselves perfectly safe. Their patron owned this town. They were Griselda's creatures to a man and woman and could have simply announced themselves and dragged her kicking and screaming away. As it was, they were not much less subtle. She tried to get away and reach another group, a real group of miners, but she was grabbed by two of the partisans and slapped. The miners she had tried to reach looked like they would protect her, but one of the men held a wooden disk up. It was a sigil of the al-Youseffi. It said that the fake miners were death to mess with by the real miners and to back away. Back away they did.

Her captors turned into an alley by the edge of the river and Ribea knew this was the last. She had to do something or suffer horror. So she turned and smiled at Ruggers, then reached under his miner's clout and twisted his yatadala as hard as she could, squeezing it like she was taking the liquid from a lemon. He screamed and let go of her, and she ran.

There was a commotion behind her as she ran, but as she approached the mouth of the alley, the dark man from the bar turned the corner and looked at her. If he grabbed for her, he was large enough that there would be no way to get loose. Ribea ran to him anyway, and when she reached the dark man, he stepped around her, drew a curved sword, and said to her, "Keep running."

And she ran. Crowds parted for her as she cried and screamed, falling to the ground, then getting up, seeking any cover she could find. There was none. No one to help her when the partisans of the Dame Griselda killed the man with the burning eyes and burst out into the street to drag her back into the alley. She ran through, hoping to reach the great hôtel and get to Princess Nazira. Ribea knew this was all she could do, hope the princess who shook hands with the commons, who stood up to the most powerful person in the land, would save her, see her clear of the evil that had entrapped her. She saw the hôtel ahead, but before she could reach it, she was stopped by hard, powerful hands. She looked up, and it was Vries, and next to him was Regnal Bish.

"What happened," Bish said.

"I was kidnapped. It was what you wanted, for me to stop reporting..." She tried to complete her sentence and could not. "They were al-Youseffi, the ones who threatened me before. They were going to torture me for something they wanted to know."

"Vries, take your men to that alley," Bish ordered. Vries nodded, punched his sergeant in the shoulder, and ran for the alley like a pack of wild beasts. Ribea watched as more soldiers, this time in town guard uniforms, met them. Their leader yelled at Regnal Bish, "What is this commotion, foreigner?"

Bish squared up on the guardsman. "Before you say that which cannot be unsaid, ask yourself who I am and what a real commotion is."

The sergeant said, "Those men going into the alley?"

Bish responded, "Seeking to save some of Dame Griselda's partisans. I believe that this woman here, a scholar, saw them beset by a pack of armed men."

The guard sergeant looked down to the alley Bish referred to. Vries and his men were coming out, weapons drawn, looking down the street. The sergeant yelled at Vries, "You, come to me!"

Vries and one of his men came out and looked at Regnal Bish, then at the guard sergeant. He stood in contemptuous silence, his great sword over his shoulder, his other hand being used to scratch his fundaments. The guard sergeant grew heated and said, "Show respect, soldier."

Vries replied, "Tasty cakes, I am a Bashi. Got a placard somewhere in my jacket that says it, which means you stand with respect, or you stand in pain with my boot up your ass."

The sergeant reached for his club, but an officer came running up from his regiment. He was about to shout at Vries when he saw Bish standing akimbo, one hand on his talwar, the other enfolding their crying Ribea. He grabbed the sergeant by the scruff of his uniform jacket and said, "Get the Dame's Master of Armsmen in the hôtel wardroom, now."

The sergeant hesitated. "Lute, this lot is a street thing."

"Now!" the officer yelled.

The sergeant genuflected, placing his palm to his chin, then ran to the hôtel. The officer watched his sergeant run to carry out his orders, then turned back to Bish. Why is your scholar out of bounds and dressed in torn char clothes? You lot pimping her out?"

"She apparently witnessed some of your lot getting a serious talking to. The Princess's Captain of the Guards was just investigating the scene. Captain Vries, what did you discover?

Vries came to a loose position that could be called attention. "Seven dead, sword wounds. Lots of blood," he said. "Dressed like miners, soaked in palm rum. Several had al-Youseffi placards in their hands. I mean, in what I presume were their hands, as most were no longer attached to any particular body. Bit of a puzzle figuring out what head, hand, leg, or what not goes with what torso, be my guess, Master Bish."

The officer seemed to Ribea to almost panic. He said to Bish, "You lot stay here," then took his men to the alley.

When the last had left, Bish grasped Ribea by the shoulders and said, "Tell me what happened, child. Who killed those people? Do it quickly, before the guard return."

"There was one, the leader. I called her the handler. She was dressed as a commoner, a worker of some sort, though not as she usually dressed. She ordered me to meet her in the rum tavern, but I refused to talk. She had six bullyrocks dressed as miners fresh from work. Dirty, they smelled; sotted with rum, but maybe that was a cover. So they were going to kill me in that alley. And when I ran, one passed me. He was dark, a Dartian, dressed in a cloak, with a beard and a scar on his face. If you found seven, then one of the handler's people remains standing!"

Regnal Bish looked at Vries, who shook his head. Bish said, "What did you find, Vries?"

"Like I said, it was a qabr. Seven dead, the woman, she says, six miners, but no man with a scar on his face. Leastwise a scar that was not put there recently," Vries said.

Bish handed Ribea to Vries and said, "The local guard are returning. Let me talk."

"Mad as hell they seem," Vries said.

"Take Scholar Ribea to the House and let me deal with the guard. Talk to no one but the Princess or me."

Vries pointed at one of his soldiers. "You with me. The rest of you protect and guard Mr. Bish here." He took hold of Ribea and gently forced her to move. His underling grabbed her other arm for good measure. They did not allow her to stop, but they did not force her hard or hurt her purposefully. As scared as she was of Vries, he was her savior for the moment. He led her into the back entrance of the hôtel and took her to a windowless sitting room. The soldier with him, a fierce-looking woman with the stripes of an under-sergeant, looked over the room until Vries said, "That is good. Guard her, Vilmia. I have to get the Princess." He banged out the door where two members of the Last Guards Regiment were looking on with worried visages. Vries manhandled one and said, "Tea and food for the Scholar." He then turned to the other and barked, "Wake up another squad and have a message sent to Life Guards. Do it now."

The soldiers broke away on their tasks and the under-sergeant closed the doorway to the room. In a few minutes, there was a knock. The guard drew her talwar and opened the door to find a servant, startled by the drawn weapons. "Tea," the servant said weakly.

"Drink a cup," the soldier said, so the servant put the service on a table, poured a stoneware cup filled to the top with tea, and drank some. Satisfied, the soldier said, "Be gone," and put her curved sword back in her sheaf.

Ribea watched as he poured a cup of tea for her. She accepted it and drank a deep drag of the brew. It was hot and welcome, some nameless local brew, smokey, overdone, but bright in the way boiled tea was. It hit her senses like a hammer, and she could feel the shakes start that said it was stronger than it tasted. She was sipping it when Princess Nazira and three prelates; Major Tedjen al-Myrra d' Stanis, Padan-General Lesha al-Andarzbad, and Kohn Sucdow d' Hazrhat entered the room. Behind them was a draughtsman with his papers and pens named Yesha d' Semini. Ribea threw herself up and said, "Princess and faithful Rasnan Kurli." She then genuflected to the floor.

Nazira said, "Get up Scholar. That's hardly needed." She turned to the guard and said, "Will you tell Vries and Bish, to meet me here?" The soldier saluted and left, securing the door behind her. Vries and Bish must have been close by because they entered almost as the soldier left, taking places at the back of the room.

Tedjen al-Myrra gestured to Ribea. "The town guard has sent messages to Dame Youseffi that this woman killed six miners and a worker. The dead were discovered still twitching from the dread assault."

Princess Nazira scoffed. "My dear Tedjen, you will find the dead are not miners or workers, but even if they were, the scholar is not a gram above forty-five and has no arms training. Are you saying she is some zakhrafat alqua made human?"

Lesha al-Andarzbad, leader of one of the great Guisarme families to the south who was attached to Crosswell for the procession, said, "Tedjen, you speak as if you are carrying a message from Dame Griselda!"

Tedjen looked nervous. "She has retired already. I have the intelligence from her master of arms."

"My master of arms would be scalped for giving you the time of day if I did not approve, but I guess the al-Youseffi are not as keen as they were once. Though they have you dancing. But I must say the princess is right. This woman is a scholar known to me by reputation. How does she kill six as you accuse her of?"

Kohn Sucdow corrected her. "Seven, my dear Lesha. She is accused of killing seven so fast that some were still twitching."

"My apologies, Kohn. This scholar killed seven. I must say, if you are carrying the water for al-Youseffi, that bucket must be quite heavy. I found one of my partisans had taken money to kick up a fuss here in this town. That is some skullduggery that needs to be added to this account of partisanship."

"My gods, Lesha," Kohn Sucdow exclaimed, "Did you scalp the curl?"

Lesha al-Andarzbad waved in the air like the issue was not one to worry over, and said, "The young woman was very sorry for her mistake. She has taken a vow of poverty and chastity and been sent to contemplate her toes at the monastery. Nonetheless, this is not a joke, and we cannot take it as one." She turned to Regnal Bish and said, "The general who I met with today says that young princess Nazira here is not going to live past the birth of her child. Is that what the Assassins have to say, Regnal Bish?"

"Please do not address me as an assassin, Lord Lesha," Bish said calmly to the noble.

Lesha al-Andarsbad replied, "Half of the scum from Tariq are wandering our streets looking for a fight, calling themselves assassins, and you want to hide behind the niceties, Regnal Bish? I am happy your lot exist and do not call you out from a sense of disgust. Just tell us what you are about here so we know."

Regnal Bish stepped forward and said, "The Great Bank holds my contract as Princess Nazira has taken a loan against her dower. A massive loan." He stopped, then added, "Perhaps this conversation should be conducted under the rose with my guild if you wish to accuse me here in public."

Lesha al-Andarsbad looked scared for a second, then cleared her face and said, "So what is that general talking about? I would never accuse you of being an assassin even if you hold warrant from the Great Bank. Though, one must inquire if the general whose name I do not use, but who is the leader of the Life Guards, has credible intelligence. Are these dead miners partisans, and when Griselda waves her cane at you, do you slit this girl's throat as well?"

Princess Nazira interceded for Regnal Bish. "My dear Lesha, you were such a fine dancer when I met you at that party when your daughter came of age. So beautiful in your purple gown of the Guisarmes. However, as young as I am, I can count the cards for you before they are on the table. The Dominion Baracks in Cycus Port is run by an al-Dinni. General Nantavenches is al-Dinni bought and paid for. He might as well use the name. There are al-Dinni in the Bank of Cycus, and they have ties to the Great Bank. Complicated? No, it is simple. The al-Dinni's are allies of the Youseffi and the Cinci, and they all look to the Camellia Throne, which my child will occupy after he or she is born. What you see is battle for my child, nothing more."

Kohn Sucdow scoffed, "See there Tedjen, you said this girl was vapid and clueless. Yet she spoke more truth in a few minutes that you have since the procession was announced. There are games afoot. Why would Youseffi partisans die in the streets of a Youseffi stronghold trying to kidnap a scholar? Because that is what I understand." He turned to the princess. "Far as I can see, you did what you could with that idea of flinging your child-father into the ocean on a pirate boat, but the band that needs paying for it packs its instruments. Believe me, child, I knew your mother from her procession. Her only choice was to flee. You should have gotten on that pirate with your so-called husband, even if it meant sharing his fate in the storm."

Nazira laughed. "Lesha, Kohn, if only I could talk to you of truth from behind this veil." She pointed at Regnal Bish. "He is a sign of our times? The Bank is nervous. The Sublime Port surrounds us with intrigue. The Dinni, Youseffi, and Cinci sense the end of the Cycus 'dustari and the great compromise and await the decks being shuffled and a new hand played out. Perhaps, though, you can tell me what would make each of you feel more comfortable about how this land is ruled. Pretend I was the Dominar, and you could speak freely without having an assassin visit you in the night. What would you say to me?" She turned to the draughtsman. "All they say, please take down Yesha." The scholar laid open a roll of scap onto a side table and opened a new bottle of ink.

Lesha al-Andarsbad looked at the draughtsman prepare his tools, and when he saw that he was ready to copy, replied, "Stop the executions. They are not helpful. How many actual arsonists or child killers have you heard of going to the strangling stakes? And how many people do you hear of losing a husband, wife, or child because of some imbroglio between the families that keep the Dominar in power?"

Nazira said, "That is fair, and I would do it." She paused. "You are, of course, right. When my child is born, I will be on those strangling racks next. My father is broken in some ways, and the Youseffi will call for it."

Tedjen al-Myrra said, "Funny this humor and ribaldry about what a princess with no power would order if the gods turned the world upside down, but such talk can be heard, and those that hear it can act. Remember that she has no power."

Kohn Sucdow laughed, "Tedjen, it is past your bedtime. I find this talk interesting and wish sorely that Dame Griselda were not hiding in her rooms of her hôtel and sending you to a contest of wits that you are only half equipped to face. What we discuss is seven dead partisans in a town we are guests in, and our own people being corrupted by Youseffi silver." He turned to Nazira. "No more bribes to minor officials to get them to oppose the will of the family and town counselors. They get money for a road, there is never any built, and then they use that money to pay off the debts of idiots to get a voice they do not deserve." Kohn Sucdow paused, then looked at Tedjen. "Idiots with their debts paid by partisans are willing to go against their own good order to stay on the money ship. They dare not make sense, or else they will find themselves swimming in place as the ship they took tacks into the distance."

Nazira nodded. "If I am princess, I cannot stop payments for roads and the like, but I can arrange for money to go to a raanan council so it won't be misused. I cannot let the Rasnan Kurli become corrupt either, but we can look to creating provincial and colonial lander councils run by raanan. It is the best I can do there," she said.

Kohn Sucdow said, "So you are saying that you will take the throne and we are to trust you to reform under the Cycus 'dustari?"

Nazira simply said, "yes."

Lesha al-Andarsbad turned to Regnal Bish. "We have not forgotten you, Assassin. Where do you fall in all this?"

Bish laughed. "If I was an assassin, I would not fall anywhere. The bank has her protected, and if she is able to pay the first payment, will remain protecting her. She is the heir even if cut off in part by her father and grandmother. The guild, if it exists, stands for keeping civilization from destroying itself. You decide how that would work."

There was silence for a minute, then Major Tedjen yelled a curse. "On the lot of your heads to talk about this under the very roof of the Youseffi." He turned and stormed out.

Nazira laughed. "Come friends," she announced. "Let us have tea."

The remaining prelates left with Nazire, leaving Regnal Bish with Ribea. He said to her when the door closed, "The dark man, would you recognize him if you saw him again?"

Ribea was confused. "Which dark man do you speak of?"

Regnal Bish nodded. "That is what I thought." He started to turn, then paused. "The princess respects you and reads each word you write. Do not betray her, scholar. I have come to believe in her, and so should you." He hesitated. "You did well tonight. Next time, tell me what you fear and see it aided."

Ribea nodded, fearful yet hopeful, and ready to write her daughter on what she had just learned.

CHAPTER XII

Yavne Town

The signs they had for him said, "Ask my patron about our mustard." It was a bit of vanity that they spelled mustard "kardhal," which was the old tongue for mustard condiment. *It was bound to be a mistake for the advertiser,* Kendre thought. Cycuns were buggy about the old tongue and were constantly using it even when they were not fluent. But the old tongue word for mustard was a bit of a stretch. In old tongue, you would say, "'aetini alkhardal." A modern Cycun, though, would say instead "marari li dê a mostarda," and would find the old tongue disturbing to hear because, cultural conceit aside, it was a dead language despite the Cycun's ability to quote a thousand poetic lines of it on command.

Still, it was a mistake. He said to Master al-Batha, "Is kardhal the best word?"

He waved his hand in the air. "You are from the Core. What would you know of the ancient tongue of my people?"

Kendre sighed. It was vainglory to try to teach a prideful person a small truth. And all he was paid to do was carry the sign. He got not one gram of silver as people bought all the mustard in the city. Dominion Mustard paid Master al-Batha for their imported and delicate condiment, two hundred grams of which were in a delicate glass jar whose top was sealed with a stopper and beeswax could cost 40 silver pieces, two hundred grams of fine silver. Kendre spent less on ten days' food without any mustard at all.

He slipped into the sign and adjusted it. It was made of boo-wood that had been white-washed for each advertisement added by Master al-Batha, and each hour he carried it into the busier parts of the city, the master gave him a gram of silver. "Procession is still in Yavne today. If you stay out until eighteen, I will put another coin in your pocket, just like always."

Kendre nodded. 18 grams standard plus five grams was 23 grams, a nice showing for the day. It had been different at one time, before the Rivuluziunariu had driven him out. And al-Batha was wrong; his home was not in the fabled core. It was just not in the outer lands where Cycus was, but try explaining that to the advertising master.

He filled his water bottles from the fountain outside of Yavne Advertisers and Associates, then adjusted the sign and sallied forth into the crowds.

Procession had caused Yavne to go crazy. Everyone with a cart and a few things to sell were selling them, from fresh water to small songbirds in boo-wood cages. The procession itself was hundreds of people who were looking for diversion. It was a crazy chiaroscuro melange of people from the city, the countryside, and even denizens from the extents of the Dominion. There was though the tenor that disturbed Kendre. People were looking to the princess as some form of savior, but that opinion was wobbly. He stood by a shady tea stand and bought some tea and heard two women talking.

"The princess is adorable, you think?" one char said, her buckets and long-handled scrub leaned by the side of the vending booth as she drank her tea.

The other woman, older, who was a drape cleaner, said, "I remember her mother doing this, all the talk of her foreign-born charm, from a great line. Then where did she end up? I do not know."

The tea vendor chimed in, "Best not speak of the mother. She was sent packing, and the reason is not one we need worry."

A man at the end of the line of people hiding from the sun and drinking tea said, "The al-Youseffi sent her packing, and unless you want your kith to be ground down, you had best hush yourself."

Kendre drank his tea silently. Wearing the sign selling mustard was his job, but he could listen to politics on the side.

The older woman scoffed, "Hopper al-Luis, when has your family earned a silver bootlicking the al-Youseffi? The Guisarmes are past."

The man addressed as Hopper protested, "The Dominar depends on the al-Youseffi, and that is where the silver is. You lot can be poor for not seeing it."

The tea seller made another cup of tea for a new customer, a traveler in shoes based on the fact he had shoe bags hanging from his body like fat ticks. He put a tea token on the counter and collected his tea. "You owe me ten coins for your son's work shoes. When does that get paid with al-Youseffi silver?"

Hopper said, "When the Cartagers' pay me for the sour cabbage they purchased and sold in the market. Gotta get paid to be paid."

It was a misquotation of the *Heshuan*, a religious work. That sort of thing made Kendre angry. "lilhusul ealaa almal, yadfae almar'u," he said.

"What was that?" the man who had misquoted the passages asked.

The older woman said, "The man selling mustard was correcting your blasphemy. It means something like 'one gets paid by paying.'"

The man named Hopper scoffed. "Then no one gets paid, eh mustard man? Have you a scholar's parchment under that sign?"

Kendre, in fact, had a scholar's parchment, just not here. "It does not have anything to do with getting paid, it has to do with serving god if one wants to be served by god."

The younger woman with the char kit said, "Hopper is an apostolical git."

"No, I just know that if no one has silver in their pocket, nothing gets done. And that is why you are a git Barbara d' Dartia." The man turned and looked at all the patrons drinking tea. "You can go all el-dari and scream that the sun is going to fry you, but when you cannot buy a gram of sour cabbage while he has a tonne to sell, and when he cannot buy a minute of your time to char his walls despite you having all the time in the world, there is hell to pay and no one spouting verses of the Hesuan such as mustard man is going to save you. And no one saves me or buys my shoes."

There was silence in the group. The shoe seller added, "Talk about the princess all you want, but her mother never amounted to anything but making a daughter, and now we have her daughter amounting to nothing but making a new baby, and that does not mean any silver in our pockets. I have more chance of earning silver from a great kith that has tonnes than from a princess who has none. Nor from a god who has never spoken to me."

Kendre remembered people from his past and losses he had sustained that put him here in this strange land advertising mustard. "You do not know what she has for silver, or how she spends it. You know what you are told by people scared of someone else, too scared to be truthful. I admit 'shoe man,' I have no intelligence about what this princess is about or why she is suddenly presented to us as the heir-mother. But I must also say you have no intelligence of her impotence. You are not a partisan of the al-Youseffi, unless your bandanna color is camouflage rather than attestment."

The tea trader cut them off. "Give way for customers who want more tea. You lot go and seek shade with someone who you will pay to talk politics."

Kendre walked back into the crowds and ambled down the Avenue of the Bards. It was a slow stroll, turning to let passers look at the sign, not blocking traffic to have a minder come to caution him. It was not good in this city. Probably it was not good anywhere. He had landed here because it was the last stop on the ferry from Cycus city, the last land he could flee to, the farthest from his mistakes he could go. Any further and he would have had to be carried to the extents. Then he stopped. There was a man staring at him. No one stared at advertisers. They tried not to, fearful that somehow the message on their sign would sneak into their brains. What was worse, he recognized the man. A face from years ago. A name that was not real. He had a scarred face, then as now, and wore a beard and a black cloak.

He looked at Kendre and walked right up to him as if all the years had not passed. He stopped right in front of Kendre and looked into his eyes, saying, "U vostru signu hè pocu scrittu."

"I do not understand you," Kendre replied in Eurabaa, but of course, he could understand the cowled man.

"Ot, ets de la gran terra de Emporia?" Man said. It was the Friza tongue of the Core.

Again pretending to misunderstand, he said, "I am just the humble carrier of signs and do not know these tongues you speak."

The man changed to a third tongue, "Binne jo net Kendre D'Haguni fan 'e minsken dy't bloeie op Denuva?"

"I have to carry my sign," Kendre said, wanting to be anywhere but here with this man. He tried to leave, but the man stopped him with his hand.

"I recognize you Kendre, and see you know me, even if you claim not be be Cestial educated." He pressed his finger on the advertising board that Kendre wore like a breast plate and added. "And I know who you are looking at as you wander with that stupid sign around your neck getting spit on by children."

"What of it, Samedi d' Ocean?" Kendre asked. They were surrounded by people enjoying the spectacle of the procession, a special type of privacy where two people could talk among thousands.

"The Princess in the procession reminds you of your princess, does she not?" the dark man asked.

Kendre scowled. "Older."

"Older!" Samedi chortled.

"I do not have knowledge of my princess, so if that is what you seek, leave me. You know my feelings for her and her brother, and you know what occurred to him." Kendre said. "They are gone from me. Can I not watch a young princess and marvel like the rest of the crowds?"

Samedi looked at the sky, then back down to the man wearing the wooden sign. "Can you have tea?" he asked, his face softening.

"I can. There is a place for common folk down the way. I will not be the only advertiser there, and you will not be the only old drunk." Kendre said with a scowl and then turned to the side alley off of Aligance Road.

In fact, the tea shop was a benighted place that serviced people with money, but not much. Hundreds of customers were crowded into the wooden structure. Rickety tables were served by crooked chairs. Samedi looked in and nodded. "Do you like the tea here?" he asked.

"No," Kendre replied. He waved and a server came by. "A table?" she asked.

"The room. He looked at Samedi, who reached into a pocket and put some silver coins into the woman's hands. She went to the service counter, set up a platter with six cups, a plate of fruit, and a liter container of tea, and went into a door in a dark corner. She then reappeared without the tray and waved them into the room. They passed by her, but she did not follow.

Kendre shut the door to the room and tossed the tea service onto the table. The teapot top flew off with a wooden thud, and coconut cuts played themselves around the table like pinion balls across a match field. "I know you, Samedi. You are right, the Purple Hippo may be years in our past, and my memory has not trailed to senescence. You may have been an old drunk, but Master Green and Master Orange saw you dance quite often if I remember. You are not just an observer interested in crying the news for the Endwall Edition or doddering over some dry books at the University. You are a meddler who thinks the world won't spin if you take your hands off the crank."

Samedi quietly took a cup from where it had stopped, righted it, and reached for the teapot. He poured a cup of tea, then did the same with a second, his face expressionless. He pushed one of the cups over to Kendre's side of the table and took the other cup to himself. He did not touch the biscuits or the fruit. After a few seconds, he said, "Doctor d' Basta, you are an observer of people. In a crowd of ten thousand, you see the ten that matter. That is a talent I need right now. An important talent. But in that skilled observational mind of yours, there is the knowledge of how I operate, no matter what bad will exists between us from fifteen years ago. Let me ask you to pay attention to the fact that I never ask without currency to pay for my desires. I could have had you beaten by ten thugs for the cost of this private room, and you would have screamed what I wanted to know as they broke each finger on your hand. You, as a Denuvani, must know how alone you are here without association, rejected by your kith, abandoned by your union, unknown by the people in this land. Fifty grams of silver and five minutes of pain buys from you anything I want in this time and place."

Kendre was horrified. It was so true. He felt the vulnerability of existing alone in a strange land. But the idea that this old man, who had played Master Green and Master Orange so often in the Purple Hippo's strange world of favors and connections, beggared to his beliefs. The world did not change that drastically. "You would not do that."

Samedi motioned for Kendre to sit down, and he did. "And there you know I have currency that does not consist of torturing you for information. Use your logic, would I play the role of Master Green with nothing to offer?"

"Then offer, old man," Kendre said, feeling the fear that his old life coming back to haunt him offered.

Samedi laughed, but it was dry and brittle. "For five days, I have watched you. You were not just wearing a sign and taking home a few silver during this procession. You were looking at the crowds. Each time Princess Nazira appears in public, you are there watching. Each time a speech is given, you and that stupid sign are present, even though one would suppose an event that has the people's attention taken would be a poor return on your investment of time."

"The Advertising Master does not understand that. He thinks a big crowd is a good crowd, even if they are watching a tragedy on stage," Kendre replied, taking the teacup and sipping some tea. It was terrible stuff, bitter like pipe-root, but always bracing.

"Thus, you would not shirk your duties. Do you ever give less than you are paid to do? I think not. You have a reason to be there and I know why, and I also know what you are finding out in broad strokes," Samedi said. He reached for the tea, drank some, then put the cup down with a grimace.

Kendre nodded. "You want me to fill you in on what I have seen, and possibly maintain this study of the procession, but what will you pay me in return?"

Samedi took out a piece of scap paper with some cursive on it. The writing was Denuvani, a neat hand. It said, "Holland returned from the war with great scars on his face. He has taken the name Cicatrice..." Kendre lowered his head and said, "Then Holland lives."

"The intelligence that reached this land of Holland's death in battle was wrong. I was there when you fell out with him over his taking up the sword. I heard that a Buccanieri pirate had cut him low, and I mourned him, as you must have. Yet I had the means to check that intelligence which you do not have. Your cousin Holland lives and has become tutor to your cross cousin Cinque. King Angelique and the rest of the Royal Family remain in deadly conflict with the Buccanieri, but as of today, all live. And if you serve me this year, then I will see you back to Denuva Land." Samedi said.

Kendre felt like a tonne of water had fallen on him. He was drowning in emotions to know his beloved Holland lived, and that the little baby Cinque, so sick that none expected her to thrive when he was banished, thrived. But Samedi lacked every piece to the puzzle block. "Geddi will not be easy to sway. When he had me tossed from the land, he was caught in the throes of nonsense about his right to the throne through the Anticu claim. His nonsense when you knew him of Rivuluziunariu has taken root. I am not fooled by his claim that this is a hobby. I heard him plotting with the Cortone and the Wiewalli, and he was mooching after Vinaldi. Only Angelique's minister is torpid and did not believe my warning. I cannot return."

"You can return to Denuva," Samedi said. "I need you to focus for me on this land of Cycus, and this Princess Nazira, give me the information I need. If you do, I will pay the debt not just with passage to the land of your birth, but return your name to you. Doctor Kendre, you could be Kendre d' Basta again, and your brother cannot stop me."

Kendre considered this. His brother was mad, but he had so many supporters, especially in his own kith. But not everyone agreed with him, and Angelique did not really know the details of his banishment. Samedi was known in Denuva; he had connections. It was his constant meddling and power brokering that gave him this. Kendre did not know how old the man was. He was old when he had frequented the Purple Hippo and that was fifteen years ago. He must be almost ninety now, but he still looked like he was hale, and his mind was clear, or so Kendre thought. It was very possible he could arrange for his return and rehabilitation no matter what nonsense his brother chirped on about ancient kingly lines of descent.

"I agree to your terms, as long as you are not seeking to harm this princess," he said.

"Quite the opposite. In my meddling would I harm a person such as her?" he asked.

Kendre shook his head no. "There is a dance around this princess. Four groups, not apparently aligned, watch her. Partisans ask odd questions in the taverns. Apostolical strangers wearing too much metal and praying too little act in ways that are not usual for their kind, confident that none will call out their behavior. I would expect that the powers would be protecting a princess on procession, but these people do not protect; they seem to be like vultures fighting over the corpse of a deer."

"Give me details," Samedi requested.

Kendre grasped up a cocoanut teacup and placed it in the center of the table. "A man claiming to be an al-Cinci partisan was asking performers if they had been invited for private performances with the Princess, and to name her staff. They were quite forceful about the issue, but while they received names of the staff that followed the princess, they gained no blackmail or advantage. They perhaps thought the Princess was lying about her pregnancy or creating doubt as to who the parent of the heir was. That was my read. This same man in armor who claims the al-Cinci kith appears with two women, a char and a hunter, in the crowds, but they are not locals. I take them to be bringing information to their kith."

Samedi said, "I do not doubt this intelligence you offer. The al-Cinci are looking for a position here, and their matron is grasping. This is good information. What else do you have?"

Kendre turned over another cocoanut and put it next to the first. "Three more women make an effort to not be seen as a group, but they are a group. Very professional. No motivation I can see, they just watch."

"They are from the Assassins. The princess does not know it, but the man they have looking after her is an assassin, and a very good one. His name is Regnal Bish, and you may have a visit from him," Samedi said.

"What should I do?" Kendre asked, feeling afraid.

Samedi tried the tea again and his face had the same grimace as before. "If you are scared, give him this tea. It is really quite bad."

Kendre replied, "That is no answer."

"It actually is. The assassins are a rule to themselves. They could do great violence, hold great power, but instead, in lands where they work they are almost a business, and they do not wantonly murder people who they have an interest in. You are safer with one of them than you would be with a more partisan people. If Regnal Bish asks you a question, tell him what you know about me," Samedi said.

"Very little, as it turns out," Kendre griped.

Samedi nodded, "And what he wants, you do not know. Now continue."

Kendre leaned down and recovered a cocoanut teacup from the floor and put it with the other two. "There are some nautical types flexing in the bars, and they are watching the procession as well. Not from town, and not even from Cycus. A lot of Dartians and some Phingeons with deck sandals and unmarked crew jackets. Not very professional, and no real leadership."

"Naseer al-Dinni's people," Samedi said. "They are pirates. You can ignore them. Someone put their leader onto a boat a month back. More than likely, they work for Nasira and do not know it now."

"There are some Cycus Port toughs following the procession. They are pretty chaotic," Kendre said, moving the third cocoanut to indicate he thought of them as part of the part of the same group as the pirates.

Samedi reached over and grabbed a mango slice and put some honey on it from a dipper and jar on the try. He ate the fruit and then took the pot of honey and put it by the coconut. "The toughs are Daniella's people. She is, or rather was, a gang boss from Cycus. Someone named Sederick Devious blew him up. That is someone I expected to be in these crowds."

"Never heard of anyone named Devious," Kendre replied. "A capital sort, is he?"

Samedi shrugged. "Everyone knows him, no one knows him. He is some sort of fixer, working on the shadows for the Princess. Other than that, I do not know. As you watch for me, look for Harmond Carr. He runs what you would call a tenement. Not a bad sort, but he was present when Daniella, the gangster I described, was killed." He stood up. "Thank you for telling me about the assassins and the al-Cinci. They are who I needed to know about." From his pocket, Samedi produced a bag that was filled with clinking coins. "Keep that sign but quit the job. Here is three-thousand, follow the procession as long as it is on the road."

"How do I tell you want I find?" Kendre asked, taking the bag from Samedi.

"I will find you. Wait a few minutes and then back to your advertising." He turned and left.

Kendre reached for the fruit plate and started eating. After a few minutes, he took the sign and walked out into the street.

Kendre arrived at his diggings, slang for what his own people would have been a tenement, and found Osmar in front with two bullyrocks, a look of hesitation on his face. He walked up, put his sign down against a bush, and waved at the property owner. "Master Osmar, is there an issue?"

The guards started, but Osmar waved his hand to calm them. "Ochoa is behind, if you must know." He paused, then added, "So am I. To pay for myself, she has to pay herself. It is the way of it, you know."

"How much is she into you for?" Kendre asked.

"Fifty coins. Plus twelve for these two," Osmar said.

One of the bullyrocks scowled and said, "You offered three each."

Osmar rubbed his bald head and scowled, turning to his employees. "Are you experts in math now?" He turned back to Kendre and shrugged. Everyone tithes the truth, or so Kendre found. It was human nature.

Kendre turned around, measured out forty coins, and turned back. "Forty to pay all. Six more if these ladies work for me for the day."

"Sixty all in," Osmar said.

Osmar considered it. "Fifty pays all."

Kendre nodded. He turned and measured out twenty more, for sixty coins in total. When he turned back, he said, "Fifty, and five for Ochoa and I, we are leaving the city. Sixty, you have some people to pack our stuff who won't get sticky?"

He nodded. "Sorry to see you leave." Waving his hand at the bullyrocks, he said, "Ochoa will be coming out. You protect her as she does her business for the rest of the day."

Kendre left the trio and walked down the little path to the diggings. Twenty round wooden doors led to twenty apartments, each about ninety square meters, with a single window that looked out into a courtyard. Ochoa was looking out one window, a club in her hand. She lived in the next apartment to Kendre with her sister Kicker, and they often exchanged comments from window to window. "Hello Ochoa," Kendre said.

"Hell, Kendre. Is Osmar out there with the Chaos Sisters?" she asked. She was a big woman who lifted stones in sacks as exercise and worked watching children for lumber workers during working hours.

"Who are the Chaos Sisters?" Kendre asked.

"Two big women, scowls on their face," she replied.

"Yes," Kendre said. It was comical that a big woman like Ochoa thought the two women she called the "Chaos Sisters" were large. Ochoa was bigger than Kendre, and the two women serving as bullyrocks were smaller than him. "They are out there. They work for you now."

"How is this?" Ochoa said.

"Why are you staying here?" Kendre asked.

He knew this was a tough question for the woman. She looked a little lost, her thick jaw and angular face taking a soft look. "Zorbo lived here."

"I paid your rent. Zorbo is dead on the longshore. He is not coming back. Be serious, his sister and you are at the end of your ropes, and this city has no connection here anymore. I just paid off your rent. You can stay and end up here again, or you and Kicker can come with me and get out of here." He walked up to the window and touched her cheek to carry away a tear that was forming. "You, Kicker, and I, we have no Kith. How much money do the wood choppers owe you?"

"It has been a hard year for them," Ochoa replied.

Kendre nodded. "And I am sorry for them, but if they owe you less than five hundred coins, I would be shocked. And they probably owe the grocers twice as much, and the grocers owe the farmers twice as much again. None of this works, and if you are like us and have no kith, then the Chaos Sisters are the ones that take the loss out of our bodies. And I bet even Osmar owes a pile of coin to someone. I have work for a year, and silver to pay. Come work for me with Kicker and we can be our own kith."

Ochoa traced a shocked look on her face. "What does Kicker get to do? She is so sick. And not just in body."

Kendre nodded. "I once knew a very sick girl who became a princess in a foreign land. Kicker is a counter. That is amazing. She may not be able to speak well, or look people in the eye, but she can count, and happens I need a person who counts things, remembers how many people pass a certain point, and how many had red hats. Just what she loves to do." He stopped for a second and saw into the darkened apartment. Kicker was in there counting and sorting rocks. She was bent, twisted like a reed pulled by two dogs. At sixteen she was tiny, but like Princess Nazira, like his beloved cousin Cinque gone for so many years from his sight, she has huge reflective eyes and lustrous black hair. While Princess Nazira no doubt was not touched, and he knew Cinque had grown strong after her ailment, the curse that ran through Kicker's brain did not make her a lesser person to the royals. He knew the devotion Zorbo held for the girl, and when he died, his wife Ochoa took up the same devotion. She was not broken, just different. "The cash lasts a year. Let us move on while it is within our reach."

"And what happens when the cash ends?" Ochoa asked.

"Maybe we can move to a fantasy island where Kicker can be a princess herself," Kendre said, not wanting to say more on the matter. "In a year, we will face another year, and Kicker will face it with us."

"Well then, what is to do?" Ochoa said.

Kendre clapped her shoulder. "Pack us up, then go with the Chaos Sisters, take some of my money, and pay off what debts you have. I have to meet the Lamplighter. The procession moves on, and we will move on with it." He took all but ten coins from the sack and handed it to her. "If we can get a used cart, just enough to get us started, something with some canvas on it, get one. I will pull it myself. Do not get an animal."

She took the silver. "When do we leave?"

"The procession leaves tonight. I hope to tag along. It is safer." Kendre turned away, but stopped. "This is a good thing for us." Ochoa did not respond, but held the silver like it was a talisman. Behind her, Kicker explained, "Two-twenty-two."

He left, knowing this was the key to escaping Yavne and staying safe as puppets of the Samedi, who was at one time known as the Darkfather, a sinister name.

The Lamplighters Guild has one official responsibility, taking care of the gaslights in Yavne. Kendre walked up to their union house and stopped in front of the guild desk. The woman who was sitter there looked up with a smile and said, "I like that mustard."

Kendre tried to bow in the board. "Then you pay for my room and food."

The woman smiled. "That is a nice thought. Next time I put mustard on my beans and rice, I will think of you and your comfortable home."

Kendre smiled back. "I have to see the Lamplighter."

"I was just going to send someone to fetch you. It is nice of you to save me the bother," She said.

Kendre felt his stomach go flat. He could only mouse out a squeaky, "Oh?"

"Just so," the door keeper said. "The Lamplighter-Major wanted to see you before sundown. This saves having a few of the boys and girls go out to see you, once you go into his office."

He entered the den of the Lamplighter-Major and was shocked to see a second man sitting with him, an older man dressed in court finery, wearing a sword and an ornamental hat. Ignoring the man, Kendre bowed and advanced to the desk, placing his last ten silver coins in front of the Guild Master. Aware that the stranger was watching, he said, "Master, I am paying promise on my duties to the Lamplighters as I am leaving the city under the employment of a master."

The Lamplighter did not reach for the money. "Do you know the name of this new master?"

Kendre said, "Yes." He then stood in silence.

The Lamplighter-Major nodded. "If you are leaving, why pay the first portion of your tithe?"

Kendre looked at the silver for a second, asking himself just that, but he knew why he did. He just had to be honest with himself. "You and your fellows are the people who protect the street, but you protect more than the streets of Yavne. I will travel far this year, and except for the capital, you and your brothers and sisters have a hand in the towns and cities of this land. Honor demands I pay someone. You are the best one I know."

"Reasonable," The Lamplighter said. He turned to the stranger. "This is my person, dear Master Bish. Courtesy says you may ask him questions, but I warn you that there are limits. Agreements exist."

The man named as Bish nodded. "Agreements exist, Master Lamplighter, I agree. I have only one question for this man. Tell me what he knows about the man he was seen with today in the forum, the man who spoke to him in foreign tongues?"

The Master Lamplighter said, "Reasonable, please answer the man."

Kendre said, "He knew who you were, and told me you would ask me about him. He did not forbid me to answer. Fifteen years ago I was a person of means, a scholar and a doctor of culture in a foreign land. I ran with a crowd though, people seeking to change the world. The man was known to us as Samedi, and he was a foreigner to my land. He was old and played the game with us, the game of secrets and ideals. Then he left."

He paused for a second, then dove in, though he should have remained silent. "He named you an assassin."

"We do not use that term," the Master Lamplighter warned sternly.

The man named Bish waved his hand. "He is not of this island. There are no assassins, my dear sign carrier. I am a troubleshooter, nothing more."

"Well, Master Bish, then man you seek and who is now my patron, names you assassin." He turned to the Lamplighter, "Master Lamplighter, may I withdraw?"

"I will enjoy a letter when you have a chance, and you may pay my brother in Kermal your arrears."

Kendre bowed. He stepped out into the waning light and looked at the lights of the city starting to flicker on as the people of the Guild did their duty.

Chapter XIII

The Sage of Maryam Hall

Nazira was weary, heavy with her child, and tired of the procession. In each town, there were people to meet. She met with the power brokers, the commoners, the old nobility of the old families, and, in her veil, sat silently while her pregnancy was shown off to all.

When her day was done, though, she had to meet each night with a long list of people she hoped to convince to become her partisans. Many were called old guards, the families who had generations before lost the struggle with her grandfather for Cycus. She had spoken with the leaders of the Sublime Port, the great bank which had entailed her money, street gangs in Seanlast and Ramsgate, herders from the upland wool cooperative, shipwrights and treeheards of Lesser Grange, and keena farmers from the lowlands.

Yet for all these visits, she had been waiting for the eldest sage of Maryam Hall, the last scholar who remembered the days before the fall the old regime. Ribea al' Jin was happier than Nazira had seen her for days, as the Sage was reclusive and rarely gave interviews.

"He is the last voice from the era before the invasion," Ribea said as they walked amidst a double guard, having been taken to the scholar's hall by carts with a cavalry escort.

"I am happy you approve, Scholar," Nazira replied. In reality, she wanted to sleep, but it was hard to deny the scholar this.

She looked over at Regnal Bish. He was still her protector and possible murderer, but his dissonance on the matter had grown in recent days, and when she grew cross with her pregnancy and lashed out at him, reminding the man that he was likely to be ordered to kill her, his face would sketch a troubled look for a second, before he reset it into a serene vanilla of nothingness.

They arrived at the door of the sage's retreat where two scholars in robes held vigil. Both bowed but remained blocking the door.

Regnal Bish said, "We are here to see the teacher."

"He is a sage," the younger of the two scholars replied. "Three of you may enter, no more."

Bish started to complain, but Nazira said, "One old man is not a danger."

Bish looked at her and said, "I am an old man, and you name me a danger."

"Regnal Bish, you are a danger in a shift with your hands behind your back," Nazira retorted. "This man is a person who reads and writes books. Besides, Scholar Ribea will burst if we do not enter and hear from this man."

Ribea, forgetting her place, said, "Oh my dear Regnal Bish, there can be no harm with seeing the man. It is amazing he has invited us at all."

There was silence before Bish relented. "As you say Princess." He turned to the soldier from the Last Guard and said, "No one in or out, Sergeant."

The sergeant nodded, then turned to quietly disperse his people.

They entered the house, and a servant greeted them. She led them to a study with a small table and overstuffed chairs. Ribea cryptically nodded with approval and said, "Baseboard air heat," but did not explain what this meant.

Nazira was guided to a chair that was across from an old man who seemed to be asleep. Nazira and Bish settled into seats further back.

"Master Sage, I am Princess Nazira," the princess said.

"Styled al-Youseffi but more properly Nazira al-Nabeel d' Kemeya," the old man said.

"Not accurate, Sage Maryam. I have never stepped foot on Kemeya. My father was born there, but I was born to Irula d' Canus Cragia in the city of Cycus Port. I have taken the name Nazira, Saeid d' Cycus."

"How interesting," the sage said, reaching over and taking a tea service and pulling it closer to him. "Not Amira d' Cycus? Not Warith Alsiyada?"

"Master Maryam, I am neither of those things," she replied.

"I find the common tongue, what we call Eurubea in scholarly circles, so fascinating in that we borrow so many terms from the old languages, both to lie and to tell the truth. The Cycus 'dustari calls for you to hold the title warith alsiyada, or walsiyada as the more vulgar say. The sounds are magical, but the words in our common just mean heir. The person who follows. The one who takes the tiller off the boat when the previous one falls out." He stopped, then said, "I shall prepare tea."

The sage made tea in slow, methodical steps. First, he took a decanter of water, poured it into a paraffin cooker, and lit the fire of a block of fuel. Then he took down a tea jar and used a wooden spoon to measure out a portion of leaf into a mortar and pestle. Using the pestle, he ground down the tea with measured chops and then placed the pestle aside and poured the pulverized tea into a boo-wood jar. When the water was boiling, he poured it over the tea, extinguishing the flame under the cooker and replacing the stone boiling-jar back into place. He made no small talk as he watched the water infuse with the tea, removing it from his holder and pouring it over a coarse strainer into a stone pot. Then each of the four cups got a paper strainer and received a portion of the tea. Finally, he removed the strainers and scraped the tea power from them into a cup for reuse. When the Sage placed the four cups of tea on a platter, he said to Ribea, "Dame Scholar, will you do the honors as I no longer have a graduate to aid me?"

"I will *Ealim jalil*," she replied. Ribea took the tea and handed it around, then supplied herself with a cup and drank from it.

"I am so old, my princess, that I remember the world before the father of our Dominar took this island for his own. I was not yet one of the Egliffs then, with their picky books filled with contracts and numbers, merely a student of the same. The Egliffs are now gone. They died from God's Fire or they and their agents were arrested and delivered to courts of the land, and those courts worked. They died, and ones like myself only lived because we were too small for the gods or the partisans of the Dominar to see," the old man said.

"Have you ever heard of the Egliffs, Mr. Bish?" Nazira asked.

Regnal Bish leaned forward. "I admit I have not. The secrecy with which Scholar Ribea made this contact and arranged for our visit is suggestive though. I have met many men and women whose names are not theirs, who live in shadows that are hard to penetrate and surround themselves in lies to protect the truth, and there is no guarantee that if I have not heard of them that their story can withstand review. Yet if one was to remain outside of the eye of my kith, so to speak, one would have to live in a tiny fortress, served by fanatic servants, in a room full of books, never venturing out, such as the esteemed Doctor Rayokes does."

Nazira turned and polled Ribea, "My good 'Scholar of the Procession.' Do you have citation to add to help me understand this story that our scholar will proceed with shortly?"

"I will, my liege. Scholar Rayokes was more known in your grandfather's era, and that is when I met him, during the procession of Irula d' Canus Cragia. He was the only survivor of the university that advised the Guisarmes prior to their destruction and the coming of Nawaz," she said.

"That is a foundation at least. Tell us your story, honored scholar."

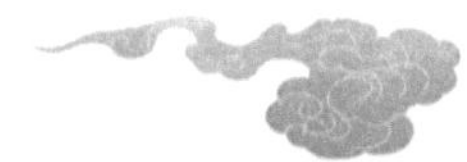

Kurile Amarosa was a tough master, but Rayokes loved the sanctuary of Maryam Hall with all of his heart. He and his fellow graduate Certiza had been studying in the hall for five years, since they were both not much past ten-years and just past grammar. They both could look forward to ten more years of work before becoming journeyers, and ten more after that before they could even contemplate submitting a dissertation for master status.

Rayokes let himself in through the front door. The hall had two scholars in residence, Master Amarosa, who was an astronomer, and Luciel Bey, who was a mathematician and a musician. Luciel had twenty graduates and five journeyers studying under her, such was the fame of her studio, but Master Amarosa was far less famous. That was fitting, given his studies. He purported to be testing the existence of god.

Not really, or not so anyone outside of the lab could understand, Rayokes thought. He had in his hands a boo-wood case of soft cream scap, leaves of which were nearly perfect in their clear soft whiteness. Amarosa needed the papers for his telescope, which was why he was not living with the greater community of scholars at Union Point University. He needed darkness, and the one thing you could count on at Maryam Hall and the mountain that towered over it was that it was dark at night. Preternaturally dark. Made worse by the agreement with the town and Master Luciel to prevent the use of candles, lanterns, or torches outside.

Rayokes went to the supply closet and opened it with his latchkey. Inside were bottles of ink, proximity arms, compass screws made of fine metal, springs, cranequins of thick wood with precise spokes, and glass bulbs of the finest quality, all of which went out of sync regularly enough to need replacing. The paper was both to write on, but also when treated with crystal find allowed pyrographic notation. Rayokes took a soy candle from a box on the wall, lit it from the gaslight, and positioned it so he could see in the dim supply room, then carefully brought the paper in and lowered it into a dispenser. On a card attached to the dispenser, he used his fountain pen to note that it now had 271 more pages in it than last count.

His task complete, he left the closet and locked the latch. He turned and nearly bumped into Finula, an older journeyer of Master Luciel. "Graduate Rayokes, how wonderful to nearly collide with you as a make my rounds."

"Journeyer Finula," he replied, "how is the singing coming along?"

The woman was Luciel's sister and acid-tongued in the best of times. "You would know if you had not abandoned my sister."

"Three years ago, and both masters agreed. My dear journeyer, it is time to set this topic aside for others," Rayokes said. "Besides, I never sang. I was and remain a mathematician. Do I not aid in your own research?"

"That is why I seek you. Do you go to the 'zujaj ealaa aljabal' tonight? What do the modish call it?" she said, smoothing out her thawb.

"A reflector," he replied. "It is not like a range finder. You do not look through it. You project what it sees on a wall, or even better, a pyrographic display. It is quite wonderful."

Finula smiled. "I am sure, and your master has a surprise for us all, it seems, tonight on the subject, but for now, I need your help. Do you have your kit?"

"I know my master says this will be a shock to all, but I am not aware of what it could be. You see, he does not confide in me as much as your master in you." Rayokes paused, then said, "I have my kit on my belt, and I can help you if you need."

Finula turned and led him into the hall of music which dominated the north face of the Hall. She opened the fourth room in the hall and ushered Rayokes in. Inside was a Denuvani of find tempered loosewood viola on a tripod. It lacked strings, but a string bench was set up next to it. Instead of strings, though, made from loose-form or animal gut, there were strings of drawn metal such as his own master used in his reflectors. He considered the strings, then said, "I understand, this is what your master has been doing with my master on all those late nights."

"What else? And now the project is mine. And the damn things do not work. They should, you should be able to tune them, but they just do not work. Not like they should," she said.

Rayokes took out his kit. He pulled a metal string for the viola and inspected it. It was metal, made from what looked like tin and iron, or some combination. From his kit, he pulled a little tenser and set the metal string into it. He then measured a length and cut it, placing it on a portable scale. "Just short of 3 grams per millimeter and just shy of 6-millimeters diameter. You intend this for a number 'five' string." He took out his workbook and ink pen and did some figures. "I guess it looks like a 130 tuned gut, if it were gut."

"Why do you say that?" Finula asked. "That is not what Tuder says."

"How did Tuder do the math?" Rayokes asked.

Finula pulled a scap notebook from her front pocket and handed it to Rayokes. "Does that make sense?"

Rayokes read it. "Only if you are drunk. He assumes your metal strings are made from bronze, iron, and tin, wrapped together in a ratio of 3-3-4." He scribbled some figures in his own book, then took a calculator from this kit and operated the slides for a minute. "That would be correct in terms of math. This string masses what a string made of those three metals wrapped together should mass. However, they are not a composite object. Like when you make rope from three types of jute. The jute each has critical failure points and stretch, but you cannot assume that they all simply combine together into a whole magically. In the case of jute, some weaves of it will begin to snap when under heavy mass and thus not contribute to the strength or resonance of the whole. Broadly speaking, there is change, but not uniform change. Obvious enough of a change that your goal of a perfect five-string is being frustrated."

"Well, how would you fix the problem? Tuder is scared to comment, thinks metal is dangerous to have on an instrument. The tunes can read God, he says," Finula mocked.

"And we know that is nonsense. But why use three metals in the first place?" he asked.

"None of the three metals worked well on their own. Tin breaks, brass does not resonate well but is strong and inexpensive. There are a number of groups that draw brass, and black iron resonates well. The three together make a pleasing tune when plucked as a single string, but are impossible to tune onto a viola," she said.

"How about a hammer dulcimer?" Rayokes asked. "You have to retune a dulcimer after every play. Is that not what the slides are for?"

"Yes. You have to retune every instrument though," she said.

"By replacing the string. Here is my suggestion. Get metal to work on a hammer dulcimer. And then start to develop a process that a player can follow each time. Tune off one key and then everyone tunes off one instrument. Once you can do that, I can help you take what you know from that and work to make the strings resonate on the viola and other instruments," he said.

"What if it does not work?" she asked.

Rayokes shrugged. "Then metal strings are not possible. At least for now."

He watched her for a minute as she approached the viola, her pride and joy, and touched the wood. She was always angry, but always driven. Getting even a gram more from her instrument was what she lived for. She was in a room with her lover, and not a piece of pegged wood coated with resins. He turned and left "them" together.

Rayokes got out of the vertical and un-clutched it to allow the cart to return down the mountain. When he turned, he was shocked and let out a scream. The reflector appeared broken. Instead of being oriented to the sky, it was slanted at the horizon with its mirrors in complete disarray. All the cranequins had been positioned at nonsensical angles, and the pyrograph was nearly vertical. He looked around in confusion and Certiza came running up and jumped into his arms. "Isn't it amazing!" she said.

"It is ruined!" Rayokes despaired.

Master Amarosa came around the corner of the workhouse and said, "No, it is serving us tonight, not as a reflector but as a device to show my life's work!"

"Master!" Rayokes despaired.

"Oh, Rayokes, do not fret. I intend to leave this reflector to you and move my work to a new observatory. You see, we have been retained by the Egliffs."

Rayokes understood. "When did they retain us?"

Amarosa said, "Last year. They have hired me to build the largest reflector on Ocean and target it on the heavens to listen in to the gods. That is my work, to prove the gods exist and find out what they are about in the sky!"

Certiza kissed his cheek, and she was wont to do and said, "Tonight we show the scholars and the largest families of the Guisarmes our new reflector, and tomorrow we reveal our labor to the world. This time next year, we will publish a book on the intelligent powers that exist in our sky."

Rayokes was sandbagged. Mad theory and nonsense were the realm of studying God as if it were a planet or a star. "Complete and utter rot," Master Amarosa called it just five years ago. Rayokes had been perfecting two lines of research, the forces that kept the moons and the planets from crashing into the ground, and its relation to the forces that caused storms to run around Ocean. He never would have tried to use a reflector to look into the sky for god. God no doubt existed, and let humanity know of his or her existence from time to time to warn the apostolic who the true power was. This, though, was horrifying.

"My Master, why have you excluded me from this?" Rayokes asked.

Amarosa reached out his hand to his graduate's shoulder. "I know you are brilliant, my lad, but I also know you are touched with superstitious dread on the gods. No one is saying you are apostolical, but this is not in your cockpit. Some wheels must be turned by others. When I transfer my studies to the Great Scope, that is what we call it, this becomes yours to keep with your valuable work."

Rayokes looked at his love, Certiza, with her round face and brilliant spray of hair. Her mind was first class, and her eyes missed nothing. She again kissed him and said, "We will get rangefinders and look at each other every day, and you can read the flags just like me. We will not be separated, I can always see you." He nodded at her and looked back at his master.

"We must prepare for the Egliffs," Master Amarosa said.

Egliffs. The secret society was neither all that secret nor really a society. Rayokes set the tea on the cookers and began to pull dishes and cups from the cupboards. He looked at his master and Certiza preparing for their presentation, and wondered at how he has missed that there was this great study and the building of a massive new reflector to look at objects as small as a hundred meters across in orbit of the planet. *How can you get the reflectors to track?* he thought. He considered some math and decided there must be a coaching element, but it would be a devilish thing to time.

Unless you used metal gears. Heretical clocks all made of metal could keep excellent time. They used precision parts fit by hand, measured and remeasured, to spin motor-dials. That was how you built a large reflector that could see objects below the orbit of the moon! Someone had stocked sweet biscuit in the cupboards, so that came out and went on plates. He realized it had been since the Yallends that he had been to the observatory. There had been so many tasks to fill like getting special paper, and he realized that was on purpose. The vertical arrived and the sound of it clutching resonated through the observatory. The first of the scholars to see Amarosa's presentation. He tried to ignore the group that came up, but one stepped up to the tea table and asked, "Any warm brew? God's, but your so-called observatory is lacking in heat."

Rayokes looked at the man. He had a set of scholar's robes and a torque of office as a rector. He had ground glass spectacles, a floppy scholar's hat, and awards made from sprigs of holly on his chest. "The water is hot, Doctor. Would you like Old Core or Mlik Tea?"

"Core, please," the scholar said. After that, there was a rush of scholars to the tea table requiring the beverage to be renewed many times. The biscuits were less favored, but soon they were out as well. When all were served and his patron had started his speech, Rayokes went down the vertical, not caring to listen to the presentation. He left the lift building, noting that they had enough torque saved for a dozen trips up and down, enough for everyone to leave the mountaintop, and then stepped off into the street where dozens of carts and footmen lined the way. He ignored their card games and laughter, walking down to the village by the switch-back path and came to the grand fountain. Men and women were filling pails with water for their homes, while workers taking off for the day stopped and talked to each other. He turned and looked at the mountain and wondered if he was really designed to be a scholar.

"Are they hearing about the end of the world up there?" a man asked.

Rayokes turned and looked at the man, a common worker, probably Dartian, here to labor in the mines. Many of the locals were superstitious of scholarship in general, but Maryam Hall was not a large place, nor much thought of. Not like the university or other schools in the bigger cities. It was likely just a consideration of the strange tower and its cryptic uses, never mind that most of their real work was making sea almanacs.

"They could be. I would not know," he replied.

"You work with the Sage of Maryam Hall, do you not?" the man said.

Rayokes turned and asked, "Who are you?"

"Does not matter. Come with me," the man said.

Rayokes was about to tell the man to leave him alone when he decided, for no good reason he could think of, to follow him. Then he found that he could not see the man if he looked straight at him, only out of the corner of his eyes. He followed him though, down to the river, over the small bridge, and out into the winding valley road south of town. They walked into darkness, then came upon a wooden barn. "Join me for some tea," the man said. Rayokes agreed.

The man started a fire. He must have been an excellent hand at that because it took only a second. The tea was soon ready, and the man handed Rayokes a cup of porcelain. He almost drank it immediately, but the man warned, "Give it a few minutes. It is hot."

It was hot, so the advice was well taken. "What is your master doing in the large building he has made about eight miles north of here?"

"Making a reflector to speak with God," Rayokes said, sipping the tea. It was still hard to look at the man, but he was not worried.

"Stop him," the man said.

"I cannot," Rayokes responded.

The man got up and walked around for a minute. "When does the unveiling happen?" he asked.

"Tomorrow. This is good tea," Rayokes replied.

"Pozno kot ponavadi." The man said, then shook his head.

Rayokes sipped his tea and then, through that, he did not understand what the strange man said. "What was that?" he asked.

"I was cursing my own stupidity, that is all. Do you know what a sledilni teleskop is?" the man asked.

Rayokes considered it. "No."

The man thought for a second, and then said, "Sledilni means to follow. In this case automatically."

"Clockwork Reflector," he said. "It is metal."

The man said something that sounded like a curse. "Sranje!" He looked at Rayokes, then asked, "Can you get home safely from here?"

"Of course, this is close to where I live." He sipped the last of the tea.

The scholar had a tear in his eyes. "I have never heard any of this?"

"Your grandfather invaded a month afterward. He invaded because God's Fire burned all the scholars, and all the kit lords of the Guisarmes. It burned my Master Amarosa, and it burned my sweet love, Certiza, and all the scholars of the secret society of the Egliffs. I do not know what they saw or what it would mean, but they all died, and then we died as a nation.

"What of the stranger? That was an oddity?" Bish asked.

"He comes around from time to time," Scholar Rayokes said. "He blames himself for the death of my master and my love, but I tell him that he cannot control the gods. He is foolish to think he can."

Regnal Bish looked skeptical as Nazira levered her gravid self up from her chair. He leaped up to help, but she waved him off. "Thank you, my scholar."

"You think I am an old fool," the scholar said.

"No," Nazira assured him. "And if I survive, I will see what I can do to help you and your people here."

"He likes you," Scholar Rayokes said.

"Wait!" Bish growled. "What does that mean?"

"Just as I say, he says the Princess is a new breed of ruler. That if given the chance and surrounded by the right people, anything is possible." The scholar chuckled. "Many years ago, I asked him why he cared, and he called himself a meddler, that he cared because we were humans. Humans under a microscope, he said."

"What is that?" Nazira inquired.

"I do not know. Ask him if you ever meet. Now, I am tired and must rest," the scholar said, ringing a bell on his table for help.

Outside of the hall, Nazira took Regnal Bish's hand and allowed him to help her to the carts. "Too many secrets are being kept from me, Regnal."

"Regnal?" Bish asked at his first name being used.

"I am keeping secrets from you, you are keeping them from me, and there is the issue of this stranger who dogs our every move. This deadly stranger, yet one who has not offered death to me or mine."

"He could be in preparation," Bish said.

"Do you believe that, Regnal?" Nazira asked. "You still keep your secrets as well."

"You know what I am now and what I may be called on to do," Bish said.

Nazira growled. "Not that secret. The secret of the island and my husband. I have a letter that he is safe still and moving to complete my task I set him."

"That secret is his, my lady. His and many others, including Oban's." Bish said, then added, "But this stranger who chases us is indeed a holder of secrets that I would like to have in a chair to ask some pointed questions."

"I will ask them with you. Is he friend or foe? I need partisans, but I fear what he is," she said, reaching the carts.

Regnal Bish replied, "You have more than you know," and helped her up for the ride back to the apartments and the procession.

Chapter XIV

Hunters

She was named Kicker. The Darkfather watched her protectively as she sat in the town center, a begging bowl by her side, chanting slowly to herself and rocking back and forth. He was not the only one watching the woman. Two of the Darkfather's associates were assured that they could have the contents of the bowl if she was protected. Another person, more sinister, watched them. The first layer of muscle was day workers. Their job was to be loudly protesting if anyone tried to hurt Kicker. The third one, who blended into the crowds perfectly, was the real danger in this game to anyone who made an attempt on the small, twisted woman who sat alone, a seeming beggar.

A person touched his back. Kendre was a Danuvani exile, highly educated, and a power in himself. The Darkfather believed in people. They did not purposely fail you if you selected them for the right task and informed them what success looked like. Kendre was filled with self-doubt, angry at what he had lost, but protective of his own people, and a master of information. He could be pressed and deliver, as long as you understood in the long run that he protected others. That was his tell, and that was his payment.

He did not look at Kendre, who carried a sign that said "Mustard," stolen from a previous employer. He looked at Kicker, like many people, pretending to be interested in how someone broken physically like she was could remain sitting, and wondering what she was muttering. In fact, the Darkfather knew what she was doing. She was counting.

"What did you find?" the Darkfather asked.

"Junior Administrator Brandon is being stalked right this second. I expect in the next hour Partisans of the al-Cinci will have him.

"Kicker is quite special," the Darkfather said.

Kendre coughed. "She likes to be useful." The Darkfather could not see Kendre's face but knew that the scholar was concerned over the danger he was bringing his two friends.

"She is well protected," the Darkfather said. "Three guards. Her work is very valuable."

"I saw two guards," Kendre replied.

"That is as it should be," the Darkfather said. "Where is this Brandon personage?"

Kendre said, "Oak Palm Estates."

The Darkfather groaned. How typical that skullduggery was always being essayed in a rum tavern. He would absolutely marvel if some dark-lantern types decided to make their way to a library or a ballpark to set up their outrages. The town was calmer today than the last four, as people grew used to the procession, and public parades gave way to the more internalized events that were designed to allow the ruling class to see the mother of the future heir, pulling on her sails so to speak. Procession was all about proving to skeptical people who were lied to on a daily basis that this one thing, the new heir, was true, a settled thing.

He left the forum and turned into an alley. Then he felt something was wrong. He turned and saw that Kendre was being manhandled by two guardsmen. He drew his yataghan, but something struck him from behind.

Nazira walked into the clearing and saw that the dark man who had been stalking her was entangled in nets and ropes, sitting under a boo-wood tree. His eyes flashed and she could feel them boring into her, making her anger fade. Nazira grabbed a firelock from Bish's belt, cocked it, and placed it on the dark man's head. "Welcome stalker. Tell me, why you should not go to the qabr today? Work very hard to convince me that your actions are not fell." She hesitated, then renewed her concentration. "And whatever trick you are playing, stop."

Suddenly, the oppressive pressure on her soul ended. The man did not change his flat, almost bored expression, but Nazira could tell something had almost switched off. His eyes, though, continued to dance.

"Have felt your presence for weeks, always lurking, like a cracked tooth. I could sense you, but not see you more than for glimpses. Do you know who I am?" she asked.

"You are the Princess Nazira. They say you will die when that baby is born." His affect was flat, as if the idea of the pistol placed to his head was the least of his worries. He spoke with an odd accent. He was not from Cycus or the Cyclone Islands, but his language was precise, like spoken from the mouth of a dancing master. He spoke Eurabaa in a distant manner, like he was thinking in a strange tongue and needed the formality of a constant translation to sustain speaking in it.

She looked over at Vries, who was holding a great curved sword in his hand, then at Bish, whose very body was a weapon. There was might enough to take the man, she was in no danger. She lifted the Dragoon Model into the air, engaged the half cock, and handed the weapon behind her, knowing one of her guards would take it. "Waqt alaiktishaf," she said to herself, from the *Heshuan*. She rubbed her head and again quoted the book of thought, "alalihat tadeu alsalam."

The man replied, "qad tamnahuk alalihat hadha alsalam." It was the proper response to the ancient book. A sheep herder might yell "The gods call peace" to a passing drover, and the response was, "May the gods grant you peace." It was old tongue that Eurabaan was born from, but again he spoke it with a crisp mechanical style. His understanding was perfect, like he had learned it by pouring over the books, seeking the perfect example of the ancient forms, but not like he was born speaking the tongue. It was perhaps a game? She switched to Amharian, "Timihiriti ā'imironi yasitat'ik'ewali." She said. It was a saying of wealthy merchants, meaning 'education armors the mind.'

He nodded. "Li'iliti hoyi t'iru ābabali newi." He was complimenting her on her mastery of sayings, again in achingly beautiful but mechanical pronunciation.

She looked at Bish, whose own education was impressive and spoke more tongues with a better understanding than her. He replied with a shrug.

Bish would put the man down because he was a danger. It was obvious. He looked at Vries, who, though dull and gritty as a soup made with sand, was cunning and could spy foul character. Vries fingered his sword, but did not seem all that bothered. "Tell me of this man, Vries."

"I picked him up at the market, Princess. He bought a book, read to some waifs down by the cordage masters, spoke of tea and cloth for purchase, talked with the carters and drovers about various options for moving wares, and had a meal" Vries said, injecting no opinion, just facts of what he saw, into his details. "He then wandered the market. It was a while before we found one of his partisans, and he tried to save the man. That allowed us the chance to get him. Vries hesitated, then said, "Princess. If not for trying to rescue his partisan, we would not have had him."

"Would you play dice with him?" Nazira asked.

Vries screwed up his face in a puzzle of misplaced muscles. The man had a face that showed conflict. His left ear was off short, while his nose bent over and was quite mobile in a way noses should not be. "If he had coin, I would, but I would worry about what is under his bonnet. He is a thinker, so it would be dice or darts, not cards or the figures. The Princess's pardon for the vices I mention."

Nazira waved it off. Vries was worried because she had arranged for this discussion at the well of hope. The well was, during the day, a gathering place just out of the city proper. There were benches where well-dippers could sit under a tarp and gossip as they waited their turn at the cascade chutes. Holders for sharp bottomed water jugs and parkades for flag-jacks, flat-bottomed leather, and collapsable water carriers that could be managed on large poles were present for the convenience of the townspeople. "Tell the Deena we will require her spring until an hour before dawn. Then arrange a place for this man to sit, two guards. You and Vries opposite at my side. The men and women to keep us clear of ears and eyes."

Her guard scattered to follower her tasks while Vries guided the dark man to one of the tables as requested.

The Deena, an old woman with a wooden claw staff, came to Nazira. "I understand you need the well," she said.

Nazira lifted her veil for a second and bowed to the women, whose position was one of village trust. "Precious Deena of Calumn High Spring, can you or your daughters bring tea to all made from the waters of this place?"

The Deena, dark-haired with dark piercing eyes, bowed low. "Our tea is humble."

Nazira looked at Oban standing in the dark. The one person who was in her entourage who was scared of the man was Oban. He had refused to show himself to the man. "Oban, can you help replace this good person's tea? We will drink hers, and she shall have ours."

Oban said, "I will." He wanted to say more, but he trailed off. Nazira looked at him and walked to where he stood in the shadows.

"What can I aid my caretaker with?" Nazira asked.

He hesitated, then said, "Some feel like him where I am from." He then grasped her shoulders. "He is not of the silence, but he has the powers. You know I cannot say more."

Nazira patted his hands and then removed them gently, placing them and her own over his heart. "Thank you, Oban. Take the Deena to her kitchen and prepare tea."

She came out and sat down in the place provided for her. A paraffin lantern was sputtering on the table, giving wan light, while a pair of beeswax candles tried reluctantly to provide more illumination, but instead were simply fox fire orbs tricking the eyes. Nazira motioned to the tepid lighting, and the guard next to Vries stepped into the shadows and returned with a pair of paper lanterns. These he tied off into the shelter's cross beams, and lit them so they provided a soft glowing base light that made a warm, almost comfortable orb of civility around the table. The lights made Nazira depressed, as she saw them as a lie. Nothing was warm or civil. A man would soon die, and the world would be no better for it. Yet the game had to be played.

The dark man was seated across from her, the dark cloak he affected removed and taken away, now dressed in a tunic of cotton and his heavy traveling pants. "Your man in the shadows does not trust me."

Nazira nodded. "He does not. Is that troubling?"

He laughed. "Kakšno igro se igramo moja princeska," he said in a strange tongue.

"And that means?" she replied.

The man shifted in his seat, then looked with sharp eyes at the princess. "I said we play a serious game in the tongue of my birth land."

Nazira smiled, but the smile was a harsh sketch on her face. "I am glad you see this. We indeed play a game. It is one of storytelling. You tell me a story of yourself. If I am satisfied, the dawn will see many things. If I am not, the dawn will not come." She paused. "I knew you in my youth. You are the Darkfather. Killed by my father."

"Perhaps not killed, my princess. Do you suspect I am not the Darkfather?" he asked.

"You are perceptive. Hadhih alsaaeat hi saeat min alhayat, yaqdunaha mithl lufat alnard ealaa tawilat al'aleabi. Do you understand the old language enough to translate?" She asked. "You seem well spoken in many tongues."

"These hours are ones of life, spent like dice rolls at a gaming table." He translated. "hadhih alsaaeat hi saeat min alhayat, yaqdunaha mithl lufat alnard ealaa tawilat al'aleabi." The words rolled from his tongue. "Again from the Heshuan. You are much better educated than when we first met."

She ignored the compliment. "I like using the old tongue. It is so clear and precise. Common has so many borrowed words, precision can be impossible. Now let us speak of why you are alive and following me. And be expansive," she said.

"I will tell the true story then, as much as I can, and I will tell it quickly, as I wish to myself know the number my die rolls, if one or twelve, or somewhere between," he said.

"I was born in the land of the Dagor-Lay, a place off any chart you have, away from any place you can visit. My father was a baron, the Water Master of the Darkfather Mountains. He was a man who controlled the great powers of water, to the betterment of my people. Our water fed many plants, drove wheels that crushed and chopped and created great energy from nothing more than the stuff of the world. And in time, my beloved parents died, and I took a wife and became myself the Baron of Darkfather Mountain, wearing the personal name of Samedi with pride," he said.

He stopped for a second. Nazira felt great sadness roll over her, understood terror and anguish. Then it was gone. It had roared out like the torrents behind them, then ceased as if it had never been. "Continue please," she said.

"My people had an illegal power. It was a thing that was forbidden for our caste and condition. It caused others to desire what we had, criminals, though the people who say which is criminal and which is not would consider us equal in our vainglory. They were the Sudosi, the people who lived in a land of ice and storms, where they had concealed themselves from seeing. The great people we called Sky-borne ignored us because we were pastoralists. They ignored them because they did not know they existed, at least at first," he said.

The man who called himself Darkfather laughed a low, mirthless chuckle. "The Sudosi were jealous of us. They wanted the power we controlled, and the green lands they lived in. They landed on our shores with great ships, marooning themselves once landed, they could not again take to the black seas. Our great general fought them, and I, with my own people formed into horrible legions, fought them as well. In the war, I sent one of my war masters to the council of rulers, the highest of our thinkers and scholars, and demanded they act. They had sat idle in debate rather than springing to defend the realms. They sent my war master back, and he died in delivering the message. They would call on the greatest of our powers, and handed me his yataghan, the weapon your men took from me, the blade of his family, and died in my arms."

Nazira nodded and waved a hand. From the darkness one of her young women, decked in green leather armor and a helm of iron and brass, a great firelock slung on her shoulder, a talwar on her belt, and with the crest of the princess proudly displayed on her back. She had the yataghan in her hand, held in a cloth rag of swaddling.

Nazira accepted the weapon. It was an odd thing. She grasped it and felt like she should throw it down. It was a terrible feeling of dread and loss that spread across her. There was also anger and loathing, distant and brooding. But below that, there was hope. Objects often spoke to Nazira, but this one was quite loud, if dissident.

Visually it was a typical if finely made blade, but it was blacked and disreputable, as if used to stir a fire. Its form was indeed a yataghan, which meant a thinner blade than a talwar, designed for stabbing as well as slashing. It could also be affixed to a pole using the clever locks built into its pommel without making it hard to wield. The cross guard and pommel were brass, while the blade was the finest iron.

She looked at her guard and said, "What of this weapon? How do you find it?"

Her guard was young but fearless, a person who found service the highest honor. Her turnout was immaculate. There was no bend in her, or sense of self, at least when she stood guard. Yet she was surprised to be asked for an opinion by her princess. "It is a mess. I tried to clean it, but it cannot be cleaned. I tried it on the cloth. It cut the cloth. It is not one of our weapons. The maker's mark is in a foreign script, and the number on the pommel is nonsense. The iron is what we call steel—forged in great heat for precise amounts of time. It bends a little but does not bow. Its back guard is clever, a T. He also has an unusual dagger, likewise made from steel. It is clean and has been rusted with blue and fined." She paused, then seemed to conclude what she was saying, leaving something off the end she had intended to give voice to.

"What does rusted with blue mean?" she asked the soldier.

"It is a practice permitted by the El-dari where metal is lightly rusted, a corruption said to remove some of the evil from the metal, making handling it less damaging to the soul. Firelocks of the very faithful have a blue patina from this process. Otherwise, we use a coating process that coats the metals of a weapon with a secondary metal. That is considered a sacrilege for El Dari,"

Nazira looked at the stained weapon in her hands. "Is this rusted with blue?"

"No, my Princess," the soldier said. "It appears damaged by fire, yet is not damaged."

Nazira handed the weapon back to the soldier, who took it away. "Are your people El Dari?" She tapped her hand on the table. "Your other weapon appears to be El Dari prepared."

The man named Darkfather shrugged his shoulders and said, "That has no meaning in my former lands. There are no El Dari, and no reason for El Dari."

"Do you not have gods in this land?" she asked.

He looked at her with no fear. "In my land, God is faith and the gods you fear are seen for what they are. God is not the gods. The gods are not God."

"Then tell me of the fate of this land, the Dagor-Lay. You were a general and fighting to defend your lands. That is a human thing in a human land and does not need gods to happen. You describe a greater land that demands rules and laws be followed, yet your people broke these laws and fought with others who did. That is all understandable," she said.

Tea arrived. Vries prepared two cups of common porcelain and filled each with the drink, then sat one by the man named Samedi, and the other in front of Nazira. She reached out and took a sip of the brown liquid. "Do you have tea?" she asked.

The dark man took his teacup and drank from it. "The sky-borne do not. They have a thicker, sweeter drink, and another drink made from effervescence. They would consider tea bitter and tasteless. My people, though, drink a tea called Bos. You have it in these lands as well, though as a rare drink that is like tea, but not as bracing." He drank another sip. "Yet I travel in tea myself. It is an interesting product. The people of your Halo take much stock of the drink, and it brings the people together in a way that defies violence. I approve of the drink."

Nazira laughed. The man so far was honest, and he was not just honest, but sharing his thoughts on things minor and dire. Time to probe his fear and hate, the things he had so far avoided. "Your people died, did they not, soldier?" She slapped the table to emphasis this point. "They died, and you did not stop it or die yourself."

The dark man put down his cup but did not grow angry or hateful. He looked lost and sad, and he seemed to be digging for a way to express great pain in an honest manner. "I did die. The leaders of my land knew that the center of the Sudosi invasion would be where that sword you saw was. They did not know the true owner would die, or that the sword would pass to me."

He hesitated, but then opened up, "It is called the abomination apocalypse, the misuse of this power I have alluded to. There are rules, limits, standards, and safeties that prevent the power from being used in a manner that would threaten the core of mankind nor allow it to lash out in great offense. Those protections are there for a purpose and should never have been removed. Yet, to my shame, the leaders of my people did this. Every last protection, war, sigil, gate, or barrier was lifted. Yet they needed a target and a target they found. That sword in my hand, in the moment when the two great armies were clashing on the great plains of the Dagor-Lay, they cast forth energies that should never be set forth. They did what no one should have done. And they died when they did so, slipping past punishment."

"Stop!" she said. "Tell me of this power you carry."

"Dwimmer, my princess. It is called Dwimmer," he replied.

She nodded, rolling the word in her head. "Continue."

The Darkfather looked down at the table. "Many died. Many more were changed in ways that no one could have predicted. The great lands of Dagoria, the entire peoples of the Dagor-Lay, the invading Sudosi, suffered fates. Some were turned horrible in mind and body. Some were frozen as if statues, timeless beings of living stones. I was served a worse fate. I and a few others were struck with deeper, invisible wounds. We are known as the forlorn for this among the Sky-borne."

He waved to the heavens and then said, "All I knew was gone. Yet the abomination apocalypse was noticed by the Sky-borne, and they sent Justicari to find someone to punish. I hid from them, first with the mistress of a spring much like this one, then in a school for people who legally manipulated the great powers that destroyed my people. Yet the Justicari did not sleep, or presume I was lost beyond the reach of their great hands of punishment. And to tell the truth, I did not care in the end. I stopped running, and they captured me. I was betrayed by another of the forlorn in exchange for her freedom. And I was cast down, punished. Yet in the last minutes I escaped and came to hide in the lands of the Halo, as you see me now."

Nazira looked into his eyes. It was the truth. Now for another push, she thought. "Then why follow me?" she asked.

The man was almost slumped, a great change from the person of pride they had first captured. He was like a paper balloon with a leak at its seam. It could no longer flow when candle air was applied. Instead, it sagged and dropped to the floor in collapse. "I traveled these islands of the Halo for years. In my mind, a great crime was visited on your people. And the first way of making this crime right is to find the people and the place who may learn of what must be known without superstition and violence. It is difficult. If my pursuers find me, they might send what you call God's fire to kill me and destroy those that know me."

"So I am to believe you are my partisan?" Nazira asked.

"You have many partisans, do you not? You have been at each stop on this procession, collecting followers, commoners, and those of rank. Should I not become a believer in your ability to fix the world, to drag your people from darkness?" he said.

She laughed. "Good. Then be my partisan." She stood. "Hand him the sword." The soldier came again from the dark, and without question handed Darkfather the yataghan. "You are free."

The man stood with the yataghan and walked around the table. Nazira could feel Vries and Bish go on high alert, and indeed, her child started to kick as well as if the small being understood that his or her mother was throwing the dice once again. Violence could break out if the dark man made one wrong move. Yet the move he made was what she expected. No one dives into the lion's den without an idea that there is a treasure behind the bite of the creatures' jaws. Not if they were sane at least. The man kneeled and reversed the blackened yataghan, presenting it to her, his head bowed.

She took the yataghan from him, looked at it, and returned it. "You are now my partisan," she said. "Stand."

He did as ordered, standing. She noticed Bish and Vries had come to the standing of honor, feet together and the back but wide at the front, hands at their side, the thumb of their right hand tucked into the fingers, the right hand with all fingers bent into a fist by the line of their pants. Their shoulders were straight, and they looked forward without expression. The soldier who had brought the sword and the guard that stood at the dark man's back likewise copied the position of honor called out. "Look at those men and women and stand like them."

He looked, then sketched a stance precisely like those of her soldiers. Nazira upended the sword, grasping the pommel at the base, leaving room above her hand. She then released the sword back to him. "I name you Darkfather, surname Samedi, Baron Darkness, arms bearer, councilor, and bondsman of my personal guard."

There was a silence as this all settled in. The candles seemed to return to their feeble state; the lantern returned to sputtering. Nazira felt tired and noted that the orange fingers of dawn were just making their presence known in the sky. "Today is a day of rest. Bring Oban out to escort me back to my quarters. Take the Darkfather in hand to prepare for the tasks ahead."

She then stopped. "You must judge how much of your power to give, but if the people seeking you come, they will find that your friends will not easily let them take you.

Chapter XV

Execution

Ribea al' Jin was screaming at her door. Nazira climbed out of bed and was lost in the darkness. She went and opened the door, and was knocked to the floor by the scholar who covered her with a thick blanket.

There was a sudden burst of light, smoke, and sound.

Nazira felt her body lifted and thrown into the air. The inn room she had been given by the traveling master was in flames, while smoke billowed forth across the smashed building. She pulled the blanket from her head and looked at the burning chaos around her.

In the roiling flames, a man in a soldier's outfit, firelock to his shoulder, approached. From the wreckage, Ribea al' Jin stood, screaming for help, covered in blood and gore, and launched herself at the intruder. The soldier, in Life Guard powder blue, raised his firelock and shot the scholar, but did not kill her. The scholar landed on the man, a piece of craggy wood in her hand, and started to plunge it into his body. He screamed, threw the scholar off, and started to reload his firelock in the flame and haze of the ruined room.

That awoke something inside of Nazira. The soldier was fumbling with his cartridge, coughing, bloody, and eyes wide from the assault. He was bearded, which was wrong as the Life Guard carried no beard, and his uniform was dirty, not with soot, but with green grass stains. Nazira reached about her, surrounded by flames, and grabbed forth a metal rod, retreating on her hands and knees like a crab as the soldier loaded and advanced on her. She came against a solid object and could not retreat any further, so she fumbled with the clumsy metal rod, coming to her knees, and held it before herself. "If you hurt my child, I will kill you!" she screamed.

The man smiled. She recognized him as the son of one of the draughtsmen, who had been described to her as a miner or quarryman. "Princess, a chest of silver if you die in this fire, so your child is the least of it." He was unsure about the firelock's mechanism, but he had it reloaded in a second and put it to Nazira's head.

He was again set upon by the scholar. Ribea al' Jin was such a small creature, that it was amazing to see her fight for her life and the life of Nazira with such terrible violence. The false soldier screamed in pain, then tossed Ribea off him and shot her again.

Nazira screamed, and the man began to again reload the weapon. He fumbled a cartridge, dropping it, then was able to get another into the firelock's chamber. He cocked it, turned it again on Nazira, and aimed it at her head. With a jerk, he pulled the trigger and nothing happened.

It was on half cock, Nazira thought with sudden clarity. The animal did not know how to return the newly loaded firelock to fire and thought the half-lifted hammer was sufficient to activate the weapon. He must have taken it loaded from a Life Guard and not recognized how to reload it once fired. He pulled with brutal terror on the trigger, his face twisting in rage, and the hammer did not fall.

Nazira battled the barrel away, and though heavy with her child, she ran down the barrel of the long weapon and stabbed her metal rod into the man's right eye. He screamed and fell back, dropping the firelock with a howl.

She grabbed up the firelock and saw a second man, one that also had a scraggly beard, with a gap in his teeth and a scar on his face, wearing a disreputable uniform also of the Life Guard. He screeched when seeing the draughtsman's son, mutilated, yelling in pain, and raised his own rifle, but screamed as a sword pushed out through his chest.

Gullen, coming from the smoke, had run him through, back-to-front, with a poniard. She tried to pull the weapon out, but it had pinned the assassin from his back to his groin. He turned and triggered the firelock, but the bullet went wide. Nazira triggered the one she held as well, but also missed in the smoke and flame.

The killers were too interested in their own wounds to further fight, dead or dying, so Nazira grabbed Ribea and dragged her over to the door, motioning for Gullen. They stumbled, dragging the stricken women through the thick haze of a burning common room, and were trapped by fire in the kitchen.

"We die here, my princess." Gullen said, coughing.

"No," Nazira replied. Two great stoves sat in the center of the kitchen, along with burning tables and the bodies of a poor washer who had been killed either by blast or the assassins. Yet in death, the washer showed the way. His hands reached out to a grill next to which cleaning buckets were sat. The grill had been displaced by him.

"Follow me," Nazira said. She reached for the metal grate and pulled it loose with a strength she did not know she had, then levered herself down. "It will slant into the main sewer."

"What if it is too small?" Gullen asked, coughing as the air turned foul.

"It must be big enough for a large child. That is how they clean it," Nazira replied. It was difficult to breathe, and she found her eyes watering in the heat and smoke.

She took Ribea and put her into the water chute, then slipped into the opening herself and started to slide down. Gullen followed her, and the three flew down the chute, unable to control their slide. Indeed, she had not thought of her own condition, the fact that while she was small as a large child, the child she had in her stomach made her quite large. Yet she made it, barely, and with Gullen, pulled Ribea up above the level of the water.

It was dark in the sewer, pitch black in fact, and the sludge water, though flowing, was thick and deep. "Grab my shoulder, do not let go," Nazira said to Ribea, then felt Gullen grab her as well.

Nazira reached her right hand out and oriented herself with the flow of the water. She moved forward, bumped into a wall, reoriented, and went forward. Time, distance, and speed were all difficult to judge. There was an echoic sound quality, dull but reverberating, and the eyes did not seem to collect any light but instead made up fake images to fool the brain. Soon though, she realized by some trick of thought and vision that there were very dim images on the walls of the tunnel. They were numbers and arrows embossed on the ceilings, visible only because they were themselves somewhat florescent despite a lack of illumination. Then the tunnel turned and turned again, and there was a firelight ahead that gave the eyes a purchase in reality. They came out into a chamber where a small group of men, women, and older children sat, all dressed in gray silky-looking coveralls.

"Not more of a step," one of them, a taller woman with her hair shaved off, said. They had a fire which they sat circled, and she was turning a trident spit made of a slender piece of metal.

"Who are you, and why do you assume to give me orders?" Nazira asked.

The whole group laughed. "Well now, sneak thief. Perhaps the orders I give should be listened to because if you step off into the drink, I will have to get your body out, assuming anyone comes asking. The other question, though, would be for me to you. Sneaks always decide that treasure is down here. There is, only it is not yours."

"I am Princess Nazira, mother of the future heir to this Dominion, and you are required to aid me. Or you can turn me in to the killers who tried to end my life and sent me fleeing into this place. Choose wisely though, but you cannot choose inaction," Nazira said.

"Well, Floe," a man snickered, "stepped your foot in the foul that time." The group laughed again.

"So that noise that shook us was something?" One asked.

One of the older women stepped down into the muck and helped Nazira, Ribea and Gullen onto the wooden bridge walks. She sat them down by the fire, then went to a chest and retrieved a large water bladder, underclothes, and the thick waders and tops the rest wore as a sort of uniform. "Migosh, you are all in taffeta and fresnel. Turn away, sots, let me clean and dress these children. One has a babe, even!"

The bladder contained a soft, sudsy, liquid soap made from vegetable fat which the woman applied using a soft brush like she was cleaning-the-char. Several other women got up and helped clean, then rinse Nazira and Gullen.

When they came to Ribea, they recoiled. "How in the world, you need the museif, child."

Nazira revived herself and looked over Ribea. Gunshot, burned, and pierced by deadly missiles, the scholar's remaining awake, let alone alive, was amazing. "You must get us to someone to help her," she said.

"We will," the woman said.

Nazira thanked the woman and felt strong hands lift her. She saw the workers were also lofting Gullen and Ribea up to their shoulders. As a group, they ran along the wooden walkways, crossing the sewer paths twice, and coming out into the sun into the arms of a squad of Life Guards.

"Hold there!" a sergeant yelled

The sewer workers put the three down, and the elder pushed up and said, "You louts, this is the princess."

The sergeant said, "Port arms. Is that you, Princess?"

"Are you loyal?" Nazira asked, regaining her feet with trouble due to the weight of the child.

"Princess," the sergeant said, "of course we are loyal. What could make you think not?"

Nazira shouldered her way through the sewer workers. "Men in your uniform attacked me and burned my room."

"That true, soldier-boy, you lot trying to do for a pregnant woman?" One of the workers said.

The sergeant turned to his squad. "Perkal, message to the General, tell 'em we have skunks in the woodshed. Malkie, off for Regnal Bish and Vries, tell them both we have the princess, alive."

"We need the museif as well," Nazira said, coughing.

The sergeant yelled, "You lot, sewer manes, pick up the princess and her people. We are going for the museif." He turned to the remainder of his squad. "Close order, boys and girls, and if anyone does not give, let them have a taste of the knife."

They walked out into the main street, where chaos reigned. People down the street were fighting the fire with a bucket brigade, while solders, town guards, and others moved wounded and dying to a large tent that had previously been used for the large meals of the procession. Regnal Bish, led by a Life Guard and with two Last Guards, came running up.

"Princess," Bish said, "the inn is burned to the ground and at least eight died."

Nazira again regained her feet and said to the sergeant, "Take Ribea to the museif and guard her as if she was me." She turned to Regnal Bish. "It was the Draughtsman's son," she said.

Bish looked angry beyond any sane measure. "More than that. The Life Guards caught several canaries who are all singing songs, and those songs lead to a woman of interest."

"The assassins were in Life Guard uniforms," Nazira replied.

"The Life Guard are angry. Four of their men and women were killed in a place of low character, and their uniforms taken. General Abd al-Nur is furious. He wants to pledge you his loyalty."

"Send a message to him. He will have his chance, but for now, show me who has killed my people," Nazira commanded.

Regnal Bish drew his small sword and nodded to the Last Guards to take positions around Nazira and Gullen. He then led them to a small tavern where soldiers and guards, armed to the teeth, stood vigil.

Regnal Bish pushed past the guards, but she stopped. "Gullen, you are wounded and dirty. Get yourself clean. I need you fresh."

Gullen did not argue, just turned and left. Nazira looked at a sergeant of the Last Guard and said, "Two of your people with her. Do not let harm come to her."

The Last Guard sergeant nodded and said, "Dahdah, Chaibi, off with you." He then saluted Nazira, and she replied by grasping his shoulder.

Inside of the inn, she stopped short. Regnal Bish was standing before Melinda al-Cinci d' Courtage, who struggled against the grasp of several Vries's men and women. Her face was bruised and smudged with fire powder and dirt, and her brown and green cloak ripped and falling off her shoulder. Vries saluted and said, "We have the rest in the farm, those that did not get burned up."

She turned to Bish. "Do you have everyone?"

Bish nodded. "The plan was to blow the building up with powder, then kill people who came out. Only the powder fired rather than really blew and they had to go in after you. We are not sure who died because the inn is still on fire. A lot of bodies, though, have come out, none can be recognized."

Nazira grabbed a soldier by the wrist who was standing nearby. "The people who tend the sewers, who are they called?"

"Muckers, my princess," the soldier replied. "They have a guild, you know."

Nazira looked around and saw Oban, tears on his face and wraps on his hand. She yelled with joy, "Oban!" She feared he was dead, but her faithful servant appeared harmed, but not seriously. "Thank God," she said.

"My Princess," he was crying, "You lived! It was all this Melinda item, you know. I spat on her!"

"And right, you should. Oban, take what silver we have, and follow this soldier." She pointed to the one who knew about the Muckers. "Give them silver."

"How much, my princess?" Oban asked.

"Make them rich," Nazira said. They nodded and left. Nazira turned to Bish and said, "Now for Melinda."

Nazira walked up to her and grabbed her face with her hands. "Did you think that I was powerless, that you could kill me and my baby?" She looked over her shoulder and said, "Drag out one of the cabal."

Several of her men and women turned, left the inn, and returned, dragging a small man with burned clothing and a leather mask hanging from his neck. Vries grabbed the man's hair and said, "This one set the explosives. Bastard is a bit crispy."

Nazira was surprised. She thought Melinda would use her husband for this job, but this was a low-level servant of the al-Cinci. Then she saw Melinda's face, and it all became clear.

"Who is this? I remember his name as Qui-Cay. Doesn't he cup bear for Pordia al-Cinci?" Nazira said.

It was all striking home for Melinda, whose normal inflated attitude was collapsing like a balloon floating away from its fire. "Release Quick-Jay now," Melinda said with an attempt at self-importance.

"Melinda, you mind yourself now. This is not your place to try and throw me. I remember Quick-Jay though. He has cleaned your bed chamber late at night, from what I hear. Was that what you paid him to blow up my child?" Nazira walked over to one of the guards who stood with a silent presence and pulled a firelock from the quiet woman's belt, pulled the bolt and made sure of the load, then pressed the weapon against Quick-Jay's forehead and pulled the trigger.

The dragoon firelock was small, using a brass shell that held five grams of fire powder to push a five-gram lead bullet, shaped in a conical form, at five hundred meters per second out. The bullet was propelled into the man's head. His eyes bulged in his handsome face, and a splash of blood came pouring out of the hole in his head. The man collapsed in a cloud of black acrid smoke.

Melinda collapsed and started to cry. "You cannot kill me, half-sister, you will pay," she wailed.

Nazira looked at the kicking man as he died. "You tried to kill me and my child. My child, Melinda. Do you understand that this is far past the games you played before?"

Nazira pulled a cartridge from one of the soldier's bandoliers, jacked open the dragoon firelock, and then realized the cartridge from the guard was much larger than the chamber of the weapon she had. Frustrated, she threw the large cartridge to the ground and yelled, "Get me the right one!"

A soldier reached into her belt pouch and pulled out a wooden ammunition carrier, sliding open the latch and pulling the two parts open to reveal twenty cartridges. She selected one of the cylinders and put it into Nazira's hand. "Sorry Princess, the dragons use smaller cartridges than our firelocks do.

Nazira nodded, then held the small item up for Melinda to see. "Such a small object, so precise. I saw them making these once. The bottom part is resin paper in which they put fire powder in, then they dip the base in passion wax. The top part is made of lead. How apostolical it all is. It is almost a sin to carry these, but perhaps only a sin if the Gods would burn us." Nazira motioned to the twitching body of Quick-Jay. "You did that. I merely was the end action of what you caused. Did you think that just because I have never taken a life, that I would not take one to save my child? I watched poor Ribea al' Jin, bloody, burned, and shot, claw away at one of the men you sent to kill me. She is dying, far as I can tell, but you warn me that I should not hurt you?"

Slowly, she inserted the next cartridge into the firelock and closed the bolt mechanism. "So much work to make this device that does such violence. So many pieces to craft. And the most decadent part is what they call a barrel." Nazira nodded to Vries, who walked back into the icehouse and led an older woman in a black cassock out with two Last Guard soldiers at her back.

The woman did not even reach Nazira when she held the dragoon firelock out again and triggered it. There was a crack and a flash from the small weapon and the woman grabbed her neck, falling to the ground on top of her executed com-rade. "We are warned from birth that metal makes the gods angry and that the gods will strike us for our sins if they see us with metal." Nazira snapped her finger, and the soldier pulled another cartridge from her cartridge box and handed it to her. She fit the cartridge into the feed ramp, pulled the bolt, and closed it again. Then she nodded.

A man was literally dragged out, screaming loudly that he was not the cause of the affair and that his son was the guilty one. The soldiers dragging him could barely control the man's struggle as he saw the bodies and Melinda tied up before him. "She did this. It was her. She promised!" the man raved.

"Shut up fool," Melinda screeched. "Do not bargain my life for a minute more breath."

Nazira again looked at the firelock. "Oh, but if we have a better tool than a firelock to settle differences. If we could sit at a table and talk rather than send bits of shell from metal tubes at each other. What is your name, man who took up arms against my unborn child?"

"Tegger, Princess, just Tegger. No family is mine, only my criminal son who crossed you and I in the world. Pity for me. Pity!" he cried.

Nazira readied the firelock and pressed it to the man's head but did not fire. "It is the waiting, is it not? The knowledge that death is a second away, but the hope that it does not come. That is my life, Melinda. You want to be me, to be princess. You think that if you kill me and my child that all the rules and all the politics that put my neck into this noose will fade away like a fey dancer spinning on the waves of a grotto, and the sanctity of the crown will settle to your brow. I understand Tegger here, at this second, as the resistance of a sear, the slippage of a mainspring, the strength of a baleen plant wire is all that keeps him from death. And the mercy would be pulling the trigger. The mercy is not holding the firelock to his head as he sits and listens to an argument he could not comprehend ... that you created with your venality." She withdrew the firelock from Tegger's head.

"So the meek Nazira is revealed, bitch." Melinda spat. "A bloody horror who kills with her own hands. A bringer of death."

"Jalib almawt you call me, yet it is my ability to bring life that is why I am standing here. You should call me jalib alhayaa, one who brings life." She then stopped. "I will prove it. Your husband is spared by me. Your child will live." Nazira turned and shot the man Tegger in the head. The man collapsed silently, but in the distance of the dark night, a scream could be heard.

Melinda struggled some more, then seemed to calm. "Sister, release me and I will protect you from father." She gulped a breath of air, and then said, "Do not shoot me, sister."

Nazira nodded. She handed the firelock back to the soldier who owned it, and then reached over and pulled a kirpan from Vries's belt. With a flash, she cut her sister's throat. Melinda tried to reach her neck, breaking away in the final seconds of her life from the soldier's grip, but Nazira threw the knife down and caught her half-sister's hands in her own. Great rivulets of blood flowed from the neck wound, and Nazira saw that Melinda looked scared.

"Be calm, sister. Think good thoughts so the gods let you into their realm. Be at peace," Nazira said.

Melinda could not speak but instead stared as her life flowed out. There was a pain in Nazira's heart. Killing her half-sister was not what she would have wanted, but her child would never be safe as long as Melinda lived, not after all of this.

Vries stepped from among his men, a somber but determined look on his face. "What should happen to their bodies?" he asked.

Nazira motioned to the door. "This is one of the most beautiful towns in our lands." She paused and wiped a tear from her eyes. "Make this wondrous place their fane. Select one of the great rocks on the tor and dig a hole under it. Then, when they are interred, topple the rock onto them and remember where you have done this. Someday I will return with the al-Cinci kith, if any live past this, and heal the breach that my knife has opened. Your men and women must remain silent to avoid the weight of this act falling on their own families."

Vries nodded. "My princess, there is nothing that would make your soldiers, either bodyguard or the fusiliers, betray your trust. I must say, though, something must be done about Lord Regnal Bish. He is too smart and well informed to not understand what you have done this night."

Nazira sighed. "Bish may not be harmed, that is my order, and remains the order. Bish is coming to our side."

"Understand, my princess. Then we will be off so as to be returned before tomorrow." Vries said, motioning to his men.

Nazira left the inn and saw two men standing in bloody whites, both with the pointed hats of museifi. One stepped forward, bowed deeply, and said, "Princess, you must come with us."

"I will." A number of her bodyguards and soldiers from the Last Guard Battalion closed in, and they all went to the tent where the injured screamed under the care of the healer.

She passed by the wounded, stopping occasionally when she found someone who was aware and touching their feet and saying a few words, then moved on, but at the end of the line of the wounded was Ribea al' Jin.

Nazira stopped short when she saw the scholar. Though swaddled, she was obviously burned and bloody. The Darkfather sat next to her, his hand holding hers. He turned and saw that the princess was watching, got up, and came to her.

Nazira said, "Can she be saved?"

"I am keeping her alive, but it is a losing battle. When a person is burned, they lose liquid from their body. She was also shot twice and cut numerous times. Her blood volume is low and getting worse," he said.

"What does this mean?" she asked.

"There are many things that can be done. I can rebuild her lost blood. I can rebuild her skin and protect her from infection. All that takes time. But one of the bullets struck what you might call the tahaal. I have used my art to repair it. I am not skilled enough to open her body. I am not actually a healer, you see. I learned my skills long ago," the Darkfather said.

"So this tahaal injury?" Nazira asked.

The Darkfather replied, "I will fight it with my art as long as I can, but she needs what we cannot give her." He reached out to her and said, "My princess, she will die."

Nazira left the Darkfather and went to Ribea. The scholar reached up, and the princess grasped her hand. "How many were hurt?" Ribea asked.

"Do not worry, friend. Do not worry. Can I get you anything?" Nazira asked.

"I must give you my book. It was in my room," she said.

"If it was in your room, then it has burned," Nazira said sadly.

"No, it is safe. Tell me it is safe!" Ribea said, crying.

Nazira turned to the Darkfather. "Have someone look for a book in the inn."

"It will be in a metal case," Ribea said.

"In a metal case," Nazira added, and the Darkfather nodded and went to the soldiers at the entrance of the tent. They returned in a few minutes with a burned and disreputable metal box. They looked at it with dread as they set it down. Some acts of bravery go almost unnoticed, but Nazira said to them, "Thank you for carrying this to us. You are not harmed by it, since I believe it contains a book, nothing evil."

Nazira opened the case, and indeed, wrapped in cloth, was a leather-bound book. She took it and sat down next to the scholar, who reached her hand up and caressed the leather cover. "It is the master copy of my best work, the story of all these towns and villages we have passed through, written for you."

Nazira opened it and saw indeed it was a fine work. While just the author's copy and not the finished work of a scribe, it was magnificent in its quality. She read a few pages, then closed it and said, "It is wonderful. The first book in my library. I wish I could give you something in return."

Ribea lay back. "Do not forget the scholars. Your father and grandfather did. Please think of us." She then began to shake, and the Darkfather pushed Nazira away.

It went that way for forty hours. Ribea never woke again, but she fought for her life, and the Darkfather was able to return her to breath and life dozens of times. But in the end, she fell into death and could not be returned. The Darkfather finally stopped trying and said, "If I brought her back, she would not be anything anymore. Better to leave her now for the Gods."

Nazira hugged her baby in her womb and cried.

Chapter XVI

Weaver

U rwa had grown up on the steaming river Rage that flowed from the valley of Vardos in the Northlands of Cycus. She was born twenty-years to the day after the battle of Ventias Crossing—which connected her to an event that defined the region in some people's minds. She thought little of that history though; it did not shear the wool from any sheep, card the wool any finer, or cause the great looms to form cloth that made any better price at the market. Being an al-Ravi from Ventias Rage meant being a weaver, and Urwa had worked since childhood to learn the techniques and arts of her guild. Her family, the sheep that grazed the shores of the rage, the clicking clack of the well-formed looms, and the steam from the vats that made lanolin, creolin, and other valuable products for sale were all that mattered to her.

And if you found a skull or a bit of leather in the pastures, you would take it to a midden reserved for the purpose near the Tea House by the bridge and leave it in case anyone who cares should visit. No one cared though. Since she was a child, no one had visited the midden where the dead slept fitfully in their deadly sleep. It was as if the battle that her elders had told of in hushed tones had never happened. The River Rage flowed down to the sea and the village of Ventias turned the hirsute product of sheep and dromeds into wool blankets, tents, coats, and cowls, to be sold to merchants from the great cities of Cycus and even to traders who would carry it across the seas. Perhaps Urwa would care about the denizens of the middens if their kin cared. They did not, so she did not.

Above the village of Ventias Rage, the valley of the Vardos breached the mountains of Cranga Voltari like a tongue rolling out from the steaming mouth of a dragon. Hot water from the river met the colder air of the plains there and created billowing clouds that sat like pregnant spiders across the land. Urwa had grown up with those billowing clouds. The valley was the lair to the master sailmaker, who called her valley Lizard's Home for the green anoles that lived in the humid, hot clime. No one from Vardos entered the valley, but the apprentices to the sailmaker brought sails down the river on dredge punts dragged by brawny vicuna and returned to their cloud-covered abode with great biers of Denuvani jute and Aletian flax.

As so, Urwa was surprised when her father, Ustis al-Ravi, invited her to dinner on her twenty-third year and beckoned for her to sit down at his table. They ate together with pleasantries when Ustis said, "Urwa, I know you intended to join a frigate and learn to be a sailing master, but I must ask you first to divert for a year, perhaps two at most."

Urwa was a bit shocked. She took a spoon of keena and mutton, then reached for a mug of mineral tea to consider, then said, "I am at the service of Ventias Rage, Father, you know that."

"I know that. And I know that since your elder sister gets my looks and your elder brother gets your mother's herds, that you have every right to make your fortune at the sea and return when you have seen the world to take up what occupation you see as correct. There are no uncles or aunts that have open situations, and you have more than earned your way here." He stopped for a second and drank his tea deep, before motioning for a khadim wajba to refill his cup with tea. The server tonight was Hamza, who was finishing her last year as a khadim wajba and learning how to shepherd. "Hamza, why cook, serve, and clean?" Urwa's father asked.

"I honor the Ventias Rage," Hamza said, pouring the hot tea into Ustis's cup.

Ustis took a drink from his tea and slammed the cup to the table. People around the room stopped to listen. "No, why for real? Not what people say, but why labor so hard?"

Hamza looked embarrassed but said, "I want to marry and have a loom of my own, and a husband or wife to tend a flock."

"And be Hamza al-Ravi d' Ventias Rage." Ustis said. "That is not a bad plan for life, as it has served myself and my wife well. And Hamza has almost earned what you were born into my daughter Urwa. A decade of filling my and other's cups with tea, and we make her our equal on the yallends of winter. Daughter, you wish to take to the sea, but I want, and the other elders hope, to have a sailmaker in town to use or looms for new products. So I want you to visit Lizard's Home, spend a year with the Master of the Valley as her apprentice, then return to our town to impart those skills to Hamza."

Urwa replied, "Father, I am honored, but why not send Hamza?"

"Because the Master of Lizard Home, the Master Sailmaker, is a difficult person. I could not name a price for Hamza to study under her. It was only when I mentioned you, my own daughter, that she gave a price anyone could afford for a year of study. And since you are a journeyman at the looms, I can see the advantage myself now that my anger has faded," her father said.

Hamza stood as if she was stuck in a spindle. "Master Ustis, am I to be a sailmaker?"

Ustis seemed to have forgotten Hamza was there. "I am sorry, Hamza. I have kept this from you, but just this morning, word came of the agreement. You are a good weaver, with your khadim wajba complete, you are a good investment for becoming our sailmaker."

"Thank you, Master. And thank you, Urwa." Hamza said, a tear rolling on her cheek.

Urwa nodded. Her father was a tricky man, and this was a setup to convince her to do what she would prefer not to do. He smiled at her, and she nodded. "Can I wait for the end of the Yallends to go?"

Ustis replied, "That was the day that I arranged for you to go."

On the first day of winter, Urwa sat with her mother packing a wood-framed drover's pack. The pack had nearly twenty kilograms of silver in lanolin jars made from alder, her best woolens, a leather work vest, stockings, a blanket, and her personals. Mother provided her with a nice woven cap, a belt of leather with tool holders, a jack knife made from obsidian, and both winter and wefting mittens that allowed her fingers to be exposed for precise work. Her father bundled himself for the wet cold that had descended on the village, ducked his head into her room, and nodded. It was time for her to go.

They left the hastings and walked down into the Dale of Rage, where the ships were quartered in the early winter. It was early, so the shepherds relaxed by their small peat fires, brewing tea. Their dromeds, dogs, and small tents of canvas dotted the rolling hills, while the sheep had gathered in clumps and not yet separated for the morning graze. The sun tried to break through the clouds, but a rain was falling, cold and spitting, giving promise of a day that would be dark.

Despite the gloom, as they passed the midden, the sun glinted off of skulls that the rain had uncovered, staring with empty eye orbits from the brown soil and dead grass. Urwa looked out of the corner of her eye, but her father caught her scared fascination with the place of death. "You have always feared them," he said.

"I have not," she replied. Her voice cracked, and she cursed to herself. "What is there to be scared of?"

"I was five when the Haseemi and the Cinci clashed here. I saw the fields of the Dale covered by bodies and watched as the Haseemi fled and the Cinci turned to the capital to support the invaders. My mother found your aunt and I hiding in a rick. It was a fearsome thing to know history was made right where you lived." her father explained. "You can learn from history."

"How to make a sail?" Urwa asked.

"Why did the Cinci fight the Haseemi here? Why did the Cinci betray the Guisarmes? Or perhaps is that there were men and women who thought they would win a battle who died far from their homes and now sit alone, unheralded in our dale." He walked on for a bit then said, "All of our plans for the new wing to the hastings, to share our breeding dromeds with the Chelties, to start a look for sails, they all fall to nothing if the land is unsettled by war and invasion. All the dead of the lower dale, they all had plans. Now they are bleached skulls in a midden of mud."

They walked on in silence after that.

The approach to Lizard's Home was foreboding, a terrible visage of some sort of nature-made hell. Hot springs bubbled in the rocks next to the narrow path that led from the Dale of Ventias to the fens along the north road. Valley was a relative term at the start of the trail; the fens were a wide, sluggish point where the river Rage met a series of boiling streams that trickled out of the rocky highlands and formed a swampy, stygian chiaroscuro of fetid, stinking life. The villagers of Ventias Rage avoided the fens at the mouth of the valley. Urwa herself had only been this far down the north road once.

The trail had narrowed to a single cart-track when they met a man in a white linen shirt and loose-lined pants. The man said, "Are you Ustis al-Rava?"

"And you are the senior apprentice to Kasimira al-Regeri?" Urwa's father said.

The man bowed in an insolent manner. "Here to make the sale, odd as it is, of a sack of silver for your daughter."

"She has the silver," Ustis said.

"Then I will take her to the master." The man bowed again, and said, "Dame weaver, I am Saqib, apprentice to Kashmir al-Regeri. And I will be your guide. Shall we leave your father behind?"

"Saqib," Ustis said.

"Yes, squire of the sheep and weavings?" the man named Saqib replied.

"If my daughter gives ill word, then you will learn the masters of Ventias Rage have long arms," her father said.

Saqib scoffed. "The master has ordered your precious daughter be placed in cotton batting. I believe not even the flies will bite her, given the master's ill humor and stern words on the subject."

"Just so you know," her father said. He then turned and touched Urwa's cheek. "You have made the right choice, and you can take to the sea with my blessing and support when this is over."

She nodded and hugged her father, and then watched as she walked off into the steamy fog.

"Do you have something better than the woolens?" her guide said asked.

She turned toward him. "I do not, Master."

"My name, as I said, is Saqib, and I am merely the senior apprentice. You call me Saqib. Only the master is master." He was taller than her, muscular, with black, long hair and a handsome, bright face. He spoke Eurabaa with a clipped accent as if he came from Kemeya or one of the trailing islands of the Cyclonidees. His stance was arrogant, superior, and dismissive, as if she was an inconvenience.

"I am sorry Apprentice Saqib," Urwa said. "I have a shift and a thawb for night wear."

"Do not call me apprentice and do not say sorry. You are sorry to the master, not fellow apprentices. Let us get you attired. Pull out your thawb and strip down." Saqib set his pack on the side of the trail, rested against a tree branch, and opened it up. Urwa likewise dropped her pack next to his and took out her white thawb.

"Give it here," he said. She handed it to him and saw that he had taken a set of clippers and a sewing kit from his pack. Using the clippers like sheers, he removed the lower half of the cloth from the garment, then cut off both arms and material from the neck. He then began to neatly and with expertise sew in a stitching to make the cut lines look like intentional art of a seem-worker. As he worked against his pack, he looked at her and said, "Get out of your clothing before you boil like a river-dad."

She nodded. Feeling the heat from her woolens, she was happy to strip them away. When she was naked, he took her woolens, rolled them tight into a carry-roll, passed a jute rope through them, and then fixed them to his pack. He then held the light summer dress he had made from her thawb to her body, took it back, and started to make alterations.

She stood before without clothing and noted there was no touch of cold. The valley mouth was a blast of hot, wet air that did not require clothing, even now, in the eve of winter. Saqib first took a linen cloth from his pack and passed it to her. It was clean and freshly laundered, a sublica like many sailors wore. When she saw it properly wrapped, he took the thawb, now cut as a tunic, and lowered it onto her over upthrust hands. "Take out a light jacket if you have one. Get used to putting on and taking of clothing in the valley."

When she was dressed, he reached again into his pack and handed her a bag of water. "Drink it all," he said.

"A whole liter?" she asked.

"Until you know the valley, you drink like it is the desert. Drink more than you think is good for you. The heat fools you, as does the wet air. I will get you soda and sugar to mix with the water as well." Saqib said.

"My first lesson," Urwa said dryly. She looked at her wool clothing hanging from Saqib's pack and wondered when she would get them back. The valley was wet and hot even in this, the depth of winter. She imagined it ten times as hot in the summer. It seemed she was stepping into a land of make believe.

"Just so," Saqib replied. "Now drink the water while I teach you the rest of your lesson." He started to repack his bundle while she slowly consumed the water in the bottle. "You master is Kasimira al-Regeri. She became head of the Sailmaker's guild in the time of the first Dominar, Nawaz. When Abelard took his place as Dominar, our master agreed to retreat to this valley. We make sails for the fleet, and we do not make trouble. Do you understand this? You may be our paid princess, but you do not make trouble."

Urwa nodded. "I understand." She swung her pack laden with silver onto her back. The man was oddly angry for merely being a guide, like he had been personally wronged somehow. He looked at her as he worked on his pack and she said, "I appreciate your lessons."

Saqib looked up at her, shook his head, then finished rigging his pack. When it was tied down, he tested its weight and made a few changes to its balance. "The master partners with some odd people, so be careful. Listen and watch and you will be ok. She has assigned you to me as a project. I will protect you." He threw his pack onto his back and reached out to her. Urwa was confused for a second, then realized he wanted the empty water bottle. She handed it back, and he attached it to his belt. "Watch and listen as we travel into the valley."

The winter sky was gray as they started up the path. It followed a steaming river, slowly climbing, but not as fast as the valley walls. As she followed the path, Urwa noted that there was snow falling between hot streams, but the watercourses remained free from ice. The valley and its riot of life and color shocked Urwa, especially the plants that were out of season thriving in the verges of the rivers. May apples and bleeding hearts sprang forth in the understory of the river, flowers that had died back with the grip of cold weather around her home village. Exotic flowers, supporting bugs and flies that she had never seen before, even in the grip of summer. It all gave the valley a primeval feeling of a world held back in time. Little bergamot trees, twisted cranberry bushes, summer flukes, and jonnies-all-blue-and-red sprang forth in their glory, completely ignorant that they were sustained by a boiling cauldron of water cascading past them or that the gray sky above concealed a cold maelstrom.

As they passed a hammock in the climbing drover-road, they passed a wooden, covered cart with big hoop-wheels by a simmering fire, some sort of temporary wayside camp. Two people in breach clouts and small hats stepped out from behind cart and blocked the path. "Saqib," one said.

"Ctailor," Saqib acknowledged. "New apprentice," he said, motioning at Urwa. "The Master chose her special from the weavers at Ventias Rage."

The man named Ctailor, bulky with muscles, holding a short glaive, growled, "My father's father fell at the battle of the crossing."

Urwa grew scared. The man's words and his demeanor were forceful and not very respectful, but she realized this was history coming back to haunt her. She hissed, "Haseemi, here?"

Saqib shook his head. "Ctailor, the new apprentice barely knows what happened at Rage Crossing." He spit on the ground and covered the gobbet with soil using his boot. "My boss is liable to sew you a shroud if you try at the panky with one of her apprentices."

The other guard was a woman of menacing aspect, likewise holding a glaive and equipped with a bow. She put her hand on her partner's shoulder and said, "None of that Ctailor, your lesson was learned, or was it?"

"Tried," the man said. "If you wanted, little girl, the Rage is a hot river.

"Failed," the woman replied. "Girl, you villagers are not loved by us Haseemi. Try not to walk alone."

Saqib took Urwa by the arm and led her on the climbing road away from the encampment. "Haseemi," he said. "You are correct, they serve the master."

"The Haseemi were the warriors of the Guisarmes," Urwa said, a statement of fact. "What are they doing here?" She hurried up the cart path and a hundred meters on she said, "They all fell at the battle of the crossing.

Saqib replied, "They excel at being worthless. Most died, from what the Master says. They died on Kemeyan lances and the swords of the Cinci. and they were hunted through the fens for days. Now the last Haseemi hide under the protection of the master. They still cleave to their history, worry it like gristle from a badly cooked lamb. And they claim a day comes when they will earn back their patrimony."

"Are you Haseemi?" Urwas innocently asked.

"I am a Guisarme bastard, but learn not to ask that sort of question here. No one comes to the swamps because they had a good place before Master noticed them. No one but you, it seems." Saqib replied.

"Why does the master permit people like the Haseemi here?" Urwa asked.

Saqib laughed. "You misunderstand the master. Have you ever met someone who collected carvings or little wooden spoons?"

The climb was growing tiring. Out of breath, Urwa said, "Of course."

"The master collects people like someone would collect unique spoons. You cannot own people, that is slavery, so she collects people who have nowhere else to go ... like me," Saqib said.

Urwa paused. "You do not like the master?"

"No," he said, pulling out a pair of one-liter water bottles from his belt and passing one over to her. "She is a good teacher, and has a plan for each thing she does, but I do not like her. She knows it. That is why she sends me to collect new apprentices." He paused and added, "I do not look for silver or fame from the master. Just day by day."

Urwa drank from the new bottle. "I am sorry."

Saqib shrugged. "Like I said, you are not a collectable spoon. You are from the weavers' guild, old family, long lines and connections, bags of silver. The Dominar leaves her be because she makes sails. I do not understand it all, no one here does, but as I said, this is a lesson, and the master is the one who is your protector. I would not forget it."

The life in the valley was amazing. Frogs sat in the broad steamy daylight as if no heron or snake was bold enough to take them while they basked. They passed by tended ponds where Haseemi toiled in their discolored waters. There were fish ponds filled with small fish that nipped at the top of fetid green water and other ponds with great floating leaves and shaking flowers on red stalks. Two women were clearing a small lake with a clothes net, gathering a harvest of fish into a big writhing mass of life destined for the garum barrels. Their heads were hidden by hats made of reeds, but when they looked up, sinister eyes stared with barely concealed malice at Urwa as if they blamed her for their lives in this magical land. The beautiful valley seemed to be scarred by some deep hate that infected everyone in it, or so Urwa thought.

Dragonflies and butterflies flitted in the broken light of the towering Fenwood trees performing charming dances, while in the evening fireflies and fenwisps put on an enchanting light show of blinking lights as they walked. Mews screamed calls from the trees and occasionally leaped into flight to catch one of the bright dancing insects, returning to their perches to consume their catches. And then through the mist, Urwa saw Master Kasimira sitting on a stone, working a bit of cloth. She looked up and said, "Thank you for bringing the village apprentice to me, Saqib," then motioned to her side, and Saqib lowered his eyes and stepped to his appointed spot. "Come up child, let us meet you." Urwa did as ordered.

"You have met my eldest apprentice, and have heard his whines, have you my dear?" Kasimra said. She was old, with crottled hands and rheumy eyes that were watery, reflecting the chiaroscuro of the jungle overgrowth. She affected a white shift cut shorter than current fashion, leather boots that were mucky from wading, and a tool belt of canvas filled with tools.

"He has only taught me as is proper," Urwa said.

The woman scoffed. "He finds concealment here from his deeds of his youth. I allow him certain extravagances because he is quite bright. He hates me, but he won't leave because the day comes when he will be a master in his own right of this valley. The dwimmer of the sheets says he will be a sailmaker. If he leaves, only blank canvas stretching out kilometers into the future exists," she said. "Your village brings silver to me, does it not?"

"My village contributed the sum you requested to see me trained," Urwa said with pride.

"To make you and your village a boundary of sails?" the master replied.

Urwa nodded. "That is the goal. There is a drought of good sheets for the expanding fleets of the Dominar. We will not be a competition with the valley."

Master Kasimira was a big woman but agile on her feet. "Making sails is magic, and you will not forget that. If you ever wish to leave, do so. I do not hold you, but I keep the silver. Your apprenticeship begins immediately. Saqib, take her to the sleeping room of the chantry and put her to work so she learns how to handle the heat."

The chantry was the central building along a wide spot in the river below the hot pools and upper falls, and the lower valley run. The building had five large weaving rooms, a dozen storage rooms, ten apprentice rooms, a kitchen, and a dining space. The two journeymen and the master had their own houses, all made from masonry. Urwa was given a room for older apprentices that was adjacent to the dormitories, but was private and ate with the journeyman and senior apprentices. Though a senior apprentice, Saqib assigned her the daily assignments and spent most of the time training her.

At first Urwa cleaned. She swept the chantry, carried night buckets, sluiced the showers, pulled lint from clappers. Then she began to separate fibers, do rough grading, spindle and pull the hard Denuvani jute and the strong, supple reed-wage of their own fetid jungle; and then, finally, she was assigned to make string, yardage, and rue-matts after a year of study and practice. She was following the path of an apprentice but far faster than any apprentice would go. Her own skills as a near master weaver were not enough to see her catapulted to journeyman training, but they were appreciated as she proved to know the lesser skills.

It was never easy. The Haseemi were threatening and contemptuous of the students, and she found that they would take advantage of her if they had the chance. The apprentices never traveled alone into the village or the woods, lest a Haseemi would find them alone and easy prey for their cruel games. Only Saqib seemed to have the freedom to mingle with them.

The village that surrounded the chantry and its work-shops was made from stone houses which, despite the oncoming winter, were snug and warm, housing Haseemi families—sometimes four or more, in four or five rooms. Each night the Haseemi brewed red tea on the peat stove set on small wooden decks overlooking the surrounding fens. It gave the village a smell of medical esters in the air. When the tea was finished and the fires put out, Urwa could see wisps in the forests, dressed in their blue-gold winter colors, glowing as they played their endless games through the heat-blasted landscape. Occasionally she would hear the Haseemi villagers gather to sing songs of war and betrayal, with young children encouraged to solo the stanzas of betrayal with ethereal-pitched voices. The songs sounded like magical enchantments until Urwa followed the words of the children in her head. Then she realized they were about the loss of honor, bodies floating in the steaming river, and the eternal betrayal of the order of Haseemi. Many songs predicted the return of the Haseemi to power, if only they could remain steely in their determination.

The master kept two journeymen in Lizard's Home; D'casio, a woman from Groenlandia, and an older man named Aabid, but D'casio left nearly immediately. When Journeyman D'casio left, Saqib became one of the two journeymen himself, despite resisting the title and proclaiming his hatred for the master. Something had happened with D'casio that had made the master furious, but no one spoke of it. There was no masterwork by the former journeyman, no dissertation or design ceremony where she was granted her robes. She left, and became a subject never broached.

Urwa was constantly enchanted by the valley of the sail-makers, despite the dangers of the people and the jungles, and worked diligently on her studies of thread and cloth.

Often she sat in the steamy night and watched the lights of bugs and mug-fishers compete in the verdant rain forest. Knowing her time was limited, she would study the small library of books on sailing and sail craft on the portico steps of the chantry. Sometimes the younger apprentices joined her, and she often ended up teaching small classes of her own on classical weaving and the fiber arts. Despite the sinister Haseemi, nights with the apprentices were fun and removed much of the stress from her rushed studies.

Kasimira herself was brilliant in a muddled way. She required all the apprentices learn how to dye, stretch, strengthen, composite, and cut the jute for sails, taking the reeds from their natural state to the wefted thread used to make sails. Though the master said they were not seamers or spinners and had their own unique techniques, she also made each apprentice learn at least a little about the process by which a plant or animal fiber became a useful product, be it a bag, a sack, a thawb, a camisole, or even a sail, and Urwa had to prove she mastered these areas. If Urwa had not previously mastered these skills, it was likely that Kasimira would never have allowed her to touch a sail, even if well paid in silver.

Urwa was working on a weaving in the workroom of her beloved chantry when one of the Haseemi villagers entered and said, "The master wishes to have you join her at the great pools." It was odd for a Haseemi to be in the chantry, but they did carry messages for the master from time to time. Her breath caught in her mouth and she turned her face away to hide her fear at the summons, for she had never been summoned to the pools.

In the hand of the Haseemi was an insulated pot of tea and two teacups. She nodded at the Haseemi and put away her weavings, then he led her on the path out of the village to the great pools above.

She made her way up the boardwalks, across the middle bridge, to the taller of the two falls where a stairway had been cut into the living rock, and then out onto a flat in the side of the notch between the two hills that defined the valley. The great pools, steaming with scalding water, were always overflowing across a dam of granite blocks and into a natural channel that formed the valley's stream. While there were smaller springs, the two pools at the top of the valley had been dammed off to control the flow of water and provide a permanent source of hot water before it ran through the valley. And there sat Master Kasimira, sipping her tea and looking at the splash of falling evening light.

The progressing winter had slowed the riot of color and life in the hot fen, but it did not completely erase it, just changed its tenor. The color of the butterflies was replaced by their great cocoons hanging from the branches of sturdy banyans. The frogs slowly hid from the cold—restricting themselves to the hotter lagoons, but were replaced by mudpuppies who trilled in the evening air from atop tree stumps and large rocks. The glow of the fireflies faded as cold ended their dances, but the fenwisps took on different colors as if to compensate for the loss.

Urwa stopped at a respectful distance, but the master said, "There is no time. Come sit by me, child."

Urwa did as she was told and started to cry. She feared the old master and her strange servants.

"Why are you crying?" the Master asked.

"It is nothing, Master. I am overcome by the heat," she replied.

The old woman looked at her and said, "Well, stop it, dear. I am dying, entering my last years, perhaps the last one.

Simple as that. And I have failed in my task of creating this valley to be one of the trade of cloth. My chosen successor left. The Dominar is at the gates waiting for my last breath. Every apprentice who has the skill will be made master, perhaps before your short time with us is over." She nodded to the Haseemi holding the teapot, who poured two cups of tea, passing one to the master, and one to Urwa. In the year since she had arrived, it had gone from the cold of winter to spring, to fetid summer, to luxurious fall, and now it was again cold in the valley despite their bubbling heat. Urwa reached for the tea and let it warm her hands.

The Haseemi placed the billy down and left. Master Kasimira stared at the retreating man with a look of displeasure in her eyes. When he was gone from sight, she turned back to Urwa and erased a worried look in her eye. "The Dominar is cleaning up things that were left broken, discarding torn cloth that nimble hands cannot mend. It is not really the Dominar, but the hands behind him which are moving to consolidate power." She paused to consume the tea, then asked, "do you understand?"

"I do not know politics, just the weaving and the sails," Urwa said.

The master nodded. "I am a torn cloth." She looked back to where the Haseemi had retreated and then lowered her head into her hands and spoke to the ground. "There will be war. I tried to make a place where time stopped, but my past has arrived and there are tears in my sheets that cannot be repaired anymore. We will be dragged away by the winds of time, and I cannot change those winds, only harness them in the sails I make," she said. "You are a sail, you must comprehend."

"I do not understand, Master," Urwa said.

"You are now a journeyman alongside Saqib, and on my death, I have named you both, along with, Aabid, Balock, and D'casio masters, even if you return to your village before my passing." She handed a swatch from her pocket to Urwa. On it was a needlepoint of a man with a beard and a dark face. The image struck fear into her.

Urwa took the cloth and looked at it. The image was scary, not warm like most needle points. It would grace no home in a frame. "Who is it, Master?" she asked.

"A face you are to recognize, my new journeyman, if it ever presents itself to you. And a story as well," Kashmir said. "Sit child. Take more tea."

Urwa did as she was told. There was a strange, mystic feeling in the clearing of the pools, and much of what the master was saying did not hold much sense. Her voice lacked the normal aggressive vim, and she was distracted by small sounds and movements in the verge. An anole sprang forth, leaping across branches, causing the master to look into the sky and watch its antics.

The master returned her gaze to Urwa. "My master was more than the lead sailmaker to the Guisarmes. She had special powers over the sails, the ability to use them to divine truth and tell the future. She claimed that weaving sails was magic. Magic that could predict the future, if you looked closely enough at the weaves you made. I never believed her, but she worked hard and made the best sails in the land. Superstition was something I think people overlooked in her."

The master looked at Urwa, perhaps expecting a response. When Urwa gave none, she drank deep of her tea and continued. "One day she called to me and said she saw fire in her sails, a great conflagration that would break the world. God's fire, she claimed, would kill most of the great families, and the rest would die in an invasion from foreign shores. She tried to tell the Guisarmes, but she was not believed." Kasimira said. "At night she would say the fires were coming, and that no one would listen.

Urwa said nothing but stared at the back of her master as she sat in thought. The master spoke mystically about her sails, but many masters found magic in the arts. They sat in silence, suljaji flowing past suljaji, each expecting the other to speak. Finally, Urwa said, "Ealim jalil, Master of Sail, you speak past where I can say."

Master Kasimira put her hand out and said, "The art of sailmaking is an art of precision, but also an art of chance; no weave is perfect. My old master, she had the eye. It is called in the old tongue, 'shiewadha.' The art of divination by reading the stitchings of cloth."

"Dajala?" Urwa said in a low voice.

The master looked away, then turned back to Urwa. "No, that is the old word for trickery and is not the right word at all. There was a man, a dark man, who believed the practice of reading the sails. He spoke with my master and believed her when no one else would. The dark man in that picture called it dwimmer, and I heard him say it. He said it was simple, for some, to understand, and impossible for others. Call it what you want, my new journeyman, but the sheets speak, and if you can read them, as my master could, then you can predict large things from small fragments of cloth. That is why sailmakers were known for divinations in the times of the old. And that is why the Dominars came for her in the night, like they came for so many in their fight to control our lands. My master disappeared. Never to be seen again. She was taken to a place where I would have been taken, that is said to be a place of horror, and if not for Nawaz and their need of sails, then I would have gone there as well. There was great violence settled on us, and my master predicted that our lands would suffer by looking at the magic of the cloth."

"Our lands?" Urwa asked.

"You, I, the Haseemi, we are all 'ahl al'ard, and we are all the victims of a violence that we cannot understand, and which I tried to create a hiding place from. Were the Guisarmes our true rulers? The Guisarmes were destroyed on the shores of time, and the rest of us cast loose into the sea tides, trying to make our way home. So many died, so many disappeared for the Dominion that is not ours, but the evil of others. I was sitting at my work when they took my master, and she did not return to us. She died, the cloth says this, and she died hard." The master looked into the hidden sky with a locked jaw.

A wind whipped up, and clouds started to dapple, opening and closing to the setting sun. "Afterward, a dark man came back to me, the one in the needlepoint, and said that I would have the same power as my master and that I would see a time when the world was changing, and that likely the same forces that took my master would take me. I did not believe him. He was a demon, and merely making a threat to me to meddle in my plans to live in exile." She stopped. "Yet, now I see the signs in the cloth. I see my end, and the end of everything, if the sky falls on us. It is driving me mad."

"I still do not understand, Master," she said. "Perhaps losing Journeyman D'casio was too much for you. Many people have breaks with their life and need to find solace and their way back to a calm mind."

"When you work on your sails tomorrow, look for messages in them. Look for an augury that says the world will be aflame. Do it for me," the master said.

"I am close to ending my time here, Master," Urwa said, standing up. "If I see anything in the sheets though, I will tell you."

When she returned to the chantry, she found Saqib and asked him about the strange conversation. "Do you believe this?"

Saqib looked up from his loom. The apprentices still followed their orders in making cloth and learning, but the journeymen were now exclusively tasked with making sails. "There was a man in my village who could tell the weather by the shape of the clouds. He was good at this, but I never could figure if he was a charlatan or a true sage. Who really cares what the weavings say to the master, as long as in the end, she makes us masters as well, and leaves us to our freedom."

One day she was proofing a great sail of jute canvas when the Master approached her. "Read the sail, Daughter," she said.

"I cannot, Master," Urwa replied. She never read anything.

The master reached across Urwa and grabbed a pot of pigment. Using a brush from her vest, she drew a circle of black ink onto the sail. "What is in the circle?"

"The warp has doubled on the weft," Urwa said. She then paused. "It does not mean the sail is faulty. It may even be stronger."

Urwa touched his hand. "You do not believe in this dwimmer!"

Saqib nodded. "Dwimmer is nonsense. The sails tell us nothing. Yet I, like you, just want to learn the craft. Her nonsense is nothing compared to her skill and what we can learn. Lie to her, say the waters are calm."

Aabid came in with the Haseemi Ctailor. They were dressed in canvas armor and held glaives in their hands. Saqib stood from his loom and locked the shuttle. Aabid handed him armor, and Saqib took up a pruning hook from behind his loom. Urwa stopped and looked at the journeyman and understood why the master was having such feelings of abandonment. They were leaving for war.

"Saqib, what are you and Aabid doing?" Urwa asked.

"Shut up, little girl," Ctailor said with a growl.

Aabid clenched his fists, but Saqib made a hand motion and they relaxed. He approached Urwa and said, "You haven't paid attention to anything in the year you have been here. You deserve the master. There is unrest in the cities. The Cinci are marching to take the capital rather than have a weak princess, her bastard offspring, or the old Dominar stay seated on the throne. Coming down from Courtage, all proud under banners of gold."

"And what do you care?" Urwa asked. "I just heard the fear of an old master who thinks her life's work is lost because her journeymen left. She will make you a master before the yallends of winter. What can you gain by marching to war with the Haseemi, if there is even a war to be had?"

Ctailor grabbed Urwa and threw her down. "Everything, you khade forsaken harpy. My grandfather died at the battle of the bridge. My father was a child. We are the last loyal warriors of the Guisarmes. The Cinci are coming down from Courtage to take the capital. If we stop them and take it ourselves, then glory for us all!"

He tried to kick Urwa, but Saqib stepped in his way. "None of that."

Ctailor grimaced and turned around, "You come along now or there will be no silver for you." He then pushed Aabid out of the room.

Saqib helped Urwa up. "You will be safe in the chantry."

"You are going with those idiots to get a sack of silver?" Urwa asked.

He backed away from her. "If I remember, you came to this valley with a sack of silver for a year of training. You are not just Urwa, but Urwa al-Ravi, born into a rich kith who has watched the world flow by without leaving their secure little glen with all their fat sheep in a score of decades. What am I? Saqib who has no kith. Saqib d' Votari if someone is being polite and thinks this steam filled valley matters. But you said yourself, the master is predicting the future based on what a sail looks like. You have not heard it, but it has been years since she has been failing like this. While you ignore the signs outside of the valley and play with cloth looms, the world around us is changing, and people like me need to reach out and grab the silver that is offered to us."

"Bleached skulls!" Urwa yelled. "I was surprised the Haseemi were so close because they have, in forty-and-more-years, never sought out their dead that stared out at me from our midden through my childhood. Ctailor's grandfather stands guard on a pile of bones and suddenly he cares and wants to avenge a man he has never known and whose remains he never sought out."

"Urwa, stay here, but spare me the lectures." He said, then turned to leave with the gathering of the Haseemi.

That night Urwa watched with the Master as the Haseemi went to war. Except for the pregnant, the old, the young, and the impossibly frail, all the people of the valley were lining up and handing out pole arms made from gardening tools and armor sewn from working vests. Balock and a few of the younger apprentices who were not going sat on the stoop of the chantry and watched, eating from a bowl of keena and steam-fired clams below them. The Master had made the tea for both of them, a bitter tisane of burdock, fancy yew, wilting yen, and coolreidze. It was dreggy and not well made—the master had no skill at making her own tea and was at a loss without her servants. Still, there was nothing better, and before long they would all be chewing burdock for want of better provender.

"They walk into death," the master said.

Urwa looked at her and shivered.

"Go look at your sails now." Master Kasimira said. "Is there no such thing as 'shiewadha?'"

Urwa knew what she wanted to hear, what Saqib said she should say, but she could not embrace the dreadful belief in the voice of the fabrics. When the master went to bed, she took to the looms in the loom room of the chantry and looked at the stretched fabric. There were flames in them. She could finally see them, but they were not from the fabric. She stepped onto the verge where no Haseemi made red tea on peat fires and even the wisps seemed subdued, and she saw a glow on the horizon. Something was burning in the glens below the valley concealed by the mists.

CHAPTER XVII

Stepmother of the Dominar

Nazira woke with a warm, snuggling body next to her. It was her son. She started to sit up and felt an arching pain through her body. Then she looked over and saw Bish sitting in a chair next to her bed. "Is this your moment?" she asked.

"We do not kill mothers right after they birth their children. You have time, some at least," he said. He then reached over and touched her baby. "He has a name, Jamil al-Youseffi d' Tariq."

"Al-Youseffi d' Tariq," she said. "Father's mother's line and title."

"A clever piece of work, attaching the young prince to the family of your grandmother," Bish opined laconically.

Nazira held up her hand. "My father's mother, please. I have no wish to be associated with my relatives from Tariq."

"And yet, perhaps you should think twice about this attitude. Dame Griselda al-Youseffi d' Tariq waits to take the child to a wet nurse, and she is a formidable woman of her own mind," Bish said.

Nazira sat up and saw that Gullen, the former dungeon master and now protector for the princess, sat in the corner, unwilling to leave the shadows. "May I have water, Gullen?"

Gullen stood up and walked to the water barrel. She seemed, if anything, smaller in the light of day, her dark hair and dark complexion part of her furtive and forgettable demeanor as much as her leg brace. She was veiled, and her only notable ornamentation was a Carver Dragoon firelock she had acquired from someplace or other, hanging across her chest on a bandolier of shells. Such an expensive and ostentatious weapon for a little shell of a person who lived to deflect notice. From the side of the barrel, she took a teapot, gleaming in the waning light of day that streamed from the windows, and plunged it into the barrel, filling it to the top. She then took a large tea service glass and brought the tea pot and glass to Nazira. She handed Nazira the glass, then filled it up from the pot.

Nazira drank the water down, then handed the cup back to Gullen. "Let Dame Griselda in," she finally said.

Bish stood up. "Are you ready, Princess? What will transpire, I cannot interfere with."

"I fully understand what will transpire. Let the old woman in." Nazira set her strength of will into place because Griselda was herself a strong will, and much older and wiser in theory.

Nazira had technically known Griselda her whole life, in that they were often in the same room together, but Griselda had never had much to say to her, and Nazira definitely had nothing to say to the old woman. Grandmother she may be, but she had never cared to show any interest in the girl who her husband had declared would be the route for the heir of the Dominion.

Griselda, as the eldest and ranking al-Youseffi, wife of the original and first Dominar of Cycus, was by her own loud commentary the first subject in the whole realm of the Cyclonidees. And to show this she traveled in great retinue, followed by her daughters, granddaughters, and a range of cowering sycophants who seemed only present to whip up a constant chorus of aggrieved muttering in support of whatever the dame al-Youseffi directed them.

Griselda was seated in a chair that had a clever arrangement of tires like a haggler's cart, but instead of an egg vendor pushing the device, it was Griselda's daughter Anamita, and Anamita's own daughter Vella. Both looked exhausted; Nazira's birth room was high in the north tower and the ramps that led to it were 300 or 400 meters long and quite steep in parts. Around the cart was a coterie of guards, lawyers, bards, medics, and others, at least twenty strong. Nazira's room was spacious, taking up the entire floor of the tower, but it suddenly closed in with the number of followers filing in.

However, despite the mass of humanity filling her birth room, it was the occupant of the wheeled cart that held everyone's attention. Griselda al-Youseffi d' Tariq held herself long-pole-pine straight, like a great stately tree rather than an aging woman. Her eyes were like firelocks, swinging to cover her target with deadly and intense purpose. Only Gullen and Bish seemed to be immune to the pan of her gaze, not that she did not try to use her powers on them. For one tableau second, she caught and held Gullen in her vision. Gullen made an obscure and obscene hand gesture while pretending to brush her hair from her face. Bish, when favored with Griselda's gaze, took a sliver of wood and picked his teeth.

Griselda held her whip stick in her hand. When Anamita and Vella parked her cart next to Nazira's bed, they tried to primp her head pillow and lap blanket, but she lashed out with several brisk whips, expertly aimed at her daughter and granddaughter's neck and wrists. They recoiled from the onslaught and backed into their Dame's retinue, practiced at allowing the blows to land without showing pain.

"So you, broodmare, you hold the heir to the Dominion and my own polity. Time to hand it over, welp. You have had enough time to say goodbye," she said.

Nazira sat up and looked intensely at the old woman, throwing every gram of spite she had into each second she took her under her angry gaze. Yet the old woman would not turn to look at her, instead gazing away into the aether. In some ways, it was like Bish, whose own eyes did not track, or seemed not to. Yet Bish's wandering eyes were not an affectation but a limitation that he used to his advantage. You never knew what Bish was looking at, what he could see. In Griselda, the failure of her to lock a person she was talking to in her vision was an affectation of power. She only looked at people to intimidate them. She had no desire for an empathic reading of people's faces she did not care about, which was both Nazira's and the court's general read on the powerful noble.

Nazira held her son close, then shot back a reply. "Jamil is not your property."

The old woman struck Nazira's bed close to her hand. "Jamil is Prince Telemark to you, and if you forget your tongue, I will have you beaten. Who do you think you are?"

"I am the woman who your own husband, the first Dominar, elected to overlook you, your son, and your other progeny for as route of the heir. And now the so-called Prince Telemark takes your name and your own lands. Is not Tariq vouchsafed to the al-Youseffis? Is not Telemark the old castle your lot calls a great estate? Does not the income of Telemark feed your hordes of useful followers? And now that money and land and even your name belongs to my son. My son! And it is your son who is taking it from you," Nazira said with sullen anger.

"Know so much, do we?" she snipped.

"Why are your daughter and granddaughter losing their heritage and birthright? If I had your power or the power you say you have, I would have supported my children and their children, unless they are utterly stupid." Nazira laughed. "I suspect you do not care for your own kith."

Slap! Griselda's whip stick came down on the bed, closer to Nazira's leg. "My kith, as you call them, do as I say, and I say they do not get to complain on this subject. My lord Telemark, whom your only connection to is birthing him, is by Dominar Nawaz Second, and confirmed by my son Dominar Abelard 'Arba'a 'Aashar' both the Seigner of Tariq, the master of Fortress Telemark, and soon the King of the Cyclonidees, the lord Dominar Cycus. And in case you do not recognize the significance of this, the baby you hold is my property, and I will be raising Lord Telemark. And he will never hear of you as long as he lives. You will be erased."

Nazira looked at Anamita and Vella, looking for the whole world like beaten slaves, and said, "They tried to erase my mother just like your daughter and granddaughter want to erase me. Yet she still exists. People on this island remember her."

"The only island of people who remember her is the island of freaks, and they are only alive because my son spared them." Griselda waved her whip stick in the air but did not smack it down again.

Nazira looked at Bish. Like always, it was impossible to tell where his crazy eyes were actually focused, but she could see the rare curdle of hatred on his face. Surprisingly, Gullen, furtive as ever, has stepped into the light and was trading glances with the old woman's granddaughter Vella.

Bish walked to Nazira's bed and gently took the child from her. He motioned to Griselda's brood servant, who took the swaddled baby in her arms and wrapped him in a carryall.

Griselda finally moved to look on Nazira, a smirk on her face. "If your forgotten mother lives, she lives as a wave girl on some broken and blasted island, servicing surf fishers for the rights to eat the guts from their catches. She is erased. My only mercy for you is that you will be saved by Lord Beijus's blade draining your life onto a dirty piece of jute, which itself will be burned and forgotten. My lord Beijus, why not do the deed now?"

Bish turned and seemed to look into the sky. It seemed to disconcert Griselda, a play of her own games. "As you say, I am Regnal Bish al-Beijus d' Khasir Aljazira, which means I neither take your orders nor respect your authority, Griselda 'um Domjini."

Nazira watched as Griselda's face clouded over. For all of her posturing, for each bit of dripping acid hate, Bish had landed a true blow to her by doing what none of her coterie would do, addressing her by the name she despised, and the only name she was entitled to. "'Um, Domjini," Nazira said to the old woman as she locked gaze on her, mouthing the words. In the old tongue, it was a warm, beautiful appellation. It originated in the farm communities of Cycus, back before the speech of the islands invaded the far reaches of the Halo. A farmer was a freeholder, or domjini. He or she, though, always was advised by the eldest woman of the clan, called walidat alduwminar, or just 'um domjini. The wise women whose duties were to teach the children of the farmstead and rule on conflicts.

Here, though, it was not an appellation of respect. The modern term, since the fall of the old polity, meant a useless thing passed over by a powerful war officer. From the term of great warmth and honor, it went on to become, and now means a useless thing, the lowest member of a military legion, a person used for sexual gratification by a coven of monks, the lowest servant in a fortress who mucks the sanitary closets.

Yet there were hidden layers in Bish's comment. It was the first time Bish had ever mentioned his dominion in Nazira's experience. It seemed nonsense; "Khasir Aljazira" meant "Lost Island," and few people in the room would track that reference. He announced himself as the "lord of the island of the freaks," the secret that people in power spoke openly about, but always with a glance to their back or into the shadows, that touch of superstitious fear.

Griselda clouded, then whipped her daughter in the face with her whip stick, cutting a deep scar in her face. Her granddaughter Vella came to Anamita's aid as Griselda yelled, "We leave now, leave off of her, granddaughter, get to my cart."

The entire retinue fell into chaos as various sycophantic side boys and girls tusked and fidgeted in an effort to achieve the proper order and position due their rank, within the limits of a small room and an even smaller hallway and ramp. Gullen took the opportunity to run a swathing cloth to Anamita and hand it to her. Anamita placed the cloth to her face and looked at Nazira, who held her gaze for a minute until she turned and left the room.

Oban went and closed the door behind the retreating retinue, tears in his eyes. When the door closed, he collapsed, sobbing to the ground. Gullen rushed to his side and silently comforted the caretaker. Regnal Bish turned to Gullen and Oban but then stopped. He slowly turned around and said, "Why did Gullen pass Anamita al-Youseffi a note?"

Nazira looked away from the closed doors and replied, "What do you mean, Bish?"

Regnal Bish approached Nazira and said, "Why did Gullen pass Anamita a note."

Gullen stood from her comfort of Oban, drew a black poniard from her bodice, and slowly approached Bish from the rear. Oban squealed and said, "Mistress, you must not do this."

Bish turned and looked at Gullen with his crazy eyes. "Indeed, you would suffer, Gullen. More than you understand." He slid his slender kirpan from his froggings and held it loosely in his left hand.

Nazira leaped from her bed and rushed Bish. He was caught by surprise as she grabbed his blade and placed it against her own throat. "Gullen gave instructions to Anamita al-Youseffi to murder dame Griselda and steal my son from his caretakers, running with him to the protections of the Sayaad Alsamak, specifically the al-Rasheedi of Bihaqi Major. Now do your job and end my conspiracy, assassin who claimed to be my mentor."

"No one calls me assassin," Bish said.

"Yet that is what you are. An assassin of the Qatil Niqaba, a prelate of the tartib almawt alqadim. I name you 'ahad 'iikhwat alsikiyn al'ahmar and demand you press your knife home and complete the tadhiat al'abria,'" she yelled, pulling

Bish's kirpan against her throat so tight that beads of blood welled from her neck.

"Your language shows you have somehow not just understood my role but read of the duties and honors of my position." Regnal Bish did not remove the knife from Nazira's neck, but instead the force of his strength and the precision of his mastery of the blade pulled it back a millimeter or two. "Yet I cannot see how your plans will succeed. You are painting the walls of your fireplace a new pastel, yet the next blaze will make the color burn black."

"Javier al-Rasheed returns with the *Remarker*. It is four days out, and I have word that he has met with my mother and will proceed to the Silent Island." Nazira used her voice with as much control as she could master. She threw these dice, knowing there was only one chance in twelve that the number would read a win. Yet she had hope, or if she failed, death would save her the misery of failing.

Bish pulled her hand from his kirpan and placed it back into its frogged sheaf. "Your husband is going to the island of Silence?"

"Yes, I have gathered many allies, but my mother informs me by courier that these are the allies I need the most. And let us not forget Standish returns with a company of marines fanatically loyal to my husband. You name my cause lost, yet I believe you do not understand the slope of the dice table, nor the effect I have had on the camber of the dice."

Bish looked down and seemed to almost cry for a second. "You think your efforts at sweating the dice in a game of angles will help you to victory, yet you do not understand what you have set into motion. And one of your game pieces is woefully flawed.

Nazira stamped her food. "You are wise yet blind. Blind like everyone to the qualities of Javier al-Rasheed."

"I am aware of his talents and how they are hidden. Yet he has a weakness, and you have sent him into the den. You speak like you know what the silent island is. Yet you do not know, despite being raised by a denizen of that island and being daughter of a person who did more to save it from genocide than any other." Bish looked at Oban. "Speak now Oban. It is the time for cards to be played."

Nazira looked at her body servant. "Oban, what do you have to say?"

"My lady. You have in your mind that you understand the island. The island was one of the most profound torture. Your grandfather cleared the land of the old guard, the people who kept the Republic alive. And he sent the worst, or the people he felt were the worst, to the island," he said.

"I know this, dear Oban," Nazira replied.

"You do not understand the dimension of it. The length of time it has lasted. The horror," he said, almost crying with the effort.

Nazira slipped past Bish and approached Oban. "Dear friend, father I never had. I agree that this place was a horror, but I call on my husband to save the island. My mother sends a message to the mistress of that land."

"I fear for Javier," Oban said.

Nazira said, "I do not." She rubbed the bald man's head, then touched his face to lift away a tear. "Oban, Javier is stronger than you think. However, I will see your concerns made right." She turned back to Bish. "Regnal Bish, time to stand on my side or be my enemy. Go to the island yourself and meet my husband. And I will send word to the al-Youseffi to bring my son to the island as well. Will you follow me, or no?"

Bish looked up, and for the first time drilled Nazira's eyes with his own, as if he had the vision of a normal man. An affectation for one struck with crazy-eye, but an effective one that said all Nazira needed to know about his sincerity. "I will send fighters from the island in the form of servants that can blend in to you. Oban, Gullen, and I will travel together to the mistress of the silent island, and I will return Oban or Gullen with messages. I am now your partisan."

Nazira smiled and said, "Then be off, gallant friends, for in a few days, the war for the heart of Cycus begins."

CHAPTER XVIII

The Terrible Storm

Saqib felt himself being rolled over. An old man was rooting through his pockets, pulling things out of his pocket and putting them onto his chest. "Water," he said when he realized he was awake and not lost in a dream.

"Shut up, you are dead," the man said.

"Where am I?" Saqib asked.

The man shook his canteen, then placed it to his lips. "You are in Qabr." The water from the canteen flowed into his throat as the man said, "Qad tajiduk alnieam."

After he drank deep, Saqib replied, "Qad tamnahuk ala-lihat hadha alsalam."

"Shut up, dead man. Let me get your things," the old man said, pressing the canteen into his hands. He pulled a few coins from a pouch and then said, "Educated, are you though. Wasted though, since it brought you here."

"Kalam majnun," Saqib said with a groan. Insane words by an insane man. He tried to move and collapse in pain.

"Dead man," the robber said, "I have many to loot, and not much time. Remain still and start dying."

"I may not die," Saqib said.

"Why not? Most of your fellows have." The man paused with his looting and said, "My name is Ustis al-Ravi. Do you have anything to say to your survivors if they come to my village?"

"Tell them you left a living man to die on the battle-field," Saqib said, then tried to spit. It did not happen as he expected, and he collapsed into a heap.

The man stood up and said, "Cousin, this one says he is alive."

"They never come and get the ones who are alive. Leave her," came a voice from out of Saqib's vision.

"It is a him, and he says he can survive," the robber said.

"Do you agree?" came a reply.

The man patted his body and then opened his shirt. "No, I think he is dead."

A woman came into Saqib's vision. "There are fifty who will die tonight." She looked over and two more men joined her. Saqib's view was soon filled with people.

The original robber said, "When the last battle hap-pened here, I was a boy, and the wounded suffered in our village for days. The Kemayans took our food, they burned our haystacks. Just like you lot this time." He waved, and Saqib felt people grab him under the arms. He passed out from the pain.

Squib woke up to the screams of men and women in pain. They were in a large structure, perhaps a barn or some-thing originally made for animals, with lofts for feed and pens that had fresh rushes on the floor. He lifted his head and saw that five others were in the pen with him. Three were in a deep sleep or a coma. One was staring at him from a bier but was missing some of his jaw and face, while another woman had a horribly deformed skull. He turned and saw an older woman who was trying to feed water to one of the unconscious casualties, their body swaddled and unrecognizable as friend or foe. "Where am I?" he asked. The noise of the screams drowned out his question, so he asked again, louder. "Lady villager, where am I?"

The woman turned and said, "You fought so hard for this village. Do you not know what you were fighting for?"

Saqib shook his head. "No, we were coming up from the Steaming Vale to Cycus Port to take the Cinci. The best place to cross the river Rage is at the turnpike, and your village commands the bridge. I do not think our leaders knew that you were hiding in ambush."

"What?" the woman asked. "Did the flaming haystacks and dead sheep not concern you?"

"The war leader said you were killing them to keep the food from us," Saqib said, groaning. He was hot from his wounds and delirious from fever, "Can I have water?"

"The sheep were killed by the al-Cinci, and you ambushed each other in the Fields of Blading when you both found the Youseffi had collapsed our beautiful bridge. And no, you cannot have water." The woman said. She lifted the dressings on Saqib's stomach. The stench was awful, so Saqib turned his head away.

"The people in the field were cruel. They kept joking that I would die," Saqib said.

"You will. I am surprised they brought you here," the woman said. She removed the bandages and reached for a bucket nearby. It had more bandages made from torn shirts soaked in creolin. She rang out one and gently placed it on his chest. The pain shot through him—he writhed in agony, holding his voice until a scream was forced from his stomach.

Then he wailed in pain greater than he had ever felt in his life. Worse than when the soldier had run him through with a lance. It was a terrible and mind numbing pain.

It slowly faded though, and he came back to reality with the woman saying something to him. It took a second, and then he realized it was, "You have to drink, or you die, but if you drink, you die. You are in a race with yourself. But you will probably die."

Then there was a light in his brain. Everyone in this little corner of the stable was going to die, not just him. He cried out, "Was it worth it?" Then he started to cry.

The woman touched his brow with a new cloth, this one soaked in water. "What were you trying to do?"

"The Kemayans were fighting, father and daughter. The Haseemi thought it was time to steal the thunder for the Guisarmes and take the capital," he said, as if it made some sort of sense.

The woman shook her head. "You fought the Cinci? That is sadness in itself." She swabbed his brow more and then started cleaning his arms.

"Why?" he asked.

"History child. Do not let it worry you. Where are your from, who can we send word to?" She asked.

"I am from the Steaming Vale," he replied.

The woman stopped. "My daughter apprentices in the Vale. Urwa al-Ravi is her name. Did she march with the Haseemi? Could she be in the field?"

Saqib shook his head. "We marched and left her with the master. She lives. When I die though, I only want one person to know. On the tea merchant *Remarker* there is a sailor named Alia D'casio."

"I thank you for news of my daughter. Word will go to the port where it is said the *Remarker* is has taken the city for the princess. And word will be sent to the valley for the master of that land, in case they have a desire to arrive here with haste, since they are but a few days away." The woman left, and Saqib fell into a fitful sleep.

When he awoke, the fever was all-consuming, and his vision was dimmed. He looked out from broken eyes and saw that Urwa sat next to him. It could be she was holding his hand. "Calm, my friend," she said.

"I am dead, Urwa," he replied. "Did you not see it in the sails? Alia told me to come to sea with her."

"You mean Journeyman D'casio?" Urwas asked.

"The same. She and I had a connection. I could have left with her," he replied, groaning with fever.

"Then why not?" Urwa demanded. "Why take to the sword with the fool Haseemi?"

"You know, the coin, the fame. War was an opportunity. Now I am killed." He started to cry.

Urwa reached out and touched his brow. "You will not die if I can help it."

"Your father said I would die," he said.

"My father is a great man at the loom. He knows not much of the heart of a sailmaker. That is what you are, a sailmaker," Urwa said.

He awoke again but had no sense of time. A heavy-set woman was sitting over him and yelled, "Urwa!"

Urwa appeared. Saqib held out his hand, and she took it. "D'casio has come to see you. We have a healer who will conduct surgery on your legs."

"Tell me of the midden," He pleaded.

Urwa frowned. "There is no need for you to hear of the midden."

"No one came for them," Saqib moaned.

"Which is not you. D'casio awaits you. The new Dominar has dispatched healers to the battles that have been fought across the island. Friend and foe alike are being treated, even if many were lost," she said.

Then he saw D'casio behind Urwa. He loved the journeyman weaver and sailmaker. "Alia," he said. She was dressed in a merchant's field uniform with the star rank of an Aspirant.

"Foolish Saqib. You went and fought with the Haseemi," she said.

"Forgive me," he replied.

"No need. This is Tabib Azar of the island of silence," Alia said.

A man with milky white eyes moved into his vision. Saqib suddenly was wracked with pain, but the pain receded. Azar was dressed in a white shalver with a kamarband around his waist. The shalver was painted with blood, as if the man had been wading in a stream of gore. "You may lose your legs, but you will likely keep your life," the man said. "Are you one with courage to live past a crippling wound?"

Saqib tried to answer, but Alia interrupted him, "I have coin to pay for his recovery. Lots of coin."

Urwa touched her shoulder. "Sailing Master of the *Remarker*, there is every reason to hope for Saqib to recover, and he has a place with the people of the Rage. My father wants a sailmaker, and I want to see the world."

Saqib looked at D'casio. If he had a loom in the dale of Ventias's rage, he could marry D'casio, have a home with her here for when she returned from the sea. He looked at her, and she at him. "If my bewed Saqib wishes to stay and your father allows him a home and a loom among the people of this dale, then I can assure you, Urwa, that my captain will see you mustered into our crew."

Saqib saw Urwa nod. "Deals such as this make for a tidy ending." Then he saw she was crying. She looked back into the sorting building at the people who waited for healing, or who were failing from their wounds. Alia D'casio looked over as well, and they all fell silent. Urwa then stepped in and said, "The Tabib has many to treat. Here, drink this." She lifted his head and gave him a bitter draught from a wooden cup. Soon he was asleep.

Chapter XIX

Sacrifice

Yadira surveyed the cluster of carts and drovers that she had assembled at the crossroads Firth Kabir, near where the sewer tunnels could be accessed. She stood beside her number two, Sabah, waif-like and deadly.

"Daniella would have loved this," Sabah said.

Yadira shook her head. "Daniella is dead, and with her the Red Hand. We have to think of the Circum Valus now. What I do not like is how complicated this has gotten. We should be in the streets brawling for our slice."

There were five carts and fifty of her girls and boys with knockers and cutters waiting for their ticket, and tens of thousands of grams of silver to gain. More, if this turned out well. She looked at the first cart, though with a bit of anguish. The damn face dancer made her nervous, and the oddity made her nervous. Not that strange beings were absent this night—there were oddities aplenty fighting for control of Cycus Port, but these two made her especially nervous.

"How many of the lads and lasses are bent, I wonder." She said it to herself, but Sabah answered, "We agreed this was a good time to find out."

The sewer grating rattled, then gave way to someone with a batter, and out came two sots in Black and Gold. Yadira said, "That's the colors of our patrons."

Sabah waved her hand in front of her face. "But damn, they should have changed. That is a stench they will not launder from those wool jackets for some time."

Yadira smelled and agreed with Sabah. The two young men from the Youseffi Family Battalion were foul and did not wear good looks on their faces. One was an officer with a talwar and a fancy torc, the other was a soldier with a firelock that he had dragged through the sewers with him. Fancy thing, if it would work now. The officer approached and yelled, "You lot, get ready for the quality."

Yadira stormed up to the officer and said, "Shut up, man. The quality is going to find her ass hung from a bridge if you yell any louder."

"I am a Youseffi officer. I am not scared of the damn princess or her rabble," he said.

"Then why are you running away sirrah?" Sabah said under her breath.

"What was that?" The officer asked.

Yadira said, "My patron said they would run away at the sight of you. Signal the quality now."

The officer made a supercilious inspection of the carts, then returned to the sewer and helped a dozen more men and women of the Youseffi Guard out, and when they were ready, carefully helping the quality.

The first out was tottery old Bentham, formerly of the Red Hand, and now just a waste of space and air. He was dressed better than the soldiers though, and immediately pulled his nasties off and replaced them with clothing from a leather bag. "Ahh, the benighted Red Hand of Magrid!" he said with insulting tones.

"We are the Circum-Valus, oh patron of filth," he replied.

"Whatever, Yadira. Get the water to wash me, and the ladies who follow," he said.

Yadira nodded and one of the drovers, a grim man with a deep face scar and a heavy beard, stepped down from his cart and started to pull from the cargo carrier water guts. He selected one, approached Bentham as he finished shucking his altogether, and sprayed water from the bladder on him. From his pocket, he handed him some soap and a sponge.

The soldiers next handed up an older, imperious woman, whose fine dress was clogged with filth. She was aided from behind by a pair of muckers in canvas work outfits. They were the only ones who seemed unaffected by the stench.

Bentham bowed, which looked silly considering his yatadala was flopping around in the freezing cold air, and said, "Mistress, we will have a fire going and throw up some blinds for you to change in."

"No fire, imbecile, just water to clean with," she replied.

"Yes, Dame Griselda," Bentham said. She stripped off her dress without ceremony, and the glum carter handed her lye soap and washed her down with the contents of another bladder.

Anamita, her daughter, came out next. "To think a Youseffi would flee the city in the sewers." She was obviously furious.

"Daughter, let me tell you, this is not the time to complain. I will remind you that Nazira item is crazy, and we have her child in tow. She killed Melinda without a second's pause, in cold blood, for no reason. You are her cousin. If she would kill her sister, do not expect mercy," Griselda said.

Anamita pulled her own dress off and turned to see her own daughter, Griselda's grandchild proper, emerge from the sewer. "Merida, help me out of this dress. And you should clean as well."

The drover sprayed each with water and handed out more soap. Yadira had never seen the granddaughter of Griselda, but she seemed to be a whipped non-entity. Given who her mother and grandmother were, the poor child never had a chance.

Merida threw off her dress. "Disgusting, and the soap is lye, why not olive oil?"

The drover replied, "I am sorry mistress, lye is all that is strong enough to clean what is on you."

More soldiers and another man in finery emerged. It was Ghent, formerly first officer on the *Remarker* when she was still in the pirate trade. He noticed Yadira and marched to her, pulling his soiled outfit off. "So you lot is who they hired for this flight from the rabid townies."

Yadira nodded. "*Remarker* is in the roadstead. You fancy to get her back?"

Ghent laughed. "Oh that is rich. There are more ships in the ocean than yon matey. No, I will eat Rasheed's heart, but the ship is no longer what I am looking for."

Bentham was first dressed, but he interrupted the rest. "Mates, come round," he yelled, and about a third of Yadira's lads and lasses broke away, drew weapons, and surrounded the Youseffi.

Griselda, covered in suds, noticed the action and said, "What the demon spawn is this?"

Bentham ignored her and watched the sewer. From its mouth came a pair of carters carrying a wooden bindle with two carry poles. They set it down, cleaned it of filth, opened it, and inside was a child in swaddling. "How is the package?"

The pair carrying it, checked the child, cooed at it, and made sure that the infant was happy and snug. The older one, a bent man, said, "Prince Jamil is hungry and dirty, but both can be solved with a midwife and a change of nappies." The second carter, a young woman with a blank face, nodded agreement.

Anamita walked over to the drover with the water bladders, took one from his hands, and rinsed herself off. Bentham held out a long dress of worsted, which she put on without underclothing. "Mother Griselda, Nazira paid me a handsome sum to rescue her son and kill you. I am doing neither. However, it is time for you to start walking back to town for some clothing since you are no longer the grande dame of the Youseffi."

Griselda growled a low growl. "Do you think you can replace me in the family?"

"The family says I can. Uncle Thales and Sayid Bockra both messaged me that if I returned without you but with the heir, then there would be a different order to the family." Anamita said, pulling her long hair from her face and tying it behind her.

Yadira said under her breath to Sabah, "Did you think Kassab would betray us."

Sabah nodded. "He cheats at dice."

Yadira nodded. "I did not know."

"Merida, get washed and dressed," Anamita said. Pirate Ghent took another water bottle from the drover and washed off Merida, then handed her another dress. She stepped away from her grandmother but did not approach her mother. Instead, she attached herself to Ghent.

"Mother, the child goes with me," Merida said.

Yadira saw as the guards and some of her own people again repositioned themselves. "Is Ghent or Merida driving the horse?" she asked Sabah quietly.

"Neither, Yadira, please step back and do not interfere." Her own second, Sabah, had betrayed her. Yadira was unsure if she should be proud or angry. She decided angry.

"Merida, Ghent, take the child. Ghulem, disarm Yadira and her people, and anyone who wants to cling to Anamita or Griselda," Sabah said.

There was a sudden flurry of posturing. The drovers and the muckers fled in the confusion, and many of her people looked to her for orders. "Sabah," Yadira said. "Three-way fights never end well, even if you have more knockers and blades."

Sabah looked at her former street boss and said, "Yadira, killing your lot is part of the deal. You kidnapped the child on behalf of the Youseffi, and you all died on this crossroads."

"That is the deal," Ghent laughed, but then he got quiet when Sabah looked at him. He looked at Merida, who was thinking the same thought, and the old woman Griselda laughed. "Done in by my granddaughter and daughter. You stupid women. We all die here."

Sabah said, "Bring the swaddling basket and the brat."

Yadira yelled at her former gang leader, "Think this one through, Sabah. Dame Griselda is not lying about Nazira. If you hurt her son, she will kill you slowly."

Griselda added, "The boy is the only way to keep the families in check."

Sabah laughed like she was insane, and Yadira thought it was possible. "Abelard and Nazira will kill each other in that town. They are doing it now! What is this babe worth other than a way for the Guisarmes and Kemayans to cling to power? But I tell you now, if Nawaz can take Cycus, so can I."

"Nawaz had 10,000," Griselda said. "I was there, he did not take this land, my own father had 10,000 as well, and the Cinci had 10,000 more. And we did not take it, we negotiated for it. It was won at the bargaining table!"

Sabah walked over to the basket and reached inside as if to make a point. She then screamed, "Where is the child!"

Only two drovers remained, but they were no longer cowering like servants or handing out water bladders. And from the cane breaks at the edge of the forest, a hundred or more haunting figures in white cloaks walked into the fields around the crossroads. Yadira drew her sword and said, "Lads and lassies, if you are with me, now is the time to step to me. Twenty of her stalwart did.

Sabah backed up and was surrounded by what had to be her own people, and there were still a small number of partisans who cleaved to Griselda, Bentham, and Anamita, or Merida and Ghent.

The two drovers threw off their cloaks. One was dressed in black and had a dirty, disreputable yataghan. The second seemed to lose his face. He was no longer a hirsute man with a grey beard, but instead looked like an androgynous youth. Griselda laughed out loud. "Oh, a dead man, a face dancer, and the denizens of the Island of Silence come to save a baby from the likes of me."

"I am surprised you remember me, Griselda," the man with the scar said.

"Oh, it was a decade ago, but you died on the strangling post, or so I thought. Something to do with Nazira's companion. They called you Darkfather, the dancing master," Griselda said.

The Darkfather bowed. "Your power has always been in knowing people. Like Hesperia."

"Yes, did you kill her?" Griselda asked.

The Darkfather shook his head. "No, another did. A long time ago, and not an issue we need address. Things are coming together tonight, Griselda, and it is time for you to choose."

Anamita yelled, "Who is this man, mother?"

"Shut up daughter. This is not the fight for you." Griselda laughed, then said, "Tell me what is coming together. I mean, the figures in the trees and cane breaks are ... well, I would never have believed it."

"The *Remarker* is in port, and her crew fight in the streets," the Darkfather said, lifting a finger to say it was the first thing.

Griselda nodded. "So she did not die in that storm."

The Darkfather shook his head. "Nazira has gotten many messages that bode well for her side doing what your husband Nawaz did. The assassins have thrown in behind her, you never had that."

"Disturbing. Are you, master Darkfather, an assassin?" Griselda asked.

The Darkfather shook his head. "No. You should know that only a few battalions of the Guard are fighting for your stepson," he said, holding up a third finger.

"My stepson is not one to engender loyalty," Griselda said with a hand wave.

The other man with the lost face stepped forward and said in a voice made of cotton, "And for the first time, the Mistress of Silence and the Silent People go to war."

Griselda seemed to accept this, as she made no comment. The Darkfather said, "We have prepared a comfortable exile for the Youseffi and Cinci who betrayed the trust of the Dominion. Or you could retreat to the Island of Silence to live on the beach in a hut of boxwood.

"And what if I take the third option?" Griselda asked.

The man next to Darkfather said in a haunting voice. "The Warriors of Silence become muntaqim min alzulm."

There was a shouting stillness that lasted for a long moment, quiet so deafening that Yadira felt she should scream to pierce it. The figures in white were unmoving, as if carved from some white stone. Griselda broke the tension by saying, "Exile my kith as you see fit, I will not resist."

The white figures rushed into the crossroads, and Griselda, Anamita, and Merida were grasped and taken away, leaving the traitors behind.

Ghent noticed this first and said, "Do I not get exile?"

The Darkfather, the baby, and even the muckers were gone. This had just become a family affair. Yadira walked calmly to a cart and climbed on so everyone could see her. Looking among those still loyal to her, she said, "Latif, get some order there. You are number two."

Latif, a small but limber man who came to the streets through the short grift, started pointed and yelling, while his people, the men and women of the Circum-Valus made traitors and soldier kneel in separate groups. When he finished, he looked up and said to Yadira, "complicated night for betrayal and sorting out who is with whom, my leader, Yadira."

Yadira smirked. "You and your lot seemed ready to go out with me."

"Seemed like the thing, mistress. Daniella got hers, but she never bent. She was blown up playing the game. I would not feel right having lived if I had not done right." Latif rubbed his beard, then said, "The white warriors are an oddity, you have a figure for that?"

"No," Yadira said. It was a "no" that had finality in the discussion.

Latif went back, pushing and bullying people into clusters. When the culling had been achieved, Yadira yelled out, "Soldiers of the Youseffi. Run for home, join the Circum-Valus, take up farming, bedevil no more or we will slaughter you."

Most ran, but a few stood up near Latif indicating their choice to join the gang and he assigned them to gang leaders with a shove and a cuff. More formality than that would happen later.

"What about us?" Sabah asked. She looked at Ghent, Benthem, and the others, but Yadira knew she meant herself more than the rest of the rabble.

It did not matter to Yadira. "Daniella used to say, one bite of the apple. You had the bite. Time to dig a hole."

Chapter XX

Silence and Darkness

The Lady Silence and the Darkfather sat contemplating the burning buildings, listening to the sounds that came from tens of thousands of people struggling for life as the sun rose on the horizon. All that they could do was done. As the Cycuns said, "The die was cast." It would hopefully show a twelve on its face.

Silence looked at the red orb piercing the horizon and said, "There are people who worship the sun. They say that you know your place in the universe by what you call the sun in your own tongue. You do not hear it often, but the people of the Halo often call her al'umu alshams."

The Darkfather looked at Silence in her white gown. "It means mother sun?"

Silence nodded. "The sun gives us life, so it must be a mother. What do your people call the sun?"

He shrugged. "When I was a child, it had one name, and now it has another. I am not much minded to wonder on this anymore." He stopped, then turned again to Silence. "There is so much for us to talk about, yet we look out on the ruins caused by a revolution and talk about what to call an orange orb. When we last parted, there was much to say, and little said. What words do you now want to tell me?"

Silence, after a long while, turned to the Darkfather. "You have not been truthful to the new Dominar." After a few seconds, she added, "And you healed her husband. Yet you covered that up? That is why I pushed you away years ago; you travel in a cloud of lies, Samedi."

"Did you tell Regnal Bish al-Beijus of our connections? Are you not protected by the assassins and obligated to be truthful?" he asked.

The Lady Silence replied, "Let me tell you a story, a story that has been erased. It is one I have contemplated for many years. A sister of yours came to our land with an idea. She wanted people to assist in some fell plan, and she bribed a group of islanders called the Egliffs to get what she wanted."

The Darkfather replied, "Hesperia was not my sister."

"Then what was she to you? She named you! No one remembers, but I do. I was there and heard her name you the Prince of Darkfather Mountain!"

The Darkfather shook his head. "Baron, and I am no longer that."

Silence laughed. "Wicked how we weave webs of lies, Darkfather, who is named Samedi. Not your sister, not your kith? But connected to you, was she not?"

"We both were criminals where we came from. She was a criminal sage, and I was a partisan of a dead land. I was exiled, and she came here of her own accord," he said.

"And she told the Egliffs a secret of power," Silence stated. "She told them that the gods watch us from the heavens."

"No, she did not say that," Darkfather stated. Then he realized it was likely a lie. She could have said that, and it would explain how the Egliffs died, trying to look on the face of god using a tube of glass.

"Then what secret did she sell?" Silence asked, sensing the prevarication.

Darkfather thought quickly. "I do not know, but in thinking on it after all these years, it is possible that while she did not sell the greater secrets to the Egliffs, that she was immoderate in her discussions. People of my kith, the kith greater than Ocean, can forget how smart the children of the Halo are. She may have said things that should not be said. That would be the first of her crimes, but she did it knowing that the Egliffs had the ability to construct a device that would do just that, try to look on the face of the gods," he said.

"And the gods killed them?" Silence asked.

"Yes, in essence, she did not tell them that the gods do not like being looked at by those they would deny exist." The Darkfather was almost sobbing when he said this. The truth speared him that much of the death and destruction that had visited these people could have been caused by Hesperia. Hesperia, whose crimes could not even be discussed without revealing too much. As he said, the Children of the Halo were clever. Teach them it was possible to build a ladder to the moon, and they would build just such a ladder.

"Then the Apostolical Egliffs died. They all died, and Hesperia went on to spend her silver," Silence said.

"Not silver. I cannot tell you what she wanted, but she wanted a thing that would bring her power. She wanted to violate a rule of her … my … our people, a rule that could not be broken. And to break that rule, she had to break other rules, rules which my and her people would strike her down for if discovered," he said.

"The lies that broke you from me," she stated. "You did not know she died at the hands of a common guard. Her hubris could not see that coming." Silence brooded for a second, then said, "Why did you not come to me when she died?"

"I did not know she died at all," he said. "When Hesperia fell to her own calumny, you could have come out and found me."

Silence shook her head. "Old man, you were much older than me, and now I am old, and you are ... the same." She stopped. "Many cannot leave the island of silence. What Hesperia did ... was horror, nothing short. I did not know I could leave the island, and when I tried ... it was too late." She stopped then said, "I am cursed, but now I see yours, ageless witness. You did not take life out of fear, and I did not take it either. But in not a few years, I will leave this world and sleep in the midden they have built on the Island of Silence. What will happen to you? Will you continue on? Is that your curse?"

He shook his head. "That is indeed the nature of my curse."

"Then cursed you are," she said, "all of your yesterdays to contemplate for what you have left behind, or like me, never grasped as you could have." She stopped, then added, "You healed al-Rasheed."

The Darkfather nodded. "I healed Javier al-Rasheed, but I did not cure him. A small push to wake him up at the right time. He will need time to be cured, if that is ever possible." He stopped for a minute more, then added, "If we discuss lies, and living in a cloud of them, Javier al-Rasheed's father was not a fisher, and his son did not run into the woods to be saved by you. Both are lies you have uttered, yet you accuse me of swimming is a stream of untruth."

Silence shook her head. "Yes, there are things she need not know. Lies cover up truths that should not be learned for the betterment of the person lied to. Her mother is at the heart of still more lies. That one and others. Pull on one string, and the blanket unravels." She waved at the city brooding below her. "What is this but a story, and that story, of what is Javier al-Rasheed, is like your own story, one that has to be told forever incomplete, because they must live with their stories. This land must live with those stories. That ship sitting in harbor must live with the stories that you and I tell, accurate or not. My preference is for almost accurate. Let the watchers wonder if every last paragraph parses true. The sun knows the truth, but is not speaking."

"Exactly," the Darkfather replied. "We both have lied to many people to conceal unpleasant truth, not for personal gain. It is not false witness, merely protective coloration."

Silence nodded, then put her hand on the Darkfather's shoulder. "I was twenty-and-one when our story was told, and you never told me how old you were or the name of your place of birth. You never explained the truth behind your oddities. Even the name you called the sun on the island of your birth was kept from me. So I kept things from you. Yet the time has arrived when those lies will wash ashore, even as you protected greater truths with a thin veil of banality. You have some truth coming to you soon," Silence said.

The Darkfather looked down at his yataghan in his lap. So much truth, so little that should be said to these people. Even if it meant he must always be alone. "What Truth do you now have for me?"

"She told me of your first wife. A secret she thought would make me turn on you." Silence said.

"She could be ruthless. My wife and daughter died long ago. It was simply not something that mattered." He hesitated, then said, "Anymore, at least. Hesperia was not above shading the truth to get what she wanted, and she wanted you to remain on the island when I left." He continued to stare at his yataghan. "Her secrets were gathering even then, when I lived on the island."

Silence said, "I should have stopped her earlier, when I found I had the powers she was looking for in the denizens-of-silence. Yet she also told me another secret, that you are forlorn. Shew was not giving you a hiding place. She was using you as a model to study in her attempt to create something different. Her deal with Nawaz was to have people to study, to experiment with. You were her model, and by studying you, she made me."

The Darkfather nodded. "I was ignorant, but perhaps I knew what she wanted of me. Indeed, we call it being forlorn. The gathering of dwimmer that wipes away the humanity of our soul but leaves something else in its place. But she had to break so many to get the ones she wanted to have and died before her process was perfected. And I had hoped her lies and spite would die with her. As you say, it cost me you, and I have many years yet to regret this."

"Do not. The cloud of lies is slowly dimming between us, Samedi. One of my truths will be revealed to you soon. That is the best we can do, for now. We can start tearing away the deadly veil that has been built between us after all these years," Silence said. Then she asked, "Did you ever return the silver to Whenua Koura?"

"I did, though it cost me you," he said.

"Not forever," she replied.

The Darkfather turned his head from the rising sun. "The sun you see is named Kappa Ceti by my people, but it was not the sun I was born looking at. To me, this sun was just one island in an ocean of light. I was born under Gamma Pavonis. Some night I will point it out to you."

"And I will tell you that you are not alone," she said.

"Thank you. Perhaps we can create again what was torn away between us," Samedi replied.

"No," Silence said. "I speak of your daughter, who is even now, thanks to Javier al-Rasheed, standing in the palace of the port of Cycus, not knowing she will soon meet her father."

The Darkfather was caught without words. He and the Mistress Silence sat together for the rest of the day until a messenger from the new Dominar called them away.

He entered the chamber where Abelard sat, propped up in a bed by an explosion of cushions. The former Dominar was frail looking, his face filled with wrinkles, his hair no longer styled to cover the place where he had been horribly injured years ago. He was staring at a fire that had been built up to keep him warm. Someone had placed a handlock by his side. The Darkfather snatched the weapon up, levered open its charging block, and noted that a doubled-loaded cartridge had been inserted thoughtfully by some regicide into the chamber. He pulled back on the ejector and caught the charge in his hand, then walked to a dresser and placed the weapon in among some bed clothing. There was no need for the old Dominar to leave that way, not in the state he was in.

The noise of disposing of the weapon cause the Dominar to look over from the fire. "I know you," he said.

"You do. You were injured as a child and I repaired the injury, as best I could," the Darkfather replied. "It is a good sign you recognize me."

Abelard looked at him with sad eyes and said, "Better if I had died then. Is that what you are here for now?" He looked at the table where the handlock had been sitting. "They came in and left me a weapon. I could not use it. I am not brave that way."

"You cannot undo my healing, poor Abelard. I wish I had done more for you all those years ago," the Darkfather said.

Abelard looked back at the fire, forgetting, it seemed, their conversation.

The door opened and Nazira, the princes and presumed Dominar of Cycus, entered her father's sickroom. By her side were Regnal Bish, Liena d' Canus Cragia, and Amina, who had chosen to adopt the appellation d' Nabeel, the old kith name for the rulers of Kemeya, the birthplace of Nawaz.

Nazira stopped and asked the Darkfather, "How is my father?"

The Darkfather turned and said, "He will not die, at least not of natural causes. Leaving a loaded firelock fit for one hand, though, is a rather pointed way to deal with his problem.

Nazira said, "That was an option that was discussed, but not approved. Regnal, who of my new subjects has jumped the gun, so to speak?"

Regnal looked chagrined. "I do not know, but I will find out."

"Can he speak?" Nazira asked the Darkfather.

"He can, after a fashion. He has had what you call brain fire. I treated it earlier, but he will never be the same again." The Darkfather touched Abelard, "You daughters are here to see you."

He turned back from the fire. "I have daughters?"

Nazira stepped between the Darkfather and Abelard. "You have two, Father. Myself, your heir, and your younger daughter who you have never met. She is named Amina, and grew up in the mountains of truth, Canus Cragia, in the lands of Codis Aletia,"

Amina stepped forward and looked at her father. She looked every bit the sister of Nazira and daughter of Abelard with her deep black hair and sharp face. "I did not know," Abelard said.

Amina looked a little scared and turned to the Darkfather, "What does he mean by that?"

The Darkfather said, "Exactly what he says. He is beyond lies now. His mind is like a child's. He may have known of you previously. He did know of Nazira, your sister, but now…"

"What he knows is not a surety." Nazira finished his sentence. I have commanded he be treated as a child.

Amina nodded and stepped forward, putting her hand on his shoulder. "You were married to Irula. She has taught me kindness for you." She hesitated. "Do you remember the island of silence?"

The Darkfather stepped forward. "The island was never his. It belonged to his father, Nawaz. He does not understand any of that though. The past comes crashing into his mind like the ocean, and thoughts are like many voices are yelling at him at the same time."

"I want him to tell me the story, to my own face," Amina said.

The Darkfather kneeled by the former Dominar and placed his hands on his head. A breeze stirred up despite the room being closed, and there seemed to be a glow that covered the men, one sitting in despair, and the other kneeling. When the Darkfather removed his hands from Abelard's head, the former Dominar traced a soft smile across his face and said, "Hello daughters."

"You have a father, my Dominar and dear Amina, but my arts cannot give you back what he was."

Nazira turned to the Darkfather. "He cannot be cured?"

"No, Dominar Nazira. He is merely helped for a short while. For him to find peace will be many years, perhaps all he has left. Like your husband, he is broken, and there is nothing that can quickly fix it." The Darkfather looked to Regnal Bish and said, "The Mistress Silence may take Abelard to help him heal."

Bish nodded, "You know the Mistress?" There was surprise in his voice.

The Darkfather nodded. "You will find the Mistress Silence has nothing against Abelard. He ignored their island, which was for the best after what Nawaz permitted."

Nazira brushed her father's hair from his brow and said, "I will visit you, father."

"I would like that, daughter. Where is your husband?" he asked.

Nazira looked stricken and said, "I must go to Javier. He must survive."

Bish moved to her and put his arm on her shoulder. "My Dominar, the Mistress Silence is not hopeful. Not at all. She has told me that some from the island who were taken by Hesperia faded and died when confronted by the truth of their experience."

The Darkfather stood and said, "Hesperia was a criminal, but now she is long dead. While your father is organically sick in a way that may heal with care, your husband has broken down by sinister tortures and forced to repair himself. Do not expect that he can return. It is not a chemical or mechanical problem that plagues him. The messages that flow in his brain are what have become stricken."

"Can I do something?" Abelard asked, his voice like a child.

"I do not think so, Father," Amina replied. "Come, let us dress you and prepare for your journey to the Island of Silence.

"I will like that," Abelard said.

Nazira left the room, followed by Amina and her newly met father, the former Dominar Abelard. Regnal Bish lingered for a second, looking at the Darkfather and Liena, then he also turned and left, leaving the two alone.

"A complicated family," Liena said.

The Darkfather nodded. "Yes, indeed."

Liena then said, "When were you going to tell me, Samedi? That is your real name, is it not?"

"Darkfather is the name of the land I am from. Darkfather Mountain. I lost everything there," Darkfather said.

"When Amina was born, I was two and had arrived as a baby on Canus Cragia. My mother had passed, and she gave me this." She pulled a small chain from her bodice and revealed a flat piece of metal that had been etched with the word "Samedi."

"She did not pass. She had sent you to safety to protect you from what has befallen Javier al-Rasheed." The Darkfather reached for the pendant and took it in his hand. "I was a prisoner and took comfort with a lover on the Island of Silence, the island where you were born. This is titanium, a cheap metal, stamped with my name and worn around my neck. The figures below are my number, which was more important than my name when this was given me. I gave this to a beautiful woman, the Mistress of Silence. She is your mother." He hesitated and said, "You may meet her if you wish. I think she wants to see what her daughter has become."

"Did you know I existed?" Liena asked, brushing aside the talk of her mother.

The Darkfather had yet to look her in the eyes. "If I had, then you would not have been raised an orphan. I am forlorn. I did not even know it was possible for me to have a child. Your mother did not tell me of you to protect you. How you arrived at the mountains of Canus Cragia on the island of Codis Aletia, I cannot say. I suspect your mother smuggled you out. Stories are never neat and easy to understand unless being told by a bard, and that bard is likely trying to pick your pockets clean of silver."

"Irula knows how I was saved, I am sure of it, but it does not matter. I will not call you Darkfather, as the rest do. I will just call you father," she said.

The Darkfather nodded. He reached out his hand and found Liena's by her side. "Your mother waits to meet you."

Liena replied, "In a bit."

AFTERWARD

Sunstar and Darkfather

Sunstar Nine felt slightly drugged. The sun was down to the horizon, and she did not remember it falling that low. She looked about the cockpit top and saw the Darkfather, the ship's new Quartermaine holding the sun-box in his hands. The man had a mysterious past but had, like her, fought in the watcher's revolution and withstood the fire of both Guisarme and Kemeyan firelocks. Yet despite his being new, she felt an instant camaraderie with the man.

"We sail tomorrow on the sunset tide." She said to Darkfather.

The Darkfather placed the sun-box down and replied, "We do." Then he left the cockpit top by the forward gangway.

Standish just missed him. "What do you make of our new Quartermaine?" She asked.

"He seems perfect for our crew, though he does not share his stories much as you might like," Sunstar replied.

Standish looked to the docks, then to the busy activity preparing the ship for its second expedition. "No, he is more than he seems, I will grant you that. Tell me when the captain comes aboard, I want to plan our last cadre meeting before we warp to Kemeya."

"I will do that Major," Sunstar looked to the fading sun and was excited about what lay ahead.

Book Club Questions

1. How does Nawaz react to the injury of his son Abelard?

2. What drives Abelard's jealousy of Nazira?

3. What is Dame Griselda's motivations to suppress Nazira?

4. What events led to Nazira "growing up"?

5. What role does Regnal Bish play in the procession?

6. What is the purpose of procession?

7. What unusual characteristics does Samedi Darkfather display?

8. How is Nazira similar to Javier with how they deal with people?

9. How is Nazira very different from Javier?

10. How does the Deadly Veil mix present and past events to tell the story of the revolution?

11. Why does Nazira soften to her father in the end?

12. How is Abelard similar to Javier and how does that effect Nazira?

ABOUT THE AUTHOR

Nelson McKeeby is a native of Iowa, born near Spirit Lake to a Navy Officer and his teacher wife. Placed in classes for slow learners at a young age, he was never able to make education work and left school by age sixteen. He immediately landed a job as one of the country's youngest live-air television directors and professional television writers, a career he has maintained since then. Nelson is neurodiverse with both autism and severe epilepsy. A long-time hitchhiker who often uses his experiences in his writing, he has also served with the Department of Justice and as a deputy sheriff.

Nelson is known for non-fiction writing about insider politics, law enforcement, the entertainment industry, and the Quaker faith. He splits his time between La Habra, California and Iowa, living with a Brazilian doctor of biology and nurse, and four cats in a multilingual household.

Discover more at
4HorsemenPublications.com

10% off using HORSEMEN10